"If I were teaching a c[...]
write a mystery, I'd m[...]
HART required reading."
Los Angeles Times

"The queen of the traditional mystery in
America. . . . [Hart's] plotting skills rival
those of Britain's Agatha Christie."
Cleveland Plain Dealer

"Always a delight."
Chattanooga Times

"I'll admit it. I'm a sucker for Carolyn
Hart's Annie and Max series."
Robert Crais

"Carolyn Hart is superb."
Green Bay Press-Gazette

"A shining star in the mystery galaxy."
Jackson Clarion-Ledger

"For those readers who place a premium
on sleuthing over the shoulders of their
mystery protagonists, Hart is hard to beat."
Columbia State

By Carolyn Hart

Death on Demand

Henrie O

Bailey Ruth

DARE TO DIE

CAROLYN
HART

AVON

An Imprint of HarperCollinsPublishers

This book is a work of fiction. The characters, incidents, and dialogue are drawn from the author's imagination and are not to be construed as real. Any resemblance to actual events or persons, living or dead, is entirely coincidental.

AVON BOOKS
An Imprint of HarperCollins*Publishers*
10 East 53rd Street
New York, New York 10022-5299

Copyright © 2009 by Carolyn Hart
Excerpt from *Laughed 'Til He Died* copyright © 2010 by Carolyn Hart
ISBN 978-0-06-145305-2
www.avonmystery.com

First Avon Books paperback printing: April 2010
First William Morrow hardcover printing: April 2009

Avon Trademark Reg. U.S. Pat. Off. and in Other Countries, Marca Registrada, Hecho en U.S.A.
HarperCollins® is a registered trademark of HarperCollins Publishers.

Printed in the U.S.A.

10 9 8 7 6 5 4 3 2 1

To PDH, Jr.

DARE TO DIE

❖ *One* ❖

IRIS TILFORD HELD tight to the Exercycle hand grips, pumped the pedals. She was the last one working out tonight in the mission gym. A cool April breeze eddied through open windows in the ramshackle building. Red, green, and purple flashed in her eyes from the pulsating neon sign above the bar across the street. She tried to block out thrumming guitars and a nasal twang singing of love gone wrong. Iris didn't like country music, but she'd closed down a lot of bars.

Her throat felt suddenly parched. A beer . . .

No. Never.

One day at a time. That's what she had to hold to, one day at a time. She pushed away memories of stuporous nights and drug-induced fantasies. One day at a time . . .

She pumped harder. That's what Kirk told her. *When the demons come, push and pound and sweat. You've got seventy-three days. Keep it up, one day at a time. . . .*

The gym in its former life had been Murray's Garage with an oil-stained floor, thin wooden walls, and a tin roof. Now the building housed partitioned sleeping areas for men and women, a kitchen and dining area, and a ragtag collection of exercise equipment. Iris wished the mission wasn't across from the bar and the neon flashes that pulled at her, but space was cheap in this seedy Savannah neighborhood where bar signs flickered and music wailed or thumped all through the night.

"Good going, Iris." Kirk's voice was surprisingly soft for such a big man. "Brought you some Gatorade." Kirk's face had the texture of beaten silver, but his brown eyes, eyes that had seen too much, were kind.

Iris felt a moment's pride. Beaten silver. She remembered that from an art class she'd taken. . . . She drooped inside. She didn't know when or where she'd been in an art class. There were so many things she didn't remember.

He held out a plastic cup in his left hand. His right arm was a stub that poked from a floppy T-shirt sleeve.

Iris realized she was breathing in short, quick gasps. She felt dizzy. Time to stop. But when she stopped, she felt the pull of the neon. She took the cup, drank greedily.

"You're doing great." His deep voice reminded her of a bear's growl, a sunny Disney bear, not a fearsome north woods bear.

She stared at him, mournful and frightened. "I got to make it better."

"Can't remake the world in a hurry." He spoke slowly, as if there were hours and days and years enough for everything. "One day at a time."

She finished the sweet orange drink, handed him the cup. "I'll ride a little longer. That helps." Iris wiped sweat from her face, pushed back a tendril of damp hair, bent again to the handlebars. As the pedals whirred, she made her decision. Part of getting well was making things right. She couldn't change what had happened at the picnic. But she could go back to the island. Nana was dead. No one there cared about her. That made it easier to return. She couldn't have endured seeing Nana's face lined with grief. She'd broken Nana's heart. At the time, the decision had seemed simple. Leave the island, leave behind her questions and fears and doubts. Instead, she'd carried misery with her, a burden that grew heavier with the passage of time.

Iris's memory was spotty. For years she'd blocked away a picture of that night, Jocelyn hurrying into the fog, a figure slipping after her. Maybe she'd dreamed that moment. There had been so many dreams. Jocelyn's death might have had nothing to do with Iris. Iris wished she could remember the timing. Once she saw one person walk into the fog with Jocelyn. Another time she remembered a different person. Which person came last? And why, this was the terrible aching inescapable question, why hadn't anyone admitted going into the woods with Jocelyn?

Iris wouldn't know until she asked. If her fears were the product of dreams, she would finally rid herself of the deep dark emptiness that accused her. If she didn't go to the island and discover the truth, she would succumb to the insatiable lust for oblivion. ·

She had to be brave.

One day at a time . . .

Buck Carlisle walked at a deliberate pace to the front hall. He was never eager in the morning to leave for his office. He moved quickly and felt young and alive only during those shining moments in his workshop. Last night he'd almost finished a white pine table with a mosaic inlay. His workshop was as near heaven as he ever expected to come, the smell of wood as he planed, the feel of tools that seemed to fit into his hand as if specially made. Often he shared those moments with Terry. His daughter was•the light of his life, her ebony dark hair cut in bangs above a round expressive little girl's face with brown eyes that brimmed with love for her daddy. He and Fran had been closer ever since Terry came, watching in wonder as a toddler became a little girl, so cheerful and kind and caring. Fran was much too restless to spend time in the workshop though she always admired what he made.

He paused in the hallway, reached out for his briefcase. The briefcase was a deep, rich tan, made of finest English leather with his initials in gold. Fran had given it to him for his birthday. As he gripped the handles, he saw himself in the elegant rococo Chippendale mirror. Nothing in Fran's house was anything less than perfect.

Except for him. He stared into puzzled brown eyes. He hadn't changed much since high school. Ten years later and his hair was still a thick, curly brown, his face squarish with a blunt chin, his expression befuddled. In a few minutes, his father would glare at him. "I expected the Addison brief on my desk this morning. For God's sake, Buck, most of the time I think you're half addled."

Somehow he'd get through the day, one more day as the buffoon lawyer in his father's office. The brief was due tomorrow.

Ten years . . . He pushed away memories. If Jocelyn hadn't died, if she'd made good on her threat, his father would have kicked him out. He'd have had to get a job, maybe ended up a finish carpenter, holding wood in his hands, shaping it, loving it. Instead, Jocelyn died and he went to college and on to law school. If he hadn't gone to college, he wouldn't be a lawyer. Fran wouldn't have married him if he'd been a carpenter. He knew that. But if he hadn't gone to college and on to law school and married Fran, he wouldn't have Terry.

He reached for the doorknob. He couldn't delay any longer or his father would be furious.

Fran Carlisle's ebony hair gleamed in a shaft of sunlight through her office window. She wasn't beautiful. Her features were irregular, her chin too pointed, her shoulders bony, her movements too restless and jerky, but everything about her was tasteful. Taste mattered to her. On the near wall hung a Richmond Burton oil on canvas with elliptical spheres in gold, blue, and white. A pebbly red-and-orange Ettore Spalletti sculpture sat on a teak stand behind her English oak desk.

She made a final entry on the spreadsheet. Fran was punctilious about recording income and expenses. For the fourth straight year, she'd made more than seventy thousand dollars. Today marked the sixth anniversary of Yesterday's Treasures. Even her snooty mother-in-law with her pale eyes and thin mouth observed that the store was exceptionally tasteful.

Fran picked up a creamy envelope, pulled out an engraved invitation. Here it was, a genteel request for her presence at the next meeting of the Palmetto Club. Since its inception in 1878, the club had maintained the privacy of its membership rolls, but those who belonged knew and their membership set them apart. To belong was the height of social success on Broward's Rock.

Fran's smile was sunny. The Palmetto Club. Life couldn't be better.

Except for the party Friday night.

For an instant, her face was empty of all expression. Annie and Max Darling had no idea the picnic pavilion held meaning for some of their guests. Those who were there the night Jocelyn died avoided coming together this time of year.

Jocelyn . . . Fran steeled herself, refused to remember.

The Darling party had been scheduled to welcome friends to the Franklin house, the antebellum mansion they were restoring. When water damage delayed their occupancy, they rented the harbor pavilion for their event, styling it as a celebration of hospitality to come.

Fran enjoyed the close-knit social circles on the island, but that very closeness made it impossible to decline a party unless ill or off island. Her fingers ached. She drew in a breath, realized she'd crushed her Palmetto Club invitation.

Cara Wilkes held the door wide. She kept her perky smile intact, a requisite for real estate agents selling to the super-rich. She knew she was perfect for her part, sandy hair in a gamine style, dangling earrings framing a narrow face, loose silk blouse, white silk slacks, a multichain necklace with bright topaz beads, peony-pink leather sandals. She was stylish enough to enhance the clients' experience, yet clearly subservient.

She appraised her quarry, a willowy brunette with wide-spaced blue eyes and a chunky balding man twenty years older. Good. Papa Bear would be eager to flex his financial muscles. Cara slipped into her patter. "You'll note the terrazzo floor in the entryway and the Bohemian glass chandelier in the entry hall. The spirit of the house"—a sardonic inner voice murmured: conspicuous consumption on a Lalique level—"is explicit in the magnificence of the main living area. Sixty-five feet in length, fifteen feet high with the dome reaching a center peak of twenty-five feet." She took two quick steps and pirouetted to gesture at the white room framed by marble pillars ridged like the trunks of coconut palms and topped by feathery bronze fronds. White marble walls were as cool as a crypt. Not an image she would share, but one that afforded her pleasure, a crypt and imaginary biers holding a willowy trophy wife and her pig-eyed husband. Light filtered through Chinese window tiles circling the central dome, providing a soft luster for the Chinese and Philippine rattan furniture.

"Harry," the thin woman's voice was breathy. "It's gorgeous. Just gorgeous."

"One of a kind," Cara chirped. "Nine bedrooms, nine baths. Ten thousand square feet. A king master suite with a Carrara marble hot tub. One of two master suites, of course. The other adjoins the Olympic-size pool. There are three living areas in addition to this grand space." Another wave of her hand. She noted a chipped nail. Not appropriate for a servitor of the upper crust. Did she care? "The theater and gaming rooms open to the back terrace that overlooks the ocean."

Harry was balding and fiftyish, his Tommy Bahama shirt open at the neck to reveal a mat of dark chest hair. His right arm was tattooed from shoulder to wrist in a blaze of purple and black. He wouldn't fit in with the Astors, but he'd moored a four-million-dollar yacht at the marina. Today's new superrich had more marbles than almost any in history and many exulted in vulgarity.

He jingled coins in his pocket. "It's got possibilities. We'll look it over. You can wait here for us."

"I'll be happy to show you—"

He cut her off. "Don't worry, babe. We won't rip off any of the fancy john seats." With that he strode toward the hallway, his bellow of laughter echoing from the marble walls. The brunette trotted to catch up.

Cara shrugged. She strolled past nineteenth-century Ottoman glass lamps, a dhurrie rug, a nineteenth-century settee covered in green-blue silk and stepped onto the piazza. The ocean was placid today.

Passionate longing swept her. If she could be a kid again and run to the water and dive beneath a wave and come up wet and sleek and happy, sure of sunny days, unaware of the heartbreak and failure that lay ahead. How long had it been since she'd been happy? She'd thought her burdened heart would mend if she came home, came back to the island where she'd once been carefree, eager, confident that every day would be wonderful. Coming home hadn't helped. She still ached inside. The days, no matter how sunny, seemed framed in gray. Now there was the Darlings' party at the pavilion.

She wouldn't go.

Buck would be there.

So would Fran.

Russell Montgomery checked the caller ID on his cell. Liz, of course. Calling to see how the meeting at the bank went. Or to ask whether he'd like coconut cake or crème brûlée for dessert. The more she did for him, the worse he felt. Liz had nursed a squirrel with a broken paw back to health. She took soup to the sick, called on shut-ins, volunteered for most island charities, enjoyed running her own antique store downtown. Yet, there was another Liz. He blocked away the memory of the fury he'd once glimpsed in her eyes, fury because she felt she was losing him.

He stood by the white pickup, red-faced beneath a grimy oversize Panama hat. Sweat stained his blue polo shirt. Mud splashes streaked his baggy khaki shorts. Wet clumps of gray dirt clung to his work boots. At the last ring, tension eased out of his body. He hadn't trusted himself to talk to her now. The misery that stained his soul was too near to the surface today.

Damn the Darlings.

His face ridged in resentment, but he tamped down the feeling as he'd tamped down feelings for so many years. He tried to focus on the here and now, gazing at the scaffolding at the side of the church. The persistent day-after-day rain had finally stopped though thunder was due this afternoon. The men were making progress with the painting. If they didn't get done by June, a thousand-dollar-per-day penalty would begin to run. He shouldn't have agreed to that clause, but he needed the job and now he was behind because of the rains. The crew was three men short. . . . That last shipment of two-by-fours was warped. . . . The flashing around the chimney needed to be replaced. . . .

Beneath the swirl of worries, he wished he'd told Liz to turn down the Darlings' invitation. Liz would have looked at him with concern, but she would have done as he asked. Now it was too late. Besides, it wouldn't be smart to offend Max Darling. He'd paid handsomely for the work on the Franklin house and he was being remarkably patient about the plumbing mess. The subcontractor hadn't shown up or returned Russell's calls for two days. Maybe it was time to ask Buck to send a demand letter.

Russell gripped the cell phone. What if he called Liz now and told her the truth? He'd never been sure how much Liz knew. Liz had always been crazy about him. After he and Jocelyn broke up, he'd started dating Liz. Several times she'd tried to talk about Jocelyn. One night he told her to leave the past alone. She never asked again.

How would Liz feel if he told her the truth? Would she look at him with loathing? He'd kept quiet all these years, but the ugliness festered inside. If he told her, maybe it would be like lancing a boil and letting the poison stream free.

He was too late, years too late.

Russell shoved the cell into his pocket, moved toward the construction trailer.

Liz Montgomery pushed with her foot to jam steel claws into the ground. She pulled on the shaft and gouged out the weed. She swung the tool over a plastic barrel to dump the weed with its dangling roots and fragments of sandy earth. A half-dozen members of the Sea Side Garden Club, all in dusty pink, wide-brimmed hats and pink-and-green-striped smocks, worked on the grounds of the Pickett house, the antebellum home maintained by the island historical society. Guided tours were available three times weekly and high tea was served every Thursday afternoon.

Liz braced the weeder against the trash bin and knelt to use a hand tool plucked from her smock. She loved the smell of freshly turned earth, the feel of dirt on her hands. She had gardening gloves, but she rarely wore them. Her verbenas were the envy of the garden club. She loved all the varieties of lavender plants. Tall spiky lavender plants grew in profusion on either side of their drive. The scent was heavenly from spring through early fall. She enjoyed making lavender potpourri and sachets, which she sold in her shop. Her beautiful flowers . . . They brought peace and joy even when she wasn't physically in her garden. She paused to rest for a moment even though the April morning was cool. In her peripheral vision, she glimpsed Fish Haul pier stretching into the Sound. She stiffened. She never saw the pier or the nearby picnic pavilion without a sense of dread. She would not think about the pier . . . if only they didn't have to go to the Darlings' party . . . Russell hadn't said anything . . . oh, Russell, do you still love her . . .

She jammed the hand tool into the earth. Again and again.

A laughing voice spoke behind her. "You're ferocious this morning, Liz. Did the weed make you mad? You don't have to kill it."

A reddish haze of anger slowly lifted. She stared at the ruptured ground and the minced remnants of the dandelion.

Annie Darling rested on her elbow and gazed down at Max, his face burrowed into the pillow. His thick blond hair was tangled, the portion of visible cheek stubbled. Night was lifting. She looked toward the window. Tendrils of rose streaked the milky sky. The view was unfamiliar. The last place she had expected to be this April morning was in a rental cabin facing the marsh. The travel clock's red numerals glowed 5:15. The last of their furniture was going into temporary storage today. The move into the Franklin house had been delayed until damage from a water leak was repaired. Max had worked hard to restore the antebellum home, but last week a newly installed toilet overflowed on the second floor. They'd gone to Charleston to attend an auction and hadn't been by the house for several days. By then, the upper floor was flooded and part of the ceiling had fallen in the dining room. With their previous house promised to new owners, Ingrid Webb had been quick to offer them sanctuary at Nightingale Courts.

The marsh was dark beneath the sky, now tinged with pink and gold. Annie felt content and at peace. Sure, their move to the Franklin house was on hold, but how lucky she and Max were to have friends like Ingrid and Duane Webb, to live on the loveliest sea island (she had her prejudices) to grace the South Carolina coast, to be happy. Soon another day in paradise would unfold. There was much to do, books to unpack at Death on Demand, a dental appointment next Monday, the worrisome concern about Emma Clyde, the disappointment of moving their planned party at the Franklin house to the harbor pavilion. Still, friends would gather and there would be time enough for many parties in their refurbished home. Nothing onerous marred her horizon.

Most of all, how lucky they were to be together.

Her fingers lightly caressed her husband's stubbled cheek.

Max murmured, shifted, turned his face toward her. His eyes flickered open. The haze of sleep disappeared. His eyes told her she was beautiful.

Annie brushed back a tangle of blond hair.

"Good morning, Mrs. Darling." He reached out and pulled her close, nuzzled her throat, then his lips sought hers.

Any day that started with love was certain to be stellar from start to finish.

∾ *Two* ∾

"THAT CAT'S DONE it again." Ingrid's shout from the front of the store wasn't amused.

In the storeroom, Annie hit the wrong key and the list of thirteen-digit ISBN numbers on her computer screen disappeared, a list that had required forty-five minutes of intense concentration to input. As she zoomed the cursor toward undo, she inadvertently flicked *c*. A single letter appeared, *c* for . . . The answer was clear. Her computer was at the mercy of a cosmic force enjoying a joke. Clearly, *c* was for cat. Or maybe chump.

"She's hissing at me." Ingrid was outraged.

Annie rushed up the central aisle, her loafers (a soft pink to match her blouse) slapping against the heart-pine floor. Even in the midst of a minor crisis, she delighted in her bookstore, the pleasing tan of the gum shelves, the vivid ranks of bright book covers, the cozy enclave devoted to traditional mysteries with a full case of Christies. (Two billion sold worldwide and counting.) Whitmani ferns glistened green and luxuriant, reminders of the Mary Roberts Rinehart days when potted greenery was the epitome of Victorian taste. The latest addition to the comfortable furniture was a heavily upholstered walnut armchair with curly feet, a tribute to Patricia Wentworth's indomitable Miss Silver, who took quiet pleasure in her Victorian furnished flat.

Annie knew that pride puffeth up. She had a quick vision of a bulbous (and likely poisonous) mushroom. However, wasn't that false pride? She would have to ask Father Patton. Surely she could be excused for her delight in Death on Demand, the finest mystery bookstore north of Miami. The depth and breadth of Death on Demand's stock included everything from the latest in thrillers (Alex Kava, Martin Cruz Smith, and Lee Child) to the most poignant tales of ordinary people and their passions (Nancy Pickard, Jodi Picoult, and Phillip DePoy). Death on Demand, in Annie's view (hopefully she wasn't smug), rivaled Murder by the Book in Houston, The Poisoned Pen in Scottsdale, Mystery Lovers Bookshop in Oakmont, Mystery Bookstore in Los Angeles, "M" Is for Mystery in San Mateo, and Mysteries To Die For in Thousand Oaks.

Annie skidded to a stop near a Charleston-made Queen Anne table. On the heart-pine floor, books lay askew atop a green silk throw with orange tassels.

Agatha stood on the table, green eyes narrowed, back arched, tail flicking like an adder's tongue.

Annie moved swiftly, interposing herself between Ingrid, standing with her hands on her hips, and the bookstore's resident black cat.

"It's my fault." Annie pointed at the remains of the exhibit she'd completed only this morning. She loved to celebrate mysteries in particular times or places. *The Penguin Pool Murder* by Stuart Palmer, *A Coffin for Dimitrios* by Eric Ambler, *The Listening House* by Mabel Seeley, *Ming*

Yellow by John P. Marquand, and *The Case Is Closed* by Patricia Wentworth afforded a fly-on-the-wall, you-are-there immersion in the nineteen-thirties.

Keeping a careful eye on Agatha, Annie reached down. "I couldn't resist the throw. I saw it in the window of Yesterday's Treasures." Annie always found it hard to pass by Fran Carlisle's window displays. The shop was a half-block from the ferry. Annie fought temptation every time she arrived or left the island. "It's the fault of the tassels. The tassels move when we have the ceiling fans on." Annie pointed up at the softly whirring fan. "We can't blame Agatha."

Ingrid might have been an ice carving. Her silvered brown hair was now cut short with a hint of curl. Ingrid looked springlike in a white cardigan with appliqués of pelicans, but her bony face was set in irritation. Obviously, in her view, the fault lay not in the stars, but in the attitude of a green-eyed cat.

Annie flapped the throw. Agatha crouched. Annie hurried down the center aisle. Agatha loped after her. Annie tossed the throw over a wicker chair in the cozy enclave. Agatha flew through the air. She snagged the throw, pulled it to the floor, and batted at a tassel.

At the table, Ingrid rearranged the books. "There's a split in the Seeley spine. It was an unblemished first." She wasn't pleased.

Annie came up behind her and slipped an arm around rigid shoulders. "Nobody's perfect. Especially not cats. Come on, let's have a mocha. Double whipped cream."

Annie led the way to the coffee bar, another point of pride in Death on Demand. She carefully measured today's special coffee from Ethiopia. The oily beans smelled heavenly. As the superautomatic machine, a birthday gift from Max, produced four shots of espresso, Annie looked over the shelves of white coffee mugs.

Each mug bore the name of a famous mystery in crimson script. She picked *Don't Go Away Mad* by Joseph Hayes for Ingrid and *Detection Unlimited* by Georgette Heyer for herself. In a flash, she mixed double shots of espresso and milk steamed with Mexican cacao, cinnamon, and a dash of almond.

She handed Ingrid her mug, lifted her own in salute. "Pax?"

A lopsided smile softened Ingrid's face. She raised her mug. "You spoil that beast."

"We all have weaknesses. One of mine is Agatha. Anyway, she's a great attraction. People love cats."

Ingrid raised an eyebrow, her narrow face skeptical.

"Okay, some people don't love cats, but most mystery readers do. Besides, Agatha never scratches anyone but me."

Ingrid's expression was wry. "Certainly that proves Agatha's devotion to you."

To Annie's relief, the front doorbell gave its tinkling peal. Glad to evade further consideration of Agatha and her foibles, Annie turned toward the front of the store.

A drooping figure shuffled toward them.

Annie looked toward Ingrid, gave a tiny nod toward the coffee bar.

Annie smiled brightly. "Hey, Emma." Annie wished she could start over. The false heartiness in her tone was sure to elicit a snarl from Emma Clyde. The island's famous mystery author, revered creator of the bestselling world-famous Marigold Rembrandt series, never suffered fools or phoniness.

A subdued clatter at the coffee bar indicated Ingrid was concocting a special treat for Emma.

Emma never looked up. Instead of her customary brisk swagger, she moved at a snail's pace, head down, spiky hair drooping. Silver roots gleamed beneath a half-inch of faded purple. Usually her brightly striped or patterned caftans swirled. Emma enjoyed relaxed-fitting clothing with an attitude. Today's caftan hung limp and looked muted, the colors obviously faded. Possibly she'd dragged it from a castaway pile. The ruby ring on her right hand was the only remnant of her usual vivid appearance.

Annie was determined to dispel the aura of hopelessness. "Emma, we've sold out of *The Case of the Cadaver's Coupe*." Of course, a new shipment was due in this afternoon in preparation for next week's book signing. "I don't have a single copy." That admission should have guaranteed a vitriolic outburst. Emma had been known to threaten a bookseller foolish enough not to stock a plenitude of her new title with banishment to the Arctic accompanied only by a Game Boy for entertainment.

Today Emma's craggy face continued to droop. Her response was a shrug. "It will go OP soon enough. Books always go out of print if there isn't a new one in the chute."

"Have you seen this month's watercolors?" Annie loved all of these books which were guaranteed to lift readers' spirits. "Let me show you. Ingrid's fixing espresso topped with whipped cream for you."

Emma let Annie lead her to the coffee bar. She settled on the high stool with her arms on the counter, her blue eyes dull. She ignored the paintings. "I'm through." She lifted the mug—Ingrid had selected *Murder as a Fine Art* by Carol Carnac—and drank automatically. She was oblivious to a puffy mustache of whipped cream. She looked at the mug, morose as a nineteen-forties' gumshoe nursing a double shot of bourbon. "OP. R.I.P. Two months and no plot. It won't come. Every time I have an idea, do you know what happens?" Her tone was mournful.

Annie and Ingrid bent nearer. "What?" Annie breathed.

Emma's square face sagged. "Nothing."

Ingrid looked puzzled. "Nothing?"

"Nothing." Emma's voice was as doom laden as the creak of a dungeon door in Poe. "The idea lies there like a dead fish. I never understood about inert elements until now." She looked at them with desperate eyes. "I should have everything I need: my sleuth, a victim, suspects who knew the victim, a title. That's all I've ever needed." Her voice quivered. "This time, I can't start."

Ingrid patted Emma's arm. "There, there. You can do it, Emma. You've always done it."

"Not this time." The words dropped with the finality of a guillotine. Absently she licked away the remnants of whipping cream.

"Sudoku?" Ingrid offered.

Emma didn't bother to answer.

"To get your brain started." Ingrid was eager.

Emma clutched her head. "Brain dead."

"I have an idea." Annie was emphatic.

Emma sighed. "I have ideas. D.O.A."

Annie felt impatient. Emma's ingenious mind had devised plots that turned on the color of a bird's feather or the muted sound of a faraway bell tolling. Surely she could pull up her socks. . . .

A tear rolled down Emma's cheek.

Annie slapped the countertop. "The solution is obvious."

Emma looked toward Annie, her gaze beseeching.

Annie was no authority on true crime, but there were classic cases. "You know Dorothy L. Sayers's brilliant analysis of the William Herbert Wallace affair?"

Hope warred with despair in Emma's blue eyes.

Annie beamed. "We'll find a crime for you, Emma. There's the Hall-Mills murders, Lizzie Borden, Sir Harry Oakes, the Mullendore shooting, none of them solved. You pick a crime and once you've solved it, starting a new book will be easy as pie."

Emma drooped again on the counter. "Pie in the sky. I'm finish—"

The front door opened.

"Ingrid?" Duane Webb's call was hurried and strained.

Ingrid's eyes flared in alarm. She moved swiftly to the center aisle. "What's wrong?"

Annie too recognized trouble when she heard it. She squeezed Emma's arm and hurried after Ingrid.

Duane, his rounded face drawn and worried, rushed to Ingrid. His bow tie was askew. Despite the fine mist outside, he was in his shirtsleeves. He held open his arms and Ingrid came into her husband's damp embrace. He spoke quickly as he always did, but his tone was grave. "Sissy's in the hospital. They think it's a heart attack."

Annie had met Ingrid's older sister from Tallahassee on a recent holiday on the island.

"Her neighbor got an ambulance and called us. I don't know what the prognosis is." Duane sounded angry as well as worried. "Nobody at the hospital will give out information. That damn privacy law again. For God's sake, nothing works right in this country anymore. One damn roadblock after another because of some damn bureaucratic idiot. I told the hospital they actually can give out information. It's their prerogative. I might as well have talked to a stone monolith. Everybody at a hospital is scared they're going to be sued. I told the neighbor you'd come. I've got the car packed. You can drop me off on your way to the ferry. I'll call around, find somebody who'll watch over Nightingale Courts and get there as soon as I can."

Annie took two quick steps. "Max and I will take care of everything. We're already there, for heaven's sake." She touched Duane's arm. "Ingrid needs you. You go with her."

Duane's staccato words peppered her. "I left folks waiting to check in. Told 'em I had an emergency. The units aren't cleaned yet. Our housekeeper's in Mobile. Her daughter's having a baby. We thought we could manage until she got back. I'd cleaned one cabin, but everything else needs to be done. Ingrid will have to go on without me."

Annie gave him a gentle nudge. "Grab your toothbrush and catch the ferry. Tell the guests your clerk is on the way. Give them free Cokes and they can relax on the deck and watch the marsh hawks. I'll be out there as soon as I make a couple of phone calls. I'll check them in and clean the cabins."

Ingrid fought back tears. "Sissy will be all right." Her voice was thin. "I know she will. Annie, bless you. All the keys are tagged. The extras hang on a hook in the office. The cleaning supplies are in the cement block building with the ice maker and washing machines." She gave Annie a quick hug, swung away.

Duane was right behind her. He was halfway out the door when he stopped and looked back. Duane was a hard-bitten former newspaper editor, unsentimental and brusque. He'd fought the dragon of alcohol, his past sorrows eased by Ingrid. He knew people. Worry puckered his face. "That girl in Six. I think she's got trouble. Maybe nothing anyone can do to help, but keep an eye out. She rented a cabin yesterday evening. She came in the rain. Alone. On a bicycle."

Max's cell phone didn't answer. Annie pictured it lying in the front seat of his new Jeep Cherokee. Sports cars, he'd told her solemnly, were part of his past. He cherished his black Corvette, but he had officially deemed it Annie's runabout, insisting her Volvo was creaking with age. Annie still drove the Volvo so Max drove the Corvette on sunny days to keep it in running shape. The Jeep was his choice for hauling. Today he would be here, there, and everywhere, putting things in place for the Friday night oyster roast. He'd insisted on handling everything. She was not to worry. Annie was sure he planned a surprise. She loved Max's surprises, but at this moment she wished he wasn't determined to avoid entrapment by technology. True, life was freer before electronic tethers made solitude an elusive quest. However, all wasn't lost. She left a message. ". . . call me as soon as you can."

Emma came up beside her. "In the rain. Alone. On a bicycle." Emma's face squinted in thought. "I can see her. Young. Dark curls tangled, drenched clothes plastered to her. Duane didn't say anything about a raincoat. Who wears a raincoat on a bicycle? Why a bicycle?"

Annie turned back to the phone. Emma's singlemindedness never came as a surprise, but it would have been helpful if she'd offered to take over the store for a while.

Annie dialed Henny Brawley's number. Again she left a message. ". . . and if you could give me a hand at the store, it would be great. I'll be at Nightingale Courts."

Emma began to pace, eyes glittering. "Alone. Did she come to the island to see someone?"

Annie grinned. Maybe all Emma needed was a good hard puzzle. Annie punched familiar numbers. Dulcet tones answered. "Breathe deeply, dear child." Laurel's husky voice was as soothing as a tai chi moment.

Oh no. Annie wasn't going to go there. Tai chi was her mother-in-law's new enthusiasm. She kept urging Annie to attend a class she was teaching. Not in this lifetime. Annie felt a moment of suffocation. She wasn't stressed. Absolutely she wasn't.

All right. She was.

How did her mother-in-law know?

Annie envisioned Laurel's patrician face framed by spun gold hair. Laurel's Nordic blue eyes would be shining with empathy, her perfect lips curved in a caring smile, the mother-in-law from . . . Annie squelched the thought. Laurel, after all, always meant well. Didn't she?

The husky voice exuded support. "You wouldn't be calling if you were in the chapel—"

Annie's eyes darted to the round clock. To her surprise it read ten minutes after ten. She regularly attended Holy Communion at ten o'clock on Wednesdays in the chapel of St. Mary's, but Ingrid's abrupt departure had deranged, as Hercule Poirot might remark, her routine.

"—so obviously something unexpected has occurred. I am thrilled—humbled—exalted—that you are seeking my help." A sigh of contentment wafted over the wire. "Henny and I have just completed our morning tai chi on my deck overlooking the lagoon. Happily a portion of the deck is covered so the swirling mist over the marsh was lovely, much as you might see in a hanging scroll of a Chinese landscape. Annie, would it surprise you if I told you that a great blue heron," Laurel's tone was hushed, "executed a most perfect Stork Spreads Its Wings?. Oh, the grace of that long golden bill, the symmetry of that curving neck, the delicacy of those trailing feathers."

Annie resisted the impulse to say that she would not only be surprised but astounded since most great blue herons of her acquaintance did not attend tai chi classes. Herons and storks were cousins so it might be assumed the exercise was patterned after the birds and not the birds after the exercise.

As was often the case in exchanges with her mother-in-law, Annie's mouth opened and closed with a sense once again that she had been bested, but wasn't quite certain how it had happened. "Laurel, I need help. Ingrid's sister . . ."

Emma paced back and forth near the counter, muttering. "Who is she? Not a stranger to the island or she wouldn't know about Nightingale Courts."

Annie spoke a little louder. ". . . so I'm going to Nightingale Courts right now."

The front doorbell sounded.

Annie looked up in time to see Emma's caftan swirling out into the mist.

"Sweet child, don't give the store a moment's thought." Laurel's laughter was a gay trill. "Henny and I will be there at once. Everything shall be splendid. Henny and I have often discussed how we would cha— That is, Death on Demand will receive our most loving and careful and insightful supervision."

Max Darling balanced near the top of the wooden ladder, one hand gripping the top step. With the other hand, he maneuvered a furled banner toward a hook projecting from the rafter. He eased the rod into the hook. With both sides secure, he started down the ladder, pulling the banner down as he went.

When he reached the flagstone floor of the harbor pavilion, he looked up. The ten-by-twelve-foot banner hanging from the central rafter rippled in the onshore breeze that swept gently through the open-air structure. If he turned, the view of the Sound would be magnificent, a light haze of fog over jade green water, sailboats scudding before the wind, steel gray dolphins leaping and diving. Instead, he focused on the banner. Maybe he should hook some trolling sinkers to each end. He had some eight-ounce sinkers.

"It looks pretty, moving in the breeze." The soft voice was admiring.

Max swung around. A much-too-thin girl—his mind amended the thought—a much-too-thin young woman, in a faded yellow blouse and age-paled jeans, stood astride a bicycle at the foot of the pavilion steps. She looked damp from the mist.

She gave an apologetic smile. "I didn't mean to interrupt."

"You're fine. Come on up." The harbor pavilion was a public picnic facility and anyone could reserve it. Since he and Annie had switched their party plans at the last minute, he was glad it was early enough in April that the property was available on a Friday night and that Ben Parotti, proprietor of the island's famed Parotti's Bar and Grill, would cater for them. If the party had occurred at the Franklin house, Max had planned to don his chef hat and serve shrimp and crab okra gumbo, baked chicken breasts with a Madeira wine and whipped cream sauce, corn pudding, and cold asparagus with a vinaigrette dressing. His signature lime shortcake, light and zesty, would have been the dessert.

Instead of asking Ben to replicate Max's dinner, they'd

settled on an oyster roast with the usual suspects from the menu at Parotti's Bar and Grill: rice with almonds, raisins, and chopped cooked chicken; apple fritters; cheese grits; curly fries; candied sweet potatoes; and pineapple-coconut cookies. A grill would offer hamburgers and hot dogs for nonoyster fans. Beer on tap, sweetened and unsweetened iced tea, assorted soda pop, and chicory coffee strong enough to march in a parade would satisfy thirst.

The slender woman propped her bike and came up the steps. She joined him to look up at the silk hanging. The banner held a life-size picture of Max and Annie, standing hand in hand on the piazza of the Franklin house, framed by alabaster white columns. The photo had been taken on a brilliantly sunny day.

Max's gaze scanned past his own image to Annie, his beautiful, fun-loving, fascinating Annie with flyaway blond hair and steady gray eyes and kissable lips, soon to be hostess of the Franklin house. Her smile would welcome their guests Friday night to what should have been their inaugural party. The banner would proclaim the hospitality they hoped to offer at the Franklin house for years to come. The ripple of the fabric made it seem as if he and Annie were moving toward the viewer. Maybe he didn't need any weights.

The visitor looked curious. "Is it an ad for a movie?"

He squinted. The banner did have the quality of a movie poster with its vivid colors and crisp images. Certainly the South Carolina Low Country had been the site of its fair share of films in recent years, thanks to the success of the hardworking South Carolina Film Commission in wooing films and TV programs.

"Nothing that grand."

The girl looked at him, recognition quick. "You're on the banner."

Max pointed. "That's my wife. The banner's a surprise for her. We were supposed to have a party in our new house Friday night. An old house, actually. But we had some water damage. Since the party was already scheduled, we decided not to cancel . . ." He broke off because she wasn't listening.

She stood beneath the banner, gazing around the old pavilion. A seat-level stone wall, conveniently placed for marshmallow toasting, framed a huge fireplace. Picnic tables and benches filled the remainder of the pavilion. More picnic tables dotted the grassy expanse between the pavilion and the harbor boardwalk. Diners could choose between the cover of the pavilion or the open-air tables.

The breeze stirred dark curls that sprang away from a thin face, emphasizing too-sharp features. She looked at the pavilion and the tables beyond on the grass, then turned toward the woods. She stood with her shoulders hunched, tense and stiff.

Max's first impression had been of the accentuated thinness that often marked models, but her hollow-cheeked face was worn, older than its years, with dark smudges beneath somber brown eyes. Max wondered if she had been ill.

She turned toward him. "A party Friday night." She brushed back the straying curls. "I hope you have a good time." With that, she gave a slight nod and hurried to the steps and down. She swung onto the bike and pedaled fast.

Max had a sense of escape as he watched her disappear behind a grove of pines. He was left in silence broken only by the caw of seabirds and the clang of a buoy, lonely sounds both.

Annie drove fast on Sand Dollar Road, hoping Sgt. Hyla Harrison and her patrol car weren't tucked in the shadows of a live oak. Annie and the aloof officer wouldn't be termed friends, but now they were friendly. Sgt. Harrison usually dropped by on her day off to order a double espresso poured into half-and-half and buy the next title in Ed McBain's 87th Precinct series. Annie's fingers clamped on the wheel. She was ready to brake if she saw a bicyclist, deer, or Sgt. Harrison.

Annie turned left from Sand Dollar Road onto a narrow, sandy twisting lane. A hand-lettered arrow pointed west: NIGHTINGALE COURTS 2 MILES. Dust churned beneath the Volvo's wheels as she passed beneath the arch of the honeysuckle-laden arbor and nosed into a parking slot near Cabin One.

Grateful that the mist had eased and the gray sky was beginning to lighten, she hurried to the manager's office. The small space was filled to capacity. As she slipped behind the counter, she was relieved when a quick count added up to five. She could handle five. Without thinking, she sucked air deep into her abdomen. "Breathe from your center, peace will follow." She almost strangled, realizing she heard Laurel's husky voice in her mind, but darned if the inflow of oxygen wasn't helping.

Ingrid and Duane had never upgraded to a computer. They registered their guests in an old-fashioned leatherbound book that had come with the property when Ingrid bought it twenty-five years ago. They did have a small credit card scanner. Two couples from Ohio, the Gormans and the Hasseldorfs, were quickly checked into Cabins Three and Four. Annie noted their license plate numbers and felt a quiet pride that she'd remembered everything. She smiled at the new lodgers. "Due to a family emergency, the cabins aren't ready yet, but they will be available within the hour. Please be the guests of Nightingale Courts for lunch at Parotti's Bar and Grill."

Smiles replaced frowns and in a flurry the couples were on their way, clutching a handwritten note to put the meals on the Darlings' tab. Annie took another centered breath and felt cool, calm, and collected. She turned to the waiting area's final occupant, a slouch-hatted, raincoat-clad figure hidden behind the fronds of a potted banana tree.

"How may I help you?" She tried not to sound hurried though she felt the minutes fleeting before the tourists would return, expecting pristine cabins.

"Took you long enough." Emma's crusty voice wasn't admiring. She ducked from behind the banana tree.

"Emma?" Annie blinked. Where and how had she arrived? Emma's maroon Rolls-Royce certainly hadn't been parked out in front.

Emma's blue eyes gleamed. "I'm incognito."

Annie's stare was blank.

Emma moved briskly toward the counter. "Marigold never tips her hand when she goes undercover."

Since it might be dangerous to her health, Annie never admitted that she loathed Emma's overbearing, red-haired sleuth. Although it was lovely to see Emma aggressive and demanding, almost, in fact, her old self, Annie didn't have time to waste. "Whatever it is, it has to wait until I get two cabins cleaned."

Emma reached for the register. "You run right along. I'm checking into Seven. I've already parked Essie Faye's son's car there." Essie Faye was Emma's imperturbable housekeeper. "He's loaned it to me."

"Why?"

Emma planted her hands on her hips. "The girl in Six. How can we keep an eye out for her if we don't know who she is?"

Obviously, the Girl on the Bicycle—a possible title?—had captured Emma's imagination. Perhaps Emma would get back on track. The subdued ghost-of-her-former-obnoxious-self would be replaced by the crusty persona Annie knew well. In Annie's private thoughts—very private—she thought of the mystery writer as Emma Center-of-Her-Own-Universe Clyde. Whatever, Emma's request seemed harmless and another cabin rented, another dollar in the Nightingale Courts coffer. "Okay. Put the register on the second shelf when you finish."

Annie's nose itched. Since her gloved hands were damp from scrubbing the lavatory in Cabin Four, she wiggled her nose, finally sneezed into the crook of her elbow. She was almost done, the cabins dusted, beds freshly made, floors swept. She glanced at her watch. She had ten minutes left of her hour and only this bathroom to finish. She reached for the mop, blinked watery eyes. Maybe she'd put in too much ammonia—

The screen door rattled. A high voice cried, "Somebody's hurt."

Annie whirled, knocking over the pail. Sudsy water sloshed onto the tiles. She moved fast, skidding on the wet floor. She pushed open the screen door.

A thin, dark-haired woman stood beside the cleaning cart near the cabin steps. She pointed toward Cabin Six. "A woman's hurt. I found her in my cabin. Hurry. She may be dying."

∾ *Three* ∾

ANNIE PUSHED INSIDE Cabin Six. A crumpled figure lay near the foot of the bed. In a shaft of sunlight from the open door, a ruby ring sparkled on an outflung hand. "Emma . . ."

The next few moments were never clear in Annie's mind. She found herself on her knees, holding a clean hand towel gently against the bloody gash on Emma's forehead.

The young woman stood in the doorway. "Can I help?"

"I think I have the bleeding stopped." Annie's cell phone was in her purse in the office. "Do you have a cell phone?" The cabins no longer had in-room telephones. Ingrid and Duane touted solitude, promising a retreat from worldly cares at lovely Nightingale Courts. Ingrid saw it as a reasonable savings, confident everyone carried a cell phone these days. If they didn't have a cell, they were welcome to use the office telephone as long as charges were reversed.

"No." The young woman moved forward. "I'll stay with her if you want to go call." She knelt beside Annie. "I can hold the cloth."

Annie was on her feet. She ran as fast as she could. When

she reached the office, her breath came in choked gasps. She punched 911.

"Emergency services."

Annie was relieved to recognize Mavis Cameron's voice. Island Police Chief Billy Cameron's wife was unflappable and capable. "Mavis, Annie Darling. Send an ambulance to Nightingale Courts, Cabin Six. Emma Clyde has a head injury. She's unconscious." Annie hung up and turned on her heel.

When Annie hurried back into the cabin, the dark-haired woman held Emma's wrist. She looked up, her eyes concerned. "There's a pulse, but it's faint. I don't know how long she's been here. I guess she was bringing clean towels and she fell."

Bringing clean towels?

Towels were tumbled onto the floor near Emma. Indisputably, she had carried them and dropped them as she fell.

Annie spoke uncertainly. "I guess that's what happened." Emma had no business in this cabin, with or without towels. She once again dropped down beside Emma, took one flaccid hand in her own, worried at its coolness.

It seemed a long time but Annie knew only minutes had passed when sirens sounded. The hospital was very near. Annie pushed up from the floor, hurried to hold the door for the EMTs.

The young woman stood near the table, her thin face furrowed. Her yellow peasant blouse was too big, slipping a little on one shoulder. A braided leather belt hitched up saggy jeans. Faded red sandals were down-at-heel.

Annie's muscles tensed, willing the techs to move faster though she knew they were proceeding with all due speed, following protocol. Most important, they made a careful examination to be sure Emma hadn't suffered a neck or back injury, then lightly applied a gauze bandage to the wound.

Annie breathed a sigh of relief when Emma was strapped onto a gurney. Emma's face, the portion not hidden by gauze, was waxy, the grayness of shock and blood loss. The EMTs, ebullient Josie Winters, who had a complete collection of Elizabeth Peters's Amelia Peabody series, and burly Jack Kramer, who had once played shortstop with the Savannah Sand Gnats, eased their burden down the steps. As the ambulance pulled away, siren wailing, a police cruiser turned into Nightingale Courts.

Annie looked at the thin woman. Annie didn't know her name, but there wasn't time now for introductions. "I've got to go to the emergency room. I'll straighten the cabin when I get back." Or maybe she could catch Max, ask him to take over at Nightingale Courts and finish the cleaning. She'd grab her purse from the office and head for the hospital. Annie pushed through the door, then stopped on the porch.

Police Chief Billy Cameron walked toward Cabin Six. Billy was six-feet-plus inches of brawn and character. His short blond hair had glints of silver though he was still in his thirties. His eyes held a sober, questing look. Billy was the island's watchdog. He'd grown up on Broward's Rock, and he took the safety of each and every citizen very seriously indeed. Billy was here because she'd called 911 and not stayed on the line.

He came up the steps. His probing gaze chided her as she stepped back for him to enter. "Mavis didn't get all the information. What happened to Emma? What are you doing here? Where's Ingrid?"

She hadn't reported a crime, but Billy knew his island. Famed island mystery author Emma Clyde lived in a multimillion-dollar beach mansion. Her discovery, unconscious from a head injury in a motel cabin, required explanation.

"Ingrid's gone to Florida on a family emergency and I'm handling everything. I don't know how Emma got hurt. I didn't find her. The guest who rents the cabin found her"— Annie looked at her watch—"about twenty minutes ago." It felt as though hours had passed.

Billy looked puzzled. "She found Emma in her cabin? How did Emma get in?"

Before Annie could reply, the young woman joined her on the porch and answered. "I guess she used her passkey since she was bringing towels." She stood aside to point into the cabin. "See, they're on the floor."

Billy looked at the woman, not the towels.

There was a moment of silence.

She drew herself up, her narrow face rigid.

"Hello, Iris." Billy rocked back on his heels. His gaze was cool. "Your grandmother reported you missing."

A pulse fluttered in her thin throat. She didn't speak.

"She spent all her money looking for you." His tone wasn't accusing, more grave and sad. "She loved you."

Tears glistened in the woman's deep-sunk dark eyes.

Annie felt as if she watched an injured bird, desperate to take flight, unable to move, frozen in pain.

Billy shifted his weight forward. "You didn't come to her funeral."

"I couldn't. I was . . . sick." Tears spilled unchecked. Iris slipped bony fingers together, laced them so tight the skin blanched. "Were you there?"

He nodded. "She was a good woman. Everyone came."

Tears trickled down her thin cheeks. "Did they play 'In the Garden'?"

Billy's voice softened. "Yes."

"That was her favorite. I sing it now. I hold to it." She lifted her chin. "I would have come if I could have. I'm sorry about everything, especially running away. That's why I've come back. It's too late for Nana, but there's people I got to talk to." She glanced into the cabin. "I'm sorry the maid fell down." Her glance at Annie was faintly accusing. "She looked awfully old to be cleaning rooms."

Billy looked at her sharply. "Maid? That's—"

Annie interrupted. "Billy, I can explain." She didn't intend to tell him the truth. At least, not in front of Iris. Annie had no doubt that Emma had rooted around in Ingrid's office, found an extra key to Cabin Six, and set out to search it, carrying fresh towels in case the occupant returned. "Ingrid's sister is in the hospital in Tallahassee. We're taking care of everything while she's gone." We could be understood to include others, such as Laurel and Henny and, as soon as he arrived, Max. That the helpers did not include Emma could be shared with Billy later.

"I see." Billy nodded, clearly reassured. Emma's unlikely presence at Nightingale Courts had been accounted for. "Emma was bringing towels—"

Annie hoped her cheeks didn't flame. She had an unfortunate tendency to turn bright red under the stress of subterfuge.

"—and must have tripped. I'll take a look."

Billy stepped inside the cabin. Iris and Annie followed.

Billy studied the bare, clean, uncluttered floor. "Where was she lying?"

Iris pointed toward the footboard. "Right there. It looked like she hit the bed when she fell. There was a gash on the right side of her head."

Billy bent near the footboard. "Here's where she hit. There's blood here."

Iris turned away.

"I'll clean it up." Annie reached down, scooped up the towels. They'd have to be washed anyway since they'd fallen on the floor. With a little cold water, she'd have the stain gone in a jiffy.

Billy lifted a hand, then let it drop. "I guess that's okay. Emma took a tumble. Maybe she got dizzy. If she lost her balance suddenly and fell hard, that would account for the head wound."

Annie hurried to the bathroom, dipped a towel in cold water. It didn't take long to clean the footboard and swipe up a streak of blood from the tile floor.

Billy turned to Iris. "Just for the record, did you see anybody near the cabin when you arrived?"

"Only a raccoon." A tiny smile touched her thin face. "That made me feel at home. When Nana played the piano, a raccoon came to listen. We'd see her in the bushes near the side window." Then, with a quick head shake, she continued in a cool, remote tone. "Anyway, I'd been downtown. On my bike. Coming back here, I stopped at Gas'n Go for some groceries." She pointed at the small brown sack sitting on the chest.

Gas'n Go was a mile and a half from Nightingale Courts. It belonged to Ben Parotti.

"The door was ajar. I pushed it in and saw her."

Billy nodded. "I suppose Emma left it open behind her since she was servicing the cabin." He waved his hand at the small plaid duffel bag lying empty on the luggage rack. "Was everything in order?"

Annie felt uncomfortable. What if Emma had disarranged Iris's belongings?

Iris looked surprised, then gave a wry smile. "You think somebody was trying to rob me? I got this outfit and one more. I got the sandals I'm wearing. A pretty stupid burglar." She walked to the dresser, opened the top drawer. "My stuff's here." She looked weary. "Sometimes I feel like everything bad happens around me. That poor old lady bringing towels and falling down. I didn't even need towels."

Billy was brisk. "Don't take blame when none's due." He moved toward the door, stopped at the threshold. "You going to stay on the island long?"

"A few days." Her face was unreadable.

"Nice time of year to be here." Billy reached for the sack of groceries. "Here, better get your stuff in the refrigerator." He lifted out a quart of milk, a box of Ritz crackers, and a small jar of peanut butter.

Iris took the milk and turned toward the small refrigerator.

Billy fished out a receipt, slipped it in a pocket.

When Iris faced him again, he offered the sack.

"Thanks. I don't need it."

Billy crumpled the sack and tossed it into the wastebasket. "Be seeing you."

Annie was behind him as they stepped outside. He paused to look down at the bike, number 16. Annie recognized the distinctive light green from Ben Parotti's bike rental shed near the ferry terminal. She waited to speak until she heard the click of the cabin door shutting. "Billy, there's something you should know." She gestured toward the office with a quick glance behind to be certain the door to the cabin was closed.

Billy gave her a sharp look, then nodded and walked with her.

Ingrid's office was understated, but welcoming. Red and yellow cushions looked inviting in rattan chairs. White pine paneled the walls. Hanging on one wall was Duane's photograph of a great blue heron feeding in the marsh, his reflection crystal clear in the water, beauty twice captured. Potted ferns glistened in sunlight spilling through a sliding glass door that opened onto a deck. Marsh grasses wavered in the onshore breeze. The tide was out. In the distance, dolphins arched in their daily aquatic ballet.

Annie gestured toward the largest of the chairs.

Billy shook his head, stood with his feet apart, waiting.

Annie remained standing, too. There was no good way to start. "I think Emma was searching Cabin Six." Was that breaking and entering? Emma hadn't broken in. She'd used a key. But still . . . Billy was a stickler about following the law.

Billy's broad face rarely revealed emotion. For an instant, his eyes widened, then he gave a short nod. "Emma was searching Iris's cabin. Why?"

"Emma's depressed." Annie heard the plea in her voice, but Billy looked stolid. "She's convinced she can't start a new book. She hasn't been eating. Ingrid and I thought it would help her, get her back on track, if she solved a mystery of some sort. Then we got word about Ingrid's sister being sick. On the way out Duane asked me to keep an eye on the girl in Cabin Six. He said she came last evening to rent a cabin. In the rain. Alone. On a bicycle. Emma was fascinated. She kept talking about it. She hurried out while I was on the phone. When I got here, Emma was waiting. She said she was going to stay in the next cabin to keep an eye on the girl. I needed to clean some cabins so I told Emma to check herself in. I guess she filched a key to Six."

Billy frowned, folded his arms.

Annie talked fast and heard the pleading note in her

voice. "Emma didn't mean any harm. She was curious. You have to admit there is something odd about arriving on a bicycle in the rain. Alone."

Billy looked pensive. "Not odd. Sad. I'd guess Iris just got out of treatment."

"Oh." The skeletal frame, the smudged darkness beneath Iris's eyes, now they made sense. "If she found Emma searching her room . . ."

Billy slowly shook his head. "I don't see Iris striking out at anyone. She was a gentle kid. She grew up down the street from me. My mom and hers were good friends. Her mom died when she was in middle school. Her grandma did her best, but Iris got into drugs. There are always a few. Everybody tells them, but they don't hear. She ran away just before she would have graduated from high school. I can check on it. Maybe she wasn't going to graduate. Maybe that was part of it. That was a bad year. Another kid died from an overdose. His sister drowned off Fish Haul pier a couple of weeks later. Some people thought she jumped because of him. A bad year." He shook his head again. "Anyway, there's no mystery about Iris." He pulled the Gas'n Go receipt from his pocket. "I'll find out for sure whether Iris could have pushed Emma. Not that I think Emma was pushed, but I like to check things out. That's why I took Iris's receipt." He glanced at it. "She paid cash at eleven-oh-three. The nine-one-one call came at eleven-ten. That figures about right for Iris to arrive here, find Emma, get you and you make the call. It's a five-minute bike ride from Gas'n Go to the cabin. We don't know how long Emma was unconscious. When did you last see her?"

"About ten-fifteen."

"Iris said she'd been downtown. I'll check it out."

* * *

Annie hurried into the hospital. Soon there would be an around-the-clock schedule set up with Altar Guild members taking turns sitting with Emma. Emma's room was at the far end of the second floor.

Annie felt as if she'd climbed a tall mountain, taking over at Nightingale Courts, cleaning the cabins, the shock of Emma's injury, racing to leave a note for Max as soon as she'd mopped up the spilled water in Cabin Five, driving fast to the hospital, hoping once again that Sgt. Harrison was otherwise occupied. There was a long wait in the E.R. waiting room. It was a couple of hours before Emma was transferred to a room and another twenty minutes before Dr. Burford walked down the hall. He nodded to her and stepped into Emma's room.

Annie scarcely remembered when the day had begun. The day had begun so well. If only it had ended well, too. She eased open Emma's door. Dr. Burford, his craggy face intent, stood at the bedside. Emma lay unmoving, her face pale beneath the neat bandage, IV in place. The nurse frowned at Annie and shook her head. Annie closed the door and leaned against the stippled plaster wall.

Her cell rang. Quickly, she flipped it open, silencing the tune, which seemed raucous in the quiet of a hospital hallway.

"Is Emma okay?" Max's voice was worried.

"I don't—" The door to Emma's room opened. "Hold on a minute."

Dr. Burford pulled the door shut behind him. Always gruff, he never wasted words. He gave Annie an abrupt nod. "Vital signs stable. Minimal blood loss. She's regained consciousness, but now she's asleep. The CT scan showed no significant brain injury. A simple concussion. She needs to be quiet for couple of days. Tell the mother hens—"

Annie knew he had experience with Altar Guild members taking care of one of their own.

"—to keep the noise level down. Emma's head will be pounding when she wakes up." He turned away.

Annie followed. "Did she say what happened?"

Burford was brusque. "Go ask a psychic. Emma won't remember where she was, much less what happened. She may not remember the day at all." With that he strode down the hall, a man in a hurry, always.

Annie lifted the cell. "Did you hear?"

"Every word. It sounds like Emma's going to be fine."

Max's voice seemed to come from a long distance. "Yes." Annie felt weak from relief. She'd felt responsible for Emma's injury. Annie shouldn't have left Emma on her own in the office.

"Annie!"

She pulled herself together. "I'm fine. Just a little hungry."

"Have you had lunch?"

The elevator door opened. Pamela Potts and Henny Brawley hurried toward her. Annie immediately felt better. Having Henny there obscurely made Annie feel that of course everything was going to be all right. Henny had that effect. Pamela was serious, kind, and always came when needed.

"Not yet." That's why she felt lightheaded.

"Meet me at Parotti's."

"I should stay here with Emma."

"She's doing great. I heard Doc say so. I'll bet the hall is swarming with Altar Guild members." Max knew the church ladies could be counted on.

The second elevator sang. Three more women spilled out and headed for her.

Annie felt buoyed. "I'm on my way."

Parotti's Bar and Grill, across from the ferry landing, was an island institution. As Annie pushed through the heavy oak door, she took a deep, satisfied breath, enjoying the mixture of scents: sawdust, live bait, hot grease, and beer on tap.

Max slid out of a booth and strode toward her. Tall, blond, and solidly built, he moved with easy grace.

She hurried toward him. When she was tired or weary or worried, emotion welled up, threatening to overcome her. She'd come so near to losing him when he was falsely—and so persuasively—accused of a crime during the hot days of August. She came into his arms, clung.

"Hey," his tone was soft, "it's okay, honey. Everything's okay." He gave her a quick hug, turned her toward the booth. "I've ordered for you. A double fried-oyster sandwich deluxe on an onion bun, horseradish mayo laced with barbecue sauce, curly fries, jalapeño cheese grits, and cole slaw."

Annie was touched. At Parotti's, Max always hoped to encourage her—by his sterling example—to order poached sole on a bed of endive. She always smiled pleasantly and ordered what she pleased. She gripped his hand until they moved apart to slide into the hard wooden booth. "Max, it's my fault . . ." and the words spilled out. ". . . I should have known not to leave Emma there by herself."

He reached across the table, placed a firm finger lightly on her lips. "Did Emma say she planned to snoop? No. Are you a mind reader? No. Case closed."

Annie felt as if she'd shed a huge burden. Truly, it hadn't occurred to her that Emma would filch a key and enter

Cabin Six. Her tense shoulders relaxed. Annie realized she was starving. She looked toward the kitchen.

Ben headed toward them, easily balancing the tray. When she'd first come to the island, the bar and grill had smelled fishier and an unshaven Ben, a wad of tobacco lodged in one cheek and with all the charm of an ill-tempered leprechaun, had slouched about in a faded red union suit and worn bib overalls. Then he met Miss Jolene, who owned a tea shop on the mainland. Their match was proof positive that love works miracles. Miss Jolene, as mistress and chef of Parotti's Bar and Grill, introduced quiche and salads to the menu, added fresh flowers in clear glass milk bottles to each table, and transformed Ben into a blazer-and-slacks-clad leprechaun, always freshly shaved and snapping Wrigley's Spearmint as he worked. Then and now, he had a finger in every island pie.

Ben unloaded the tray with practiced ease. "Any word on Ingrid's sister?"

That Ben was aware of Ingrid's hurried departure came as no surprise.

Annie picked up the oyster sandwich. "Not yet. Ingrid will probably call tonight." Annie took a bite. The sandwich was perfection, fried oysters crisp on the outside, succulent on the inside, onion bun toasted with a dash of butter.

"Too bad Emma got hurt trying to help out. I hear she fell down." Ben looked puzzled. "Emma's sure-footed as a mountain goat." He gave a bark of laughter. "And just as ornery. They say Iris Tilford found her." He slid the tray under one arm, settled back on his heels. "Iris came in on the ferry last night. She's been gone a long time. It gave me a turn to see her. She looks like she's been through a wringer. She waited for me, asked if I still rented bikes. I opened up the shed, got her a good one."

Annie remembered the sturdy green bike propped by the cabin door. "Iris was out on her bike this morning. She'd stopped at the Gas'n Go. She found Emma when she got back. It's lucky she wasn't out all day."

Ben looked thoughtful. "It surprises me Iris came back with her grandma gone. Iris missed the funeral. I wonder if she's home to stay." He glanced at her glass. "I'll freshen up your tea."

As Ben moved away, Max poured the rest of his Bud Light into the frosted glass. He averted his eyes as Annie added a splash of tartar sauce to her condiment-laden, cornmeal-crusted oysters. "There should be limits."

Annie resisted the temptation to add another splash of tartar sauce. "How about steamed shrimp for dinner?" The cabin had a small kitchenette and she'd bought a pound of shrimp yesterday and fresh spinach and homegrown tomatoes. She felt virtuous. Of course she loved healthy eating.

Max shook his head. "One serving of steamed fish doesn't balance out that." He pointed at her offending plate. Annie licked a streak of barbecue sauce from one finger and gave him a sunny smile.

The wooden door creaked open and Billy Cameron walked in. He paused to adjust his eyes to the dimness, then raised a hand in greeting and walked toward them.

Max started to rise and Billy waved his hand. "Keep your seat. Saw your cars outside. I thought you'd be glad to know everything checked out with Iris. Libby Callahan saw her talking on the pay phone by the ferry just as the ten-thirty bells chimed at St. Mary's. Iris was still at the pay phone ten minutes later when Libby came out of the yarn shop. It's a good twenty-five-minute bike ride to the Gas'n Go, another five minutes to Nightingale Courts. Iris's clear from the time you last saw Emma until Emma was found at eleven-ten. So,

Emma fell down and that's all there is to it. Which is what I expected."

"Have a cup of coffee with us." Max slid closer to the wall.

Billy grinned. "It's Wednesday and that's Miss Jolene's coconut cream pie day."

Ben arrived with the tea pitcher. "Hey, Billy. One coffee black and pie coming up."

"Make that two pieces of pie." Annie swiped one last curly fry through ketchup and gave Max another sunny smile.

As Max and Billy debated the finer points of mullet versus mackerel as bait for blue marlins, Annie spooned the creamy pie with its exquisitely toasted fresh coconut flakes and began a mental to-do list: grocery-shop to replenish the Nightingale Courts soda and snack counter, wash soiled sheets, pick up flowers for Emma—

Without warning Ben's hoarse words echoed in her mind: *. . . sure-footed as a mountain goat.*

Annie looked toward Billy, then shrugged. It was silly to let Ben's offhand comment make her uneasy. Billy had checked everything out. Iris certainly hadn't surprised Emma in her cabin and pushed her. Besides, as Billy had made clear, there was no mystery about Iris Tilford.

∽ Four ∾

EMMA'S EYES BLINKED open. She looked vague, then her gaze, lucid and baffled, settled on Annie. "My head hurts."

Pamela Potts, soft blond hair swaying in her haste, reached out to adjust Emma's pillow. "Now, now, we need to be quiet and rest."

Emma glared at Pamela. "Where am I?" It was a snarl.

Annie felt a curl of delight. What a great start for Friday. TGIF. Doc Burford had been reassuring, but it had worried Annie that Emma had slept most of the time since her injury on Wednesday. Now, finally, Emma was awake. Moreover, she was herself, crusty, overbearing, and demanding despite her pale face, bandaged head, IV, and wrinkled hospital gown. Annie smiled, said softly, "In the hospital."

Annie moved closer with her vase filled with pink carnations. She was glad she'd waited until this morning to bring the flowers. They would be absolutely fresh and aromatic. She pushed aside an oblong planter with lovely trailing blooms of lavender. As her hand touched a bloom, she smiled at the sweet familiar smell.

Pamela took a deep breath. "Oh, what a glorious scent. Liz Montgomery brought the planter. They are her very own Homestead Purple." Pamela clutched the planter, held it near the bed. "Can you smell them, Emma?"

Emma's eyes glittered. "Of course I can smell. It's my head that hurts, not my nose."

"Lavender." Pamela was as ecstatic as a high priestess at a flower-laden altar. "Lavender has great healing properties." Her tone was earnest. "Lavender lifts depression, eases nausea, and soothes insect bites. Liz is so thoughtful."

"I'm not depressed," Emma snapped. "My stomach would be fine if I had some food, and I don't itch."

Pamela replaced the planter and reached for the carnations. "Here are Annie's beautiful carnations." She held the vase close for Emma's inspection.

Emma's nose wrinkled. "Spicy."

Pamela nodded happily. "Carnations and cloves both contain eugenol. That's what gives carnations their heavy scent. And did you know," she positively chirruped in happiness, "eugenol is a colorless liquid phenol used as an antiseptic by dentists." Pamela placed the vase next to the planter. "The Altar Guild sent a dozen red roses"—she pointed to a gorgeous bouquet among several vases on the windowsill— "and they smell heavenly, too."

Emma was no longer listening. She lifted a hand to her head. She looked uncertainly around the room, slowly sank back onto the pillow. Her blue eyes glazed over, closed, fluttered open. In a startled tone, she said, "I was walking—" She stopped, as if she'd run into a wall. "Something reminded me." Her gaze slid from the partially raised window sash to the open bathroom door to Pamela standing near the chair to Annie at the bedside table. "Something . . ." She shook her head, winced. Her fingers touched the bandage. "What's this?"

Pamela poured water from a carafe into a plastic cup. "We had a little fall and bumped our head."

Emma's gaze at Pamela was withering. "*We* didn't do any such thing." She struggled onto one elbow, winced.

"Do you want to sit up?" At Emma's nod, Annie pushed the control and the head portion of the bed rose.

When Emma was comfortably settled, she waved away the water. "Coffee. I need coffee."

Pamela looked uncertain. "Do you think that's wise?"

"Wise be damned." Emma's cheeks turned pink.

Annie hurried to intervene. Emma liked Pamela, admitted Pamela was true-blue, but even at the best of times Pamela pushed Emma dangerously near the edge. This wasn't the best of times. "Pamela, maybe we should check with the nurse and see if we can get coffee and some breakfast for Emma, too."

Pamela always seized an opportunity to serve. When the door closed behind her, Annie slipped into the chair next to the bed. "How are you feeling?"

"Like death warmed over." Emma's eyes gleamed. "That was the title of a Mary Collins book. She didn't write enough books."

Annie agreed. The California author published six novels to critical acclaim between 1941 and 1949, then disappeared from the annals of mystery writers.

Emma glowered. "I don't remember falling."

Annie nodded. That's what Doc Burford had predicted.

Emma once again gently touched the bandage. "What happened?"

Annie hesitated, then began delicately. "You were at the

store. We were talking about a guest at Nightingale Courts who arrived on her bicycle in the rain."

There was no flicker of memory in Emma's cornflower blue eyes.

"Ingrid got word her sister was sick. She and Duane had to leave in a hurry. I promised to take care of everything while they were gone. You came out to Nightingale Courts." Obviously, Emma had no idea she'd been engaged in illegal behavior. Annie made a quick decision. Billy had assumed Emma was engaged in housekeeping. Annie was a firm believer in not disturbing sleeping dogs. "You took towels to Cabin Six"—Annie watched Emma closely—"and the guest found you unconscious. Apparently you tripped and banged your head on the footboard."

"I tripped?" Emma's eyebrows rose. "That was stupid." She brushed her fingers across the bandage. "How long have I been here?"

"You fell Wednesday. It's Friday morning." As far as Annie was concerned, it was definitely TGIF. She'd always loved Fridays, but this one was special: Emma was going to be fine, Ingrid had called to say that her sister was doing well and might be able to go home this afternoon, the weather was early April perfect, sunny and cloudless, with a high in the low seventies, and tonight she and Max would greet their friends at the harbor pavilion.

"Not until next week?" Max frowned.

Russell Montgomery swiped at his cheeks with an oversize bandanna, his face red despite the shade from his Panama hat. "The plumber's tied up in Bluffton. He swears he'll get to the Franklin house by Monday at the latest."

Max switched his gaze from Russell's defensive expression to the shining columns of the Franklin house. The pillars glistened ivory white, and the moss green of the tabby walls had the muted glow of sunlight slanting through seawater. Max's impatience seeped away. Russell was doing the best he could and the date that they moved in scarcely mattered. When he remembered how near he'd come to having a broken life—jailed for a crime he hadn't committed and rescued only by Annie's bravery and Billy's honor—a delayed move was no big thing.

Max's gaze turned back. His smile was genuine. "Thanks, Russell. Hey, we're looking forward to seeing you and Liz tonight."

Russell's face stiffened. "Yeah. That'll be great." He wiped the kerchief against his neck, stuffed it in a pocket, and forced a smile. "Yeah. And thanks for cutting me some slack on the house. I'll get it done." He gave a short nod, then turned and strode away, his work boots crackling on the oyster-shell path. He slammed into his truck.

Max watched as the pickup disappeared behind the live oaks. Had he offended Russell? Maybe his irritation over the delay had been too evident and the reference to the party seemed patronizing.

Max shrugged. Whatever. Nothing was going to diminish his pleasure in the party. Wait till Annie saw that banner!

Annie pushed the six-packs of Coke deeper into her trunk. She wedged the Sprites next to the grocery sacks. When Ingrid and Duane got home, they would find everything in good order.

Annie glanced at the sky, the sun beginning its afternoon downward arc. Errands and a quick grilled chicken salad at the Cosy Corner Tea Shoppe had taken most of the day. If she hurried straight to Nightingale Courts, she could finish her tasks and have time for a dip in the pool before getting ready for the party. She felt a squiggle of eagerness. Max had firmly insisted she was not to come near the pavilion until a quarter to six. He had everything under control and all she needed to bring was her party face.

She turned on the motor and drove out of the parking lot. However, she swerved left instead of right, heading for Death on Demand. Some desires could not be denied. After all, Agatha would have missed her. Which reminded her that Dorothy L., their good-humored white cat, also needed playtime this afternoon. In her equable fashion, Dorothy L. was tolerating their temporary quarters at Nightingale Courts with her usual equanimity.

Annie found a shady spot beneath a weeping willow in the harbor parking lot. She walked fast to the wooden steps to the boardwalk. The shop fronts curved in a semicircle facing the marina. Gleaming yachts, sportfishing charters, sleek cruisers, sturdy outboards, and sailing dinghies rode at anchor. Laughing gulls cackled overhead.

Annie stopped at the top of the steps and stared. Women in bright spring clothes milled outside the front door of Death on Demand. She recognized Friends of the Library members, tennis players, golfers, quilters. . . . High voices rose in good-humored conversation, then there was forward movement. "The doors are open . . . such a lovely idea . . . Absolutely novel . . ."

Annie followed the crowd and squeezed inside the bookstore. She glimpsed Henny at the cash desk. Their eyes met. Henny grinned and turned a cheerful thumbs-up.

Laurel's beguiling voice, soft yet always heard, lifted above the chatter. "My dears, welcome. We have gathered to enhance our minds, bodies, and spirits. We shall explore the yin and the yang." Her smile was beatific. Her hands rose as if in benediction. Laurel's spun gold hair was perfectly coiffed in a Peter Pan cut. Her classic features offered ageless beauty. Standing in the center of the coffee bar area, she was elegant in a red silk tai chi uniform, the jacket with traditional loop-and-knot closures, the slacks loose fitting yet beautifully styled, soft white leather shoes a dazzling counterpoint. Her blue eyes were dreamy yet acutely aware of each and every person present. That perceptive gaze reached Annie.

"Oohh." Laurel's sigh of pleasure elicited smiles. "How lovely. Here is our dear Annie. We owe the grace of our surroundings to Annie, who shares with this fortunate island her devotion to books that elevate character, just as tai chi elevates bodies and souls. I have allotted fifteen minutes before we begin our tai chi"—it was as if she bestowed a treasure sought by many and achieved by few—"for each of you to purchase the book of your choice and to view the mystery paintings above the fireplace." Now her glowing smile was almost beatific. "You will note the lovely watercolors. Many of you may not know the history behind the paintings. Members of our island watercolor society volunteer to provide the paintings. After the contest ends every month, the paintings are raffled off by the society to raise money for scholarships. This month our artist is Gus Winship, who teaches art in the high school. Aren't his paintings wonderful!" Laurel waved a graceful hand at the watercolors.

Every month Annie hung five paintings, each scene representing a critical moment in a superb mystery. Henny Brawley was the runaway winner of the contests, which afforded coffee for a month and a free (noncollectible) book. Henny hadn't paid for a cup of coffee in months.

Obediently, the tai chi neophytes turned toward the paintings. Appreciative oohs and ahs rose.

In the first painting, a petite silver-haired woman with sparkling black eyes and a turned-up nose held a pistol with casual ease and dropped several boxes of bullets into the pockets of her red shirt-jacket. A flaming redhead in an orange Auburn T-shirt and floral stretch leggings gingerly gripped a handgun. A rifle leaned against the wall near a stack of moving boxes.

In the second painting, the wine cellar was dark and shadowy, lit only by a candle set on a small table. A man tied to a chair was dressed in finery, the latest fashion in doublet and breeches. His face looked highborn but there was an air of dishonor about him. An imperious figure, with aristocratic features, spare high cheekbones, and zeal-burned blue eyes, stared at the captive coldly. Three men stood at the foot of the stairs, a huge redhead, a slender young man with intelligent dark eyes, and an elegant blond dandy. Behind them on the steps, a pale young woman in a green velvet dress with a white collar watched with haunted eyes.

In the third painting, a fiftyish blonde with a face well seasoned by living trained a shotgun on a trim man in a dark suit. A slender blonde, perhaps ten years younger, used her foot to nudge a gun out of his reach on the floor. The well-kept interior of the trailer, with comfortable chairs and the casual disarray of happy living, books, and children's toys, was in stark contrast to the burning and dangerous fury in his grim face.

In the fourth painting, a gorgeous blonde grappled with a Rhodesian ridgeback in a graveled parking area, skinning her elbows and ripping the knees of her jeans as the lean, powerful dog struggled to escape.

In the fifth painting, a dark-haired leggy young woman ran full tilt down an aisle between stacked merchandise in a department store storeroom, throwing picture frames, candles, wreaths, Christmas ornaments, pots and pans as she tried to escape her pursuer.

Annie looked at the uplifted faces and felt a surge of hope. Maybe this month the contest would be won by someone other than Henny. After the watercolors were admired, the women fanned through Death on Demand, eagerly scanning the shelves.

Annie approached her mother-in-law in awe. "We've never had this many customers in April."

Laurel beamed. "Seek and ye shall find."

Annie almost pointed out that Laurel was mixing cultures, then, as often in dealing with her mother-in-law, Annie remained mute.

Laurel traced a finger delicately across the green-and-gold dragon embroidered on her jacket. "Everything has gone splendidly." She turned to the coffee bar to pick up a notepad.

Annie looked at the coffee bar. Agatha stretched on her back atop her red cushion, eyes half open, paws apart. If she'd been in a cartoon, an appropriate caption would read: *Glutton at rest; Indifferent to owner's absence.*

"I poached a chicken breast for Agatha with a sauce of mashed sardines. Of course"—Laurel's laughter was light—"she may be a wee bit demanding at future meals. However, I knew"—Laurel's gaze was bright—"you wanted only the best for Agatha. Such a sensitive creature."

Annie resisted an impulse to pour ice water over Agatha. It had taken months to wean her overweight feline from soft food to a twice daily portion of reduced-calorie dry food, months punctuated by sulking and outright attacks. A wee bit demanding . . .

Laurel touched Annie's shoulder. "My dear, such rigidity. I have a solution. But first"—she tore a sheet from the notepad and gave it to Annie—"here are the calls you've received. I kept a careful record. I invited everyone who called to join us for our exercise and meditation and to bring a friend. In addition, I made a few calls of my own." She waved her hand at the filled aisles.

The cash register sang. Annie hurried to help Henny at the cash desk. As Henny scanned credit cards, Annie handled cash payments. There were two left in line when a gong sounded.

Startled, Annie jumped and grabbed at the countertop to keep her balance.

Henny pushed a sales receipt to the customer and leaned toward Annie. "Tai chi encourages balance, harmony, grace, and beauty."

The last customer pushed a twenty-dollar bill and a paperback edition of Tim Myers's *A Mold for Murder* toward Annie. "Tuck a credit in my book. I'll pick it up after our class." She turned to hurry to the coffee bar.

The gong sounded again. A hush fell.

Laurel gestured to Annie with the mallet. "Come forward, Annie. I know you will·want to help me lead your wonderful patrons in our exercises. Please, let Annie through." She swung the mallet at a bronze gong on the center table and the deep resonance filled the room.

Women moved aside and a path opened.

Henny whispered, "Five hundred and forty-two dollars and sixty-three cents."

Annie folded the sheet of phone messages, tucked it in

her pocket, and swept to the coffee area. She embraced her mother-in-law and turned to face the assembled tai chi enthusiasts.

Laurel folded her hands and bowed. Hands folded, everyone bowed to her in turn.

A beat late, Annie clasped and bowed.

Laurel's tone was warm, inviting, as soporific as a gentle waterfall. "We'll begin—Annie, dear, place your feet parallel, toes pointed straight. Bend your knees. Wrists loose, allow your arms to float . . ."

Annie turned the Volvo into Nightingale Courts. Five hundred and forty-two dollars and sixty-three cents . . . She wondered if she'd ever get the hang of Stork Spreads Its Wings. How did anyone wave one hand in one direction, the other in another, bend knees, point one foot out, lift a foot as if swinging over a log, and breathe at the right time? If the class continued, would Laurel teach it?

Laurel in Death on Demand every week?

Five hundred and forty-two dollars and sixty-three cents . . .

As Annie slid out of the car and tucked the keys into her pocket, she touched folded sheets of paper. She pulled the phone messages out of her pocket. Laurel had pointed with pride to her careful recording. The messages were liberally annotated with Laurel's thoughts.

Annie stopped in the shade of a willow and laughed aloud. Max would love this message with Laurel's editorial additions: "The dentist's receptionist called to confirm your appointment. She sounds like a Viagra ad. There is nothing sexy about a filling. I almost suggested she consider voice lessons to achieve a more professional tone—cheery but bland—then decided the moment might not be opportune. Your appointment is at ten o'clock Monday. I assured her you would come."

Laurel had adorned a message left by Pamela Potts with smiley faces, exclamation points, and heavily scored under-lining with the editorial comment: "Pamela is such a dear, but she does reiterate, doesn't she? Below is an expurgated version of her call."

As she read, Annie heard Pamela's earnest voice in her mind: "When I helped Emma dry off after her shower this afternoon, she was quite gruff when I accidentally touched her back. That's when I saw the bruise below her right shoulder blade. I was shocked, a big, purple spot with a circumference of almost four inches which as you will admit—"

Annie's smile faded.

"—is rather large. I told the nurse. She looked at it and said it was a bruise. I replied that I knew it was a bruise. The nurse said people who fall often sustain many scrapes and bruises and the attending physician would have noted the bruise and concluded it posed no threat. The nurse said the bruise would go away." Annie imagined Pamela's soft voice, aggrieved and impatient. "Of course, it will—"

At this point, Laurel had put within parentheses: (Pamela takes discursiveness to a height not achieved by even the most skilled politicians.)

"—go away. The point is, how did it get there? As I un-derstand the accident, Emma fell forward, not backward. Please call when you have a moment. I am uneasy. I hope you can reassure me. Did Emma perhaps lurch backward, then fall?"

Annie had planned to carry in the groceries. Instead, she

took time only to grab a stack of fresh towels and hurry to Cabin Six. White curtains were closed in the front windows. No green bike was propped next to the steps.

She unlocked the door and called out, "Housekeeping," to no response. As she stepped into dimness, she felt a prickle down her back. Just so had Emma Clyde entered this room Wednesday morning.

Annie flicked on the light. The room was cheerful, wicker easy chairs with red and yellow cushions, oak bed with a green comforter, lacy eyelet curtains fluttering from the draft of the open door, three lime green walls, the fourth a marsh scene with fiddler crabs in the mud and a yellow-crowned night heron stalking forward, one foot forever lifted in a step.

Annie left the door ajar. Though she still held the towels, she didn't move toward the bathroom. To her right, a TV sat on a dresser. A compact refrigerator was tucked between the dresser and a chest. To the left of the entrance, a small table sat beneath the window. The bed and two wicker chairs completed the furnishings.

Annie figured distances. Emma was found crumpled near the foot of the bed. If she had fallen backward and struck the edge of the dresser, she wouldn't have been found on the floor near the bed. The edge of the dresser was sharp and couldn't account for a large circular bruise beneath her right shoulder blade.

There had been traces of blood on the footboard. If Emma fell full force and struck the footboard, she would have fallen precisely as she was found.

Why did she fall? The vinyl tiled floor was clear and smooth. Unless something was lying there and she'd tripped, the floor afforded no reason for an accident. The floor was clear when Annie knelt beside her. Could Emma have had a dizzy turn? That was possible.

Neither dizziness nor tripping explained a bruise on her back.

Suddenly Annie heard a long-silent voice from her memory: *A hypothesis must include analysis of all possibilities.* She remembered her mystery-loving uncle Ambrose from whom she'd inherited Death on Demand and his insistence that all successful mysteries accounted for every fact.

She'd failed Uncle Ambrose's test. She hadn't even considered the most simple explanation: Emma's bruise had no connection to Cabin Six. She might have thumped against a nozzle in her hot tub or been the unfortunate recipient of a whack from a broom handle when standing in line at the supermarket. That bruise could have occurred a dozen different ways prior to Wednesday morning. Annie blew out a breath of relief.

Whenever the bruise occurred, it hadn't been caused by her fall.

Unless . . . Annie looked at the space behind the partially open door. When Emma entered the room someone could have stood behind the door. As it shut, the unseen figure could have jumped, fist bunched, slamming Emma forward.

However, and she could almost smell Uncle Ambrose's pipe smoke, that possibility required a desperate need by the assailant not to be seen. Iris Tilford had no reason to hide her presence in the cabin she'd rented. In any event, Billy had checked and Iris was nowhere near the cabin when Emma fell.

Did Emma surprise an intruder?

Annie looked across the room. Between the bathroom and a kitchenette, a sliding glass door opened onto a small deck that overlooked the marsh. It took only a moment to reach the door and grab the handle. The door opened easily. It had not been locked. Which proved nothing. Perhaps it had been unlocked for days or weeks.

If it were open Wednesday morning, an intruder could have entered that way.

But Iris had found nothing out of order among her few possessions.

Annie slid shut the sliding door's lock. Whatever the fact Wednesday morning, no one could now enter the cabin from the deck. Confident she'd hear Iris on the cabin's front steps, Annie checked the top drawer in the dresser. There were a green-and-white-striped blouse and white cotton slacks. Two bras, two panties, and a neatly folded turquoise shorty nightgown completed the inventory.

Annie closed the drawer. The other drawers were empty. She found nothing in the chest. The duffel was empty, too. A frayed navy blue Atlanta Braves sweatshirt hung in the closet. In the bathroom, there were a comb, hairbrush, deodorant stick, makeup kit, toothbrush, and toothpaste.

There was nothing worth stealing. Iris's belongings were remarkable only for their meagerness. Annie added a towel to the rack and turned away. Whatever road Iris had traveled in coming to the island, she'd carried little with her except perhaps memories and sadness. As Billy had made clear, there was no mystery about Iris Tilford.

Envisioning a lurking assailant in her rented cabin made no sense.

Annie clutched her cell phone and reminded herself to be patient, but she paced restlessly as she listened to Pamela Potts's high, sweet voice: ". . . good of you to call and I suppose you are right. Emma could have suffered that bruise another time. I'm afraid we'll never know for sure. Emma doesn't remember anything about being at Nightingale Courts. Although it seems an odd coincidence and I thought," Pamela's tone was faintly accusing, "you were always suspicious of coincidences."

Once again Annie felt uneasy. Was the bruise a coincidence? If Emma had lost her balance in the cabin, she could have lost her balance another time. Annie brushed away the memory of Ben describing the author as sure-footed as a mountain goat. Pamela began to reiterate everything they'd discussed. Annie looked yearningly at the open car trunk and sacks waiting to be carried inside. Her patience expired. She interrupted. "Tell Emma I'm glad she's feeling better and we'll miss seeing her tonight. Oh, golly, Pamela, I have to run. I'll talk to you at the picnic." She clicked off the cell, feeling vaguely guilty. But she had much to do and little time.

As Annie retrieved the last of the groceries, Iris rode up on her bike.

Iris braked. She stepped off the bike and asked softly, "Is the lady okay?"

Annie balanced the sack as she closed the trunk. "Emma's doing fine. She's conscious and none the worse except for a headache."

Iris looked relieved. "I'm glad." She looked toward her cabin. "Has anybody asked for me? An old friend said she'd come and I hope I'm not late."

"No one has been around for the last hour or so."

Iris nodded and swung onto the seat. Dust puffed as she rode on the crushed oyster shells.

In the office, Annie unloaded the sack. As she placed the last Sprite in the refrigerator, tires crunched on the oyster-shell drive. Annie hoped no one was arriving to check in.

There was no reservation for the night. She hurried to the window and saw Cara Wilkes's late-model white Lexus convertible. Cara had represented the buyers of Annie and Max's previous house on Scarlet King Lagoon. Annie wondered if there was some kind of problem with the new owners. The car didn't stop at the office. Cara drove straight to Cabin Six.

Annie smiled. It was nice that someone was welcoming Iris home.

When the last clean towel was shaken and folded and the fresh stack placed in the housekeeping closet, Annie brushed back a limp tendril of hair. She was hot, tired, and thirsty. She glanced at her watch. A quarter to five. She intended to arrive at the pavilion at a quarter to six. It was going to be a great party. She didn't have to worry about having a good time. She always had a good time with Max. That morning she'd unpacked a new Irish linen shirt trimmed with open-work embroidery and a long swirly skirt with matching embroidery above the hem. The shirt and skirt were the delicate light blue of a robin's egg. Her new sandals were a perfect color match. Max would reach out and take her hand and tell her she was beautiful and his eyes would tell her more.

She locked the housekeeping closet and hurried across the hummocky grass toward their cabin. She had time for a swim before she showered and dressed. The cabins at Nightingale Courts curved in a semicircle near the marsh. Three years ago Ingrid and Duane had built a pool in the center of the grassy area in front of the cabins between the palmettos that lined the oyster-shell drive and a stand of pines.

In the cabin, Annie changed into her swimsuit, slipped on thongs. She didn't bother with a cap. As she came down the steps, a towel over one arm, she glanced toward Cabin Six. Cara's white car was gone. The green bicycle rested on its kickstand. A solitary figure stood on the deck behind Cabin Six.

Annie was halfway to the line of palmettos when she stopped. She turned to look. The deck behind Cabin Six was no longer visible. But she knew what she'd glimpsed in her peripheral vision, a thin, forlorn, too-alone woman staring out at the marsh, shoulders drooping, a picture of defeat and sadness.

Annie wanted a quick dip, a plunge that would refresh her for a festive evening. She had no time or energy to waste.

A long-ago memory bobbed, bright as a beach ball bouncing in the sun, her mother's sweet and thoughtful voice when Annie had sloughed away a phone message from a too-earnest, too-plump, too-hungry-for-friendship girl in her class: "Don't pass by on the other side." Annie returned that call and discovered a bright, sweet, kind girl who'd grown to be a charming woman whose friendship Annie still treasured.

Duane had asked Annie to look out for the girl in Cabin Six. Duane had known sadness. Ingrid's kindness had lifted him up.

Annie turned and walked slowly toward Iris's cabin. It was all well and good to offer understanding. Yet, what right did Annie have? She was a stranger. How could she help Iris? What was she going to say? She skirted around the side of the cabin. The nutrient-rich scent of the marsh was pungent and wonderful to Annie though outlanders sometimes called the smell a stench. The tide was out. Fiddler crabs swarmed on the chocolate brown mudflat. Egrets stepped high, beaks flashing to snatch a crab.

Iris heard the crackle of the oyster shells. She turned.

The late afternoon sun wasn't kind to her sallow, worn face, emphasizing dark shadows beneath her eyes.

Annie reached the steps to the deck. "Hey, Iris." Silence fell. Feeling uncertain and intrusive, Annie forced a smile. "I'm going to take a swim in the pool and wondered if you'd like to join me."

"A swim?" Iris spoke as if the words were strange.

Annie was suddenly certain it had been a long time, measured both in time and emotion, since Iris had slipped carefree into the inviting blue waters of a swimming pool.

Iris's thin face held an instant of eagerness, then the light in her eyes faded. She massaged one wrist. "Thanks. But I"—she stared down at the old planks—"I guess pretty soon I'll ride my bike for a while."

It was a lame excuse.

Annie understood only too well. She knew—no one better—that Iris had no swimsuit. "Please join me. I hate to swim alone. I know you're only here for a few days and you may not have a swimsuit with you. Ingrid—she's the lady you rented from Wednesday night and I'm helping out while she's gone to be with her sister—has a stack of suits in the"—Annie caught herself in time from saying the one-piece suits were in the snack shop. She'd be sure and remove the sale price if Iris agreed— "office and they're for guests who forgot to bring a suit. I'll run and get one for you." Annie's smile was warm. "The water will be perfect."

Iris stared for a moment like a child offered an unexpected gift. Her sudden smile was shy. "That would be very nice."

∼: *Five* :∼

THE WATER WAS perfect, not too warm, not too cold. With her dark hair sleek against her head, Iris looked younger and almost carefree.

Annie concluded, ". . . and I inherited the bookstore from Uncle Ambrose. Max followed me to the island." She'd run away from New York and Max because she cared too much. She was sure they didn't belong together. Max was rich; she was poor. Max was laid-back and casual; she was intense and hardworking. Max enjoyed subtleties; she was direct and open.

"Now you're married." Iris trailed fingers through the water. "It's like a fairy tale. And you lived happily ever after."

Annie's throat felt tight. "Happily ever after . . ." Her smile disappeared. Once, she'd trusted that her life and his were charmed. Not now. Never again. Life and happiness were fragile at best. Sunny days could be gone in an instant.

Iris's dark eyes were empathetic. It was as if a cloud slid across the sun and both of them were in a shadow. She looked at Annie gravely. "What happened?"

Annie gazed at Iris's burdened face, too old for its years.

Annie was often asked about a time that was seared in her memory. She was quick to discern the curiosity of those seeking sensation, much like TV viewers feasting on the raw emotion and exhibitionism of reality shows. Instead, Iris looked at Annie with eyes that had known sorrow and fear. Was it better to push pain deep inside, hope that time would blur memory? Or was it better to confront the past?

Annie ducked beneath the surface, came up with water streaming down her face, fresh and cool. She'd not intended to reveal her heart to a stranger when she invited Iris to swim. "Last summer Max was accused . . ." She felt again the terror of sultry August days when Max was suspected of murder and damning facts piled against him until there seemed no way to save him.

Iris floated in a plastic ring and listened. When Annie finished, Iris spoke slowly. "Everybody has troubles. Even people like you. I guess I thought I was the only one."

"Do you have troubles?" Annie's voice was gentle.

Iris's face crinkled in thought. "Things are better now. I belong to AA and NA." Her face held a question.

Annie reached over the water, patted a bony arm. "I never had to fight that kind of battle. You have great courage."

"One day at a time." The oft-used words were a bulwark, a hope, a prayer, a plea. Iris looked past Annie at the rising tide and the spartina grass wavering in the onshore breeze. "I have things I need to clear up. Sometimes I don't remember things. When I do remember, I'm not sure what really happened. I've tried to tell the people I hurt that I'm sorry. That's why I came home. There are people I need to see."

Annie remembered Cara Wilkes's sleek white convertible. Cara hadn't stayed long. After she left, Annie had found Iris sad and alone on the deck.

Iris looked wry. "See, I've got things to ask, but nobody much wants to see me. I bring back things they don't want to remember. Maybe I should leave."

Annie wondered where Iris would go and to what kind of life?

Suddenly Iris's face hardened. "I can't let it be. When things aren't right, you have to do what you can."

Annie had no words of wisdom. She knew better now than to murmur that everything would work out. Maybe. Maybe not.

A faraway deep-throated blast signaled the arrival of the five-thirty ferry.

Annie shot straight up in the water. "The ferry's coming in. I have to be at the pavilion in fifteen minutes!" She could do it. Max always marveled at how quickly she showered and dressed and was on her way, with her hair damp but curly, a touch of makeup, and a smile. The crisp robin's-egg blue linen shirt and skirt waited for her in the closet. It was time to share laughter and friendship and food.

In three swift strokes, Annie was at the ladder. On the deck, water streaming in rivulets from her brief hibiscus-bright suit, she looked down at Iris, alone in the pool. Iris had nowhere to go, no one to welcome her, and peanut butter and Ritz crackers in her cabin.

"Iris, please come with me." Annie's smile was sudden and warm. "We're having an oyster roast. Ben Parotti's sweet tea with fresh mint is the best on the island and the view of the bay from the pavilion is great." But who was she to tell a native islander? Annie rushed on, aware of Iris's limited wardrobe. "It's down home. Everyone will be casual. There's a mixture of people. You'll probably know a lot of them." She made a quick decision to leave the linen outfit in the closet, substitute a striped red-and-white tee, jeans, and red sandals.

"A party at the pavilion." Iris's expression was a mixture of uncertainty and trepidation. "The last time I was there . . ." Her voice trailed away.

"Please come. Then you'll know you're home." The pavilion hosted every kind of event from fund drives to school groups to political rallies to private parties. "Do you remember how the harbor lights spill across the water after the sun goes down?" Annie loved the harbor after dark, the smell of creosoted timbers and saltwater, the soft whisper of the sea against the pilings, an occasional glimpse of faraway lights as cabin cruisers sailed past carrying their passengers to nearby docks or faraway ports.

Iris stroked to the ladder. She looked up, her face resolute. "I'll come." She climbed up the ladder. "I'll be quick." She walked away.

Annie stared at the thin hurrying figure. She'd hoped to offer friendship, yet Iris seemed grim, as if she were fulfilling a duty.

The heavy throb of guitars, drums, and piano echoed from a stage set up halfway between the picnic tables and a grove of pines. A gangly young teenager with a white stripe of hair bristling from a shaved head painted red belted out "You're Sixteen." A hand-painted sign hung from the stage: THE RED HOT MOHAWKS, appearing every Saturday night at The Haven, a buck a couple. Max taught tennis at The Haven, the island's recreation center for teens. Now she understood why he'd casually mentioned the Mohawks over the last several weeks. The vocalist moved back and forth on the stage, bending and stamping, apparently heavily influenced by a vision of an Indian powwow. Annie was glad the band was on the far side of the tables. The sound was loud but not loud enough to make guests shout to be heard.

The pavilion sat on a slight rise overlooking the harbor. There were tables in the open-air pavilion, but Max liked his picnics to be beneath the stars. Their party was set up for the picnic tables that dotted the sweep of sandy ground between the pavilion and the boardwalk. Annie admired the centerpieces she'd designed, hurricane lamps with candles in the center of each table. Black anchor line was coiled around the bronze base of each lamp.

Ben Parotti's face was flushed from the heat of the roaring hickory fire beneath a sheet of steel balanced on concrete blocks. Bushel bags of oysters were piled nearby and a stack of water-soaked burlap bags. Miss Jolene directed two women behind a line of steam tables. Hot dogs bobbed in bubbling hot water. No Low Country oyster roast was complete without chili dogs and squash casserole, plenty of draft beer and sweet tea.

Sheets from the Broward's Rock *Gazette* covered one stone table. Oyster knives paired with stainless steel mesh oyster gloves were ranged around the perimeter of the table. When the roast began, Ben would steam the oysters for five to ten minutes, then shovel them onto the shucking table and everyone would set to work. They had invited forty guests, so Ben had five bags of oysters ready to steam, figuring around twelve to fifteen oysters per guest. Once a plate was loaded with oysters, the steam tables would be next.

"Come on, Iris." Annie ran up the steps to the pavilion. Guests walked toward the pavilion from the oyster-shell parking lot. She had barely arrived in time to greet the first arrivals. She skidded to a stop, stared up at the brilliant banner.

Max strode toward her, grinning, his arms open. The breeze ruffled his thick blond hair. He was handsome and happy, delighted in the banner, in the moment, in her. "One of these days, we'll greet our guests on our own front porch. Until then, this"—he gestured at the rippling silk—"is the next best thing."

Annie came into his embrace. "Max, the banner's wonderful." She smiled at him. "How did you ever think of this?"

He looked up at their images between the sparkling white Ionic columns. "We couldn't greet everyone there, so I brought the Franklin house here."

Song lyrics boomed over the mike. Voices called out. Steps sounded behind them.

Annie remembered Iris. "Come meet Iris Tilford. She's the one who helped Emma when she was hurt. She's staying at Nightingale Courts and I talked her into coming tonight. She's from the island."

Iris hung back a little. The breeze ruffled her hair, tugged at her blouse and slacks. She looked uncertainly at Max.

Max reached out to shake her hand. "It's nice to see you again." He saw Annie's surprise. "Iris came by Wednesday morning when I was putting up the banner. I told her it was a surprise for my wife." He grinned at Iris. "Thanks for keeping my secret. It's great you could come tonight."

There was a flurry of arrivals and Iris edged away. A little later as the smoke billowed from the hickory fire and the sun spread a glory of rose across the water, Annie saw Iris standing alone near the old live oak that island lore traced back to the days when privateers made Broward's Rock their base for sorties against the British.

Annie took a step, then stopped. Marian Kenyon, the *Gazette*'s gimlet-eyed chief reporter, a bottle of Bud in hand, sped across the hummocky ground to plant herself in front of Iris. Whippet lean, Marian always moved fast. Her unruly black hair with its frosting of white appeared either unkempt or windblown depending upon the attitude of the viewer. Marian and Iris appeared to be acquainted. Annie was well aware that the island was a small and tight society, especially for natives. Despite her years of visiting when her uncle was alive and the time she'd spent living on Broward's Rock, Annie was often surprised at the intertwining of family and relationships that weren't always apparent to an outlander.

Billy and Mavis Cameron waited until Annie and Max were free before climbing the steps. Billy looked casual and comfortable in a red polo and khaki shorts. Mavis was more animated than usual, her pale cheeks flushed with eagerness. "Kevin's thrilled that you hired the band for tonight." She pointed toward the stage where her son thrummed the bass guitar. "Honestly, I hated those Mohawk haircuts at first but they are having so much fun I don't mind so much now. I just hope he lets his hair grow back one of these days."

A harsh twang signaled a guitar string out of tune.

Billy clapped Max on the arm. "Good thing you don't expect perfection." Billy's smile suddenly faded. He squinted toward the live oak. "There's Iris Tilford. I'm surprised she'd come to the pavilion."

Annie was puzzled, much as she had felt when Iris accepted the invitation to the picnic as if it were a duty. "Why wouldn't she come here?"

Billy's face creased in thought. "She wouldn't have good memories. But I guess there's a lot of water under the bridge. Or, actually, the pier. It's good if she's past all of that."

Mavis tugged on his arm. "Kevin's waving at us." Hand in hand, Mavis and Billy hurried toward the platform.

"Annie, hey. This is fun. I'm so glad we could come." Liz Montgomery's conventional smile didn't reach her wide-spaced blue eyes. She was as always immaculately coiffed, her prematurely white hair bright and crisp, and stylish. Tonight she wore a pale blue linen long jacket over matching trousers. Russell stood a step behind her. His face was somber. Max enjoyed playing golf with him and he'd been pleasant to work with as they restored the Franklin house, but tonight he seemed as distant as the waning crescent moon. He gazed toward the live oak and Iris.

Liz's voice was pleasant. "Everything looks beautiful. I love the way candles glow in hurricane lamps." As she gestured toward the picnic tables, she saw Iris. For an instant, Liz stood absolutely still, then she turned back to Annie. "The hickory smoke smells wonderful. We haven't been to an oyster roast since New Year's." Her island accent was as soft and throaty as the coo of mourning doves. "Nobody does oysters better than Ben. Oh, there's Fran and Buck." Liz lifted a hand in greeting. "Come on, Russell. Fran's waving at us."

They moved away and Russell hadn't said a word. So much, Annie thought, for social graces.

Liz and Fran came together in a social embrace that reminded Annie of the stylized movements of Laurel's tai chi class. Russell and Buck shook hands.

The breeze stirred Fran Carlisle's black hair. She and Liz joined a group of women clustered around Henny Brawley. Henny was gesturing toward the water. Russell stood a few feet away, arms folded, and looked determinedly at Ben's fire.

Iris was alone again. She moved out of the shadows and walked slowly toward the group of women.

Buck's usually genial face folded into a frown. He glanced

at his wife, who was deep in conversation with Fran. Buck hesitated, then stepped toward Iris. They met near a weeping willow. Buck was a big man and his bulk made Iris appear even frailer. She stared up, her face grave.

Cara Wilkes strolled up the steps, smiling. "Hey, guys." As she looked past Annie and Max, her smile slid away, making her look much older.

Annie knew she was watching Buck and Iris.

Cara's jaw muscles ridged, then she swung back to her hosts, once again with a smile. "Great day for a picnic."

"Oysters ready." Ben's hoarse shout sounded over the voices and music. He carried a shovel full of steaming shells to the prepared table. Laughing and talking, guests swirled toward the table.

Crackles and snaps and occasional mutters rose as gloved hands poked the short-bladed knives into the shells. As soon as one guest moved on, plate heavy with opened shells, another set to work.

As dusk fell, the picnic tables filled. Annie scanned the crowd. She felt quick relief when she spotted Iris sitting next to Laurel. As always, Laurel was spectacularly lovely, her beauty ageless, golden hair framing chiseled features. Laurel was smiling and listening attentively. Annie felt a surge of thankfulness. Laurel was often unpredictable, but her kindness was a constant. It was no surprise that she was drawn to the loneliest guest.

Annie settled at a far table with Billy and Mavis Cameron, Pamela Potts, Henny Brawley, and Edith Cummings. Edith was both an old friend and the island's accomplished reference librarian. Edith could discover any fact a patron fancied, including the best wildlife viewing season in Pungo, N.C. (a personal favorite of Annie's because the best

season(s) listed were spring, summer, fall, and winter, and
who could quarrel with that?), the highest level in British
peerage below a prince (a duke), and the recipe for a Black
Russian (1½ ounces vodka and ¾ ounce Kahlúa).

Edith pushed aside another emptied shell. "It would be
piggy to eat twenty oysters."

"I don't think pigs like oysters." Pamela's gaze was, as
always, serious and sincere.

Billy grinned. "Pigs like a lot of stuff. My dad raised
Large Whites. We fed them corn and barley meal, but Big
Mama, our sow, was crazy about snails and once she ate a
corn snake. She would have loved a good oyster roast."

Henny wiped a smear of chili from her chin. "Oysters are
good. Chili dogs are great."

Annie flashed her old friend a fond smile. Henny looked
elegant in a white cotton blouse and twill slacks and a striking black sweater adorned with embroidered white daisies,
a perfect accent for her clothes and a perfect weight for the
suddenly cooling April evening as the sun began to sink into
the Sound. Henny was the kind of woman Annie admired:
smart, incisive, quick-thinking, and adventurous, a WAAF
pilot in World War II, an English teacher, a two-time Peace
Corps volunteer after retirement, and, of course, a mystery
authority. She had delighted last week in pointing out to
Annie the little-known fact that the office of Charlaine Harris, bestselling author of the Sookie Stackhouse Southern
vampire series, was decorated with black-and-white photos
of New Orleans grave art. Annie wondered if Charlaine
Harris enjoyed Sarah Stewart Taylor's mysteries that celebrated funerary art.

Mavis leaned across the table. "How's Emma feeling?"
Mavis's blue eyes were filled with concern.

Henny spooned chopped onions on her dog. "Great. I checked her out of the hospital this afternoon and took her home. She sent her regrets. I'll run some oysters over in a little while."

"That's wonderful." Annie's oyster knife slipped and she was grateful for the protection of the glove. "I don't suppose she remembers anything about her fall?" If only Emma's memory had returned and the question could be settled.

Pamela swung toward Annie, used her oyster knife for emphasis. "That bruise on Emma's back worried me to pieces."

Henny's eyes narrowed. "Bruise on her back?"

As Pamela described the purplish splotch between Emma's shoulder blades, Annie pushed away a residue of uncertainty. To suppose Emma had been attacked opened up an ugly chain of thought with no basis in fact.

Billy finished the last of his beer. "Emma fell forward. Traces of blood on the footboard proved that. There was nothing in the cabin to account for an injury to her back." He mounded mashed sweet potatoes on his spoon. "A bruise like you describe had to be caused some other way."

Billy's calm response reassured Annie.

Henny grinned. "She doesn't remember Wednesday or, oddly enough, her struggle with the Slough of Despond, which, being Emma, was translated into writer's block. I left her at her desk, fingers flying on the keyboard. She's started a new book. In this one, a young woman shows up one evening at a tourist court on a sea island riding a bike in the rain. Nobody knows who she is or where she came from."

Annie looked at Billy.

His blue eyes were amused. A slight nod assured her he would be discreet. "Funny thing how head injuries affect people. Hey, Annie, have you had a piece of Miss Jolene's Key lime pie yet?"

Velvety darkness emphasized glowing lights strung among the live oak trees. Luminarias gleamed every few feet on either side of the paths that bordered the picnic area and led to the boardwalk and the woods. The waning crescent moon seemed pale and distant. It was nearing eleven. Max climbed the steps to the bandstand. He was no more than a dimly seen shadow until he reached the platform and the flash of the strobe lights.

Max borrowed the sticks from the drummer and sounded a brisk rat-a-tat.

Voices murmured as guests, indistinguishable in the darkness, moved nearer the bandstand.

"Ladies and gentlemen, tonight you've enjoyed the music of the Red Hot Mohawks. I want you to meet Elrod Phipps, vocalist; Kevin Cameron, bass guitar; and Clint Guthrie, drums. Let's give them a big hand."

The applause was strong and mixed with a few cheers. The young musicians beamed.

Annie smelled a faint scent of violets. Without surprise, she heard Laurel's throaty murmur from the dimly seen figure next to her. "How dear of Max."

Annie agreed wholeheartedly. She gave Laurel's slender hand a squeeze.

Ben poked at the mound of ashes beneath the sheet of steel to be sure the fire was doused. Miss Jolene had long since maneuvered the steam tables into the catering van and departed. Ben and two of his staff stayed behind to take care of cleanup. The band folded up the lights and picked up their instruments.

. "Good night, my dears." Laurel blew a kiss to Max and wafted toward the parking area.

As the guests dwindled to a diehard few, Annie moved around the picnic area seeking Iris. Annie walked all the way to the boardwalk, grateful for the luminarias. Uneasiness plucked at Annie when she reached the iron railings, damp from spray as the dark water slapped against the seawall. She looked up and down the boardwalk. Lamplights glistened every hundred feet, shedding a pale radiance. To her left, the shore curved. Midway to the peninsula, Fish Haul pier jutted into the Sound. The boardwalk was empty. Darkness shrouded the pier. To her right, a cluster of lights marked downtown and the ferry dock.

A solitary man walked a black Lab. He was the only moving figure on the boardwalk.

Annie turned and hurried back to the picnic area. The last farewells were sounding. ". . . had a great time." "The men's grill at eight?" ". . . a real feast . . ."

When she reached Max, she felt breathless. She gripped his arm. "I can't find Iris. Have you seen her?"

Annie hunched over the wheel of her car, brights on as she searched the road ahead. She didn't dare drive faster. Deer crossed the winding roads after dark, deer and possums and raccoons, sometimes even cougars and wild boars. Annie clung to the hope that Iris had chosen to walk back to Nightingale Courts and not thought to tell Annie. The countervoice in her mind argued, "That would have been rude. Iris wasn't rude." Even if Iris had not enjoyed the evening—Billy was surprised she'd been willing to come to the pavilion—she'd been appreciative of the invitation and would surely have known that Annie planned to take her back to her cabin.

The dark tunnel beneath live oaks ended finally. The headlights illuminated the honeysuckle bower that marked the entrance to Nightingale Courts. A single lamplight shone. Annie wheeled into the drive, saw cars parked in front of two cabins. She noted that the old car Emma had borrowed to come to Nightingale Courts on Wednesday was no longer in front of Cabin Seven. She braked at Cabin Six, left the Volvo's lights on. They shone on the green bicycle on its stand by the steps. The windows to Cabin Six were dark.

Annie's throat was dry as she slammed out of the car and ran up the steps. The door was locked. She knocked and called. "Iris? Iris?"

There was no answer.

Annie took the extra time to get a key and open the door. The cabin was empty.

Annie stared at the place on the floor where they'd found Emma and felt a cold rush of fear.

Max quartered the picnic grounds, the beam from his flashlight sweeping below tables, behind trash bins, under shrubs, around trees.

Max's cell chimed. Annie had made certain he had it on before she left. He flipped it open. "Annie?"

"I checked the cabin. It's empty. Max, where can she be?"

Max looked out at the dark water with foreboding, but he kept his voice even and measured. "She could have gone home with someone she knew. It's not like she's a stranger on the island. . . . Rude? Yeah, I guess. Sometimes people don't think. . . . Right. Call Billy if you think you should. I'll keep looking."

* * *

"She may have gone home with a friend." Billy's voice was patient.

Annie gripped the cell with one hand, the steering wheel with another. Once again, she held her speed in check and was able to jam on the brakes as a deer turned a startled face into the lights, then bolted into the woods. Annie pushed on the accelerator. "I don't think she had any friends." Annie knew her voice was thin. It was Iris's loneliness that had cried out for comfort when Annie saw Iris on the cabin deck after Cara Wilkes left. "Emma got hurt in that cabin. I'm afraid for Iris."

"What's Emma got to do with Iris?" He sounded bewildered.

"I don't think Emma fell." As Annie spoke, she felt certainty. "It's like Ben says, Emma's sure-footed as a goat. She didn't fall down, she was pushed."

"Annie, you aren't making sense." Billy sounded irritated.

"What if someone was hidden in Iris's cabin Wednesday morning? Emma came in and somebody whammed her from behind and she fell into the footboard and that's how she hit her head and got a bruise on her back."

He took a deep breath. "There's no proof that bruise didn't happen another time. But let's say you're right and somebody was in Iris's cabin. Why knock down an old woman? Why not say, 'I'm waiting for Iris. She's not here right now.'"

"Maybe the person was determined not to be seen."

He made no reply, but Annie felt his resistance, solid as a boulder. "Iris said she came back to the island"—Annie turned into the parking lot behind the pavilion—"because she wanted to find out if something she remembered or didn't quite remember was true." It was hard to give a sense of Iris's uncertainty and worry and ultimate decisiveness from those moments of honesty in the cool water of the pool. "She said people didn't want to talk to her. What if somebody was afraid of what she might remember and came to her cabin to be sure she didn't have something written down? Maybe tonight Iris remembered."

"If she remembered, so what? Do you think somebody pushed her off the pier? Did you see anything tonight to suggest she was in danger?"

"People weren't friendly, the ones I think she knew." How threatening did that sound? Maybe she was conjuring trouble out of nothing. "Liz and Russell Montgomery. Buck and Fran Carlisle. Cara Wilkes."

"They knew her." His tone was cool. "Maybe they didn't have any reason to be happy she was back. What happened? Any quarrels?"

"No." The admission came reluctantly. "I think that Iris," Annie spoke slowly, trying to communicate the force of Iris's determination, "knew something that troubled her, something really bad, but she wasn't sure."

"Maybe something tonight triggered a memory," Billy suggested, "and she went home with somebody and they're talking it over. Maybe that's why she didn't tell you she was leaving. She was caught up in the past. And maybe," Billy's voice was matter-of-fact, "she couldn't stay away from the sauce."

Annie stopped next to Max's Jeep in the parking lot behind the pavilion. "Oh." It hadn't occurred to her that Iris might have lost her never-ending battle, the hunger for alcohol, the quivering need for a drug. Maybe that was the sad answer to her disappearance.

"She'll turn up." Billy was relaxed. "You're chasing shadows, Annie. There's no reason to worry about Iris."

Max swung the flashlight toward the brooding darkness of the pines. "I've looked everywhere but the woods. She's not anywhere on the picnic grounds."

Annie stared at the towering pines, a dark mass beneath the starlit sky. The breeze rustled the limbs high in the air. Frogs chortled from a pond.

"Let's go home, Annie. Maybe Billy got it right. Maybe being back on the island was too much stress and she started drinking."

Annie remembered Iris's thin face and burdened eyes. "She was making it. One day at a time." But what if she hadn't made it? What if she had wandered into the woods, collapsed in a stupor? Annie thought about snakes and alligators and bobcats. She would never be able to sleep, imagining Iris passed out in the woods, vulnerable to attack. "Let's take the path through the woods to the pier." Billy had alluded to the pier; something there had been bad for Iris. If she had too much to drink, maybe she had been drawn to the pier.

When they reached the pines, the sounds of the night enveloped them, courting frogs, wind-stirred palmetto fronds, cooing chuck-will's-widows. Max's flashlight poked a beam into a tunnel of darkness created by the forest canopy above and the heavy undergrowth bordering the path. They moved slowly, swerving here to avoid a fallen limb, there to jump a dank puddle. A nearby thrashing signaled a creature alarmed by their presence, a deer or raccoon or possibly a cougar.

With every step, Annie looked for any evidence of a

plunge into the forest, smashed ferns or broken saw-palmetto fronds. Nothing appeared disturbed. They were nearing the end of the path and the opening on the other side of the woods near the harbor. Tension eased out of her neck and shoulders. If Iris wasn't in the forest, they would have done all they could to search for her.

Suddenly Max's hand closed hard on her wrist. His light swept up toward the canopy, leaving the trail in darkness, but she'd already seen Iris, lying facedown, unmoving, hands splayed on either side of her head.

Annie made a small whimpering sound and found herself in Max's tight embrace. "Don't look."

But she had looked.

Iris wasn't facedown dead drunk. Iris was facedown dead, her dark hair ruffled, a shiny black cord tight around her neck.

∴ *Six* ∾

THE POLICE CAR shot past them, stopped near the path into the woods. Billy slammed out of the cruiser, leaving on the headlights to illuminate the entrance. He strode toward Annie and Max. They waited midway between the woods and the boardwalk. Water slapped against the pilings of Fish Haul pier, the sound loud in the stillness of the night.

When Billy reached them, Max gestured at the woods. "She's on the main path. Strangled."

Billy's face was grim. "Did you touch anything?" He reached back to tuck his uniform shirt into his trousers.

"I checked for a pulse." Max glanced down at one hand, smudged with dirt. "I got some mud on my pants when I knelt beside her. You'll find a depression there. I tried not to make any other tracks."

"ID certain?" Billy looked at Annie.

Iris had worn her best outfit to the party, green-and-white-striped blouse, white slacks, red sandals. The dangling ends of the black cord had looked harsh against the green-and-white stripes.

"Yes." Annie rubbed red-rimmed eyes.

Another cruiser and the crime van slid to a stop, training more lights on the trees. Car doors slammed. Stocky Lou Pirelli's cheeks were dark with stubble. His red Braves sweatshirt hung halfway down cutoff jeans. Sgt. Harrison's hair was neatly braided, her uniform fresh and crisp. Both carried Maglites.

The brightness at the edge of the woods emphasized the dark mass of the pier, its sole illumination a single light at the far end.

Lou Pirelli gave Annie and Max a quick nod, turned toward Billy. Sgt. Harrison ignored them, her pale eyes intent on Billy.

Billy gestured toward the path. "Victim in the woods on the main path. Strangled. We can't touch anything until the M.E. certifies death. Lou, go to the west entrance to the woods, come this way until you see her. Go slow, look for anything, everything, trash, footprints, broken brush."

Lou nodded and loped toward the picnic grounds.

"Sergeant, get the strobe lights and cameras. Set them up near the victim."

Harrison hurried toward the van.

A shabby black coupe with a battered fender squealed to a stop behind the police vehicles.

"Doc Burford's here." Max squinted against the glare of the lights.

Face thunderous, black bag in hand, the island's burly medical examiner bulled toward them. Annie knew anger carried him. Doc Burford fought death with ferocious tenacity as the island's most beloved GP. As M.E., he encountered deaths that shouldn't have happened, drownings, car wrecks, drug overdoses, fires, murder. To have life stolen infuriated him.

Iris's life was stolen.

His expression remote, Billy glanced at Annie and Max. "You can leave now. Please come to the station at nine tomorrow. Bring the party guest list, plus I need to know who Iris spoke to at the picnic." He nodded at Annie. "Don't clear out her cabin. We'll do that. And get some fingerprints."

Annie knew that Billy was remembering her belief that someone had hidden in the cabin, knocked Emma forward. If only she'd told Iris of her suspicion.

Oyster shells crackled underfoot as Doc Burford hurried toward them. His face bleak, he grunted hello, turned to Billy.

"This way, Doc."

As the men disappeared into the woods, Annie shivered, cold from the offshore breeze, cold from the icy ache deep inside. "I should have warned Iris, told her I thought someone hid in the cabin and hurt Emma. Iris might have been scared. Maybe she wouldn't have gone into the woods."

Max took her hand, gripped it hard. "Emma's fall looked like an accident."

"Pamela told me about the bruise on Emma's back." Annie's voice quivered. "Any fool should have put it together."

He slipped his arm around her shoulders. "Everyone thought Emma fell."

She was grateful he understood her anguish, the empty feeling of having failed to act when action mattered. It might have made no difference if she'd warned Iris. But, oh, it might have saved her.

Max gently turned her away from the woods. "Let's go home, honey." They walked through the silent picnic area, the tables ghostly now, all traces of laughter and life gone.

Annie carried with her the memory of Iris's thin face,

burdened by sorrow. Iris had fought a good fight, one day at a time, until the days were no more.

The tremulous moan of a screech owl broke Annie's shallow, fitful sleep. They'd left open the sliding door to the deck. Annie watched the rippling curtain, smelled the heady scent of the marsh. She lay as still as she could, trying not to disturb Max.

The late watches of the night often spawned formless fears, phantasms that danced at the edge of consciousness, darting from the dark places of the soul, leaving corrosive trails. Iris's death was another reminder of the fragility of life. No one was safe. Not ever. Not anywhere. In an instant, everything could be lost.

Swept by anguish, Annie rolled up on her elbow. The hounds of death bayed in her heart. She flung an arm across Max. He was alive and living and so was she and there was goodness and love no matter how dark any night might be. She held tight to him.

He came awake.

Her lips found his, warm and living and loving.

The sun slanting through the window of Billy's office Saturday morning emphasized the pouches beneath his eyes, eyes reddened by lack of sleep. His fresh uniform already looked wrinkled. This was one Saturday morning he wouldn't spend mulching his roses. Two crumpled Coke cans topped discarded papers in an overflowing wastebasket. He had likely been at his desk since dawn. The files stacked on his highly varnished yellow oak desk tilted a little to his right. His stepson Kevin had made the desk in a woodworking class. One leg was shorter than the others, but Annie knew

Kevin's desk would be Billy's pride and joy as long as Billy Cameron was chief of the Broward's Rock Police.

Max pulled out a straight chair for Annie, took one himself. He handed a sheet of paper to Billy. "Here's the guest list."

Billy scanned the list. "Did you have any no-shows?"

It took some figuring, but they pared the list to thirty-three.

Billy scratched through names. "I'll add the band members and Ben Parotti's staff."

Max leaned back in his chair. "I'll bet Kevin can vouch for the band members. I remember they hung out in front of the bandstand during their break."

Annie remembered, too. The boys were too excited at their prominence to step out of the limelight.

For an instant, a smile reached Billy's eyes. "They thought they were as hot as the Jonas Brothers. We'll interview them, but the path into the woods was behind the stage. I don't expect they saw anything helpful. However, the catering steam tables faced the pines. Maybe we'll get something helpful from Ben's crew."

Annie pictured the steam tables. They faced the picnic area. The picnic tables were perpendicular to the woods. None of the guests looked directly at the path.

A grim smile twisted Billy's face. "Of course, someone not on your list may have shown up. We'll ask. Trouble is, half the time people don't remember anything right." Billy put the list on the desk. He stared down at it, absently rubbed a varnish-sticky hand against his trousers. "I hope to God somebody saw something. Or maybe she talked to someone and that will give us a lead." He glanced at a notebook. "You said Liz and Russell Montgomery and Cara Wilkes noticed Iris and Buck Carlisle talked to her. Anybody else?"

"Marian Kenyon talked to Iris early on. Iris sat with Laurel at dinner." Annie hesitated, then reluctantly said, "Buck looked kind of menacing when he walked toward Iris, but maybe that was because he's so big. Cara saw them and frowned."

Billy doodled in the margin, his expression stolid.

"I know." Annie felt despairing. "It doesn't sound like anything at all. But there was something between Buck and Iris, something more than saying hello."

"I'll ask." He didn't sound encouraged. "Maybe we'll get a lead from Iris's cabin. If not, we've got a crime that occurred anytime after dinner and the end of the picnic. She was struck from behind, either stunned or knocked out. She fell forward. The killer flipped the cord under her neck, pulled it tight. Quick, silent. No mess, no noise, nothing to link up to anybody. The cord came from one of the centerpieces on the tables. There won't be fingerprints, not with gloves handy for cracking oyster shells. Using the black rope from a table means the murder was premeditated. A guest doesn't cram a length of line in a pocket without a reason."

Annie's throat felt dry. A quick tweak and the cord had been pulled away from the hurricane lamp, ready to use. "Iris told me she came back because she had to clear something up. You said she ran away from the island. Why did she run?"

Billy rubbed his neck as if it hurt. "I got out the old files." He tapped an orange folder. "Ten years ago in April, Jocelyn Howard fell off Fish Haul pier. She drowned. An accident. Frank handled it." He was reporting a fact without any hint of criticism. "You know how careful Frank was."

Dyspeptic, hardworking Frank Saulter had been chief when Annie came to live on the island. He'd suspected Annie when murder occurred at Death on Demand. Annie and Max had discovered the truth, and Frank had been their good friend ever since. Frank would have checked every angle.

Billy flipped open the file, his face thoughtful. "Jocelyn's brother Sam died of a cocaine overdose a week earlier. The kids at the sports picnic—"

Annie felt sad. Iris had accepted the invitation to last night's party as if it were a duty. The pavilion and its nearness to the pier must have been a grim reminder of Jocelyn's death.

"—told Frank that Jocelyn was upset. Some of them were surprised she came. Nobody noticed when she left but one girl said Jocelyn was going to come home with her. When the girl couldn't find her anywhere, she raised an alarm. They didn't find her. Her body turned up out in the Sound two days later. Frank thought she'd jumped. He didn't see any reason to make that public. The family was suffering enough. The coroner ruled accidental death by drowning. A week after that, Iris's grandmother reported Iris missing. She was seen leaving on the ferry. She caught a bus to Savannah. We never picked up her trail after that. She was officially listed as a runaway."

Annie leaned forward. "Iris said something wasn't right and she had come back to the island because she needed to clear up some things. She ran away right after Jocelyn died. Does that mean Jocelyn's death wasn't an accident?"

"That remains to be seen." Billy spoke with finality.

"Does the file"—Annie pointed at the orange folder—"have the names of the kids Frank interviewed?"

Billy rolled his pen between his thumb and forefinger. "Why would you want to know?" His voice was crisp.

"Someone at our picnic murdered Iris. I want to know which of our guests were at the pavilion when Jocelyn died." Annie's gaze challenged him.

"We're on top of this investigation." Billy's expression was mild. "That's our job. You've done your job by coming here, helping us out." He pushed back his chair and stood. He was a commanding figure, well over six feet with a fullback's build.

Max put his hand on Annie's elbow, gently tugged her to her feet, turned them toward the door.

Annie wanted to resist, but Billy obviously didn't intend to share anything about his investigation. Why was Billy refusing to answer? Didn't he understand that she felt responsible for Iris's presence at the picnic?

She stopped at the doorway, looked back at him. "I urged her to come to the picnic." She kept her voice steady, but it took effort.

Billy gestured at the stack of folders on his desk. "You and Max have nothing to do with Iris's death. There's a lot of history here, miseries you didn't know about and can't change. You can be sure of one fact, Annie, when a murderer decides to kill, that murder will happen one place or another, one time or another."

Annie wished she felt comforted. "You'll find out the truth if anyone can." Her gaze told Billy that she admired and respected him. "Max and I don't want to interfere, but I feel like I owe Iris. I can't walk out of here and forget everything that's happened." Would she ever forget? Would she ever draw a breath or take a step with the confidence that those she knew and those she loved were safe? "What harm would it do for us to know more about what happened to Jocelyn? Wasn't the investigation closed when her drowning was declared accidental? Isn't the file on Jocelyn Howard's death public record now?"

Billy got his bulldog look. Annie had seen that same expression when he continued to investigate after the mayor and the media had convicted Max of murder in the public eye. "I can't accommodate you. That file has been reclassified."

Annie persisted. "Reclassified as what?"

"An ongoing investigation. As such it is closed to public inspection. Thanks for coming in." He picked up a folder, obviously ready for them to leave.

Max looked puzzled. "Who reclassified it?"

"I did." The answer was succinct, the intent clear. His face was stern. "I know you both want Iris's murderer found. You are upset because she was killed at your party. You want to nose around, see what you can find out, try to help, but finding her murderer is my job. You're outsiders this time. Iris was an island girl. If I can't find out what happened to her, no one can. She walked up that path with someone she knew, someone out of her past, someone determined to prevent her from revealing anything about—" He broke off. "Anyway, someone moved fast. We're dealing with a clever and dangerous killer. I don't want you two to get out in front of us."

Max moved to Billy's desk, reached across to grip Billy's hand, shake it firmly. "We understand. We won't get in the way." He returned to the door.

Annie glared at Max, then swung her hot gaze back to Billy.

Billy looked at her calmly. "Listen up, Annie. I figure you were right. Someone hid behind the door in Iris's cabin and shoved Emma when she walked in. The decision to kill Iris had already been made. The intruder couldn't afford to be seen. One hard push and Emma slammed into the end of the bed. Emma could have died, too. Iris's murderer will attack anyone who is seen as a threat." His blue eyes softened.

"You guys make a difference for this island. Keep safe. For me. For all of us."

Max poked his head into the laundry room. "We're agreed?"

Annie's face was mutinous. "I never thought you'd back Billy up."

Max felt hollow inside, the uneasy emptiness that presages disasters. Billy had spooked him. The foreboding in his old friend's eyes had hit Max hard. Billy sensed danger and there was Annie, his lovely, sexy, bright, funny, kind, volatile Annie, eager to mount battle against an unseen, unknown foe. Clearly Iris, for all her uncertain memories of the past, never expected to be struck down. There was no hint that she had warning of the blow which stunned her, made her easy to strangle.

He took two quick strides, cupped Annie's face in his hands. "Billy's a good cop, right?"

"Of course." Her response was emphatic.

Max persisted. "He knows all the background, right?"

"I could help. I could talk to people."

An icy breath touched him. Annie might think she was subtle, but her efforts would be transparent to the people involved. Thank God Billy had closed the Jocelyn Howard file. Those were the names Annie would match against their guest list.

He pulled her close. "Promise me you'll keep out of this." He stroked a strand of blond hair back from her solemn face, gazed deep into steady gray eyes. "I don't want you in danger." Death had been very near Annie when she discovered the secret to the Franklin house last spring. Death had waited behind the door in Cabin Six Wednesday morning at Nightingale Courts. That Emma suffered nothing worse than a concussion was sheer luck. Death had walked through the woods last night.

Annie looked up, her expression softening. "You and Billy are overreacting big time." She took a deep breath. Her answer mattered to Max. "Okay. I'll keep out." One promise was made, but another broken. She'd offered friendship to Iris. Iris had looked like a child offered an unexpected present when Annie invited her to the pool. Now Annie felt she had turned her back on Iris.

Annie measured detergent, dropped it into the washer, and loaded sheets. For an instant, she wanted to rebel. She could find out more about Iris and her friends in a day than Billy would manage in two weeks. No matter how well he knew his island, he was the chief of police. When he asked questions, answers would be carefully given and much left unsaid.

She could . . .

No, she couldn't.

She'd promised Max. They'd both learned hard lessons last summer. They now understood and never needed reminding that safety was an illusion and death might be waiting around the next corner. That knowledge deepened their gratitude for the happiness they knew. A few years ago Max might not have worried so much on her account. Now fear for her was quick to come. She had to do her part to reassure him. No matter how much she wanted to seek justice for Iris, she had given Max her promise and she would honor that promise. That was part of their bargain, each could always count on honesty and truth and respect from the other. Yes, she could ask questions, find out more, but she couldn't double-deal with Max. Not now. Not ever.

She slammed down the lid, turned the knob, heard the rush of water. Water . . . Yesterday afternoon, she and Iris had swum in the pool, Iris thin and bony in a borrowed suit. Annie sighed. She'd known Iris only a short time, but she'd glimpsed a sweet nature and great courage.

Surely there was something Annie could do. If she couldn't seek Iris's murderer, certainly she could remember her life, pay tribute to a spirit now quenched.

Spirit . . .

The word danced in her mind and with it a sudden memory of Amarillo and Maria Elena Chavez, her best friend in high school, and Maria's annual preparations for the Day of the Dead. Maria Elena loved the skull candies and dancing skeletons, but when she lighted the black clay candles on a small altar of brightly painted tiles in the shape of a cross, she was, as she joyfully told Annie, remembering with love and happiness those gone before, especially Tío Felix, who loved to play the accordion and had a mustache like a walrus, and Abuela Maria Francesca, who made the best cochitos in the whole world and always saved the largest pig-shaped ginger cookie for Maria Elena. Maria Elena fashioned a poster for each loved one with a photograph and a tribute to the Honored Spirit.

Peace washed over Annie, soothing as yesterday's pool water. Max couldn't complain if she created an Honored Spirit poster for Iris. To do a good job, she would need to find out more about Iris and the life she had lived and try to capture in words and images a gentle spirit that had fought through much difficulty. She murmured a small promise, a promise she was free to make. "Iris, I'll make you a wonderful spirit poster."

* * *

Max squinted against brightness as the Jeep plunged out of the gloom from the live-oak tunnel into the sunny drive of the Franklin house. From the outside, there was no hint of the water damage within. Soon he and Annie would be at home in the old gray-green house with its newly painted white shutters and majestic white columns with Ionic capitals on the first level and Corinthian on the second. He was willing to be patient, but he wanted to make sure there had been some progress on the repairs. He curved around the house to the back and was pleased to see Russell Montgomery's mud-streaked white pickup parked next to a plumber's van. Maybe the plumber had finished his other jobs earlier than promised.

The back door stood ajar. Max stepped inside. "Hey, Russell." For a man who'd grown up in Yankee land, as islanders described any area north of Richmond, it hadn't taken him long to learn how to speak: Hey for hi, palmetto bugs for roaches, tall cotton for perching in the catbird seat. Maybe he'd learned tall cotton from Texan Annie along with highfalutin for pretentious and tacky for low class. Max grinned and took the stairs two at a time.

Russell met him on the landing. "Hey, Max." Russell tilted back his sweat-stained Panama, revealing a white stripe on his forehead. He was a good two inches taller than Max and bulky with muscular arms and shoulders. The sleeves of his cotton shirt were rolled above the elbows. "It looks like the plumbing will be done by Tuesday, then I'll get a crew on the ceiling. I hope by the end of the week you can move in."

"That's great. When you know the definite date, I'll call the movers." Max wished he could start putting books in the library today, but he should get back to Nightingale Courts and help Annie with the cleaning.

Russell's pale blue eyes stared at Max. "I heard about the trouble in the woods last night. What happened?"

Max wasn't surprised that Russell knew. Likely most islanders knew that Iris Tilford had been strangled in the pavilion woods Friday night. The *Island Gazette* didn't publish on Saturday, but it wouldn't take Marian Kenyon's lead story in the Sunday *Gazette* to announce murder. Word spread like a ground fire in a small community, a call here, an encounter there, like sparks leaping from tinder-dry grass to turn a forest into an inferno.

With the question, Max recognized a change between them. Russell was no longer a contractor dealing with business. He was a man intent on getting information, his gaze wary and calculating.

"A woman was strangled." Max made the flat statement. His voice was bleak, as bleak as his memory of that frail body facedown on the path.

Russell's right eyelid fluttered. "I heard it was Iris Tilford." That telltale flutter of his eyelid continued. "I saw her at the picnic. Did you invite her or did she just show up?"

Max was tempted to ask Russell what difference it made. Iris came. She was dead. But if he didn't answer, Iris was left not only dead but devalued, tagged as rude, bumptious, unwelcome. "Annie invited her. Nobody knows what happened. Billy Cameron will figure it out. Anyway, I appreciate the progress on the repairs. Thanks for coming out on Saturday." He turned to go.

Russell stepped after him. "Annie invited her to your party? How come? How did Annie know Iris?"

Max stopped and faced Russell. The last thing he wanted to do was suggest the idea that Annie had some special bond with Iris. Max made his voice easy, agreeable. "Iris was staying at Nightingale Courts. We're staying there until we can move. Annie and Iris took a swim yesterday afternoon and they got to talking. Annie thought she seemed lonely and decided to invite her to the party."

Russell looked grim. "What did they talk about?"

Max shrugged. "Nothing much."

Russell's eyes narrowed. "They must have been pretty chummy for Annie to invite her to your party to celebrate the Franklin house. What did Iris do, tell Annie her life story?"

"Why would she do that?" Max tried to lighten his voice, sound as if none of this mattered. "Inviting Iris was no big deal. Annie thought she was nice and she didn't have any-where to go and it was Friday night so Annie invited her. You said you saw Iris Friday night. I guess you knew her pretty well."

Russell shrugged. "We went to school together." His voice was cool. "She left the island a long time ago."

Max took a step toward him. "Why did she leave?"

Russell's face was suddenly empty, as empty as his voice. "I guess she wanted to get away. I don't suppose we'll ever know."

Annie pulled a hot sheet from the industrial-size dryer. She'd never appreciated how hard housekeeping staffs worked. Though it was only midmorning, her shoulders ached, she was sweating like a marathoner, and the list of tasks to be done rose in her mind like the Himalayas jutting abruptly from the plain. She might be in tennis shape; she wasn't in cleaning shape. Annie gathered an armload of sheets, still hot to the touch, and carried them to the folding table.

"Annie." The call was sharp.

Startled, Annie turned toward the washroom doorway.

Fran Carlisle stood framed in sunlight. Despite skillfully

applied makeup, she looked haggard and worn. Her air of distress was in sharp contrast to the elegance of her coral sateen sundress. One slim hand gripped the doorframe. "Cara called me. Is it true? Is Iris dead? Did she die last night at the picnic?"

Never beautiful, always stylish, Fran walked into every room with the air of a princess, expecting admiration and deference as her due. To see her distraught was shocking.

Annie struggled against the too-clear memory of Iris lying dead on the path in the woods. "She was strangled."

Fran shivered. "That's what Cara said. I didn't believe her. Where was Iris? Who found her?"

Billy had been definite that she and Max weren't to be involved, but Annie knew the facts would appear in Marian's story tomorrow. Nothing she could tell Fran would compromise Billy's investigation. In a monotone, Annie described Max's search and their grisly discovery.

Fran listened with staring eyes. "On the path in the woods. Oh my God." Fran held a hand to her throat and turned away. She walked out of the washroom door into the sunlight and sat on the wooden bench in front of the office, face empty.

Annie came after her, stood a few feet away. "I'm sorry." Annie knew her words were inadequate. "Was she a good friend?"

Fran's makeup was stark against blanched skin. "We played together when we were little." Tears spilled down her face.

Annie wished she could retract the question. Fran's distress made the answer only too obvious.

Fran drew a ragged breath, wiped at her face, turned to Annie. "Are they looking for a stranger?"

Annie had a devastating vision of the cord twisted and tied behind Iris's neck, the black line that had looped around the hurricane lamps, part of a centerpiece celebrating life on a sea island. "No." No stranger had taken advantage of steel mesh gloves on the shucking table to pull free the line meant for decoration and carry it into the woods.

Fran's eyes widened. "How do you know?"

Annie made a helpless gesture with her hands. "Iris was killed with a cord from one of the picnic table centerpieces."

"That's dreadful." The cry was hopeless and despairing. "Are they sure? Cord looks alike. Someone from outside could have brought it."

Annie shook her head. The answer was inescapable. Someone at the picnic, someone they knew, had pulled black cord loose from a centerpiece on a picnic table and tucked it in a pocket or purse.

Fran wrapped her arms tightly across her chest. "I hate the pavilion."

Annie knew enough now to understand. "Because of Jocelyn Howard?"

Fran pressed her hands against her face as if blotting out an unbearable sight. Her hands slowly fell away. "You know how it is in high school, everybody has a group. We hung around together, Jocelyn, Iris, Cara, Liz, and me. We were all there the night Jocelyn went off the pier. Except for Sam, Jocelyn's brother. He had . . . died. Buck and Russell were his best friends." It was as if the words bubbled from deep within, not ordered or thoughtful. "We were all there again last night." The words came slowly, as if saying them hurt.

Fran lifted a shaking hand, brushed back a strand of hair. There was a faint spicy scent of carnation. Annie was sure it was an expensive fragrance. Everything about Fran was expensive, including silver bracelets that jangled on one thin arm and the deep green of an emerald in a delicate gold setting. "It all seems so long ago, but none of us forgot Jocelyn." Fran's face was haunted. "She was upset that night. Everybody said that's why she jumped from the pier. When Iris ran away, I wondered if she knew something. Something was terribly wrong that night. Jocelyn was upset, especially with Russell. But he wouldn't push her off the pier. She must have jumped. She couldn't swim. We all knew that. Whenever I think about her, I remember how Russell treated her that night. He did his best to stay away from her. They'd broken up a few weeks before the picnic. After she died, he looked awful. I thought he felt guilty because he'd been mean to her." Fran pressed a shaking hand against her mouth. The emerald gleamed in the sun.

Had Russell avoided Jocelyn because he was the kind of person who didn't want to be around unhappiness? Or was the reason deeper and darker? "You said he was mean to Jocelyn. What did he do?"

Fran abruptly came to her feet. "Forget what I said. I don't know what happened that night." She rubbed her temple as if it ached. "Iris ran away not too long afterward. She came back to the island and somebody killed her." She spoke slowly as if listening to her own words, trying to adjust what she knew with what had happened. "Maybe Iris saw someone with Jocelyn, but I don't know anything. I don't know anything at all."

Annie's voice was sharp. "You have to tell Billy Cameron."

Fran looked shocked. "About Russell? That would be crazy. It would be like accusing him. He could have been mad because Jocelyn was acting odd that night. They could have quarreled about anything. He'd been accepted at The Citadel. After they broke up, maybe she wouldn't let go. Breaking up's no reason to kill anyone. We were just kids. Look, promise you won't say anything, especially not to Billy."

Annie would never do anything to hamper a murder investigation, but this time she'd been told not to meddle. Billy had already decided the death—murder?—of Jocelyn Howard was connected to Iris's murder or he wouldn't have closed the file. That meant he would be talking to those present the night Jocelyn drowned. If Fran had seen Russell and Jocelyn quarreling, so would someone else.

Fran mistook her silence for resistance. "If you tell Billy, I'll say you're lying." Her face was thin and sharp and hard. "I mean it. Buck will have a fit. I don't know anything. Oh, I wish I hadn't come. But I had to know if it was true about Iris." Her face twisted. "Poor little Iris." Fran turned and ran toward her car.

As Fran's silver Lexus slewed around the arbor, spewing dust, Annie wished too that Fran hadn't come. Now whenever Annie encountered Russell Montgomery, she would wonder what happened the last time he saw Jocelyn.

∴ *Seven* ∾

THE SMALL OFFICE was cramped. An unlit cigar rested in a stained ceramic ashtray amidst a sea of folders on a battered gray metal desk jammed between rows of old-fashioned wooden filing cabinets. Above the cabinets hung bulletin boards filled with tacked-up photos of babies and small children, hundreds of them. Behind the desk, the blinds were hiked high in the single window to afford a clear view of the Sound. Between more filing cabinets, a narrow door stood open, revealing pale green walls and rattan furniture with bright cushions.

A tall woman in blue scrubs smiled at Max. "Doc will be here in a minute. Would you rather wait in his lounge?" She pointed to the partially open door.

Max shook his head, puzzled. There was a main lounge and he vaguely knew waiting areas were available on all floors. "Why does he have a lounge off of his office?"

"He fixed that up years ago. It's a big room, fancy. It was supposed to be his office. Instead, he took the little anteroom. He said the big room was perfect for families in trouble. There are waiting rooms, but none of them are private, and he said sometimes people need space and he damn well—you know how he talks, big and gruff—was going to see they had time to themselves when their hearts were breaking. There's been a lot of trouble in that room, I can tell you, but at least folks don't have to mourn in front of strangers." Her eyes were soft. "The board gave him trouble about it. Doc said hospitals were for people that hurt, not the doctors who worked there and he didn't spend much time in an office anyway."

"Stow it, Bess." Dr. Burford stomped past his nurse. He was in crumpled scrubs and his slipper-covered feet slapped against the marble floor. Bristly gray hair poked from beneath a cloth cap.

She nodded equably and left.

Burford closed the door, held out a hand to Max. "They're washed. Just delivered twins to the Magruders." He smiled and his craggy face was relaxed.

Max felt a grip of iron, pumped in return.

Burford peeled off the cap, settled behind the cluttered desk. "You and Annie in the market for twins?" A deep laugh. "Have to make your own. About time, I'd say."

Max grinned in return and pulled up a straight chair. "One of these days." The Franklin house would be perfect for kids, lots of rooms, a big backyard. . . .

"What can I do for you?" Doc picked up the unlit cigar, poked it in the corner of his mouth.

Max pulled himself back to the present. "Do you know when Iris Tilford's body will be released for burial?"

Burford's face folded into a heavy frown. "Thursday, I imagine."

"Does she have any family here, anyone to make funeral arrangements?" Max met Burford's inquiring gaze. "Annie and I want to help if we can."

"I'll check. I don't think there's any family left. I attended her grandmother. Fine woman. Iris broke her heart. Iris ran away not long after Jocelyn Howard drowned. I would have wrung Iris's neck if I could have found her." Burford frowned. "Not the best way to phrase it now. There's no doubt about how Iris died. Strangled. Who knows what she got herself mixed up in. But I'll give Iris one thing. She was clean when she died. No alcohol, no drugs." His face folded in sadness. "And no luck. She died too damn young. All of them were too young, Iris and Jocelyn and Sam Howard. The Howard kids were fraternal twins. I like delivering twins. Two for the price of one. Makes me crazy to see them die young."

Max understood Doc's rage. Jocelyn and Sam dead at eighteen, Iris at twenty-eight. "I guess you did the autopsy on Jocelyn Howard and it was clear that she drowned." Accidental death by drowning had been the verdict and that would have been based on the autopsy.

Doc Burford was suddenly very still behind his desk, his face inscrutable. Abruptly, Doc stood. "Jocelyn drowned. No evidence of other trauma. I'll let you know when Iris's body will be released." He lumbered past Max, opened the door, and strode away, head down.

In the hall, Max watched until the burly figure of the doctor turned a corner and was out of sight. Max frowned as he walked out into the hall. Doc didn't want to talk about the autopsy of Jocelyn Howard. Why?

Annie carried the extra keys to Cabin Six in her pocket. It was unlikely anyone would try to filch a key as Emma had but Annie felt better having them with her. She closed the door on Cabin Five and stripped off plastic gloves, welcoming fresh air on sweaty hands. She tossed the gloves in a plastic trash bag on the cleaning cart. As she gripped the bar of the cart, she was uncomfortably aware of Iris's cabin and the green bicycle on its stand near the front steps. No one had arrived yet to string up police tape and put the cabin off-limits.

Annie pushed the cart toward the shed. Her cell phone rang. She stuck her hand in her pocket and felt the coolness of the keys to Cabin Six as she grabbed the phone. "Hello."

"Annie, Duane here." The line crackled. "I'm an hour from the ferry dock. Ingrid's staying until her sister's well enough to be on her own. I'm coming back to take over at the Courts. You can relax now and get back to the store. I'll see to everything."

His strong voice sounded cheerful and upbeat. Annie took a deep breath and told him of Iris's murder.

There was fizz and crackle and silence. "Damn all." He was gruff. "She'd had a hard time. I knew it when I saw her."

Annie recalled Duane's words Wednesday morning. *She came in the rain. Alone. On a bicycle.*

"I invited her to the picnic." Annie's voice broke.

"Doesn't matter." He had an old newsman's disdain for unwarranted assumptions. "If somebody decided to kill her, another place and time would have served as well. Feel sorry she's gone. Don't feel bad for what you did. Feel good about liking her. She needed for somebody to like her." He cleared his throat. "Anyway, thanks for taking up the slack for us. You're off duty now." The connection ended as most conversations with Duane ended, abruptly.

Annie was glad for his call, glad to know Ingrid's sister was recovering, glad to know Duane was on his way and she could return to her life, glad most of all for his brusque reassurance that her connection to Iris had perhaps yielded some goodness, but, most of all, not caused harm. She put the cell in her pocket, again felt the keys.

In the pale April sunshine, the semicircle of cabins lay quiet. The only car was Annie's Volvo parked near Cabin Two. An egret stood near the edge of the marsh. The on-shore breeze stirred the tall bird's elegant trailing white plumes. Head immobile, yellow beak straight, the bird lifted one thin leg, its claws extended, graceful as any ballerina. The only sound was the soft clatter of palmetto fronds. No car neared, announcing its arrival on the oyster-shell drive.

Any minute a police cruiser would arrive. A final search would be made of Cabin Six. Yesterday Annie had looked through Iris's belongings and found nothing, no hint of past or present. Iris hadn't carried a purse last night. A purse likely held no clue to her murder, but the contents might provide a link to her recent past. Once Annie could have hoped Billy would share information that wasn't a part of an investigation. Not now.

If she wanted to find out anything about Iris's life off island, now was her chance. How could she do an adequate tribute if she knew nothing about Iris from the time she left the island until her return? Last week and the week before and the weeks and years before then, Iris had been some-where. Someone knew her and could tell Annie whether she had a job, if she liked to go to movies, if she read or played games, what made her laugh.

What harm would it do to try to find a name or address?

Annie gave the clearing a final searching glance. She was alone with only the egret to observe her. Quickly, she pushed the cart into the shed, grabbed a new pair of plastic gloves, pulled them on. Her heart thudded as she walked swiftly to Iris's cabin. She pulled out a key, unlocked the door, and stepped inside, closing the door behind her. She breathed shallowly, feeling nervous and uneasy. She'd better hurry. She mustn't be found here by Billy or one of his officers.

She moved across the room to the sliding door to the deck. She opened it and saw a towel and swimsuit draped over the railing. Annie felt a physical wrench. This time yesterday Iris had been alive.

Annie forced herself to continue. She turned back into the cabin, leaving the sliding door ajar. She found Iris's purse in the top drawer of the dresser. The soft beige crocheted bag had been casually dropped on top of the nightgown. Annie carefully lifted it, unhooked a clasp, and spilled out the contents on top of the dresser. She was struck by what it didn't contain: no cell phone, no sunglasses, no compact, no paper, no billfold, no credit cards, no driver's license.

No wonder the purse had been so light. It held only a clear plastic change purse, lip gloss, an eyeliner, a small packet of Kleenex, a red tin of Altoids, a neatly folded Savannah bus schedule, a once-crisp square of green cardboard with the Serenity Prayer. Annie snapped open the change purse: a Social Security card and two twenties, three fives, six ones, eighty-six cents. Tucked between two twenties was a small square card for the Mission of Hope, founded by Brother Kirk Doyle.

Outside a door slammed.

Annie committed the name and address of the mission to memory, returned the handful of possessions to the purse, and dropped the bag in the drawer. She hurried across the room and out on the deck.

Behind her, she heard the rattle of a key. "This one works,

Hyla." Lou Pirelli's drawl was satisfied. "We don't need to find Annie. If you'll get the tape, I'll look things over."

On the deck, Annie pressed against the rough wood siding of the cabin and eased to her left. She risked a quick look around the corner. Sgt. Harrison was opening the back of the crime van. Lou would be entering the cabin. With a quick breath, Annie swung over the side of the deck railing, dropped to the sandy ground, and darted to the next cabin.

She reached the office unseen by Lou or Hyla, and the tightness eased from her shoulders. She found a pad, wrote down Brother Kirk Doyle, the mission name and address, and the last line of the legend: ALL ARE WELCOME HERE.

Max traced the letter A that he'd carved several years ago in the top of the wooden table. Next came the ampersand, then *M*. He'd left the indelible marks at Ben Parotti's invitation. Only regulars were invited to decorate the wooden tables in the booths. Parotti's Bar and Grill was a constant in his life and Annie's, always welcoming, sometimes a refuge. He watched Annie, listened to her halting words, wished as so many have often wished that events could be changed, the past reversed. . . . *Nor all your Tears wash out a word of it.*

Max listened to memories of Maria Elena and Amarillo and the Day of the Dead.

"I'm going to honor Iris." Annie took a gulp of the grill's bracing tea. "I know how to find out more about her." She held up a hand to forestall his protest. "I'm not going to do anything that will bother Billy. Although"—her eyes dropped—"I did sneak into the cabin before Lou and Hyla got there."

Max frowned and sighed. He wished he had a nice big cage and could put Annie inside with a stack of her favorite mysteries, the latest by Archer Mayor or Elaine Viets or Laura Lippman.

Annie's smile was beguiling. "As my mom used to say, don't let your face freeze or you'll look like a gargoyle forever."

Despite his irritation, he laughed. He could never resist Annie's smile. Still, he shook his head. "Don't you ever think before you act? What if you'd been caught?"

"What's she done? Besides host a murder." Marian Kenyon, dark hair frowsy, knocked on the end of the booth. "Anybody home? Got room for a starving waif?" Without waiting, she slid in beside Annie, twisted to scan the room. "Yo, Ben."

Ben turned toward them, resplendent in a pink blazer, blue Oxford cloth shirt, and navy slacks. His sartorially suspect days before he married Miss Jolene, who had upscaled her new husband as well as the bar and grill, were a distant memory.

Marian pointed at Annie, yelled, "Whatever she's getting, double it, plus a side of cheese grits with jalapeño and a choc raspberry malted with a shot of sweet tea as a chaser." Marian slumped against the wooden back. Her stare was glassy. "You ever write eighty inches in an hour? Cruel and unusual. What did I come up with? Eighty inches of not much. I interviewed Billy, I got out the back files, I traced the family, I got pix. Billy's close-mouthed on this one. I couldn't get him to link last night with Jocelyn Howard's drowning, but readers can put two and two together. I mean, how likely is it that Iris Tilford comes back to the island and gets killed at a picnic in the pavilion, the same place Jocelyn Howard was last seen? There's always been a lot of spec about the Howard death. I got all the facts in and I beat the deadline."

She shot a look of loathing at the wall clock. "Actually, I still have twenty minutes, but I don't have anything else to write about the Tilford kill. I want some pathos. I want some heart. I want some soul."

"Marian." Annie looked at her with eyes full of misery.

Marian's face twisted. "Iris was my baby sister's best friend. I watched Iris grow up. I watched her life unravel. I used every skill I had trying to trace her when she ran away. No luck. Nada. She comes home and . . ." Marian pounded a small fist on the table top. "Does anybody care? Do her old friends have a kind word to say? Either no comment or vague blather about a former classmate. There's a lot more than six degrees of separation, make it a continent."

Ben arrived with a tray and unloaded a tumbler for Marian. He looked at her. "Billy getting anywhere?" Ben was well aware the *Gazette*'s star reporter knew all the news, including news that would never be printed.

Marian shook her head. "As far as the cop shop can find out, nobody saw anything, nobody heard anything. No physical traces. Weapon of opportunity. Unless the killer confesses, this will be the unsolved crime of modern time."

Ben rubbed his leathery cheek. "Poor damn kid. She worked for us for a couple of years when she was in junior high. Sweet as pie. It was in high school that she got fuzzy. Moved in slow motion. Didn't show up. Dropped things. I had to let her go when she spilled chili on the mayor. Damn hot chili." Ben didn't sound grieved. Mayor Cosgrove hustled for the island but lacked personal charm. "I'd already warned her a couple of times. I tried to get her to go for help, but she claimed she wasn't on drugs. I knew better. Where's she been the last few years?"

Marian's face screwed into a ferocious frown. "I'd say

Iris didn't know where she'd been most of the time. Savannah mostly. I talked to her last night. She didn't say much, but I connected the dots. Vague as mist. I'd bet she'd been on the street for a long time. She said she was living with friends. As far as I could find out this morning, she might have dropped in from Mars. If anybody knows her address, they're not telling."

Max saw Annie's lips part and kicked her under the table. She picked up her tea, drank deeply.

Ben nodded. "I saw her on the ferry, but I don't know where she came from. I'll get the malted." He turned away.

Marian's head swivelled toward Annie. "Speaking of dropping in, how come she was at your party? Billy said she was a guest."

Max pushed the bread basket with jalapeño cornbread toward Marian. "Hot and good. The butter's fresh. The invitation to the picnic was a last-minute thing. There's no story there. We're staying at Nightingale Courts until the Franklin house is ready. Iris was in Cabin Six. Annie and Iris got to talking and Annie asked her if she'd like to come to the picnic."

Marian's eyes narrowed. She gave Max a short stare, fastened again on Annie. "You and Max are staying at Nightingale Courts. I got that. An unknown woman checks into Cabin Six. You say hello. That I can buy. You like people. But then you asked her to your party? Come on now, Annie. Spit it out. How did that happen?"

"It was no big deal. Like I told Russell when I saw him out at the house today." Max kept his voice pleasant though he felt grim. Marian was the nearest thing to a human vacuum cleaner, sucking up everything in her path with an uncanny talent for uncovering anything hidden. "Annie and

Iris took a dip in the pool and Annie thought she might like to come to the party."

If Marian had been a bird dog, she'd have gone on point. "Jeez, Max, you would have thought I asked *you* a question. I asked Annie. Last I knew Annie was a big girl, able to talk and walk and chew gum all at the same time. Let me try again." She faced Annie and her eyes glistened. "Annie," Marian enunciated loudly, "why did you invite Iris?"

Annie's eyes warned Max.

He understood. The more Annie didn't answer, the harder Marian would pry. He gave an infinitesimal nod.

Annie was casual. "I decided to take a swim before the party. Iris was standing on her cabin deck. She looked lonely so I asked her if she'd like to swim. We had a good time. I didn't want to rush off to a party and leave her there so I invited her. Like Max said, it was no big deal."

"What did she look like?" Marian slipped a notebook from her purse, began to write.

"Thin." Annie's voice was soft. "Pretty. Dark eyes and dark hair and a sweet smile. She was a good listener. I told her about last summer when Max and I were in trouble. And then—"

Max felt uneasy but if he interrupted, Marian would be like a terrier after a bone. Better to let Annie talk. Surely there was nothing that could bring harm to her.

"—she said she hadn't realized people like me had troubles. I asked her if she had troubles. She said things were better, that she belonged to AA and NA. I told her that she was brave. She said she was trying to make up for things in the past and that's why she came home. She said—"

"Maybe we'd better leave it at that." Max gave Annie a hard stare. He was firm with Marian. "You've got enough for a story."

Marian hesitated, shot an anguished look at the clock. "Eight minutes. Yeah. I got to go. Keep my food for me. I'll be back." She slid out of the booth, headed for the door in a dead run, shouted over her shoulder. "Thanks, Annie. Iris deserves something bright, something besides diagrams of the woods and police handouts."

Annie walked swiftly on the boardwalk, breathing deeply of the slightly fishy ocean smell, welcoming the bustle and charm of the marina with boats ranging from modest sailfish to multimillion-dollar yachts. She always felt she was coming home when she entered Death on Demand. Dispossessed from their old house, barred from their antebellum home-to-be, this was her world with its glorious new book–old book smell, shining heart-pine floors, rich scent of brewed Colombian, a memory of Uncle Ambrose's pipe smoke, and glorious Agatha, queen of cats and dictator of her domain.

Annie felt the usual lift when she saw the small gold letters at the lower right of the front window: PROP. ANNIE DARLING. She looked through the plate glass and blinked in surprise. She'd taken great pleasure in her display, putting a trowel and dirt-stained canvas gloves next to two potted azaleas, one pink, one white, and gardening mysteries that evoked the rich smell of freshly turned dark earth: *Death in the Orchid Garden* by Ann Ripley, *The Blue Rose* by Anthony Eglin, *Trouble in Spades* by Heather Webber, *Summer of the Big Bachi* by Naomi Hirahara, and *Ghost Orchid* by Carol Goodman.

Instead, toy soldiers now marched in formation. A Union Jack and the Stars and Stripes hung from flagpoles behind a battered canvas-covered canteen and a miniature troop train. A poster of *Allies Day, May 1917* by Childe Hassam rested on an easel. Annie nodded approval when she saw the books with their roots in World War I: *The Murder Stone* by Charles Todd, *Angels in the Gloom* by Anne Perry, *Pardonable Lies* by Jacqueline Winspear, *The Mark of the Lion* by Suzanne Arruda, and *Twenty-Three and a Half Hour's Leave* by Mary Roberts Rinehart.

They were all wonderful books, but it seemed a little presumptuous that her gardening display had been preempted. A neatly printed card taped to the easel announced:

The Lucy Kinkaid Memorial Library will host free lectures by Henrietta Brawley every Thursday evening in May offering a perspective on The Great War through fact and fiction.

Annie understood. Henny was a retired teacher, a past president of the Friends of the Library, and a World War II veteran. No doubt she'd created this window display. Okay. Death on Demand always supported the library. Besides, it would be churlish to be miffed by such obvious enthusiasm and dedication to superb mystery fiction. Annie brightened. No doubt the great mysteries set during or after World War I would be part of Henny's presentation. She'd be sure and stock more copies of the books displayed and add Carola Dunn's delightful twenties mysteries with their link to the Great War.

Annie's smile slipped away. For an instant, she'd been immersed in her own wonderful everyday world. If only she could be caught up in thinking about ordering books and not drained by the words that now never seemed far away: *She came in the rain. Alone. On a bicycle.*

Annie took a deep breath, remembering Laurel's chirpy instruction to lift her arms and embrace the world, breathing all the while, and smiling.

Annie assumed a relaxed posture and curved her arms above her head. How did it go? Reach up and pull down a cloud. That was the ticket, envision clouds, fluffy white-as-divinity clouds.

The door opened, the bell jangling.

"Dearest Annie." Laurel's husky voice had never been warmer. "An excellent beginning. I was watching through the window. You are burdened and tai chi can lift that burden."

Annie stepped inside and found herself in the central hallway of her beloved bookstore with Laurel executing graceful motions and murmuring, "More fluidity. Let us hold our arms as if we embrace a ball, one of those gloriously light beach balls with the dearest red-and-yellow stripes. . . ."

Mesmerized, Annie made her best effort to gather clouds, bathe in the spring, and shrug shoulders like a big bear despite fending off Agatha, who seemed to take flowing arms as a personal affront. Annie had a little difficulty with Stork Spreads Its Wings, but came back strong as she grasped a sparrow's tail.

Agatha crouched, green eyes gleaming, mouth open in excitement, tail flicking.

Without missing a beat, Laurel stroked Agatha's arched back, made a soft cooing sound.

Agatha sat back and began to purr. She lifted a paw.

Annie was adamant with herself. Cats did not do tai chi.

The purr intensified.

Annie shot her cat a resentful glare.

"Now, now, dear Annie." Laurel's smile was beatific. She

moved as gracefully as, well, as a stork spreading its wings. "Breathe deeply, let go of all tensions, be free of petty emotions."

Annie didn't want to appear petty to her mother-in-law. She managed a smile, likely not beatific. In passing, while stepping over a log, she gave Agatha a pat.

Agatha's paw swiped out.

Annie jerked away.

"Smoothly, dear child, smoothly," Laurel murmured.

Annie concentrated upon being smooth, envisioning a milkshake dappled with caramel. And yes, she did feel better, more relaxed, less stressed when they concluded. Agatha even jumped up on the cash counter to be adored.

Laurel beamed approval. "You have great promise."

Annie's antenna wriggled. Was that Laurel-speak for: Sweetie, you're lousy, but there's always hope?

"Great promise." Laurel was emphatic, clapping her hands together. "Let's celebrate. You're going to love the changes to the coffee bar." She sped down the center aisle, gracefully, of course.

Annie followed, trying to retain smoothness. Changes?

Laurel set to work behind the counter. "Jamaican sodas are perfect after exertion. The hibiscus tea is already brewed." She poured from a pitcher into a glass filled with ice. She turned to an expanded array of syrups. "I'll add a splash of passion fruit syrup and soda." She splashed, stirred, and garnished the tall glass with an orange slice. "Here you are."

Annie would have preferred an espresso topped with whipped cream, but refusing would have been churlish. Was there a pattern here? Annie tasted the tea hesitantly and found the flavor unusual, but compelling. "Delicious. It will be a wonderful addition to our menu. Laurel, you and Henny have done a great job. I certainly appreciate the help while Ingrid's been gone. I know you will be happy to learn that Duane's back and I can take over here."

Graceful hands waved like sun-kissed clouds. "Perish the thought. Henny and I are here to shoulder any burden. You have too much to do to return now." Laurel beamed. "I spoke with dear Max. He told me of your wonderful plan to honor Iris. He said tomorrow afternoon you planned to go to Savannah to the mission."

Annie put down her glass. *She came in the rain. Alone. On a bicycle.*

"Oh my dear. I know." Laurel came around the counter, slid onto the next leatherette stool, took Annie's hands in hers. "Such sadness. But you made her welcome."

Annie looked into Laurel's kind blue eyes. Last night Laurel had reached out to Iris. "You did, too." Though it often seemed to Annie that her mother-in-law was never quite of this world, Laurel had a shepherd's instinct and she gathered strays with warmth and caring.

Laurel's eyes had a faraway gaze. "I understand being alone."

Annie heard an undertone of sorrow. Laurel had been much married, sometimes widowed, sometimes divorced. She attracted men from nine to ninety with her beauty and a vibrant delight in life that lifted everyone around her.

Laurel looked into her glass, as if remembering. "Iris was standing beneath the willow by herself. I asked her to join me. We walked to one of the faraway tables. We had a lovely visit. She told me about growing up on the island. When she was little, she loved to go to Blackbeard's Beach because she thought treasure was buried there. She dug and dug but she mostly found bottle caps and bits of plastic. Once the water brought in a perfect sand dollar. Since it was dead, her grandmother let her keep it. They bleached it and she painted it pale purple and called it Pansy. She was Iris and her shell was Pansy. She said her grandmother told her that was God's way, to bring unexpected treasures when we'd given up."

Annie pictured a suntanned little girl and a purple sand dollar on a string around her neck. Annie blinked away sudden tears. "Laurel, you gave Iris back some happy days."

"I hope so." Laurel looked grave. "I'm afraid"—her fine brows drew down into a thoughtful frown—"that something upset her later. I saw her walking toward the pavilion and her face looked old, old and drawn. I almost started after her. Oh, how I wish I had. A group came between us, and I lost track of her." Laurel sighed. "That was the last time I saw Iris. I called Billy and told him." She looked sad. "He asked if I noticed her after dinner talking to anyone or going into the woods with someone. I wasn't able to help him."

Annie gave Laurel a quick hug. "You've helped me. Now I have a happy memory for Iris's poster. When I go to the mission, I won't find out about happy days, but I'll find out about her courage. I'm sure of that. I'll pick the best of everything for her poster."

Laurel brightened. "Going to the mission is a wonderful idea."

Annie tensed. Laurel was quick to share thoughts, emotions, and information to all comers, especially if she felt praise was due. Clearly she wouldn't hesitate to tell everyone, friends and strangers alike, about Annie's plan to create a spirit poster for Iris and how Annie and Max were traveling all the way to Savannah for information. If word got back to Billy Cameron about their Sunday afternoon plans, Billy might wonder how Annie knew about the mission. He would by now be well aware of the contents of Iris's purse and would certainly have talked to Brother Doyle. There wouldn't be any harm in Annie and Max talking to Brother Doyle. However, it would be better if Billy didn't know about their trip. If Billy put two and two together, Annie would have some explaining to do, especially since she and Max had solemnly promised not to get involved. She didn't think the idea of a spirit poster would impress Billy.

Annie bent near, whispered. "That's a secret. Don't tell a soul."

"Oh." Laurel's eyes glowed. "I understand. There's more to this than appears on the surface. Oh, my dear, wild horses shan't drag a word from me. My lips are sealed." She crossed her arms, glossy pink nails lightly resting on the shoulders of her pale blue silk blouse.

Annie gulped more tea. She'd gone from bad to worse. Laurel now believed she and Max were involved in the investigation. Maybe Annie should confess, explain that she'd entered Cabin Six and discovered the address of the mission. She gazed into eyes filled with admiration. Laurel would be enchanted with a surreptitious entry and even more convinced Annie and Max were seeking clues.

The bell at the front door sang.

Annie dropped from the coffee stool. Maybe it would be a customer. She'd get Laurel involved. If she and Annie plunged back into the everyday business of selling books, Laurel would see that Annie wasn't involved in the investigation of Iris's murder.

She was midway up the central aisle when she saw the postwoman, a newcomer to the island who'd been, as she enjoyed telling everyone, a carrier in Minneapolis, where the elements made mail delivery as difficult as any polar expedition, but she surmounted every obstacle with her determination and dedication to the United States Postal Service. Her name was Helen and she took herself and her job very seriously.

Helen marched forward, listing a little from the weight of the heavy pouch hung over her left shoulder. Light brown hair safely in a snood, wire glasses magnifying stern brown eyes, thin lips compressed, she clutched a wad of mail in one hand; in the other she held up a single envelope.

She planted herself in front of Annie. "Postal regulations are clear. It is prohibited for any mail receptacle to be used for nonofficial purposes. And"—she leaned forward, continuing in a hiss—"it is absolutely forbidden for a letter lacking postage to be placed in an official receptacle. Mailboxes must not be used for the transmission of unauthorized material. Such acts undermine the sanctity of the mails. It is the responsibility of the owner of the mail receptacle to prohibit such illegal acts. Moreover," Helen's voice rose higher, quivering with outrage, "this letter lacks not only a stamp but there is no return address. It is your responsibility to inform the author of this missive as to the proper use of mail receptacles."

Annie wasn't irritated. Instead, she felt a little spurt of happiness. How nice to deal with ordinary, everyday nonsense. She kept her face attentive and grave. "I will definitely see to it." She held out her hand for the letter.

Helen yanked it back. "Forty-one cents postage due."

When Helen was duly paid, she once again ignored Annie's outstretched hand. "All mail," she said in a grim tone, "will be properly deposited in its official receptacle."

A few minutes later, Annie returned from the end of the boardwalk and the rank of pull-down letter boxes for boardwalk merchants. She dropped catalogs, magazines, and assorted bills on the front counter and looked at the envelope with her name printed in tiny capital letters.

It was sealed. She'd expected to lift the flap and find a casual note. She used the letter opener and slit the envelope. She pulled out a folded sheet, opened it. Small printed letters in all capitals were stark in the center of the page:

BUCK WALKED INTO THE WOODS WITH
JOCELYN THE NIGHT SHE DIED.

∴ *Eight* ∴

BILLY CAMERON TAPPED a quart-size plastic bag that held the anonymous letter. "I wish you'd called. I would have picked this up."

Annie looked surprised. "You're busy. I didn't want to take up your time."

He looked at her quizzically. "Didn't it occur to you that anybody could see you walk into the station? I'm trying to keep you and Max safe. You brought Iris to the picnic. The murderer has to wonder what Iris told you. You know and I know there's nothing that gives us a lead, but murderers run scared." Billy was suddenly stern. "Don't discuss the contents of this letter. But," he said, frowning, "you need a reason to explain your visit here this morning."

He was right. She would have been noticed going into the station. People would wonder and some would ask. She nodded. "I'll tell everyone you had more questions about the guest list."

"All right." He looked again at the letter. "This may mean the murderer is trying to focus attention on Buck. Or this may be gossip and someone thought we should know but doesn't want to get involved. I'm sure there's been a lot of talk over the years about Jocelyn's death. I think most people believe she committed suicide."

Annie wondered if Billy realized what his statement revealed. Clearly, he saw Iris's murder as the result of Jocelyn's drowning. "Someone knows a lot about the night Jocelyn died."

Billy shrugged. "Maybe, maybe not. There are lots of possibilities: The information is true, half true, or a lie. It was sent to help solve Iris's murder, to divert us from something else, or to cause trouble for Buck Carlisle. Or"—his gaze was again troubled—"somebody wanted to see if you hotfooted it over here."

Annie wished she didn't feel exposed and vulnerable.

"But you got the note, you came. I'll deal with it." He started to rise. When she made no move, he frowned.

Annie took a deep breath. "Billy, I know something."

"Annie, you promised to keep out of the investigation."

She lifted a hand to forestall his attack. "I kept my promise. I haven't tried to find out anything about Iris's murder." Or Jocelyn's. "I'm not horning in on your investigation. Instead," and she felt buoyed by her decision, "I'm making a spirit poster for Iris. I'm going to talk to people who knew her and find out nice, funny, happy things about her life."

Billy's thick blond brows bunched. "Iris didn't have a nice, funny, happy life."

Annie felt mulish. "Everybody has good things to remember. Everybody."

"You'll steer clear of the sports picnic, what happened there." It wasn't a question. It was an order.

She raised a hand as if taking an oath. "I promise."

Billy nodded. "What have you found out?"

"It wasn't my doing." She was delighted to offer proof that anything she learned came to her without her instigation. "Fran Carlisle came to see me." Annie felt as if she were betraying Fran, but Billy had to know. "If you talk to her, please keep me out of it."

"That's easy enough. Annie," his voice was reassuring, "stop feeling guilty about everything. Of course you have to tell me what Fran said."

Annie felt relieved. "What she said may be important. The anonymous letter writer may have it all wrong." She described Fran's emotional visit. "Jocelyn may have been in tears because of Russell Montgomery."

Billy's gaze was cynical. "Maybe, maybe not. For all we know, Fran's scared that an old quarrel between Buck and Jocelyn will surface so she comes to see you to shift attention to Russell. Maybe there's no truth at all to the note and it was written to point suspicion away from . . . others."

Annie felt rebuffed. Billy wasn't going to talk about Jocelyn's classmates. Yet Annie knew their identities. Fran had remembered the once carefree group of friends: Fran, Buck, Liz, Russell, and Cara. They were at the sports picnic the night Jocelyn Howard died. Jocelyn's brother Sam, who had also been one of the group, had died of a drug overdose the week before. Annie had no picture of Jocelyn or Sam, but she knew the others. She saw each face as she thought of them, intelligent Fran, likable Buck, dignified Liz, intense Russell, elusive Cara.

If Billy wouldn't talk about them, perhaps there was hope that he had a lead to someone else. In any event, Annie wasn't a player. All she wanted to do was to create a spirit poster for Iris.

* * *

Annie looked toward the harbor as she walked to her car. A sloop with gold and green sails scudded near leaping porpoises. Two shrimp boats rode the jade green water in the distance. Seabirds circled above them, waiting for a succulent meal. She reached the Volvo and looked toward Main Street.

After a moment, she dropped her car keys back into her pocket. Billy hadn't intended to focus her attention on her friends, but he had. She played doubles with Fran, Liz, and Cara. Max played golf with Russell. It had been special to Max and Annie to have friends who remembered the same movies and songs and TV shows. They were Annie and Max's friends. They had been Iris's friends. Wasn't it almost like an accusation that she hadn't spoken a word to any of them except Fran—and that had been Fran's doing—since Iris had been killed?

There was no law that she had to ignore them. Just because she and Max were staying clear of Billy's investigation, she didn't have to treat their friends like pariahs.

Annie looked across the street. A discreet sign in front of a tabby building announced: CARLISLE, SMITHERMAN, AND CARLISLE, ATTORNEYS-AT-LAW. A maroon Harley with chrome-plated shocks was parked at one side. Buck Carlisle loved raising a dust trail on the island's back roads. If he was in his office on a Saturday afternoon, he likely was catching up on the week's work and wouldn't mind a visit. Annie gave a decisive nod and crossed the street.

Buck Carlisle's office was small but attractive. Annie recognized Fran's unerring taste in the russet glow of the maple desk with matching bookcases. The office furnishings were new and of the best quality. Only the tall, dusty, beige law books were old. Two French windows, uncluttered by drapes or shutters, looked out to the harbor. One of Buck's hand-turned wooden bowls gleamed in the sun on a coffee table. Annie was always surprised by the delicacy and beauty of Buck's woodwork.

Buck made the office seem even smaller with his broad shoulders and stocky build. He sank down on the slate gray leather sofa beside Annie. He was casual in a yellow polo, faded jeans, and running shoes. His brown hair was tousled, his square face open and appealing. He reached out to take her hand, his expression earnest. "Fran said she'd talked to you. I almost called, then didn't know if I should." He sounded uncertain, bewildered. "It's a nightmare. It's like those awful days after Jocelyn died. We had a terrible time when we were seniors." His brown eyes were sorrowful. "Jocelyn and her brother died that spring. Iris ran away. I always thought she left because she was trying to forget everything bad. Her mom had died a few years before. People can only handle so much. But now, everything's crazy." He looked bewildered. "Why would anybody kill Iris?"

"It does seem crazy." Annie felt safe and normal. Buck was exactly as he always was, kind and friendly and open. "I didn't come to see you about what happened. It doesn't do any good to think about how she died. Instead, I want to do something in Iris's memory." Annie described a spirit poster.

Buck's face softened. "That's a swell idea." He gave her a grateful look. "Everybody will want to help." He leaned back against the sofa, the tension easing from his body. "Iris and I had a lot in common." His gaze was faraway. "Nothing came easy for us in school. She and I were yellow birds in the first grade." He shoved a hand through his curly brown hair. "Mrs. Blake put the readers in three groups, blue birds, red birds, and yellow birds. Everybody knew what it meant. Blue birds could read anything. Red birds stumbled. As for the yellow birds . . ." He squinted his eyes in a puzzled frown. "I hated being a yellow bird in front of everyone. I knew I wasn't very smart. But one day, something wonderful happened. Mrs. Blake wanted us to sing 'The Bear Song.' You know, one person sings and everybody else repeats the line. She asked Iris to stand up and start. I guess Iris was sitting at the first desk or something. I don't know why she picked her. Jocelyn was always Mrs. Blake's favorite." There was no rancor in his tone. "Jocelyn was everybody's favorite, beautiful and kind and sort of shining. When she walked into a room, you didn't see anybody else. But that day Mrs. Blake called on Iris. And"—wonderment shone in his face—"it was like we heard an angel. Iris's voice was high and clear and sweet and perfect. We all sat there and stared. Nobody knew Iris could sing. Mrs. Blake looked stunned. She was kind of a horsefaced old gal, gruff, impatient, demanding. It was so quiet, Iris looked scared, like she'd done something wrong. She started to cry. Mrs. Blake went over to her and put her arms around her and said, 'Thank you, honey. That was beautiful. I should have known a yellow bird would sing the best song.' For years after that, Iris and I picked each other up when we were down. She'd look at me and say, 'Yellow birds sing the best songs.' When I took first in a woodworking show when we were seniors, she came up and hugged me and whispered, 'Yellow birds sing the best songs.'" His eyes reflected remembered hurt. "My folks didn't come to the show. Dad had a bar dinner. If I'd been on the football team, he would have come to the game. I wasn't good enough even for third string. So what good was it that I could make a beautiful bowl? But Iris came." He stared at Annie with mournful eyes. "She'll never be a yellow bird again."

Liz Montgomery reminded Annie of a Dresden shepherdess. Annie wasn't sure whether the thought was engendered by Liz's round pliant face and flowery dress or the multitude of porcelain in her small but exquisite shop. It was easy to imagine Liz in a hat with streamers and rose-colored muslin against the backdrop of Victorian bisque figurines in soft pastel shades, cups and saucers that were elegant at teas two hundred years ago, mid-Victorian hand-painted and gilded tea sets, and a Gainsborough lady figurine from early-twentieth-century Japan. Treasures adorned every shelf and table.

"Annie." Liz didn't smile. She came slowly forward.

Annie realized with a small shock that she was accustomed always to seeing Liz with her lips curved in a slight smile. Today there was no hint of cheer.

"I saw you going into the police station. What's happening?" The question was almost harsh. "Do the police have any suspects?"

Annie felt uneasy. Liz assumed Annie had inside information about Billy's investigation. She had to make it clear that she wasn't involved. "I have no idea. I don't know anything about the investigation. Billy asked for the guest list for the picnic." It wasn't necessary to say she and Max had delivered the list early this morning.

Liz frowned and her cool gaze never left Annie's face. "I suppose the police will talk to everyone who knew her. Well, Russell and I barely said hello last night. Max told Russell you had a long talk with her." Her unwavering stare was faintly hostile.

Annie wasn't surprised that Russell had already told his

wife about his conversation this morning with Max. "Not really. She and I had a swim out at Nightingale Courts and that's why I invited her to the picnic. It was very casual."

"Russell and I were surprised to see her." There was no indication it had been a pleasant surprise. "We said hello but didn't have a real chance to talk." She shook her head as if she regretted the short interlude. "Everything was fine when we left. I waved good-bye to Iris." Something shifted in that seeking gaze, perhaps a flash of fear or perhaps the momentary shock of confronting eternity. Beringed fingers clutched at her amber necklace. "What happened?"

Annie turned her hands palms up. "No one knows. Apparently Iris went into the woods with someone."

Now the fear in Liz's eyes was unmistakable. "Who?" The demand was sharp.

"I think Billy—" Annie stopped. She couldn't go around reporting what Billy had said. "I don't know."

Liz's blue eyes narrowed. She was shrewd enough to know Annie had started the sentence with one thought and ended it with another.

"I don't have any idea what the police are doing." Annie talked fast, trying to get past the awkward moment and the suspicion in Liz's eyes. "That's not why I came. I just visited with Buck about a tribute to Iris." She described the spirit poster.

This time there was no rush of approval. Liz's round face was as unmoved as the forever frozen, milky white porcelain cheeks of a statuette. "I wish I could be helpful. But," Liz's tone was icy, "I'm afraid nothing I remember about Iris would be appropriate."

Annie found herself on the way out. ". . . need to run some errands . . . glad you are bearing up so well . . . such a dreadful end to your evening . . ."

Her last glimpse of Liz in the shop doorway supplanted Annie's image of Liz as a quaint figure with the much more impressive figure of a focused woman with memories she would not—or could not—share.

Annie hesitated at the entrance to Yesterday's Treasures, then reached for the antique bronze knob. Once begun, her canvass for memories of Iris would look more suspicious if abruptly ended. If she spoke only with Buck and Liz, the others would wonder why. She had no doubt that Iris's classmates would be in touch and Annie's visits discussed. Annie had a distinct feeling that Max was not going to be pleased with her afternoon.

As if on cue, her cell phone chimed. Annie turned away from the shop, moved to one of the cast iron park benches with a view of the harbor. She smiled at the caller ID. "Hi."

"I talked to Father Patton and he'll be glad to do the service."

As always, the sound of Max's voice lifted her.

"We're looking ahead to ten o'clock Friday. There isn't any family left. I'll take care of the obituary. Marian said she'd help. I'm at the store. I thought you'd be here, but Laurel told me about the note. What does Billy think?"

"Could be something, may be nothing. Anyway"—and she felt virtuous—"it's in his hands. I told him about my spirit poster and now I'm checking in with everybody to get some nice memories of Iris."

An instant of silence in the ether was a clear reminder that Max was no fool. "Everybody?"

"Max," she tried not to sound defensive, "it's terrible if we don't have anything to do with our friends. It's as if we're declaring them suspects. I decided I owed them more than that and since I need memories of Iris, I'm dropping by and visiting. That's all I'm asking for. Buck gave me a sweet memory."

"No questions about murder." Again it was a demand, not a question.

"I've already promised Billy." Did both Max and Billy think she was untrustworthy?

"Good. Make your visits short and sweet. And then, let's take some time for us." He sounded determined. The dead could be mourned, but life was to be lived.

Fran's shop was as eclectic as Liz's was predictable. Oaxacan clay statuettes were displayed on a Hans Wegner teak wall cabinet. African tribal masks hung from a Victorian iron hat tree. Yet the overall impression was not a hodgepodge but a collection of amazing vitality and exuberance. Fran's shop had been written up in *Southern Living* as one of the most unusual in the sea islands, offering glimpses of exotic worlds.

Fran stood behind a counter filled with cut-glass perfume bottles. A musky scent rose from a wooden bowl filled with potpourri. Fran's stare was wary. "I saw you go into the station."

Billy's concern was quickly proven correct.

Fran's voice was clipped. "Did you tell Billy about Russell and Jocelyn?"

Annie felt stung. "I didn't have a choice. I had to go see him anyway about—" She broke off. The last person she wanted to tell about the anonymous note was Buck's wife. "Something that had nothing to do with Russell."

Fran's eyes glittered. "About what?"

Annie felt miserable. "I can't tell you. It had nothing to do with Russell. But when Billy asked if I'd talked to anyone about Jocelyn at the sports picnic, I had to tell him what you said."

The silence between them was stiff and strained.

Annie took a step nearer Fran. "Let's not quarrel. We all want Iris's murderer caught."

Fran's angular face looked tired and worried. "Of course we want the murderer caught. But I intend to make it clear to Billy that you misunderstood what I said." She was decisive. "Sure, Russell was upset that night. Why not? Sam was his best friend. He didn't want to talk to Jocelyn. Guys can't handle emotion. That's all it amounted to."

"I'm sure Billy will talk to Russell, clear everything up. Anyway, that's not why I came to see you."

Fran heard Annie out. She was pensive. "A memory of Iris? She was always there. She hung around us."

Annie wondered if Fran sensed the picture she painted, Fran a part of a group, Iris peripheral.

"She was like a ghost that last year, never quite real." Fran turned her hands over in helplessness. "I don't know if that makes any sense. I don't know any way to say it better. I didn't have any idea what was wrong until Sam died. That's when I heard whispers, that he was on drugs and that Iris sold them to him. I couldn't believe it. But when she ran away, I knew. It was awful." Her look was bitter. "Sam was the handsomest guy in our class. We all wanted to date him." Fran's eyes filled with tears. "I can't talk about Iris now. I don't want to remember." Whirling, she moved from behind the counter, disappeared through a beaded curtain into a back room.

Annie parked in front of the Montgomery house. She didn't want to get out of her car and knock on the front door of the two-story yellow stucco home that overlooked a lagoon.

Russell had built it and the house was comfortable and welcoming. Or had always been so in the past.

Annie no longer felt sure of welcome from the group that had known both Iris and Jocelyn. Maybe talking to them was a big mistake. So far, she'd done nothing but reinforce the idea that she was meddling in a police investigation. That wasn't what she had intended.

She forced herself forward. Maybe Russell wouldn't be home. Annie walked slowly up the walk. A buzz saw whined in the distance. Russell had recently mentioned expanding the deck. He was having a busman's holiday this sunny April afternoon.

He saw her as she rounded the corner of the house. The buzz saw's shrill whine was cut off. He swiped his hands on his khaki shorts and walked toward her, big, muscular, attractive. But his face was wary.

Annie felt small inside. She wondered if he'd talked with either Liz or Fran.

"Hey, Russell." She hoped she didn't sound as craven as she felt.

He suddenly frowned. "Is everything okay at the house? The plumber's there even though it's Saturday. He's promised to keep after it until everything's fixed."

It was such a relief that he connected her visit with the Franklin house and not with Iris that she managed a tentative smile. "Everything's fine at the Franklin house. We aren't thinking much about the house now. Not after what happened last night. I'm upset that I asked her to our party and something awful happened. I'm putting together a memorial for Iris and I'm talking to people who knew her, asking for good memories. I hoped you could help."

He looked startled. "Well, sure. I'll talk to Liz—"

Annie interrupted. "I just spoke with her a few minutes ago." Annie didn't tell him his wife had declined to contribute. Maybe that wasn't playing fair. At this point, she didn't care. She'd set out to talk to those who'd known Iris. She was going to finish the task even if it left her friendships in shambles. She braced for another rejection as she sketched what she had in mind.

Russell looked thoughtful. "I felt sorry for Iris. She never seemed to belong. She was always around, but she didn't have fun like the rest of us. Liz was always nice—"

Annie nodded and wondered why Liz didn't have any good memories to share.

"—but Liz is always nice to people. Iris was real quiet. I think a lot of it went back to her mom and Hootie. Hootie was her pet owl. She'd raised him from when he was little and must have fallen out of a tree or something. Everybody said he'd die and she was stupid to try to take care of him. She didn't pay any attention and the owl didn't die. We were maybe nine or ten then. Maybe it would have been better if the owl had died right off."

Annie pictured the huge eyes of an owl, heard in her mind the plaintive cry. "What happened?"

"Her grandma had fixed a big wire cage in one of their trees. Hootie got out. Somebody shot him." Russell kicked at a pine cone on the ground. "That happened not long after her mom died. I think that's when Iris kind of went her own way. Sometimes I thought she had a look like an owl, a real distant stare."

The modest gray wood cottage sat high on pilings, safe from storm surges. A wraparound deck afforded views of the Sound and the salt marsh. Annie was pleased to see Cara's

convertible parked beneath the house. Annie wondered if
Cara would provide a memory. At least she'd come to see
Iris at Nightingale Courts though it was after Cara's depar-
ture that Iris had appeared lonely and troubled.

Annie hoped Cara would offer more information for Iris's
spirit poster. Annie was grateful for Buck's and Russell's
insights. She would find a photo online of a brilliantly yellow canary. Last year she'd taken a night photo of a barred
owl in their backyard. She would likely never know whether
Iris's owl was a great horned or a barred, but the photo
was arresting, a frontal shot with those huge eyes. "Here's
looking at you," they seemed to say. Iris would be pleased.
Annie needed more to be satisfied with her poster. She had
no intention of giving up. She would keep on looking for
memorics, on the island and on the mainland.

As she walked toward the cabin, the sound of her footsteps on the oyster-shell drive was lost in the throbbing
whop-whop of a low-flying Coast Guard helicopter. Annie
looked up, shading her eyes. She wondered if the bright
orange Dolphin was returning to the Savannah air station
from a usual patrol or if a boater was in trouble somewhere
on the Sound.

The path approached Cara's cabin from one side, affording a view of the deck overlooking the marsh. Cara stood
at the railing, facing the undulating spartina grass and the
green water beyond.

The roar of the rotors was loud and intense. Annie came
near, close enough to call out. The shout died in her throat
as Cara turned away from the view.

Cara's head hung down. Tears streaked a mottled face. She
clutched a portrait frame against her chest. She walked heavily to a rattan chair and sank into it, a figure of despair.

Annie hesitated, then turned away. Cara was alone, deliberately, decisively alone, plunged into a private torment. This was not a moment she intended to share. Offering solace would be an affront.

Annie hurried to her car, started it, backed and turned in the drive, grateful that the fading roar of the rotors masked her departure.

What had she seen and what did it mean? Was Cara's grief for Iris? That would suggest a relationship far deeper than anyone knew.

If so, Billy should know.

Annie's heart rebelled. She wouldn't reveal Cara's heartbreak unless she had no choice.

❖ *Nine* ❖

AT THE COFFEE hour after the early service, Cara Wilkes was slim and attractive in a stylish pink bouclé jacket and matching skirt and pink leather heels. She wore her usual dangling necklace. This two-strand set alternated white and pink beads, a nice accent for her suit. Her short-cut sandy hair glistened in a shaft of sunlight. Her makeup was perfect, the pink lip gloss matching the beads. Cara was animated, talking a mile a minute, waving her hands for emphasis. There was no trace of yesterday's distress.

Annie had wrestled through the night with her unwanted knowledge. If Cara's tears were related to Iris's murder, Billy should know. But there might be no connection.

In any event, she needed to ask Cara about a memory of Iris.

Annie glanced toward Max. He was deep in conversation with Father Patton. Annie skirted several groups, waited until Cara was free, then hurried to her. She'd scarcely started to explain when Cara interrupted.

"It's a lovely idea. Buck told me all about it." Cara smiled warmly. Her eyes were soft, then with a quick breath, she said brightly, "Fran wants to help, too. She's sent you an e-mail. Buck said she was too upset to talk to you yesterday." Cara suddenly looked somber. "We've all been upset since Iris died. But I love the idea of a spirit poster, something beautiful for Iris." Cara linked arms with Annie, drew her nearer the parish hall's French window, which opened to a terrace. "Come outside and let me tell you about Iris."

The air was clear and clean and cool, April fresh before summer's onslaught of heat and humidity. They sat on a wooden bench near a fountain. The soft splash was a cheerful background to Cara's quick words. "Iris and I were both raised by our grandmothers. I wore these today for Iris." Cara touched the necklace. "She made the necklace from beads she'd taken from some broken-up old jewelry of her mom's and gave it to me for Christmas when we were twelve. I loved jewelry even then. Iris and I always hung around together at Christmas. Our grandmothers were friends. We didn't have much family. At school programs, everybody else had moms and dads or at least moms. We always felt kind of hollow when everybody else had their families around. Iris was funny. Do you know one thing she really, really loved?"

Annie waited with a smile. Cara's eagerness was infectious.

"Olivia Newton-John's music. All because her mom loved it. 'Magic' was Iris's favorite. Everybody made fun of her because that wasn't cool when we were kids. U2 and the Red Hot Chili Peppers were big for us. But Iris said every time she heard 'Magic,' she thought of her mom. When she sang, I thought Iris sounded like Olivia. She would like for that to be on her poster."

She looked past Annie. "There's Fran and Buck. I'll tell

her you'll look for her e-mail." With that she was on her feet
in her usual swift fashion and rushing toward the window.

Annie looked after Cara with a feeling of reassurance.
Unless Cara was a superb actress, her sadness yesterday
afternoon had no link to Iris.

But Cara hadn't mentioned her visit to Nightingale
Courts.

Maybe that wasn't a good memory of Iris.

Max waved away a wasp circling near the fragrant white
blooms of the mock orange shrub. Annie always said the
heavenly scent of mock orange was particularly appropriate
for a shrub in the cloister between the chapel and the church.
Mock orange grew to ten feet in height. He might plant
the shrubbery in a crescent near their pond at the Franklin
house. However, the blooming period was short lived.

He leaned against a pillar and felt at peace with the world
as he waited, enjoying the tolling of the bells as parishio-
ners strolled toward their cars. Annie had stepped into the
chapel to light a candle for Iris. He looked at the massive
red wooden door, pictured her kneeling in the small alcove,
light slanting through stained glass to turn her blond hair
to gold.

Annie was safe now.

The unexpected thought startled him. He shook his head.
Billy's grim concern obviously lurked in his subconscious.
Annie wasn't involved in the investigation. She'd found a
positive outlet for her sadness about Iris's death. She was
excited about Cara's upbeat offering for the spirit poster.
He wondered if Father Patton would approve if they played
"Magic" at the service.

Of course Annie was safe. There was nothing to worry
about.

* * *

Annie moved fast through the back door of Death on Demand. She'd left Max at Nightingale Courts, whipping together a great Sunday brunch. Happily, it never took long to drive the length of the island. She wanted to check her e-mails. When she received the e-mail from Fran, everyone except Liz would have contributed to Iris's spirit poster.

Agatha jumped up on the computer desk. Annie gently touched heads with her, stroked silky fur. "Don't try to tell me you're starving. I set your automatic feeder." The latest in cat food dispensers both opened a can and dispensed dry food. It couldn't get any better at a cat Waldorf.

Agatha purred and looked as though she was smiling.

Annie smoothed Agatha's coat and clicked to Outlook Express:

Hi Annie,

Sorry I got upset when we talked yesterday. I remember Iris had a way of seeing things differently from everyone around her. In sixth grade, she was in the school play. It was a story about the War. The Yankees were trying to find hidden silver. Yankee soldiers threatened to kill a slave who'd stayed with the family because the men were gone and the mistress was sick and there were three kids. Iris played one of the kids. In the play, they were supposed to refuse to tell the hiding place. Instead, Iris told the soldiers the silver was in a burlap bag down in a well. Everybody was scandalized and Mrs. Tucker, our speech

teacher, was irritated and said Iris
had ruined the play and wanted to know
why had she done it. Iris said when she
looked at Walter, who was playing the
slave, and thought somebody was going to
hurt him, she had to speak out and save
him. Mrs. Tucker gave Iris a hug and
said having a kind heart was better than
the best acting in the world. I thought
it was funny. Maybe she never could tell
the difference between what was real and
what was make-believe.

* * *

Annie took a deep satisfied sniff. Nothing smelled as good
as their kitchen on Sunday morning, even when it con-
sisted of a small oven and two-burner range and compact
refrigerator in a rental cabin. Max was a culinary genius.
Breakfast after early church was always special. Today he
was topping potato and bacon pancakes with poached eggs
and hollandaise sauce. Max turned off the blender. He was
ready to add melted butter to the mixture of egg yolk, lemon
juice, mustard, and wilted watercress.

Annie straightened one of the place mats. Ruby macaws
looked poised for flight on navy linen place mats Henny had
brought back from Brazil. Annie put out whipped butter to
soften and poured fresh orange juice. All the comforts of
home. She glanced through the sliding glass door at green-
ing marsh grass shimmering in the morning sun. Soon
they'd be on the ferry heading toward the mainland, breathing the salty scent of the sea and watching dolphins.

A thunk sounded at the cabin's front door. Perfect timing.
The Sunday morning *Gazette* had arrived. She retrieved the

newspaper, discarded the ads, and placed the front section at Max's plate. She kept the sports section to check the scores of the Rangers and Astros. Some passions a girl from Texas never lost.

Max carried the laden plates to the table. He averted his gaze as Annie added a dash of ketchup to her hollandaise.

Annie ate contentedly, propping the baseball page against her orange juice. "Max, the pancakes are divine." After all, it was Sunday. And Michael Young had four hits and—

"For God's sake." Max slammed a hand onto the table. His face was hard and furious.

Juice slopped over the edge of her glass onto a picture of the Yankees' Alex Rodriguez hitting a home run.

"Look at this." Max thrust the front section toward her.

Annie took the paper. She saw the headline. She'd expected it, but the large black letters destroyed her pleasure in their morning, plunged her back into sadness:

MURDER MARS PAVILION PARTY; POLICE REPORT NO SUSPECTS

Former island native Iris Tilford, 28, was strangled in the woods adjacent to Harbor Pavilion Friday night . . .

Max was impatient. "Not the lead story. The inset."

Annie was glad to stop reading the lead story. She knew everything it contained. Her eyes moved to the black box with inset boldface type:

Iris Tilford's last afternoon sparkled. She swam in the pool at Nightingale Courts with a new friend, felt the coolness of sky blue water, remembered good times and bad.

Annie Darling was Tilford's hostess as she was at the fateful party Friday night. A local merchant, Darling, along with her husband Max, is known for community support and outreach. Darling was at Nightingale Courts, serving as manager while its owners were out of town because of family illness.

Friday afternoon Darling reached out to a young woman who'd been down on her luck but was fighting her way back to sobriety through AA and NA. Darling recalled these moments with Iris Tilford:

She was pretty . . . dark eyes and dark hair and a sweet smile. She'd had troubles but she said things were better since she'd joined AA and NA. I told her she was brave.

Darling was reluctant to discuss their conversation at length, but admitted Tilford said she'd returned to the island because of events in her past.

Whatever Iris Tilford shared with her new friend, Darling was quick to invite Iris to a party hosted by Darling and her husband at the harbor pavilion.

Iris Tilford saw faces from her past Friday night, but she didn't live to tell what they meant to her.

"Oh." Annie looked at Max's angry face, eyes narrowed, jaws tensed. "It sounds like Iris told me a lot about the past."

Max's tone was rough. "I'll call Vince. Get a retraction."

Annie shook her head. "That would make it worse. The old no-smoke-without-fire." She glanced down at the bold type that shouted the importance of its contents. "Actually," her voice was hopeful, "anyone reading it in a hurry wouldn't think much about it. People skim everything."

Max looked grim. "The murderer won't read it in a hurry." His gaze fastened on Annie. "From now on, it's you and me together. Day and night." His expression softened. He reached across the table, took her hand in his, held tight. "Not exactly hard duty."

Laughing gulls circled above the ferry, their distinctive hyena cackle rising over the water slapping against the hull. Whitecaps rippled across the Sound. In the distance, a freighter rode low in the water. Except for them, the passengers had remained in their cars. She followed Max up steep steps. They stopped at a railing, the wheelhouse behind them.

She felt the sharpness of the breeze. Only a few days before, Iris Tilford had taken the ferry to Broward's Rock. Had she been fearful? She was embarking on an effort to discover the truth of part of her past. She must have felt the breeze and the warmth of the sun.

Iris had been alive.

Annie gripped the railing, felt the burn of tears.

Max's arm came around her. He pulled her close. "Don't cry." His voice was soft.

"Iris was trying to do the right thing. Now she's gone."

"None of us know how long we have." Max touched her cheek.

"I'm frightened." It was scarcely a whisper. She felt as if she'd touched the edge of eternity. Iris had been here and now she was gone. Forever. The world seemed huge and alien and empty.

His embrace tightened. "Don't be scared. Don't lose faith. Or hope. Despite all evil, there's goodness, too. Hold to that."

Annie drew strength from his nearness. Whatever was to happen, she had set herself a good task and she drew comfort from it. She was going to create a tribute to Iris.

Once again she looked at the softly green water, glad for the breeze and its reminder of life and feeling. Annie wondered if they would be welcomed at the mission. Would Brother Doyle be willing to talk about Iris? Had he known her well enough to have memories to share? Could Annie find the peace she sought and the reassurance that life could be well ordered and safe?

She felt a tug on her arm.

Max's gaze was intent. "Penny for your thoughts?"

The mainland came into view, a dark smudge on the horizon.

She gave him a reassuring smile and made her tone cheerful. "I hope Brother Doyle will talk to us."

Max was positive. "Why wouldn't he? We're going to have a good day." His eyes told her more than the words, told her he was there, she was fine, life was good. "After we go to the mission, let's catch the buffet at The Lady and Sons."

"I'd love that. Although we don't really need two fabulous meals in one day." Annie enjoyed Paula Deen's famous restaurant though the lines of eager customers often stretched around the block. She and Max weren't in a hurry and it was a lovely day to be outside. The restaurant closed at five on Sundays, but a late afternoon buffet could serve as an early supper. She could already taste the deviled eggs, made with mustard as deviled eggs should be. They'd be home in time to reassure Dorothy L. that she hadn't been deserted in the cabin.

As the ferry chugged toward the dock, Annie wondered if Max wanted to delay their return to the island as long as possible. Was he afraid her efforts for Iris's poster might encroach on Billy's investigation? Max didn't need to worry. She would keep their bargain. She wouldn't ask anyone anything that related to Iris's murder.

The mission was a sagging building on a down-at-heel street that spoke of loss and despair and hard times. Kirk Doyle led Annie and Max toward a corner of the converted garage. As they walked past Exercycles and a treadmill, none in use, conversation died. Perhaps fifteen or twenty people of all ages and races, including women and small children, were seated at several trestle tables, eating Sunday dinner on plastic plates. There was a smell of braised beef and yeast rolls and apple pie. Dress ranged from neat and well worn to tattered and soiled.

Quick, wary stares accounted them strangers from a world many had never known or long ago left behind.

Doyle welcomed them to a small, cluttered office. An electric fan perched on a wooden stool stirred the air in the windowless office but did nothing to dispel a muggy undertone of mold, damp, motor oil, and rotting wood. As he closed the door, Annie tried to put away the awareness of broken lives.

The empty right sleeve of Doyle's worn black suit was pinned up. He used his left hand to swipe at the seats of two straight chairs, perhaps noting Annie's tropical green yarn sweater and long matching skirt with a profusion of jungle flowers and Max's crisp white shirt and navy worsted slacks.

Doyle waited until they were seated, then turned another straight chair around and straddled it to face them instead of sitting behind the desk. The casual posture made his stiff gray hair, weathered face, and hulking presence less intimidating. "How can I help you?" His voice was gruff but sincere.

Annie saw sadness and patience in his dark eyes. She scooted to the edge of her chair. Could she make him understand? "Mr. Doyle—"

He brushed away the title. "Kirk will do."

She told him about Iris, their afternoon in the sun, the fateful invitation to their party, and how she wanted to honor Iris.

"A spirit poster?" A smile softened his somber face. "I like that very much. I can tell you some things about Iris. I've known her since December."

Annie was surprised at the sharpness of her disappointment. What could he have learned about Iris in that short time?

"The nights were cold. December's hard for folks like Iris. Christmas is coming, but they don't think it's for them. Have you ever heard church bells ring on a Sunday morning when your head hurts and your guts want to spill out? You're outside, without anybody to love you and nobody to love, not knowing that Jesus is holding out his arms for you with the greatest love on earth. Folks like Iris have lost their way. Some of them never knew the way. She came in the middle of the night. I heard a knock at the alley door. Her face was bruised and swollen. She was limping from where she'd been kicked. She had no coat. She was drunk. She said two men at the bar next door hurt her, but she got away from them. She asked if she could hide. I didn't want to disturb the women's section. We've got four bays left from the days when this was a garage. I scrounged from demolition sites and put up beaverboard so we have the men's area and the women and children's area. I got some blankets from the storeroom, made a pallet for her in here." He pointed at the floor near their feet. "The next morning I brought her breakfast. She hadn't eaten in three days. We talked. She'd come to the end of everything. She wanted to die. I told her God wanted her to live. She started to cry." Kirk massaged a hump in his nose.

Annie wondered what long-ago bash had broken it, knew the bone hadn't been set, wondered if cool damp weather made it ache.

"She wanted to get well. I helped her get into treatment." He looked at them sharply. "Do you know what kind of courage it takes to fight addiction? There's pain and sickness and panic and always the darkness inside that drove a soul to drugs and drink in the first place. Iris had that courage. She had seventy-four days when she left to go back to her island. You can put those days on your poster, proud days, hard days, but the best days she'd ever known."

Hot tears slipped down Annie's cheeks.

"Tears are balm to hurting hearts." His smile was sweet. "Don't grieve. Iris is in a better place now. 'And God shall wipe away all tears from their eyes; and there shall be no more death, neither sorrow, nor crying, neither shall there be any more pain: for the former things have passed away.'"

Annie heard the familiar words from Revelation. But "I'm crying because she had such a sad life and then when her life was better, someone killed her."

"She lives in the hearts of those who knew her. You can put your poster where others will see it—"

Annie nodded.

"—and they can admire courage and be better for knowing Iris."

"I'll make a place in my bookstore, a table near the fireplace. I'll make up a lending library and ask readers to bring books that have touched their hearts. Anyone can borrow them, return them, or keep them."

Kirk reached to his desk, picked up a stack of cards. "And these."

Annie took the cards containing Al-Anon's heart-touching, life-changing Twelve Steps. "And these," she affirmed.

Max smiled at her. He turned to Kirk. "You saved Iris's life."

Warmth seeped from Kirk's craggy face. His face looked bleak. "And lost it for her. I told the police officer from Broward's Rock, Sergeant Harrison. I encouraged Iris to go back to the island, make amends." He picked up one of the cards, read Step Eight aloud: " 'Made a list of all persons we had harmed and became willing to make amends to all of them.' "

Annie reached out, held Max's hand.

"Iris got into drugs through a friend. The friend had access to them, but didn't use them." Kirk looked past Annie and Max, as if seeing faces they would never know. "That's how kids get hooked. A friend has drugs, shares them. Every so often there's a particularly vulnerable person like Iris. Once started, she couldn't stop. She'd do anything for the drugs. She agreed to deliver drugs to other kids in school. Everyone thought she was the supplier, but there was someone behind her who didn't use drugs. Iris took the money but it all went to her friend. She got drugs free. Then a boy died. His sister came to Iris, accused her of killing him. Iris said it wasn't her fault, she was only the go-between. She told the sister the whole story. Iris said she was high, not thinking straight, but when she realized her own supply would be cut off, she told her friend what she'd done. She saw the sister walk with her friend and later she didn't see them anywhere. When the girl drowned, Iris was afraid. I asked her what she thought had happened. That upset her. She'd pull away from talking about it, saying maybe she was all mixed up about that night."

Annie's throat felt tight. "Who had the drugs?"

He shook his head. "Iris didn't say. She always said 'my friend.' She said it worried her that no one came forward later and admitted being with the sister and yet she was almost sure the sister walked away with her friend. Iris also thought she remembered someone else going into the fog with Jocelyn. She knew there could be an innocent explanation. Still, she felt haunted by Jocelyn's death. Iris wasn't sure how much was a dream and how much was her own guilt and how much was actual. She thought she would know if she went back to the island."

Sunset bathed the marsh and Nightingale Courts in crimson. An egret stepping daintily in shallow water looked touched by flame. A great blue heron might have been a statue. Frogs in the lagoon croaked and bellowed. Chuck-will's-widows gave their haunting call as they skimmed, seeking moths. On the deck behind Cabin Seven, Annie sipped cream sherry and Max lifted a frosty bottle of Beck's as they watched night fall.

Max looked toward her. "Give it a rest." But his voice was understanding. There was no hint of criticism.

Annie buttoned her cardigan against the chilling night, but her heart felt warm. She took comfort from the empathy in Max's dark blue eyes, the compassion in his face. He wanted her to be freed from distress at Iris's struggles, but he knew she had to work her way to peace. "I keep thinking about Iris, coming back to the island, trying to lay ghosts to rest. She looked almost stricken when I invited her to come to the pavilion, but she came. That was brave. I wish she hadn't." Annie clenched her hands. "Friday night Iris must have realized who walked into the woods with Jocelyn." Had memory come clear through the haze of time and drugs?

"Billy will find out." Max's tone was final.

Brother Doyle had told Sgt. Harrison of Iris's intentions. Billy now knew why Iris had returned to the island. His instinct that Iris died because of Jocelyn had proved to be true.

Annie's cell phone pealed. She put down her glass, retrieved the phone from the patio table, glancing at caller ID. "Hey, Henny. . . . I'll be back in the store tomorrow. . . . Sure. That will be great. . . . I love the new display in the front window. . . . Henny, were you teaching when Iris Tilford was in school?"

Max turned to listen. Dorothy L. stirred in his lap, gave a sleepy mew.

"Let's talk tomorrow. I'm trying to find out more about her for a tribute. See you then." Annie closed the phone, smiled contentedly. "Henny is a great friend. And your mom can always be counted on." Annie completed the sentence in her own mind: . . . *despite a world view that borders on the unhinged.* As soon as the thought came, Annie scolded herself. For all her wacky ways, Laurel was good-hearted and well-meaning. "Anyway," Annie added hurriedly to mask a twinge of guilt, "Laurel and Henny did a wonderful job at the store. Though I'm afraid," her tone was rueful, "they see this as the start of a continuing involvement. Henny said she

had some more ideas to brighten things up. But I'll be glad
to see her tomorrow. She remembers Iris."

Annie struggled up from the deep sleep that is near oblivion
with jumbled thoughts of a jellyfish sting and a diesel truck
belching smoke and screeching brakes. Hot pricks came
again and with them a muzzy awareness of her surroundings. A strange room. No, not strange. Their cabin at Nightingale Courts. The broken ceiling at the Franklin house had
put them here so the door to the bathroom wasn't where it
should be and the blackness that loomed like the mouth
of a cavern was only the plate glass doors overlooking the
marsh.

Dorothy L. seized Annie's foot through the thin sheet.
She wailed, high and demanding. "Stop it," Annie hissed,
trying not to wake Max. She moved her foot. Dorothy L.
leaped with a piercing cry.

Max slept with his face in the crook of an elbow, his
breathing slow and even.

Annie grabbed at the chubby cat. They hadn't dared let her
go out at night in a strange place. A marsh hawk or alligator
or gray fox could spell quick death. Once they were safely
ensconced at the Franklin house, Dorothy L. would learn
her new territory. Until tonight, she'd cuddled quiescently
between them. Annie clutched Dorothy L. and struggled to
move her sluggish, sleep-drenched body, still cumbered by
a dream of foul-smelling trucks. She slid her feet into cold
Crocs, shivered. "Sorry," she whispered, "you're going to
have to sleep in your carrier." Annie stumbled toward the
corner where they kept the carrier. She was on her knees,
pushing a reluctant Dorothy L. inside, when she heard an
odd, metallic sound.

As she slid home the latch and came to her feet, she turned toward the door. She hadn't heard a car. Her nose wrinkled. Something smelled gassy. Odd in the middle of the night. Had a car pulled in and someone knocked at the office? The sound didn't come again.

Likely some noise had roused Dorothy L. A raccoon might be at work.

Dorothy L.'s shrill meow pierced the silence.

Annie turned back toward the carrier. What in the world was wrong with Dorothy L.? She must sense a predator, some kind of danger. The insistent meow continued, loud and frantic. In a minute Max would be awake. Well, she was his cat, he could deal with her. Annie picked up the carrier. Maybe she should put the carrier on the front porch. Actually, the car might be the best place.

As Annie reached for the doorknob, a whoosh sounded behind her. The noise was ominous, totally out of context. Something was terribly wrong. Something alien and inexplicable was happening. She whirled around. Orange light glowed beyond the sliding glass doors. With horrifying quickness, flames danced against the plate glass. Fire blazed, orange and yellow and red.

"Max!" Annie's scream rose above a crackling roar. Still clutching the handle of the carrier, she flung herself toward the bed, pulled at his arm. She pulled and tugged and called.

Max flailed awake and struggled from the bed, unsteady and confused, his voice groggy. "What's wrong?"

"Fire!" She screamed to be heard above crackles, hisses, and pops. Hot smoke assailed her. "We've got to get out." Dorothy L. meowed, high and strident, without stopping. The carrier wobbled in her hand as the cat lunged.

Max was a dark shadow in the hellish orange glow from

the sliding glass doors. She pulled at his arm and they turned toward the door. Annie shouted, "I've got Dorothy L." She came close behind, a hand on his back.

Max stopped at the door, fumbled to find the knob. His muscles bunched. He grunted with effort. "The door's jammed. I can't budge it. We've got to go out the window." He turned and grabbed her arm.

Annie gasped for air against thickening smoke, the smell acrid and harsh. Dorothy L. scrambled back and forth in the carrier, meowing frantically.

Heavy smoke obscured the glow from the deck. They moved blindly in a thick haze faintly tinged by orange. They could no longer see. They might be moving in any direction.

Horror pulled at Annie. They didn't know the way to the window. They couldn't get out.

Max crashed into an obstacle. "This way."

Annie barely heard his shout. She felt caught in a maelstrom, flames licking near, choked by oily smoke. Sirens shrilled above the cacophony of the fire.

Max's grip on her arm was hard, imperative. He steered her forward. The carrier bumped against her leg.

Suddenly, above the fire's roar, glass crashed, air poured inside, burning embers and sparks spattered them, hot and hurtful.

"Get to the goddam window." Duane's shout was hoarse, desperate.

Annie was never certain whether they homed to his shouts or whether they moved instinctively into the life-giving swirl of air. Max pushed her ahead of him. Flames flickered against darkness. Water sizzled as it met fire. Wetness splashed inside, cascaded over her. At the gaping hole that had been a window, Annie froze. Flames flickered everywhere, reaching inside.

Water gushed at the window, a steady strong stream that sloshed toward the roof and washed through the broken window to drench her.

"Jump, dammit, jump." Duane's shout rose above the fire.

Annie swung the carrier up and pushed it through. "Get the carrier." Thankfully, the weight shifted away. Dorothy L. was safe.

"Jump!" Duane's shout was almost lost in the mind-numbing roar of water and flames.

Fire blazed above and on either side. The smell of smoke and charred wood choked her. Max swept her up and thrust her into the night. Strong arms reached up and took her.

She twisted, screaming for Max.

A canvas-gloved hand pummeled her, beating out sparks on her nightgown. She was lifted, carried past the tangle of hoses. She struggled to be free. "Ma'am, please. You're all right. Here . . ." And she was thrust forward.

"It's okay, Annie." Duane reached out to grab her. "They got Max out."

She sagged against him and looked toward the cabin. Dancing flames illuminated firemen in white plastic helmets and bright yellow gear.

Duane's smoke-smudged face glowered at her. He held Dorothy L.'s carrier under one arm. "Damn fools. You almost got killed saving a damn cat."

Annie felt tears streak her face. "She saved us. You saved all three of us."

Max, blond hair darkened by ash, stubbled face set and angry, bare-chested and limping, streaked with grime and dirt, his tartan boxers plastered against him, came toward her, his arms open.

She ran to him, held him tight, breathed smoke and Max and the marsh. All that mattered in the world was his body next to hers.

~ *Ten* ~

THE PUMPER TRUCK headlights illuminated the cabin as the roof collapsed. Sparks swirled up within a dark column of smoke shot through with flame. Water slammed into the cabin from four hoses. Firefighters, two fire trucks, the fire chief's sedan, three police cars, and an ambulance jammed the clearing in front of the cabins.

Face grim, arms folded, Billy Cameron stood near a police cruiser, watching. The Ohio vacationers, disheveled in hastily donned tees and shorts, huddled near the office. The bigger man kept yelling. "Turn one of those hoses on our cars. . . . We've got rights. . . ."

Duane bunched his hands into fists, stalked toward the loudmouth. "Shut up." He waited until there was silence, stalked back to Annie and Max.

"Somebody started that fire. I smelled gasoline when I came outside." Duane looked toward the blaze. "That's why the cabin's a goner. Gas was splashed all the way around it. Thank God the firehouse is close."

Annie had smelled gasoline before the fire began, smelled it in half-sleep, mixed the sour stench into a dream of smoke-belching trucks. She huddled in a lawn chair, a fire truck masking her view of the flaming cabin. She had no desire to watch. She and Max would have died if not for Dorothy L.'s insistent cries and Duane's courageous rescue. She and Max had been enveloped by fire, noxious smoke choking them. She tried to stop trembling. Despite the warm blanket wrapped around her, her teeth chattered.

"Here." Henny Brawley handed Annie a plastic cup. "Hot tea. Drink it." Henny was impeccable, hair brushed, makeup fresh, warm-up jacket zipped against the offshore breeze. She handed a second cup to Max. "I'd offer Scotch but you'll need a pain pill. Not a good combo." She glanced at his feet.

Max sat with his feet propped on a small webbed stool covered by a blood-spattered towel. A redheaded EMT with the build of a sumo wrestler held a Maglite trained on Max's feet. The second EMT, thin and rangy with a bald head and a snake tattoo crawling across the back of one hand, stemmed the bleeding with small pads, then covered Max's feet with clean gauze and tape. "Need to get you to E.R. They'll clean the wounds with Betadine, remove the glass, and stitch up a couple of deep cuts. They'll take X-rays to make sure they don't miss anything. Glass shows up on X-rays. We'll get the gurney." His soft British accent seemed incongruous on a Southern sea island.

Max looked pale and tired. He twisted to look toward the gutted cabin. "I need to talk to Billy." He gave Annie a worried glance. "The front door wouldn't open."

"There will be plenty of time for that." Annie knew Max was hurting. The Crocs had saved her feet from injury, but he'd stepped barefoot on glass shards from the broken window as they escaped. Lines of pain pulled at his mouth.

Max handed the plastic cup to Henny, managed a faint smile. "Do you always careen around the marsh after midnight, carrying hot tea for wounded friends?"

Henny gestured toward dark water and the shoreline that curved, forming a small bay. "I was on my deck across the bay. When I saw flames, I knew it was Nightingale Courts. I called nine-one-one and came over to see if I could help."

"With hot tea. Thanks, Henny. If it hadn't been for Duane . . ."

Annie grabbed Max's hand. "And Dorothy L."

Henny reached down for the carrier. "I'll bet you want to thank her in person."

Annie shot her a grateful glance. Dorothy L. was a guaranteed stress buster.

Henny eased the carrier onto Max's lap. Max opened the grill wide enough to slip his hand inside. "Good girl. Brave girl. Smart girl." Some of the tension eased from his body. "She's purring. I can feel the rumble in her throat."

Annie smiled. She'd always known that Max was Dorothy L.'s preferred person, but that was all right. Dorothy L. now had carte blanche. Whatever she wanted, she would have. Annie gradually began to feel warm, warm and safe and cared for.

A purple Chrysler PT slewed around the Nightingale Courts arbor, rocked to a stop in front of the office. Marian Kenyon slammed out of the car. A bandanna corralled frizzy dark hair. A Gamecock sweatshirt flopped to the knees of faded jeans. She held a notebook. A camera dangled from a strap around her neck.

Marian skirted the police cars, ignoring Sgt. Harrison's shout, and came even with the nose of the first truck. She lifted the camera, clicked rapidly.

Sgt. Harrison, freckled face grim in the light from the spots, marched to the reporter and gestured emphatically toward the office.

Marian tried to duck around her and move toward Billy.

Harrison blocked the way, gestured again.

Marian turned and surveyed the motley gathering in front of the office, the vacationing couples in dry clothes, a grimy Duane in a once-white T-shirt and red shorts, Henny stylish in a peach warm-up, and headed straight for blanket-draped Annie and immobilized Max.

The EMTs maneuvered the gurney next to Max. "Okay. We're going to roll you over—"

Max ignored them. He snapped shut the grill, handed the carrier to Henny, and swung his legs toward the ground. "Hey. Marian." His tone was curt.

Marian stopped in front of him. She looked at the bloody towel and her face furrowed in empathy.

The slender EMT clamped a restraining hand on one leg. "Hold up, buddy. You won't be walking on these babies for a while. You got some deep cuts on the right heel and left instep."

Max's tensed muscles slowly relaxed. He glared up at Marian. "You almost got us killed, you and your story about Iris talking to Annie. You scared the murderer and we got trapped in a burning cabin."

Marian suddenly looked diminished, older, her gamine face forlorn.

Annie pushed up from her chair, stumbling as her feet tangled in the trailing blanket. She gave Marian a hug. "You didn't mean to cause us trouble." She turned, held out a hand to Max, tried to keep the blanket from sliding to the ground.

Marian's eyes glistened with tears. "I was trying to gig Iris's friends. Her so-called friends. Nobody would give me anything."

Max was unrelenting. "You gave someone the idea Annie knew a lot."

Marian stared at the flame-laced column of smoke, her face drawn in misery.

Henny lightly touched Max's arm. "A murderer sees threats everywhere. It probably didn't take Marian's story to put Annie in danger. Everyone on the island knows people talk to Annie." Her smile was sweet. "That's why we love her."

The maroon Rolls-Royce glided into the turnaround drive at the emergency room. Emma Clyde parked by the main door between NO PARKING signs. Emma considered such signs aimed at lesser mortals. Moreover, at this late hour, or very early hour depending upon perspective, the drive was empty.

Annie had hesitated to call Emma from the hospital, despite Henny's earlier assurances that Emma had offered them refuge and would be quick to come. In fact, Annie's cell rang as Max was being checked out. A wide-awake Emma said she would be there in a jiffy, explaining she'd been alerted by a friend in the E.R.

The automatic door wheezed open. The orderly pushed the wheelchair outside. Annie followed, grateful to escape the antiseptic smell of the hospital. A ratchet of frogs sounded from the lagoon at the front of the hospital. The air felt cool and silky. She was grateful for Henny's warm-up jacket. She smiled at the flaming hibiscus on Max's shirt. Duane's T-shirts were too small, but he'd found a floppy

Hawaiian shirt and khaki shorts for Max. Max's hair was uncombed, he was unshaven, and his bandaged feet were elevated. Max sagged to one side of the wheelchair, sleepy from the painkiller.

Emma bustled from the car. Her spiky hair, purplish in the glare of the hospital lights, looked droopy but that was the only sign of disarray. Of course, her usual costume, a flowing caftan, was unlikely to reflect hasty dressing. This caftan blazed with coral and white peonies against a black background, an interesting fashion combination with black leather Reeboks. The caftan's bright colors made it definite that Emma had regained her combative spirit.

Emma stopped at the bottom of the sloping ramp, planted her hands on her hips. "I've seen drowned rats that looked better. As Marigold tells Inspector Houlihan, 'Call me next time before you get in trouble. I could save you some wear and tear.'"

Emma was a sport to retrieve them from the emergency room although Annie had protested that they could stay at the Sea Side Inn. Emma insisted she was eager to put them up and her home was always equipped for guests with a ground-floor guest suite, perfect for a wheelchair. However, Emma quoting Marigold frazzled Annie. At the best of times, she loathed Marigold Rembrandt, Emma's sleuth who enjoyed making Inspector Houlihan look like an idiot. This was not the best of times.

"But"—Emma seemed to realize she was booming and dropped her voice—"I don't imagine I looked great when you found me comatose in Cabin Six. Turnabout's fair play. Tomorrow when you are once again sleek rats"—she chuckled at her own humor—"we'll gather round the campfire and talk about the strange events that have occurred at

Nightingale Courts." She reached for a handle and a rear door of the Rolls-Royce opened as smoothly as the door to a bank vault. The muscular orderly transferred Max smoothly to the seat, gave them a brisk smile, and turned away with the wheelchair.

Emma gestured toward the trunk. "Henny brought over a collapsible wheelchair. Dorothy L.'s already comfortable in your quarters." She was matter-of-fact.

Annie was too dazed to do more than nod. Henny once again had proven her resourcefulness, providing comfort for their cat heroine and producing a wheelchair in the darkest watch of the night, smoothly as a magician exchanging a scarf for a rabbit.

Annie sank into the seat next to Max. The Rolls-Royce flowed away from the hospital, majestic as a luxury liner and just as comfortable. She reached over the driver's seat and gave Emma's shoulder a squeeze. "Thank you." She sank into the feather-soft embrace of the leather seat, but she carried with her an indelible memory of fire and fear.

Annie opened the slats of the shutters, looked out at a paved terrace that ended at the dunes. As the ocean breeze swept inland, the sea oats bent toward the house. Beyond the dunes, green water glittered in bright sunlight.

A knock sounded on the door of the sitting room. Annie hurried to the door.

Emma's tall, thin housekeeper, cheerful, unflappable Essie Faye, smiled and gestured at two suitcases near the door. "Mrs. Brawley brought them. She left a note."

Annie tucked the envelope under her arm and carried in the cases. Behind her Essie Faye set the table in the sitting room and arranged dishes on the buffet. "Smoked salmon, sliced Vidalia onions, cream cheese and capers, scrambled eggs with country-cut bacon and cheese grits, mixed fruit. If you need anything more, let me know."

"Thank you, Essie Faye. Everything looks wonderful." As the door closed behind the housekeeper, Annie hurried to the bathroom and nudged the door. Sitting on a wooden bench, Max was half in, half out of the shower and half soaped. He scrubbed with a cloth. "Remind me to shake the hand of the next person I see in a wheelchair. What a hassle—and mine is temporary." He spoke cheerfully, but he was pale and Annie suspected his feet throbbed. He'd shaken his head at pain pills this morning, saying only that he was okay and he didn't want to feel fuzzy, he had work to do.

Annie flapped the sheet of paper. "Henny's been busy." Annie read aloud:

Ben came up with the folding wheelchair and opened the lock shop to make keys for the Volvo and the Jeep. The Volvo's in Emma's drive. Plus there's a hand-operated electric golf cart. A friend of mine had it converted when she broke her leg. Max can scoot anywhere on the bike paths. Ben's expecting you both at the tag agency for new driver's licenses. Ben also came up with a key for the units where your stuff is stored for the move. I found boxes with clothes and picked out several outfits.

Annie had forgotten that Ben ran the lock shop and tag agency, but his finger was in most island business pies.

Marian Kenyon's in a blue funk over the sidebar in Sunday's paper. She wants to make amends, promises to share every scrap of info she has on the Howard deaths. Laurel will see to the store. I'm going to check my class notes for the year Iris ran away. Let me know when you want to talk.

Max was cautious not to bump his feet as he dressed. When he rolled to the table in his wheelchair, Annie poured him a cup of coffee and brought filled plates.

"Max, we've got to find out—"

He held up his hand. "Breakfast first, Mrs. Darling."

Despite her sense of urgency at the passage of time and her focus on fighting back against their attacker, Annie found she was voraciously hungry. They both ate huge breakfasts.

Annie refilled their coffee cups.

Max's face was grim. "Someone wants you to die and I'm trapped in a wheelchair."

Annie gestured at the domed ceiling of the sitting room with its elaborate frescoes. "It will take more than a tin of gas to set Emma's house on fire." Dorothy L. stretched in comfort on a velvet pillow in a window seat.

For survivors of a fire, they appeared remarkably unscathed, except for Max's bandaged feet and the telltale lines of pain at the corners of his mouth and a splotch of red on Annie's arm from a burning ember. Thanks to Henny, they were both attired in their own clothes.

"Don't try to change the subject. Look, Annie"—his voice was calm and reasonable—"there's no point in taking chances. Deirdre's been wanting you to visit. This is a good time. It's great weather in San Diego."

Annie smiled. "It's always great weather in San Diego. We'll plan a trip. Your sister is a lot of fun." Annie didn't complete her thought. Deirdre was quite entertaining except that she expected guests to fully participate in her current enthusiasm. The last time they'd seen Deirdre, she was deeply engaged in training ferrets to play soccer with a Ping-Pong ball. Her mother's daughter, but that was a thought better left unexpressed. "We have unfinished business here."

Max's eyes glinted with determination. "Let me handle this. Next time the murderer may have a gun."

Annie wasn't swayed. "Oh sure, I'll take up tatting, maybe try out for a little theater role while you chase around the island"—she refrained from staring at his bandaged feet—"so you can get shot and I'll be a brave little widow. I don't think so."

He looked at her. Despite a clear effort, his lips flickered into a reluctant grin. "You don't think so?"

"No." She smacked the table for emphasis. Silverware rattled.

He spread his hands in surrender. "I should have known better. You've never ducked a fight and you won't start now. All right, Nora."

She was scared deep inside, but there was liberation in confronting danger. They could no longer stay on the sidelines. This was now their fight. She managed a grin. "All we need is a wire-haired terrier, Nick." She glanced toward the window seat and a somnolent Dorothy L. "But hey, we've got a smart white cat." Her smile slipped away. "We didn't set out to get involved. Now we don't have a choice."

She reached across the table, gripped his hand, his wonderful, strong, alive hand. The two of them together could handle anything.

She hoped.

* * *

The wheelchair sped across the marble flooring of Emma's main hall. Max was getting the hang of maneuvering it. Annie hurried to keep up. Sunshine flooded through a skylight, turning the mist from the waterfall near the front door into diamond-bright sparkles.

Annie poked her head into the drawing room. Gold-leaf baroque columns framed a dais. In a turquoise caftan, purplish hair now fashionably spiked, Emma sat in an oversize teak chair with crimson cushions, chin on hand, staring seaward.

Annie hesitated. Clearly their hostess was communing with the muse, sleepy from too much breakfast, or posing for an *Architectural Digest* photo.

Without looking back, Emma gestured peremptorily. "Come in."

Annie was impressed. Either Emma had eyes in the back of her spiky-haired head or exceedingly acute hearing. As they approached the dais, Annie saw their reflection in a mirror.

Emma nodded toward the bone white divan that faced the dais, the queen granting audience to her courtiers. "Come join me." She nodded approvingly. "Sleek rats this morning." Before Annie could drop onto the sofa, Emma continued briskly. "I've put the book aside to join the hunt."

When neither spoke, Emma pursed her lips, her stare flinty.

Annie realized applause was expected. Emma was making the most generous offer she could make, choosing to help old friends rather than devote every thought to her manuscript. "Emma, that's grand."

Emma gave a regal smile, the queen of crime sacrificing for her friends.

"Absolutely grand." Max was hearty. He kept his face suitably grave, but his eyes glinted with amusement.

Homage paid, Emma nodded gracefully. "It is my pleasure. I will likely spell the difference between success and failure. I've applied Marigold's acuteness to the problem."

Annie maintained her admiring gaze. Emma was bright, quick, and clever. If only she wouldn't present her own thoughts as Marigold's. But friends must be forbearing with friends. "And what," Annie asked brightly, "does Marigold think?"

Emma's bright blue eyes gleamed. "Marigold points out that Iris Tilford was staying in Cabin Six at Nightingale Courts. That's where I fell. What was I doing in that cabin?"

Emma was nobody's fool, and now she had every right to know. Annie was matter-of-fact, her tone carefully neutral. "You were intrigued when Duane told us that Iris arrived alone on a bicycle in the rain. You took a key from the office"—Annie refrained from using the accusatory filched instead of took— "and slipped"—here she substituted slipped for sneaked—"into her cabin, carrying towels so you could pretend to be housekeeping. Now it seems obvious you didn't fall. Someone was behind the door who was determined not to be seen."

Emma's eyes widened. "I should have known. When I wrote the scene, I realized that Marigold must search the cabin if she hopes to find out anything about the girl. Marigold obtains a passkey and pretends to be a maid and takes towels. An intruder is hidden behind the door and Marigold is struck down." Emma lifted stubby fingers to lightly touch the small bandage on her forehead. "Clearly my subconscious knows what happened." Her gaze became distant, misty, as if she plumbed far recesses of her mind, hunting, seeking, hoping. "If only I can remember . . . I almost remembered in the hospital when you came." There was no trace of the imperious author in her voice. She sounded uneasy. "I almost remembered that instant before everything went dark. Something in the hospital brought it back."

"I was at the hospital. And Pamela." Annie had been delighted when Emma glared at them, her old demanding, impossible self.

Emma stared into the distance. "Pamela." She waited, slowly shook her head. Her gaze settled on Annie. Another slow shake of her head. "It's here." She touched her fingers to her temples. "Something in the hospital triggered a memory. Though"—she was ruminative—"I don't see how that will help. Marigold walks into the room. She's looking straight ahead. She's pushed forward. She's thrown into the bed and knocked out. Obviously, she has no glimpse of her attacker." Once again Emma brushed the small bandage. "That's how it happened. That's why my back is sore. I must remember to go back and put a bruise between Marigold's shoulder blades. Marigold can't see her assailant, but still she's gained some knowledge, there is some fact that she knows, something that matters." Square face set in determination, Emma announced, "The way forward is now clear. I will leave the overt investigation to you and Max. I must write the book."

Annie stood beside the pink golf cart with a matching pink fringe. Max awkwardly swung himself into the seat. His face stiffened with pain as a foot banged against the side. She hurried around to reach for the wheelchair, but he was already folding it to swing it into the cart. "I can manage." He lifted worried eyes to her. "Why don't you come with me?"

She understood. He wanted her next to him. He wanted to keep her safe. But she wasn't ready to give in to fear. "I'm fine." She may have spoken a little loudly. She was aware, more aware than she had ever been, of the fragility of life. The slant of sun on Max's face, the blue of his eyes, the smell of the sea, the rustle of a magnolia were beautiful. She felt tears inside and a quick rush of anger. She was fiercely determined to live with Max in happiness on their lovely sea island. She would do what had to be done. "I'll be fine." Possibly she might meet danger, but that was the price to be paid for freedom. "We're going to find out what happened, Max. I can't run scared. You go to your office. Find out everything you can. I'll come as soon as I've talked to Henny."

◡ *Eleven* ◡

ANNIE LOVED THE view from Henny's deck. The incoming tide was flooding the spartina grass to its tips. A great blue heron stood immobile. Suddenly its head shot down, long black plumes quivering, to snatch a brown snake from the water. A tufted titmouse sang its sighing song as if in applause. When the tide ran out, the mudflats would be exposed, steaming in the warming sun, a hint of how the marsh would burgeon with life in summer.

Henny placed the tray with a pitcher of iced tea and glasses brimful of ice with a garnish of mint. They sat at the wicker table.

Annie crushed the mint, drank tea, and smiled at her old friend.

Henny placed a plate near Annie. "Icebox cookies. I know they're your favorites."

Small things bring happy memories. The old-fashioned recipe always carried Annie home to Amarillo and her mother cutting her a slice of the refrigerated dough to eat before putting the cookies in to bake.

Henny handed a high school annual to Annie, ornate gold letters bright against a dark blue faux-leather cover.

Yellow sticky notes protruded from pages. Annie turned
to the first marker, a full-page portrait of that year's homecoming queen, Jocelyn Howard. Annie was glad for the
April morning in the marsh, brimming with life, a coun-
terbalance to the sadness generated by the long-ago picture.
Pictures of Sam Howard and Jocelyn Howard and Iris
Tilford now held the mournful fascination of photographs
taken when death must have seemed far distant. Only the
observer is aware that time was running out.

In the senior class section, the first note in Henny's elegant handwriting was beneath the photograph of Elizabeth
Katherine Ames:

*Liz was a good student, diligent, careful, precise.
Never an original thought, but capable of absorbing
information. She was always serious and tried her
best. She was a dusty blonde then. Her hair turned
white when she was in her midtwenties. Liz usually
managed to be near Russell Montgomery. He was nice
to her, but he never saw anyone but Jocelyn.*

I'm very much afraid Liz hated Jocelyn.

Annie would have found that last sentence shocking a
week ago. "Last week I would have laughed at the idea of Liz
hating anyone. Not anymore. She was like a piece of granite
when I asked her for a memory of Iris. Malevolent granite."

Henny looked away. She took off her glasses, drew in a
breath.

Annie was surprised. Had Henny found Annie's charac-
terization of Liz offensive?

Henny's face folded in a worried frown. "Unproven ac-
cusations can ruin lives."

"That's true." Annie met her uneasy gaze. "But someone tried to kill us last night."

Henny nodded, replaced her glasses. "That's why I have to tell you. But I've never known if my suspicion was right." She took a deep breath, spoke quickly. "Jocelyn's car was vandalized in the school parking lot. A brick was thrown through the windshield. A pine grove screens the parking lot from the school. I was on the way to my car. I had a dental appointment. I saw Liz hurrying in a side door. It was during class. She could have had a hall permit to take care of some kind of errand. But there was something furtive about her movements. Later I heard about the damage to Jocelyn's car. At the time, Jocelyn was involved in a campaign against cockfighting. There had been other incidents, but they all happened late at night at the Howard house. The attack on her car was attributed to the men behind the cockfights. But I always wondered." Henny looked sad. "It would take great anger to throw a brick that hard."

Annie looked into her old friend's concerned gaze. "We may be seeking someone driven by anger." As she envisioned a young, furious Liz with a brick raised high, Annie turned to the next marked page.

Stanley George Carlisle IV smiled into the camera, his face a younger, fresher, less stressed version of the man Annie knew. She looked at the yellow sticky.

Buck often had a lost look, especially when his parents were around. With the kids, he was popular. He was friendly and kind to everyone. He always got there with his schoolwork, but it took effort. Nothing academic came easily for him. He was a big guy, but he wasn't an athlete. That made high school hard for

him because Friday night lights shine pretty bright on
the island.

Annie needed no explanation. High school football was a
religion in the South.

Sam Howard treated Buck like a flunky. He called
Buck "sonny." Sometimes, when Sam and the other
football guys were together, he'd ignore Buck. Kids
are vulnerable at that age. It's desperately important
to belong. Hanging out with Sam was Buck's ticket to
the inner circle. Sometimes Buck was in, sometimes
he was out.

I may have been wrong, but Buck appeared more
shaken by Sam's death than seemed normal. He was
distraught, unresponsive in class for several weeks. He
seemed devastated. Certainly the death of a friend can
be shocking, upsetting. But there was something more
here, something deeper.

Annie was startled. "Do you think Buck's gay?" Buck
was virile and exceedingly attractive to women. There was
always undeniable awareness between heterosexual men
and women, whether or not acknowledged. She absolutely
didn't think Buck was gay.

Henny was decisive. "I'm not talking about sex. As a matter of fact, Buck and Cara—"

Annie looked at Henny in surprise. Buck and Cara? Buck
was married to Fran.

"—were inseparable most of their senior year. I don't
know what happened. I think Buck and Cara quarreled. They
started avoiding each other. As for Fran, she was dating off

island. She had an aura among the kids because she had a big romance going with an 'older man.'" Henny smiled. "He was probably in his twenties. I heard he was a bartender at Frankie's where she worked on the mainland. But when Cara and Buck broke up, Fran went after Buck. They were dating by the time of the sports picnic. As for Sam, he always had a circle of girls for easy sex. They weren't important to him." Henny looked regretful. "Iris was one of his conquests. She was anybody's girl who'd look at her. You know the scene. Not the popular girls, the ones with respect for themselves, but the girls who are desperately hungry for attention and deep down don't feel they have any worth. It isn't that nice girls don't have sex. They do, but not one-night throwaway hookups. Iris was available, though she and Sam did seem to be a pair that spring. I remember being surprised, but, frankly, it was just another indication of Sam's willingness to use people without caring for them. But when Sam died, Buck stumbled through the weeks like a ghost. I don't think it was grief. If I didn't know better, I'd say he looked guilty, as if he'd done something dreadful."

Annie gazed at Buck's young smiling face that gave no hint of trouble. Although if she looked hard, perhaps weaving in what she knew with what she saw, there might be uncertainty in his gaze. Buck lacked swagger. He'd been a yellow bird since he was a little boy.

Henny shook her head. "I must be wrong. After all, there's no question how Sam died."

The next sticky marked Jocelyn Mary Howard's class picture. The beauty of classic features seemed poignant now.

Jocelyn was a quintessential princess. She expected everyone always to do everything to please her, yet she

*was basically thoughtful. It's hard to know how Joce-
lyn would have turned out. She was bright. A superb
debater. I rather thought she might be a lawyer. If she
believed something was right or wrong, she wouldn't
be budged. She loved animals. She led a march on a
body shop near Shank swamp—*

Annie pictured a rundown area of the island with dilapidated houses, a seedy bar, and a few businesses that started,
failed, were reborn, never quite succeeded.

*—where cockfights were held every Monday night.
They were run by a couple of tough brothers, Joe and
Gus McCoy. One night a kerosene-filled pop bottle
filled with a burning rag stuffed in the neck was tossed
on the Howard front porch and caused some damage.
Several nights later some shots were fired into her
upstairs bedroom window. The attack on her car happened about this time. Jocelyn led another march and
this time she had every charitable group on the island
involved. Almost two hundred people showed up.
Frank Saulter started twenty-four-hour surveillance
on the body shop. Finally the guys left the island. The
local SPCA gave Jocelyn a medal.*

Annie looked at Jocelyn's bright, clear gaze and resolute
mouth. Jocelyn was beautiful. She was well aware of her
beauty and expected admiration. Yes, she was a princess,
but she was more than a pretty girl. "A brave princess."

Henny's dark eyes were somber. "Brave, perhaps fool-
hardy. I'm afraid she was unable to see a threat. If Frank
had been a good-old-boy cop and hadn't backed her up, she

might have been hurt. That last night she may not have realized she was pushing someone too far."

Annie pictured the end of Fish Haul pier. A girl stood at the railing. Had her companion pointed out at the water, spoken of a boat or a light? As Jocelyn bent forward had a hard, violent push sent her flying down to darkness? Had death come as a surprise?

Annie's gaze moved to the next photo: Samuel Edward Howard. The golden boy, handsome, commanding, a Friday night hero.

Sam gloried in being the quarterback. He moved through the halls as if he owned them. He was the handsomest, richest, most athletic senior. Russell was a linebacker. Sam treated Russell almost as an equal. Did I like Sam? He could be appealing. He had charm. I'm not sure he had a heart.

Annie turned pages to the yellow sticky at Frances Fay Kinnon's photo. Even as a high school senior, Fran had an aura of success, stylish hairdo, expertly applied makeup, perfect posture, a smile that exuded confidence.

Every class has one: the girl most likely to succeed. Fran came up the hard way, single mom with a drinking problem, food baskets from the church, second-hand clothes. As soon as Fran was old enough, she started working part-time. She was quick to pick up manners and styles from her classmates. She learned to go to the Junior League shop in Savannah and pick up really beautiful clothes on the cheap. She worked at Parotti's until she figured out she could make more money from big tips at Frankie's, a swanky restaurant on the mainland near the ferry dock. I never doubted that Fran would do whatever it took to lift herself in the world. It made her admirable if not especially likable. She was too self-absorbed, too driven to be appealing. She used the same focus in school. She was a top student and it paid off. Every year Letitia Campbell—

Annie knew Letitia Campbell, a steely-eyed, elderly woman who had run the Altar Guild at St. Mary's for years. The family had lived on the island for two hundred years and managed to stay wealthy despite wars and declines in rice and cotton. When one avenue closed, a canny Campbell found another. Letitia's late husband made another fortune in electronics and her sons were entrepreneurs in Atlanta and Dallas.

—provides a four-year scholarship to Clemson, Letitia's alma mater. The scholarship is awarded on the basis of scholarship, character, and need. Fran was hands down the winner her year. Buck went to Clemson, too. I think she made up her mind she was going to be Mrs. Stanley George Carlisle IV and return to the island as part of the social class her mother never belonged to. Buck and Fran married right after graduation.

Annie felt sad. "I think Fran's scared for Buck." Annie repeated Fran's revelations about Russell.

Henny was thoughtful. "Russell seemed to be trying to stay away from Jocelyn at the picnic."

The next yellow sticky marked the photo of Russell Robert Montgomery.

Annie was struck by the marked difference in Russell then and now. His face had been lean; now it was heavy. His eyes then were somber, his expression guarded; now he appeared genial if still somewhat reserved.

Russell looked haunted after Jocelyn died. Again, just as with Buck and Sam, I felt there was something more, something deeper than loss. In fact it had been obvious for a couple of weeks that Russell was avoiding Jocelyn. That could have made him feel guilty after she died, especially if he suspected she'd committed suicide. Russell was from a military family. His father was a retired Marine colonel. Col. Montgomery went to The Citadel. Everyone knew Russell had to go there. He was grim about schoolwork. He would have been scared to go home if he brought in poor grades. Russell served in the Marines for five years before he came back here and got into construction. His father had died.

The short, crisp sentences on the sticky note revealed a boy under the thumb of a domineering father. "If his father hadn't died?"

Henny swirled the tea in her glass. "I have no doubt Russell would still be in the Marines. I think they came back to the island because of Liz. She's from a big family and she missed being home. I don't think Russell was glad to be back."

Annie wondered if Russell's antipathy to the island indicated guilt or did it simply reflect reluctance to return to a place with unpleasant memories of a controlling father? If Liz favored coming home, was that an indication she had nothing to regret? Or was the pull of family strong enough to overcome a past that she was now desperate to hide?

The last sticky marked Cara's class picture. There was no aura of sophistication. Cara Jane Jackson's sandy hair hung in a smooth page boy. Her young face was open and eager. Those were not qualities Annie associated with Cara Wilkes of the gamine haircut, shadowed eyes, and aloof expression. She'd worn a simple cotton top. Now Cara flaunted the latest in expensive leisure clothes, accented by dramatic baubles and bangles.

When Cara and Buck quarreled, it was like watching a rose shrivel from fire blight. She turned sarcastic and bitter and was quick to take offense. I ran into her a few times after that. Buck and Fran went to Clemson. Cara worked part-time and put herself through Armstrong State. After her grandmother died, she stopped coming to the island. I was surprised when she moved back a couple of years ago. I've always wondered why. She's turned into a smart, fashionable woman. I think she does well selling real estate. She's pleasant and friendly, active in the community, and yet I sense emptiness when I'm with her. She's a shadow of the girl I once knew.

"Do you know anything about the man she married?" Annie was well aware that half of all marriages end in divorce. A recital of that statistic never addressed the searing pain of parting. When love turned cold, the wound might heal but there were always scars.

"Nothing. No one on the island, to my knowledge, ever met him or knows anything about their life together or what happened."

"She came home." Annie wanted to believe in at least one friend. "Surely if she had anything to do with Jocelyn's death, she would never have returned."

Henny said quietly, "Buck is here."

Indeed he was. What if it was Buck who had been threatened by Iris's memories? What would that mean to Cara?

Annie looked up at Henny. "Friday night Iris must have remembered who she saw walking into the woods with Jocelyn. But if she remembered, why did she go into the woods with that person?"

"She must not have been certain." Henny looked out at the marsh.

Annie looked, too, drawing comfort from the peace and beauty of the water and the rustle of the cordgrass in the onshore breeze.

Henny sighed. "Or it may be that Iris was reassured, that an explanation was offered. Possibly the claim was made that Jocelyn jumped from the pier and that had been kept secret to protect her mother."

Annie was indignant. "Why was Iris so foolish?"

"That's easy to understand." Henny's tone was sad. "Iris wanted to believe Jocelyn's death was an accident. Don't you see, if Jocelyn died because Iris warned the drug dealer, then Iris would have to face the terrible truth that her actions caused Jocelyn's death. Another hand would have pushed Jocelyn from the pier, but Iris would know that she was responsible. That would be a terrible burden."

Annie understood. Iris desperately wanted to believe that her fears were unfounded, that her memory was faulty. She must have been quick to accept a glib explanation and so she walked into the woods with death.

Annie felt a hot rush of anger. She gestured at the yearbook. "They all seemed to have secrets. We have to find out more."

Annie summed up what she'd learned from Henny. "There were all kinds of unhappiness in that group." She looked at Max in dismay. "I don't know if any of it helps us much."

Max tapped his pen on the yellow legal pad. "If Buck acted guilty after Sam Howard died, that's big. Why would Buck feel guilt about a friend overdosing on cocaine? That only makes sense if Buck supplied the drug. Maybe Jocelyn found out. Maybe Buck's the one Iris saw with Jocelyn."

Annie had a sharp memory of Buck's poignant description of two yellow birds. Could he recall the little girl who'd meant so much to him if he'd killed her?

"Forget friendships for now." Max's voice was hard. "One of our friends tried to kill us. It may have been Buck."

Annie knew he'd not missed her woeful look when he spoke of Buck. She looked at him ruefully. "You don't miss much. You always read my mind."

"I wish I could read some other minds." Max pushed away the pad. "Did Liz smash Jocelyn's windshield? Does she have that kind of temper? Why was Russell avoiding Jocelyn that last night? Does Fran know something about Buck and Jocelyn that has her scared? What did Cara and Iris talk about when Cara came to Nightingale Courts Friday?"

"We'll find out. I'll ask them."

"We'll ask them." The correction was quick and firm. "And maybe Emma will keep writing and figure out everything for us."

Annie grinned. "I didn't think Emma would quit writing for long. I expect she's thrilled to have a reason to focus on the book. Do you suppose she's convinced that if she keeps writing she'll figure out what happened when she was hit?"

Max was wry. "If she believes it, maybe it will happen. At the least, we'll get her fictional take, which may or may not be helpful."

Annie was a trifle jaundiced about Emma's plots, which had a distressing tendency to turn on invisible inked messages and clues turned up in buried chests. Feeling guilty at her negative thought, especially since Emma was the bestselling author in the store next to Agatha Christie, Annie said hurriedly, "Actually, Emma's a sweetheart to put us up. She's usually oblivious to the world when she's in the middle of a book."

"I imagine she's given us the best help of all. Something in the hospital room hinted at her attacker." He looked searchingly at Annie. "You searched Iris's room. You can make a list of everything you saw, compare it to the hospital room, see if you can find a link."

Annie gave him another cool glance. Was he picturing her settled at a table in Confidential Commissions, safely out of the action, perhaps permitted a foray to the hospital? *In your dreams, Nick.*

Barb plunged into Max's office. Her Dolly Parton–blond, beehive hairdo quivered in outrage. "I'm sorry I'm late. I went by the Courts and I've never seen anything so awful, the cabin a burned-out shell, all black and fallen in." Barb's eyes were huge. "I don't see how you ever got out."

Annie was quick to give credit. "Dorothy L. woke us up and Duane got us out. We're all right." Physically that was almost true except for Max's cut feet. Emotionally?

How long would it be before she took life and safety for granted?

"Well, Billy Cameron just called and I told him things have come to a fine pass with murderers and arsonists running loose on the island. He had the nerve to tell me there was one murderer and one arsonist and thcy were the same."

Annie knew Barb's anger wasn't directed at Billy. "You shouldn't have scolded Billy. He's doing his best."

Barb stood with her arms akimbo. "Then why isn't he out looking for whoever set the fire? Why's he wasting time coming over here? I don't suppose if you knew who set the cabin on fire, you'd be keeping it a secret, but he's on his way over."

∾ *Twelve* ∾

BILLY CAMERON DROPPED a tool with a thin oblong blade and rounded wooden handle on Max's desk. "Got this out of my toolbox. Handy when you're scraping paint. We found four putty knives just like this one at the cabin. One jammed beneath the front door, one between the sashes of the side window, one in the bathroom window, one in the sliding glass doors. There's no way you and Max could have got out. You were locked in better than any jail cell."

Annie folded her arms tight across her front. "I heard a metallic sound. I didn't know what it was."

Billy picked up the tool, balanced it on a broad palm. "Gas splashed all the way around the cabin, putty knives jammed home. Somebody trapped you easy as gigging frogs in a pond. If it hadn't been for Duane, you would have burned to death. I don't think the smoke would have got you first."

Annie stared at their old friend's grim face. She wished she could push away his measured words, but she couldn't. Just as she couldn't forget the horror when roaring fire and roiling smoke surrounded them and they had no way out.

Billy hitched his chair closer to Max's desk, looked from

one to the other. "Tell me everything you know, everything you guess, everything that's happened from the time you first saw Iris Tilford to the fire."

After all, it didn't amount to much. Brief contacts with Iris. Cara Wilkes's visit to Iris's cabin. The anonymous note at Death on Demand. Fran Carlisle linking Russell Montgomery to Jocelyn Howard. Annie's efforts for Iris's spirit poster, kind tributes from Buck and Russell and Cara, hostility from Liz, a delayed response from Fran. And, of course, their visit to the mission Sunday afternoon.

Billy rubbed a thumb against the handle of the putty knife. "So you know that Iris fronted for someone else in dealing drugs."

Annie remembered the warmth of the sun, the coolness of the water in the pool. "Iris came back to the island because there were things she had to figure out. Brother Doyle said Iris told Jocelyn how Sam got the cocaine. Later that same night, Jocelyn died. Iris was afraid she remembered someone walking into the woods with Jocelyn."

Billy's face folded into a heavy frown. "Once a killer, always a killer. Iris didn't have to be killed. So what if Iris saw—or thought she saw—someone with Jocelyn! That didn't prove anything. No one will ever prove Jocelyn's death was anything other than an accident or suicide."

Annie nodded. "Maybe not. But this is a small island. How do you think one of her classmates would like to be publicly accused of drug dealing?"

Billy looked stubborn. "No proof. Iris's word wasn't worth much."

Max shrugged. "Maybe not, but an accusation like that could ruin a marriage, destroy a business, break friendships."

Billy turned the putty knife in his hands. "Killers don't care about anyone but themselves. The decision to murder Iris was made shortly after she came back to the island. The attack on Emma proved that. Someone came to Iris's cabin and searched to be sure Iris didn't keep a diary or have letters or papers that might be a link."

Max looked hopeful. "Do you know who Iris contacted on the island?"

Billy leaned back in his chair. "Cara Wilkes said Iris called and asked her to come by Nightingale Courts. Fran Carlisle said she called and wanted to talk about the sports picnic. Fran told her she didn't remember much about that evening except it was so sad."

Max's expression was cynical. "I'm sure both Cara and Fran claim all was pleasant, just a phone call between old friends. But one of Iris's old friends killed her." Max pulled a legal pad nearer. "Okay. Here's what we've got." He talked as he wrote. "One, Iris supplied cocaine to Sam. Two, at the sports picnic, Jocelyn accused Iris. Three, Iris told Jocelyn that she was the go-between and named the supplier. Four, afraid of cutting off her own supply, Iris told the drug dealer that Jocelyn knew. Five, Iris returned to the island, determined to lay to rest her fear that Jocelyn's death wasn't an accident. Six, Friday night Iris must have asked someone at our party about the night Jocelyn died." He finished writing. "And Annie's picked up a bunch of personal stuff. There was a lot going on among the classmates."

Annie's look at Billy was grave. "I talked to Henny. She knew them all. Iris hung around with Sam that spring. Henny thought he was using her for sex, but now we know she had cocaine." Annie felt sad. Iris had longed for love. "Liz was crazy about Russell. Henny thought maybe Liz had vandalized Jocelyn's car." Annie could hear Henny's quiet voice: *I'm very much afraid Liz hated Jocelyn.* "Russell and Jocelyn had broken up. He tried to avoid her at the picnic. After she died, he acted guilty. Buck seemed deeply upset after Sam's death. Buck and Cara had dated but they quarreled and that's when Fran went after him."

"Oh, those golden high school years." Max's voice was wry.

Annie shivered. "They had a hard time. But one of them caused Sam's death and that is probably behind everything that's happened. We know the drug dealer was Iris's friend. We know who her friends were. We can be sure of one fact, the drug dealer was at the pavilion ten years ago and on Friday night." She looked at Billy.

"I've checked out the people who were at the sports picnic and at your party. It's a short list." Billy ticked them off one by one, clicking the edge of the putty knife against Max's desk. "The other seniors that year, Buck and Fran Carlisle, Russell and Liz Montgomery, Cara Wilkes. The only other guests Friday night who were at both parties are Henny Brawley, Coach Butterworth, and Darlene Hopper."

"Darlene Hopper?" Annie looked puzzled.

"One of the servers in the steam line." Billy clearly didn't consider her to be important. "Darlene was in the same high school class, but not part of that crowd. I've talked to all three about the night Jocelyn drowned but didn't get much. There's no reason to consider Darlene or Henny or Coach as suspects. None of them are even outside probabilities to be the dope runner. Iris wouldn't have described any of them as a 'friend.' There was a flare of drugs that spring. After Sam Howard died, we didn't pick up on any more drug dealing. I figure we had an amateur at work, somebody in the class, and that's how Iris came to be the go-between. In addition, I can knock Darlene Hopper off the list Friday night. She was working at the steam table and was never gone long enough to have connected with Iris in the woods. I didn't get much out of Darlene. She didn't remember a lot about the sports picnic and Friday night she was too busy dishing up food to pay any attention to the party. She wasn't helpful. I guess she doesn't like being part of the help."

Annie wondered if it would do any good to talk to Darlene. Ben Parotti could tell them how to find her. Henny hadn't mentioned Darlene. Obviously, she hadn't considered Darlene part of Jocelyn's crowd.

Billy massaged the back of his neck. "We've got a long way to go." He looked at Annie. "You talked to Iris's friends for your spirit poster."

Annie knew he hoped for something from her, some kind of lead.

He watched her closely. "Tell me how you felt with each of them."

Haltingly, she tried to distill the essence of those moments. "Buck was kind. He knew what it was to struggle, to be in the shadows. Liz wouldn't give me anything. I think she's scared for Russell. Fran was angry because I told you what she'd said about Russell. She didn't want to talk about Iris. Russell must care about animals. He remembered how much Iris loved her pet owl. Cara was sweet. She and Iris must have been awfully close."

Billy looked disappointed. "You didn't sense danger?"

Danger. These were her friends. She'd laughed, had good times, spent sunny days with them. Annie shook her head. "If one of them intended to kill us," she kept her voice steady with an effort, "you think I should have felt something?"

"When I was a young cop on the mainland, a sergeant told me never to ignore a sense of uneasiness, and, if I felt scared, get ready to fight." His expression was thoughtful. "I don't believe anyone who kills ever feels at peace. Unless there's a strain of viciousness, that memory has to hurt. But one of them has had a good long while to get good at hiding emotion. Like ten years. Killing takes a lot of emotion. Striking down Iris was a response to fear of exposure. Maybe you talked to the murderer before the decision was made to set the cabin on fire so you wouldn't have picked up a feeling of threat."

Max was grim. "The trigger for the fire was the story in the Sunday *Gazette*. That was after Annie had talked to them."

Billy lifted his shoulders, let them fall. "Marian's story made it sound like Iris told Annie a lot. But it could be the killer saw Annie bring that note to the station and thought she was involved in the investigation. It could be that Annie talked too much about Iris."

Max leaned forward. "You've checked out everybody at our party. Do you have a suspect? 'A person of interest'?"

Billy shrugged. "Suspects? Sure. I got suspects, Iris's friends. I have five on my list."

Annie ticked off names in her mind: Fran and Buck Carlisle, Liz and Russell Montgomery, and Cara Wilkes.

"A person of interest?" Billy flexed his fingers as if his hand felt stiff. "Not yet. Maybe I'm a moon shot away from ever having a person of interest. People talked to Iris. They admit that. Nobody was spotted leaving the picnic with her. Last night, Duane got a glimpse of somebody in dark clothes on a bike, but that was the last thing on his mind. When the door didn't open or the window, he figured they were blocked. He picked up a chunk of firewood and busted out the window for you, then used the hose to splash down the wood and give you a chance to get out."

Annie pictured flames leaping high, black smoke, and a hunched figure on a bicycle disappearing into the woods.

Max looked eager. "Man? Woman? Are there any tracks?"

"Duane saw a dark shape, but he didn't have time to do anything about it. He had a fire to fight. We found the bike's trail in the woods. Nice tracks." Billy's voice was dour. "They match a bike we found abandoned in the parking lot at St. Mary's. A tourist reported the bike stolen this morning from condos near the forest preserve. He hadn't bothered to use the chain and lock. We found an empty gas tin near the deck. It's got fingerprints." Billy didn't sound enthused. "Some of them were pretty smeared so the last person who hauled it probably wore gloves." He slumped in the chair, a man numbed by exhaustion and frustration.

"A bike taken from a rental condo. Maybe a filched gas tin." Max drew a big zero on a legal pad. "If you pick up prints, they may not lead anywhere."

"We'll see if there's a match with any of the five. If we trace the tin, we'll ask when it was last seen. A defense attorney could have fun with that one." Billy was sardonic. " 'Chief Cameron, when did you last see the gasoline tin in your garage?' I answer, 'Last Saturday when I mowed the yard.' 'Chief, do you lock your garage?' I say, 'No. Who does? We live on an island.' The defense attorney paces around for a minute, then opens up a box on the defense table. 'Chief, is this your gasoline tin?' "

Annie would have laughed, but there was nothing funny about gasoline splashed on the cabin that could have been their pyre.

Max sketched a thumb, crosshatched it with lines. "I'll lay a little bet the prints match those of a guest at our party."

Billy's gaze was sharp. "How do you figure?"

"Put yourself in the murderer's skin." Max drew a bicycle. "This isn't a careless criminal. Iris was killed with a cord from the centerpieces. A bicycle was used that couldn't be linked to anyone. I'm sure the tin was deliberately left behind. If so, it can't be linked to the murderer. What are the odds it incriminates someone else?"

Billy slowly nodded. "Probably you're right, though it's possible Duane was on the scene quick enough to panic the murderer." He looked soberly from Annie to Max. "You almost got snuffed last night. I tried to keep you two out of this. It didn't work." He pushed up from the chair. "If you talk to your friends, maybe they'll be willing to say more than they would to the police. Right now, I don't think you are in any danger. The murderer's breathing easy. Obviously, I talked to you after the fire last night. I haven't shown up at anybody's door with a warrant. The killer has to figure the story in the *Gazette* was a crock and you don't know anything." He pushed up from the chair, clearly weary. "That's a pretty good deal." At the door he paused and looked back. "Don't push your luck. It's dangerous to taunt a tiger."

Barb poked her head in Max's office after Billy left.

"I'm halfway through the list." She flapped a sheet that contained names and phone numbers of guests at their party Friday night. "Most of them either never noticed Iris or didn't know her. Martha Farrington was a friend of Iris's grandmother. Martha saw Iris walking up toward the pavilion around seven. Martha said Iris was walking like she had something she had to do. Martha said she looked like a ghost. But hey, maybe that's a touch of drama since Iris was killed."

Annie felt her heart squeeze. "Was anyone with Iris?"

Barb was regretful. "She was alone. I'll keep calling."

Annie fought away disappointment. They were no further ahead. Why had Iris hurried to the pavilion? Had she arranged to talk to someone? Was she following someone? Had she remembered what happened ten years ago?

"Good work, Barb." Max was pleased. "The more we know, the more people we can exclude."

Annie was glad Max felt encouraged. She didn't share his satisfaction. Maybe they had excluded people, but so far they hadn't connected Iris with anyone after supper.

Annie wondered if she had it backward. Perhaps a guest saw Iris hurrying to the pavilion and slipped away from the party, carrying a pair of shucking gloves and a length of black cord.

"You'd think somebody would have seen something." Barb was disgusted. "I was sitting at a table not far from the path and I never looked that way. Why would I? The party wasn't in the woods. I'll keep trying." She glanced at her watch. "I'll order in from Parotti's. The usual?"

Annie opted for cole slaw as well as hush puppies with a fried clam sandwich. Max chose grilled flounder.

As Barb left, Max flipped to a fresh page. "I don't think Barb's going to get much information over the phone. By now the word's out all over the island about the fire last night. Let's say someone saw something odd Friday night. They may keep quiet because they're scared. We've got to offer some protection. And," his tone was determined, "an incentive."

Quickly he sketched on the pad, ripped off the sheet, and handed it to Annie.

*If YOU saw someone enter the woods at Harbor
Pavilion
FRIDAY NIGHT
with
Iris TILFORD
Call Confidential Commissions
CONFIDENTIALITY PROMISED
$10,000 reward for information
leading to the arrest of Iris Tilford's murderer*

Annie admired his drawings in the margins, a path into pine trees, a cell phone, and a stack of greenbacks. "I'll take it out to Barb."

"Tell her to run off two hundred copies. After lunch she can post them around town, leave stacks at the library."

Annie put Max's sketch on Barb's desk with a note. When Annie returned, Max was again writing on the legal pad.

Annie thought the flyer might be a help, but their best hope was to find out where Fran, Buck, Liz, Russell, and Cara were when Iris walked toward the pavilion.

Max finished writing with a flourish just as Barb walked in clutching two brown bags with telltale grease spots. "I saw your note. I'll print up a flyer right now."

"Have lunch first." Annie spread paper towels on Max's desk.

"I'll eat while I work. Back in a flash."

True to her promise, Barb returned in minutes with a bright yellow sheet.

Max spread several of the flyers on his desk. "I like the print size." Barb had used huge flame-red letters. The flyers were definitely eye-catching. "They look great. Paste 'em up everywhere."

Barb nodded. "Will do." She hurried out.

Annie took another bite of her fried clam sandwich, wiped one hand on a napkin.

Max concluded writing with a flourish. "Here's what we need to find out." He handed her the legal pad:

1. *Get Marian Kenyon's notes on the deaths of Sam and Jocelyn Howard. What were the results of the autopsy on Jocelyn's brother Sam?*
2. *Check with Frank Saulter on the investigation into Jocelyn's death. Why wouldn't Doc Burford talk about the autopsy on Jocelyn Howard?*
3. *Talk to Coach Butterworth.*
4. *Why did Jocelyn come to the sports awards picnic? Her brother had died the previous Friday.*
5. *Did Buck and Jocelyn quarrel at the picnic?*
6. *What happened between Jocelyn and Russell?*
7. *Did Jocelyn suspect either Buck or Russell of giving the cocaine to Iris?*
8. *Was Fran trying to implicate Russell? Was she protecting Buck?*
9. *Did Cara tell Billy the truth about her reason for coming to Nightingale Courts to see Iris?*
10. *At the hospital, what reminded Emma of the attack on her?*

* * *

Marian Kenyon bumped the pop machine in the *Gazette* snack room. With a rattle, two cans dropped into the trough. Marian retrieved them, placed the sodas next to a stack of folders and several notebooks on the scarred Formica-topped table. "You like peanuts in your Coke?" Marian avoided looking at Annie as she offered an opened packet of salty peanuts.

Annie declined. Some Southern favorites were not to her taste, including peanuts bobbing in Coke, boiled pig's feet, and sweet tea.

They settled on opposite sides of the table, Marian busy with notebooks and folders, her face averted.

Annie slid a bright yellow flyer across the table.

The reporter read it swiftly. Her eyes glinted. "This'll get everybody talking. It's too late for this afternoon's paper, but I'll write a story for tomorrow." She sagged back in her chair, again avoided looking at Annie. "I didn't mean to put you in danger." She could scarcely be heard.

"Of course you didn't." Annie reached across the table, gave Marian's arm a quick squeeze.

Marian looked up. Her face brightened. She lifted the Coke, slurped and munched, said mournfully, "I wonder if I'll ever be savvy enough to remember about unintended consequences. It frosted me when nobody gave me anything personal after Iris was killed. All I got was vague responses. *A former classmate. Someone I knew a long time ago. I said hello to her, but we only talked for a moment.* Anyway"—finally she gazed directly at Annie—"I'm sorry as hell about you and Max. I've got a new mantra: Count the cost, stupid." She pointed at the folders. "I've scoured my files for anything that might help. I've made copies of a bunch of stuff. Let me tell you what I know that never made it into the *Gazette.*"

Annie opened a notebook, pen poised to write.

Marian drank more Coke. Her face furrowed in remembrance. "It was foggy the night Jocelyn disappeared. There were maybe sixty kids and parents at the sports awards picnic. Two faculty sponsors, Coach Butterworth and Henny Brawley.

"They had a big bonfire in the pavilion, but the lights

aren't too bright. You could walk a few feet away from the pavilion and the fog swallowed you up. From what I found out, the picnic was subdued. Foggy, chilly, and the Grim Reaper lurking in their minds. Sam Howard had been found dead of a drug overdose a week earlier. Everybody was surprised when Jocelyn showed up." Marian flipped open a notebook. "She came late. Kids got glimpses of her, talking to different people. She was wearing her brother's letter jacket. The program started at eight, student athletes receiving their letters. When Sam's name was called, nobody came up for the patches. Sam had been varsity in three sports. It got real quiet. Coach gave a tribute to him. Nobody mentioned Jocelyn. They thought she was too upset to come forward. Sam was one of the golden boys. Here's a picture."

Annie looked at the smiling face of a handsome boy with curly chestnut hair. His expression held a hint of swagger, his green eyes were confident with an almost arrogant gleam.

"He was found next to his car in the forest preserve. An early morning jogger spotted him and raised the alarm. Nobody'd reported Sam missing yet. He'd told his mom he was going to the movies. His mom thought he was in bed when she got the call. He went to the movie. There was a triple bill that night and nobody noticed when he left. Nobody knows where he went or what he did after he left the movie. He wasn't seen again until his body was found. I don't know if they ever found out anything more. When the autopsy report showed cocaine, Frank dropped it. I guess he figured Sam had gone to the preserve for a snort and ended up dead. Maybe too much coke, maybe a weak heart. Since the death was deemed accidental, I was able to get a copy of the file. I drew a sketch of the death scene."

The drawing was meticulous. A road curled among trees. A squarish car—labeled Jeep—was angled off the side of the road, the hood nudged against a tree trunk. A stick figure lay in the road behind the car. A notation read: *Car registered to Samuel James Howard, found one-quarter mile from preserve entrance, keys in ignition, letter jacket with his billfold in the backseat. Two credit cards and thirty-two dollars in cash in billfold.*

Annie studied the drawing. "Why was his body in the road?"

Marian licked salt from her fingertips, shrugged. "Why not? Maybe he liked to sniff coke outside. Maybe he got woozy and got out of the car. Bottom line: no other trauma, healthy Caucasian male aged eighteen, verdict accidental death from cocaine." She upended the Coke, drank greedily. "I talked to some kids, promised them I wouldn't squeal, and I got the lowdown that Sam was a big alcohol and drug man so where's the surprise. There are always a few in every class and sometimes they're the golden boys who have it all, looks, money, personality, and a streak of I'm-invincible, gonna-do-what-I-wanta-do. I don't figure there was any mystery about what happened to Sam. As for Jocelyn, everybody interviewed said she was really upset at the sports awards picnic. They figured she came because the kids were getting their emblems for the various sports and Sam had lettered in football, basketball, and tennis."

At Annie's high school, guys received jackets, girls cardigan sweaters. Each sport had an emblem.

Marian took a last gurgle of Coke. "Everybody noticed she had on her brother's letter jacket. That was spooky because his personal effects, including the jacket, had been returned to the family that afternoon." Marian shuffled through papers, handed Annie another photograph.

Annie felt haunted by unfinished lives. Jocelyn had been lovely, a blue-eyed blonde with a confident gaze and smile. She was as golden in her way as her brother had been.

Marian crushed the soda can. "One of the girls said Jocelyn looked awful that night, pale and shaky, her eyes red from crying."

Annie studied the photograph, made when the future looked bright with expectations of happiness, excitement, fulfillment. That last night, Jocelyn struggled with grief. Was she upset because her brother was gone, distraught at the finality of death? Or was she upset with the living?

Frank Saulter finished the last crumb of angel food cake, placed the fork and plate on Max's desk. "I don't know what's better, the cake or the lemon icing. Barb's wasted as a girl Friday."

No one appreciated his secretary's culinary skills more than Max. When time hung heavy, she created amazing treats in Confidential Commissions' small kitchen. She also cooked when stressed. Today, she'd talked on the phone, posted the reward flyers, tallied results of her survey, and whipped a dozen eggs for the cake, while regularly checking on Max's well-being and muttering imprecations about nasty, lowlife people who set things on fire.

Frank glanced at the wheelchair. "Glad you can get around. I bunged up my feet once. Coral. I expect you hurt like hell."

Max's feet throbbed. But the haze of pain was better than the haze of pain pills. Maybe the pain helped him concentrate. "They make it easy to remember somebody out there doesn't like Annie and me." Max appreciated Frank's question because, in addition to indicating concern for his comfort, it was also an oblique recognition that Frank understood Max had a very personal interest in seeing Iris Tilford's murder solved.

Max chose his words carefully. Frank Saulter had been a superior police chief, honest, careful, thorough. Like Billy Cameron, he was an island native. Frank knew his island and its people. That was a plus in leading to answers that weren't always obvious unless you were aware of families and their histories. That knowledge also meant an emotional tie to many of those involved in investigations. "I asked Doc Burford about the autopsy on Jocelyn Howard. Doc cut me off. What did the autopsy show that he didn't want to reveal?"

Frank's hawklike features folded into a frown. He could be genial. Since his retirement, he had seemed to relax and smile more often, but in repose his face reflected a somber nature, perhaps formed by years of dealing with unhappy lives and grim realities. "The Howards ran to trouble. Not being an island boy—"

Max knew he'd never be a real island boy. When he and Annie had kids, that would be their birthright.

"—you wouldn't know much about the family. Five generations on Jocelyn's mom's side, the Hilliards. Now they're all gone. Mary Grace Hilliard was an heiress, married a golfer she met at some country club up north. He was a drunk, ran his MG into a live oak one night, leaving her with two kids, Sam and Jocelyn. Mary Grace was a sweet lady, but she drank too much, too. She may not have been a sober mother, but she loved those kids. After they died, it was like watching a leaf crumble into little pieces. She got thinner and thinner and one morning she didn't wake up."

Frank stared into the distance, seeing a picture Max

couldn't see. "When I went to the house to tell her about the report on Jocelyn, Mary Grace's first words were, 'It was an accident, Frank. My girl never jumped into that water. She hated water. She wouldn't even go in a swimming pool.' She got up and walked away from me. She stared out at the ocean, then buried her face in her hands and sobbed." Frank looked old and tired. "She hurt so bad I wouldn't have been surprised if she'd died right there in the room. Her boy dead of a drug overdose, her girl gone a week later. Do you think I was going to tell her that Jocelyn drowned and that it looked to be an accident but"—Frank's dark eyes were bleak—"maybe it could have been suicide because of the circumstances?"

Max was puzzled. "Her brother's death?"

"Sam's death knocked Jocelyn down. She was upset and crying at the awards picnic. Everybody thought she was grieving for Sam. Maybe so, maybe not." His face folded into lines of sadness, a man who had seen heartbreak, knew it too well. "She was pregnant."

Max was quick to object. "Come on, Frank. An unmarried girl getting pregnant hasn't been a scandal for a long time." Maybe a hundred years ago, a distraught young woman might choose to die or resort to possibly deadly backroom butchery, but now? Unwed mothers were no rarity. Girls opted to have babies and raise them alone every day.

The former police chief gave a brief, sour smile. "I didn't just fall off the turnip truck. Jocelyn was from a good Catholic family. She'd been accepted at Loyola. She had to be between a rock and a hard place. If the baby's father wouldn't marry her, maybe she didn't see any way out. Add that stress to depression over Sam and it spelled suicide to me. Should I have told her mother? Then Mary Grace would have fought the anguish that Jocelyn hadn't come to her, hadn't asked for help. Worst of all, Mary Grace would have lost not only her son and her daughter but her grandchild."

Max was silent. Frank had made the best decision he knew to make at the time.

Frank pushed up from the chair. "Doc and me kept it quiet. Mary Grace died two years ago. Thank God. They're all gone, the Hilliards and the Howards. Nothing can hurt Mary Grace now." He paused in the doorway, looked back. "I would have kept my mouth shut now except Iris Tilford's murder proves I was wrong. Jocelyn didn't fall or jump. Somebody pushed her, and Iris knew too much."

∿: *Thirteen* :∿

As she came out of the *Gazette* office, Annie glanced across Main Street at Parotti's Bar and Grill. Darlene Hopper might be at work. Was it worthwhile to try to talk to her? Darlene hadn't been part of Jocelyn's group of friends, and Billy Cameron was confident there hadn't been time for Darlene to walk into the woods with Iris. Still, Darlene had been in that class, and she was among the handful of those who had been present at the pavilion Friday night and ten years ago. Maybe Henny could tell her something about Darlene.

Annie walked to the railing at the edge of the harbor, stood in the sun, and welcomed the breeze. She punched a familiar number on her cell.

After the fourth ring, a voice message announced: "For the next few days, I'll be working at Death on Demand. Come by for coffee and conversation and pick up your copy of Sue Grafton's latest. What's up with her alphabet this time? See you soon."

Annie's smile was quick. She realized it was the first time

she'd smiled that day. *Thank you, Henny.* She punched the bookstore number, still smiling.

"Death on Demand, the best mystery bookstore north of Miami. How may I help you?"

Annie loved Henny's cultivated voice, which had reached to the back seats at so many little theater productions.

"Henny, you're wonderful."

"Thank you. It's mutual. What's up?"

Annie's smile fled. "Darlene Hopper was in the same class as Iris and the others. She was a server Friday night and she was at the awards picnic ten years ago. Do you remember Darlene?"

"From school? Oh yes. I didn't mention her this morning because she certainly wasn't part of that group." Henny paused, then murmured, "All God's children."

"All God's children?"

Henny sighed. "I'd like to say that I always treated students equally. Sometimes it was difficult. I'm old enough to know there is a spark of divinity in every person. But," her tone was rueful, "some people are adept at hiding every evidence of that. Darlene was uncooperative, bristling with anger, mean-spirited. And profoundly unhappy, of course. I thought highly of Jocelyn because she was kind to Darlene. Darlene adored Jocelyn. From a distance. Darlene never tried to be friends with Jocelyn, she just watched her. That would have worried a lot of people. It didn't bother Jocelyn." Henny's tone was admiring. "Darlene was heartbroken when Jocelyn died. She didn't finish school. She stayed on the island. A big family. Not a very nice family. She's worked at the grocery and later at Parotti's. Ben has a kind heart."

Annie felt a chill. "She told Billy Cameron she didn't pay any attention to Jocelyn at the sports awards picnic."

Henny spoke quietly. "I doubt very much that she told Billy the truth."

Branches interlocked above the blacktopped bike path. Ferns poked from scrubby undergrowth. Crows clamored. Max suspected the crows had sighted a fox. The somber, secluded pathway was in tune with Max's thoughts. Jocelyn Howard was pregnant when she died. That changed everything.

The golf cart careened around a curve. Max slowed. This was no time to end up mired in the dank, green-scummed swamp water that bordered the path. It was another half mile to the cemetery. He wasn't sure his idea would work out. First he needed to spot the grave site, then he could make a pitch to Billy. If Jocelyn's body were disinterred, could a forensic pathologist determine the DNA of the fetus? Even if that wouldn't be possible after all these years, the threat of DNA testing might be enough to scare a statement from Russell. If he wasn't the father, he'd be eager to see that proved as well.

Jocelyn may have died because she demanded the father acknowledge the baby. Or she may have died because Iris told her the name of their classmate who provided the cocaine that killed Sam. There was only one certainty. Jocelyn was murdered. Iris's death made it clear that Jocelyn did not jump or fall from the pier. Jocelyn was pushed.

The golf cart emerged from dimness. Ahead a dusty gray road led into the island cemetery. Markers dotted family plots lying among live oaks and palmettos. Birds chittered. Squirrels darted. A small weathered gray wooden building that served as the office was tucked among willows, not far from the marble-faced columbarium.

Max stopped the golf cart in front of the office. He swung out the wheelchair, opened it. He grimaced as he maneuvered himself into the seat. Damn, his feet hurt. But he was beginning to feel at ease with his new transport.

The office was shadowy inside. "Hello." His call was met by silence. A small notice on the counter listed a telephone number and advised that the cemetery was open from dawn to dusk. An arrow pointed to an interactive screen for those seeking information about grave-site locations.

Max rolled nearer. He touched the icon for grave sites. A pop-up offered the alphabet. He tapped *H*. Names appeared. He scanned down to Howard, Jocelyn, C48. He returned to the desktop, touched the map icon.

He studied the map and let out a sigh. He'd had great hopes. Now they were ashes. C48 was a niche in the columbarium.

Remember, man, that thou art dust, and unto dust thou shalt return.

No one would ever prove the identity of the father of that long dead baby.

Seabirds cawed. A bold crow hopped near the garbage pails. It was cool and shadowy in the alley behind Parotti's. The smell of garbage mixed with the scent of the sea and the odor of hot cooking oil. Annie understood Henny's murmured "All God's children" as she stepped back a pace to avoid a stream of cigarette smoke. Darlene Hopper's stare was sullen. A stripe of red blazed in her dark hair. Silver rings glinted from eyebrows, nose, ears, and lips. Purplish tattoos covered her plump arms from shoulders to wrists. Reddened hands from dishwashing emphasized the darkness of the tattoos.

"I know who you are." Darlene's tone wasn't friendly. "I worked the food line Friday night." She took a deep drag on the cigarette. "I wish I hadn't left before you found Iris. That must have been exciting."

Annie controlled a flare of anger. Was Darlene as callous as she sounded? Or was the sardonic remark thrown out to see if it rankled? "You knew Iris."

Even Darlene's fingers were tattooed with tracery of a spider's web. Her shoulders lifted in a faint shrug. "In school. She was a dork."

This was not the time or the place to defend Iris. One day soon the spirit poster would be finished and Annie could push away all memory of Darlene's meanness. For now, Annie forced herself to speak without animus. "You were at the sports picnic the night Jocelyn Howard died."

Darlene's hand, the half-smoked cigarette pinched between thumb and forefinger, stopped midway to her ring-pulled lips. "Jocelyn." Her face softened. Her voice slid to a depth of sadness. "She was always wonderful to me. Until that night. I knew she went out with Russell. But that was what everybody expected. She was homecoming queen. He was a football star. But I never thought about them . . . not like that." Her voice trailed away. "I wish I hadn't run away from the picnic. Oh God, if only I hadn't left. If I'd known what she was going to do, I'd have stayed with her, helped her. But she yelled at me and I ran away. I went home. I didn't find out she was missing," Darlene's voice was dull, "until the next afternoon. I went to the pavilion and helped look. I walked through the woods, back and forth. We didn't find her. She wasn't in the woods. She was in the water."

"She was your friend?" Annie tried to connect the elegant princess with Darlene.

"Friend?" It was as if Darlene repeated a word from an unknown language. She blinked at Annie. "I wasn't one of Jocelyn's friends. Everybody wanted to be her friend. Liz and Cara and Fran. Iris hung around them, but she didn't count. And there were Sam's friends, Buck and Russell. None of them were special like her. I always sat close to her." Darlene's voice was proud. "Hopper. Howard. We had English together and Spanish and history and math. Jocelyn smiled at me every day. She was beautiful, her hair, her face. Perfect. Like sunset on the water. Or the sky when it's so blue it makes you ache inside. Our lockers were next to each other. Her locker always smelled good. Once I asked her what made the locker smell so nice, like a field after rain. She said it was sachet. I didn't know what that was, but I didn't tell her that. I just told her it made me feel good when she opened her locker door. The very next day she brought me a little lacy bag of sachet. Rose, just like hers." Darlene looked at the burning cigarette. Her nose wrinkled. She dropped the stub, ground it beneath a dirt-stained sneaker. Perhaps the rank smell of tobacco dimmed the sweet memory of rose.

Sadness washed over Annie. Darlene had created a fantasy based on Jocelyn's casual kindness. How little Darlene's own life must have afforded her in the way of love and caring.

"That was very nice of Jocelyn. I see why you found her so special." Annie picked her words carefully. "What happened that last night?"

Darlene's lips trembled. "She was unhappy and Russell looked mean. I was worried about her. I decided to hang around in case she needed me. I could have walked back to the fire with her, held on to her." There was a depth of

longing in her voice, all her customary bravado and disdain
and anger shed.

Annie understood more than she wished to know. Darlene
had seen herself as a rescuer, a white knight restoring a beloved lady to safety and esteem. Darlene had built a dream
in her mind with herself as heroine, but the dream had no
reality.

Annie wondered if she was within reach of understanding
Jocelyn's death. "Russell looked mean?"

Darlene's face hardened. Anger burned in her eyes. Red
patches blotched her sallow cheeks. "He wouldn't talk to
Jocelyn. He ducked away every time she started toward him.
Russell's so big and ugly. I hate him. Finally, she came up
behind him and caught his arm. She was crying. He looked
like he wanted to push her away. She pointed outside the
pavilion and they started walking that way. The fog made
everything hard to see. You could only go a little way
and everything was all blurry. I went after them because
I wanted to protect her." Tears slipped down Darlene's
cheeks. She made no effort to brush them away.

"I suppose it was private away from the pavilion." A private place for a desperate girl and the boy who didn't want
to talk to her.

"Private. Quiet. I couldn't hear a sound from the picnic.
It was like being in a cloud somewhere. I came closer and
closer. I wanted to reach out and touch her. She was crying.
Jocelyn told him she needed help. Russell said he couldn't
do anything, that his dad would kill him, that he had to go to
The Citadel. I didn't know what he was talking about. Jocelyn grabbed his arm. 'I'm not talking about the baby. I don't
care about your dad or whether you go to The Citadel. You
should have thought about that before you said you loved

me. But you've got to help me tonight—' I didn't mean to, but I guess I called her name. I couldn't believe it. Jocelyn and him. I started to cry and she turned around and saw me. I wasn't thinking and I stepped toward her and she"—Darlene choked back a sob—"screamed at me to go away, leave her alone, stop spying on her. I turned and ran. I never saw her again. I didn't know she'd jump off the pier."

Annie was stunned. Jocelyn pregnant, Russell the father, and a confrontation. "You didn't tell anyone?"

Darlene slumped against the wall. "What good would it do? She was gone. Russell would lie. I didn't want people talking about her. I wanted everyone to remember her the way she was, beautiful and clean and perfect."

Annie looked into red-rimmed eyes. Darlene had not been able to save Jocelyn, but Darlene had guarded the world's picture of her.

"If I'd known she was going to jump—"

Annie's voice was sharp. "Jocelyn didn't jump. She was pushed." Annie reached in her purse, pulled out the bright yellow flyer, thrust it at Darlene. "That's why Iris came home. She saw someone walk into the woods with Jocelyn at the sports picnic. Iris was afraid Jocelyn's death wasn't an accident. Iris came back to the island to try to find out the truth. Somebody strangled her to keep her quiet."

Darlene stared down at the flyer. One hand came to her chest, pressed against it as if to quiet a racing heart. She stood rigid as steel.

"That's why we have to find out what happened the night Jocelyn died. Are you sure she meant that Russell was the father?"

Darlene stood mute. It was not so much that she ignored Annie as that she was unaware of Annie's presence. Darlene looked up from the flyer; her eyes wide and fixed. She flexed thin, spiderweb-tattooed fingers, curled them tight, crushing the flyer.

Annie tried to break through that wall of silence. "Don't you see? Friday night Iris went into the woods with someone. She was strangled with the cord from a table so it had to be a guest who killed her. Iris must have been persuaded that everything was all right. Maybe the murderer promised to show her what happened with Jocelyn."

Darlene stared into the distance. "Jocelyn." The word was thick and slow as if dredged from deep within. Abruptly, she pulled off the stained apron, flung it on the ground. She was short and chunky in a tie-dye T-shirt and tight jeans. She turned away.

"Darlene." Annie moved after her. "Please . . ."

Darlene yanked a rusted blue bike from a rack and flung herself on it. She hunched over the handlebars, pedaled away fast.

Max rolled the wheelchair into the main entrance of the high school and recognized the familiar school smell, a combination of wax and antiseptic and the scent of baking. Hurrying teenagers, loud and boisterous, opened a path that closed behind him. He checked in at the main office, grinned at dark, intense Angie Taylor, the receptionist who also volunteered at The Haven. "Hey, Angie. I'm here to see Coach Butterworth."

"Hey, Max, glad you and Annie are all right." Angie's big brown eyes looked shocked.

Max wasn't surprised that she knew. Very few on the island would be unaware of the fire. "Thanks. We were lucky."

Her brows drew down in a frown. "You hurt bad?"

"Scratched-up feet." Maybe tomorrow the pain would ease some. "I borrowed a wheelchair. I'm doing fine. Do you know where I can find Coach?"

She gestured to her right. "He has lunchroom duty, first serving. Everything goes real smooth when Coach is on duty. The lunchroom's down the hall and to the left through the double doors."

Max found the stocky coach standing near the terrace exit. The coolness of steel blue eyes belied his genial expression. "Yo, Max."

They shook hands.

Butterworth glanced at the wheelchair. "I hear you and Annie had a close call last night."

"Yeah. Too close."

A whoop and scuffle sounded behind him.

Butterworth looked past Max, didn't raise his voice. "Cool it."

Two bulky teens in sweatshirts and jeans abruptly pulled apart and lumbered past. "Yo, Coach."

When they were past, apparently well aware that the coach's steady gaze followed them, Butterworth looked at Max and yanked a thumb toward the terrace door. "Quieter outside." He spoke loud enough to be heard over the lunchroom hubbub. "I can see through windows. Don't make me be in a hurry to come back in." He held the door for Max.

The terrace was cool and quiet. The onshore breeze fluttered weeping willow fronds, rattled magnolia leaves, bent the cordgrass in the salt marsh. Butterworth stood with his back to the marsh, looking through windows into the lunchroom. He went right to the point, making it clear that Iris's death and its probable cause were a topic of faculty discussion. "Maybe we should have tumbled to something when Iris went off the rails after Jocelyn died. She dropped out of school, left the island. Nobody put two and two together. Now it looks like we were stupid. Everybody thought Iris was scared because of drugs. Later, after she ran away, we heard she'd supplied cocaine to Sam. Now, it sounds like there was someone else behind her."

"That's what she told someone later." Max saw no reason to mention Jocelyn's pregnancy. If it wasn't the reason for murder, let Jocelyn and her baby rest in peace.

"If"—Butterworth's eyes crinkled in thought—"the drug dealer was at your picnic and was also at the pavilion the night Jocelyn died, the list is pretty short."

Max waited. He didn't need to tell Coach the names.

Butterworth jammed his hands in the pockets of his khakis. "Loose words can ruin lives."

Max remained silent.

Butterworth looked weary. "You came near dying last night. If I know anything, I have to tell you." His face folded in a frown. "My wife's been a Girl Scout leader for years, ever since our girls were young."

Max knew this mattered.

"She comes to all the school events. She knows a lot of the girls. Not the guys, unless they're on the football team." He rubbed knuckles on his cheek. "The fog made everything out of kilter. It was like being in a dream. It's hard to remember what happened when. And it's been ten years. The best I can recall is that about fifteen minutes before the awards ceremony, my wife asked me to come with her to the woods. I was pretty short with her. I was trying to get the patches in order. I had some parents helping, but we were running late. I hated that because I knew everybody wanted to get done with the evening. We'd had a pretty big turnout. Even more parents came than usual. Maybe because of Sam's death. It was tough because all the guys were upset about Sam. It was going to be hard to get through the program without somebody breaking down. Hazel—my wife—said I needed to check the woods. Hazel was going back to her car for a jacket when she saw Cara Jackson slipping out of the pavilion. Hazel didn't think it looked right so she went after Cara. She saw Cara follow a couple into the woods. She said Cara looked sneaky. Besides, the kids weren't supposed to leave the pavilion grounds. Hazel was too far away to know who the couple was. About the time we got close to the woods, Buck Carlisle came toward us. He wasn't an athlete but he came to the picnic for his sister Jodie. She was a top swimmer. I stopped him and asked what was going on in the woods. Buck said Jocelyn was upset about Sam." Butterworth's eyes were somber. "Buck looked like somebody'd kicked him in the gut. I thought I understood. Sam was his friend and here was Sam's sister going to pieces. I almost asked Hazel to go into the woods and find the girls, but I decided everything was probably okay. Cara had seen Jocelyn and Buck and followed them. She would help Jocelyn. I felt reassured. Maybe I made one of the biggest mistakes I've ever made. I told Hazel we should give Jocelyn space. It wouldn't help anything for us to go after her, maybe make her feel worse. By this time Buck had disappeared into the fog. I went back to the pavilion and got the program started. For a long time afterward, I'd wake up in the night and wonder if I'd gone into the woods I might have been in time to keep Jocelyn from jumping. Now it looks even uglier."

* * *

Annie reached the mouth of the alley and walked to the corner of Main and Broward. She had a good view of the harbor, the ferry dock, and downtown with its one- and two-story buildings, some old and weathered, some more modern with stuccoed walls and tiled roofs. The harbor pavilion was a block to her left.

She looked in all directions. Darlene was out of sight. She was distraught and in a hurry. In a hurry to do what? Annie felt uneasy. There had been a determination in Darlene's hurried departure that suggested she had some action in mind. Could she know some fact that linked one of her classmates to Iris? In any event, Billy needed to know what Darlene claimed to have heard between Jocelyn and Russell.

Annie glanced down Main Street. She was a half-block from Liz Montgomery's store. Annie felt a sudden emptiness. If she repeated Darlene's story to Billy, Liz and Russell would suffer.

She had no choice. She had to tell Billy. Annie walked steadily toward the police station. She was halfway there when her cell phone rang. She smiled at the caller ID. She stopped on the boardwalk, again welcoming the cool and fresh onshore breeze. "Max, listen." She spilled out Darlene's revelation.

Max interrupted. "Frank told me this morning that Jocelyn was pregnant. It makes sense that Russell was the father. It will never be proved. I went to the cemetery. I found Jocelyn's urn. She was cremated."

Annie was never willing to picture cremation. Her mind pushed away images of flames and a body reduced to ashes. She said quickly, "Maybe nothing can be proved by DNA, but Darlene heard Jocelyn say Russell was the father."

"That's what Darlene told you." Max was matter-of-fact. "Maybe she heard that. Maybe she didn't. Only she and Russell know for certain what was said. But Billy needs to know. Where's Darlene?"

"She jumped on her bike and rode away." Annie felt a sudden catch in her throat. "I'd better hurry and tell Billy. Maybe he can find her, keep her safe."

"Safe?" Max's query was sharp.

"Darlene was distraught when I told her Jocelyn was murdered. I don't know what she might do." Annie pictured Darlene pumping hard on the bicycle pedals. "She said Jocelyn's name and rode away."

"Billy can find her. But Russell isn't the only one who needs to answer some questions about the sports picnic. Coach Butterworth told me . . ."

Annie remembered the block letters of the anonymous note: *Buck walked into the woods with Jocelyn the night she died.*

". . . but Coach didn't go into the woods. He thought Jocelyn was with Cara. I called Billy. He thanked me and said he'd be in touch with Coach. I'm sure Billy had already asked Buck about the anonymous note. I imagine Buck claimed he left Jocelyn in the woods and didn't see her again. There's no proof Buck didn't do exactly that."

In Annie's mind, it was as if a bright shaft of light circled two moments in time: Jocelyn leaving the pavilion with Russell, Jocelyn and Buck walking into the woods. "We have to find out whether Jocelyn quarreled with Russell before or after she was with Buck."

"We can try." Static crackled on the line. Finally, Max said quietly, "Maybe the timing mattered. Maybe it didn't. Jocelyn could have gone into the woods with Buck and Buck left her alive. And then she and Russell walked away from the pavilion. Or she and Russell quarreled and later she went into the woods with Buck. And on to the pier."

The reception area of Carlisle, Smitherman, and Carlisle reminded Max of appointments in a funeral home, dark cherry wood, gray walls, subdued lighting, a solemn aura of calm and repose. Max rolled the chair to a stop at the counter.

Ellen Nelson, a scratch golfer, looked up from her computer. Max often played a round with her husband Paul. A tall, angular brunette, Ellen exuded competence. "Hey, Max. What can I do for you?"

"Is Buck in? If he's free, I'd like to see him."

"I'll check. He's pressed this morning." She pushed the intercom button. "Max Darling's here and would like to see you."

There was a pause. "Max? All right." Buck sounded weary.

Ellen came around the counter and held the hall door.

"Thanks." In the hall, it was hard to roll the chair on the thick gray carpet.

Buck was waiting in his open doorway. He waited as Max wheeled inside, then closed the door. He walked toward his desk, then swerved to the window, holding up a hand to protect his eyes against a sharp glare of sunlight. He tilted the shades up to redirect the light. "The light hurts my eyes."

Max stopped the wheelchair near the desk.

Buck settled into his desk chair. He rubbed his face. "I've got a headache that won't quit. I guess it's because I overslept. Dad's furious with me. I was late getting here for a conference call. Anyway, I'm running behind." He glanced at papers and legal pads strewn on the desktop.

Max stared at Buck. Buck overslept. A figure had slipped through shadows, carrying a gas tin, to fire an inferno. Only Dorothy L.'s frenzied cries and Duane's quick action saved them. This morning, Buck overslept. Either Buck was innocent as a lamb or he was explaining away his late arrival at the office.

Buck looked puzzled. "What's wrong?"

"It's tough not to get enough sleep." He'd never thought Buck especially clever. If Buck was playing an ingenuous role, he was very clever indeed. Max's gaze never left Buck's tired face. "Annie and I are running a little short today, too."

Buck massaged one temple. "I heard. That's awful." There was nothing but sympathy in his expression. "Are you guys staying in another cabin?"

"No." Max didn't elaborate. Although word spread fast on the island, Max had no intention of announcing their whereabouts. Max pushed away memories of fire and fear. He wasn't here for a social visit or legal consultation. Maybe challenging Buck wasn't smart, but the time for innocuous questions was long past. "What happened between you and Jocelyn Howard in the woods at the sports picnic the night she drowned?"

Buck's face slowly hardened. "I could ask what the hell business is it of yours." He slowly came to his feet, met Max's hard stare. "I guess I know the answer. Somebody tried to kill you and Annie last night. Billy Cameron's got it all worked out. Jocelyn was pushed. Iris saw her with somebody." He took a deep breath. "Billy thinks the murderer set your cabin on fire because Annie talked to Iris. All I know for sure is that Jocelyn and Iris are dead. I'll tell you what I told Billy." Once again he rubbed his head. "The sports picnic was awful." There was remembered pain in his voice. "Jocelyn was upset because of Sam. She wanted to know where he got the cocaine. I guess she figured I would know since Sam and I were friends. I told Jocelyn all I knew." He looked straight at Max, eyes steady. "Sam bought the stuff from Iris. I told Jocelyn and I left her in the woods. Alive. I swear she was alive." His voice broke.

"What did Jocelyn say when you told her?"

Buck's gaze dropped. He moved his hands, cracking the knuckles. "She was going to talk to Iris."

Max leaned forward. Why wouldn't Buck look at him? "But what did she say to you?"

Buck swallowed. His voice was thick. "She cried. I couldn't stand hearing her cry."

"Did she run ahead of you out of the woods to go hunt for Iris?" Coach had told Max that Buck came out of the woods. He would have seen Jocelyn if she'd run ahead of Buck.

Buck hung his head. "No." The sound was muffled.

Max stared at him. "You left her there in the woods, upset and crying?"

Buck looked miserable. "I couldn't do anything to help. Nothing was going to bring Sam back, and I couldn't stand seeing her cry. I left her there. She was alive." His voice was loud. "She was alive. I never saw her again."

Annie stood with her back to the harbor, arms folded, surveying the picnic area and the woods beyond. A cloud slid over the sun. April is capricious, its tantalizing hint of warmth easily discouraged. Annie wished for her sweater, but she'd left it in the car. She'd grab it in a few minutes before she met Max for lunch at Parotti's.

Her visit with Billy had been brief. He'd thanked her, not

indicating what he intended to do with Darlene's information. Of course he would check her claims out, but Annie felt uneasy. Why had Darlene hurried away? Obviously, she was shocked and shaken that Jocelyn's death had been murder. Perhaps her precipitous departure was easily explained. She needed time and space to deal with her anguish.

Yet, there had been a sense of purposefulness in Darlene's departure.

Annie walked past a row of palmettos. The serving stations had been set up just about here, conveniently close to the picnic tables. Annie smoothed out wheel tracks in the sandy ground. Three servers: Miss Jolene, Darlene, and another older woman. Barb would have her name.

Annie took two steps. She'd not paid a great deal of attention when she'd gone through the line, but she rather thought Darlene had been at the middle station. Annie pretended to spoon fried zucchini or lift corn on the cob with tongs. She looked up.

Her arm remained in its make-believe posture as she stared beyond the picnic tables at the entrance to the woods. A lamppost was only a few feet away from the path. She recalled the lights Friday night, luminous and golden, designed for beauty not stark illumination. Yet there was sufficient light that anyone walking into the woods would be visible for a brief moment.

Especially from this vantage point.

Annie hesitated. She'd intended to take a brief look, then walk to Parotti's to meet Max. Instead, she took one step, then another toward the woods. Her throat felt dry. She didn't want to enter the dim woods. The woods hadn't been safe Friday night, but of course there was no danger now.

Annie forced herself to move forward. She stopped in

the center of the picnic area and glanced at her watch. She slipped onto a bench, pictured the centerpieces. It was the work of only seconds to pretend to tweak free a length of cord, put it in her pocket. Another pocket would hold the shucking gloves.

As if smiling at a fellow guest, she gestured toward the pavilion. "I'll be back in a minute." Once away from the table, the guest would be swallowed up in the dusk, face and figure indeterminate. As Annie saw it, Iris must have passed near the murderer's table, walking toward the pavilion, likely on her way to the women's restroom.

Annie walked up to the pavilion. Friday night the pavilion tables hadn't been used so the only visitors would be those coming up to the restrooms.

When Iris came out of the restroom, a familiar voice called to her. There were so many ways a conversation might have occurred, but whatever was said, Iris had been persuaded to come into the woods.

Annie came down the path, turned left to reach the entrance to the woods. There would have been a brief moment when Iris and the figure beside her moved through the amber light from the lamp.

That moment was unlikely to have been noticed by the guests, absorbed in conversation and food. The picnic tables sat end side to the woods so the path was in their guests' peripheral vision. Only the servers faced the entrance. The bandstand was between the woods and the picnic tables. The musicians had their backs to the woods and the path.

Annie drew a quick breath and plunged into dimness. Squirrels chittered. An unseen pine warbler's distinctive *wip wip wip* chirped nearby. She kept a moderate pace as if walking with a companion, talking. She brushed aside ferns, carrying with her the memory of Iris's huddled body. As she came around another curve, crime tape hung limply across the path.

Annie averted her gaze from the area marked off by the tape. She dropped back a step as if casually falling behind a companion. She imagined yanking on the gloves and grabbing a thick branch, sturdy enough to be a club. She cracked the weapon through the air, jolted it to a stop neck high. In her mind, Iris sagged to the ground. Annie knelt, pulled free the cord, looped it . . .

She waited a full minute. The caw of a crow sounded a dirge.

Jumping to her feet, Annie ran lightly back toward the picnic ground. She paused to quiet her breathing before plunging out of the woods and moving quickly past the lamppost. She returned to the center table.

Annie looked at her watch with a sense of wonder.

∽ *Fourteen* ∾

ANNIE PUSHED THROUGH the heavy wooden door of Parotti's. She was instantly comforted by the chatter of voices, bursts of laughter, and familiar smells of wood shavings, fish bait, and grease.

Max's wheelchair was folded next to their favorite booth. He smiled and called out, "Food's coming. Your favorites."

Annie wished that all she cared about was a fried-oyster sandwich with a double dash of tartar sauce. She hurried toward him.

As she came nearer, his smile slipped away. "Annie?"

She came close, reached out, took his hand, his wonderful, warm, reassuring hand. "Did you know"—her voice was high—"you can leave a table at the pavilion, kill someone, and be back in eleven minutes?" She pulled away, slid onto the opposite bench, welcoming the hardness of the wood, the carved tabletop decorated by so many of Ben's customers, including them. She reached out and touched the heart with their initials that Max had gouged one happy summer night. "No one would notice you'd been gone." She lifted her face, looked at him forlornly. "Killing Iris was easy. No one would pay any attention when someone left a table to go to the pavilion or get seconds or talk to someone else."

Max poured hot coffee from a serving thermos into her mug, handed it to her. "Drink this."

Annie drank, grateful for the warmth, but the steaming coffee didn't touch the cold deep inside. It was a relief to tell Max about her walk into the woods. The words built a bridge from her solitary journey to the bright cheer of Parotti's. She could almost block out her reenactment and the dark images it evoked.

Almost. Not quite.

Max shook his head. "You shouldn't have gone into the woods by yourself."

Annie was impatient. "There was no one to see me. I needed to look. Now I know how Iris was killed." She bent forward. "Darlene may have seen something. Or someone." Annie put the salt and pepper a few inches apart. She placed her knife horizontally opposite the shakers. She tapped the small space between the shakers. "That's the entrance to the woods. The serving line"—she touched the knife—"was directly opposite. Your view between the salt and pepper is Darlene's view Friday night of the path into the woods."

Max pulled out his cell, punched a number. "Mavis, this is Max. I've got a couple of things I'd like to tell Billy." Max waited. "Hey, Billy. After I talked to Coach, I went by to see Buck. I asked him what happened that night at the sports picnic. Buck claims Jocelyn wanted to know who sold the cocaine to Sam. He told her Sam got the stuff from Iris. Buck insists he left Jocelyn alive."

Annie knew every nuance of Max's voice. She felt a curl of sadness. Not Buck. Please, not dear, likable Buck.

"I guess that's not news to you. For what it's worth"—

Max's expression was troubled—"I know Buck pretty well. I would have told you he was one of the most honest men I know." The words came slowly, reluctantly. "Buck looked at me, the kind of ingenuous look the best liars have when they're putting on a spin. Buck lied to me when he told me about his conversation with Jocelyn. I can't put a finger on what sounded false. I can't prove he lied, but he wasn't telling me everything. That's as near as I can come."

Max listened, then nodded. "I know. You have to be able to connect someone with Iris at the party. Maybe there's a way. Annie went to the pavilion a little while ago. You'll want to talk to her." He handed the cell to Annie.

Annie retraced her steps for Billy. ". . . I stood exactly where the serving line was set up. Darlene Hopper looked directly toward the entrance to the woods. There's a lamp-post and enough light to recognize people. Only the servers faced the woods. The band members had their backs to the woods. Guests sitting at a picnic table look either toward the pavilion or the Sound. So the servers—"

Billy cut in. "Hold on a minute." There was a sound of rustling papers. "Yeah. I got it here. Three servers, Miss Jolene, Trudy Valdez, and Darlene Hopper. Miss Jolene and Mrs. Valdez both came to the island after Iris left. Neither one knew her."

Only Darlene.

"Good work, Annie. We're looking for Darlene. If she saw anything, we'll get it out of her."

Annie spoke fast before he could hang up. "I timed everything. . . ." Once again dark images moved in her mind. "Everything may have happened in as little as eleven minutes." Less time than it took to enjoy a good cup of coffee and a piece of Miss Jolene's Key lime pie or dance a shag or balance a checkbook.

A voice spoke in the background, the words indistinguishable. Billy was abrupt. "Got to go. But your guess is as good as anybody's. If Iris and her killer were only together for a few minutes, Darlene may be our best hope. We'll find her. ASAP."

Annie clicked off the cell. She replaced the salt and pepper in the center of the table, realigned the knife by the spoon. "If Darlene doesn't know, Billy may never be able to catch the murderer."

Max looked upbeat. "I've got a feeling he'll break the bank with Darlene. Why would she have raced away if she didn't know something? You said she looked like she was on her way somewhere as fast as possible." He looked past Annie, smiled. "Hey, Ben."

"Yo, Max." Ben Parotti's usual smile was absent. His sleeves were rolled up though he was still natty in a red-and-white-striped shirt, red polka-dot bow tie, and khaki trousers. He deftly served their plates, flounder with mushrooms and sour cream and grilled asparagus for Max, fried oysters on an onion bun and hot German potato salad for Annie. Two unsweetened iced teas. He shot them a harried glance. "If that's all you need, I got to get back to the kitchen."

As Ben strode toward the kitchen, Max forked a steaming piece of flounder. "Something's hassling Ben."

Annie wasn't worried about Ben. "Probably a crisis in the kitchen. Or maybe he and Miss Jolene are crossways."

"That's as likely as snow in July." Max cut an asparagus stalk. "Whatever's wrong, the food's still the best."

Annie welcomed the sandwich, the onion bun hot to the touch, the fried oysters lightly battered and crisp. She wished her thoughts could be as cheerful as her meal. "Billy's got it right. We need proof."

Max nodded. "If Darlene saw one of her classmates go

into the woods with Iris, everything may unravel for the murderer. If that happens, you can feel good about it. You're the one who broke through with Darlene. We've helped Billy a lot." Max ticked off what they'd learned. "Russell was the baby's father, according to Darlene. Buck is hiding something about his talk with Jocelyn. We've given all of that to Billy." He dredged a piece of flounder through the creamy sauce. "I don't think we need to worry about the murderer setting another blaze or coming after us with a gun. We've been in and out of the police station. It's obvious we've reported everything we know to Billy. The murderer's still free so it's obvious we don't possess dangerous information. When Billy finds Darlene, we may be able to get back to normal."

Annie took a last bite of the sandwich. Normal seemed long ago and not within reach. "I wish."

Max was ebullient. "Darlene will make all the difference."

Annie felt buoyed by his good humor. "Maybe she will."

Hurried steps sounded on the wooden floor. Ben approached with his tray. "Dessert?"

Annie shook her head, surprised at his departure from the usual proud listing of Miss Jolene's daily delectables.

"Not today. Tell Miss Jolene we're saving up for Saturday night and her eggnog icebox cake." Max looked toward Annie.

Annie smiled. At least once a month, they came to Parotti's on a Saturday night. The cake was one of her favorites and only available then, a magnificent concoction of butter, confectioners' sugar, egg yolks, egg whites, bourbon, pecans, and Miss Jolene's homemade pound cake.

Annie looked up at Ben. "She can count on us."

"That'll be good." He was perfunctory. "I'll put the bill on your tab."

Annie realized Ben truly wasn't himself, abstracted and lacking his usual genial patter.

She reached out to touch his arm. "What's wrong? Is there anything we can do?"

He gave them a weak smile. "Wash dishes maybe." He stretched out moist red hands. "When you asked to talk to Darlene, I figured it was extra to her break. That was an hour ago and she hasn't come back. I phoned her twice, left messages. Trudy's home sick so I've got to handle the floor by myself plus serve. I've got a call in to my cousin Norma. She'll help us out. Darlene should have told me she had to leave. I had her on a short leash anyway. A lot of the customers don't want to see all those tattoos. She may come back, but there won't be a job waiting for her."

"Oh, Ben, it's my fault. Darlene was terribly upset." Quickly, Annie explained.

Ben's face softened. "Darlene's always had the short end of the stick. I won't say anything." He bent to pick up their plates, stacking the silverware. "That was a bad year. Two kids dead, now another one gone. Drugs are poison. I wish kids would listen."

As Ben turned away, Annie called after him. "Can I have Darlene's phone number?"

He turned back. "I'll get it for you."

"And her address?" Darlene would have filled out a job application with her personal information, including her Social Security number.

Ben nodded. "Sure. Back in a sec."

As he hurried away, pausing long enough to refill tea glasses at one table, Max looked up from the wheelchair. "What do you have in mind?"

Annie looked determined. "I want to find Darlene. She'll run scared of Billy. Maybe she'll talk to us."

* * *

The onshore breeze rustled the pink fringe of the golf cart. Annie smiled at Max. "What a fun way to get around the island."

Sitting sideways in the driver's seat, Max dexterously shoved the wheelchair into the golf cart space, carefully swung his feet into the cart. "You'd be surprised at the speed I can get out of this baby."

Annie punched the number provided by Ben. As she listened to the rings, she shook her head. "Nothing ever surprises me about you and speed." She'd had too many white-knuckled rides in Max's 425-hp MerCruiser powerboat.

A tinny voice spoke, Darlene's answering message: "Catch me another time. If you can."

Slipping into the cart, Annie waited for the tone. "This is Annie Darling. Please call me." Annie left both her cell and store numbers. Why should Darlene bother? "You had a good view of the path into the woods Friday night. It's important to know if you saw Iris and if anyone was with her. Or contact the police. We'll pay out the reward either way. Remember that this information—if you have it—can put you in danger. If you have a name, stay away from that person. Don't take any chances."

Max gave her a swift glance. "Do you think she may do something stupid?"

"I hope not, but I've been scared ever since I stood where she served." The picnic grounds had been empty this morning. Silence had pressed against Annie as she faced the dark woods. Silence and remembered horror.

The electric cart rolled smoothly across the street and sped onto a bike path.

They'd gone perhaps fifty feet into the forest, quite

cool beneath the canopy of trees, when Annie reached out and touched Max's arm. "We aren't making a sound. You'd better slow down or we may careen right into an alligator."

"The path's too cool for a 'gator to be lounging around. But a passenger's peace of mind is important." He slowed until they reached a narrow paved road that angled toward the northeast.

Annie clung to the side of the cart as the golf cart picked up speed. The road was bumpy. Fishing camps and cabins dotted this end of the island. The occasional house was modest, though some were well kept.

Max slowed the cart to turn off on a dirt road. Clouds of dust rose beneath the wheels. In another half-mile, he followed a narrow, dark, and twisty lane that was scarcely more than two deep ruts. The golf cart jolted beneath low hanging branches. Undergrowth choked the dark woods.

The cart reached the end of the lane. Ramshackle wooden cabins curved in a semicircle. Tar paper covered some windows and patched some wind-damaged roofs. A rusted pickup was jacked up on the far side of the clearing. Annie looked around in dismay. "She lives here?" Growth-choked pines cast long shadows over the cabins. Algae scummed a neglected pond.

Max nodded. "Number Five." The cart rolled to a stop. Cardboard replaced several panes of a front window. The surviving panes were dirt-streaked. A yellowing sheet served as a curtain, covering the front window.

A chained German shepherd near Cabin Three growled, lunging against his restraint. A raccoon with one paw in a tilted garbage can lifted his head to watch them.

Annie stared at the dilapidated cabin. "It's desolate." She

swung out of the cart and hurried to the door. There was no bell or knocker. She rapped on the panel, waited.

The dog growled, deep in his throat. Pine boughs sighed in the breeze.

Annie knocked again. "Darlene, if you're here, please talk to us."

The door remained closed.

At the harbor, Max waited in the golf cart and watched Annie drive away. She'd promised to go straight to Death on Demand. He felt the farther she was from this end of the island, the safer she was.

Annie had agreed they'd done all they could do to find Darlene. Now it was up to Billy. Annie had gone the extra mile, trying to find Darlene to urge her to talk to Billy. Maybe they'd get a lead from the flyers Barb had posted around town. He felt uneasy. Billy had warned them: Don't taunt a tiger. Was Darlene taunting a tiger?

Max drove the golf cart along Main Street, then turned toward the harbor. He stopped on the boardwalk and breathed in the salty scent from the Sound. He watched sails puff on sloops and seabirds circle near a shrimp boat. He envied the absorption of a solitary fisherman at the end of Fish Haul pier. He wished he could slip back into his easy island life. Not yet. Would it do any good to confront Buck, demand to know what he was hiding? Max almost turned the golf cart toward the law office, then shook his head impatiently. He needed more than instinct to shake Buck's story.

It was time to get back to Confidential Commissions, see if he and Barb could nose out some fact, any fact, that would give them a lead. He smiled as he turned the cart south, knowing he would make a minor detour. One of the great charms of the Franklin house was its nearness to downtown.

He'd check and see if any progress had been made in the repairs. By the time he got back to Confidential Commissions, there might be some responses to the flyer. Max followed a bike path to Bay Street.

He felt content as he turned into the drive to the Franklin house. Soon, he and Annie would move in. He eased the golf cart to a stop in front of the two-story tabby house with piazzas both downstairs and up. The house sat high on tabby foundations. No matter what category hurricane hit the island, the Franklin house would likely be safe from the storm surge.

It wasn't until he swung out his feet that he stopped in dismay. Sure, he had a wheelchair, but there were no ramps. Damn.

Oyster shells crunched behind him. Russell Montgomery's white pickup curved toward the house, stopped behind the golf cart. Good. Russell could give him a progress report. Maybe he'd have a firm date when the house would be available. Max lifted a hand in greeting as Russell swung heavily down from the cab.

Russell was crisp in a blue-and-white checked shirt, khakis, and work boots. His face was in shadow beneath a broad-brimmed Panama. He moved like a man ready to fight, hands bunched into fists, stride bullish.

Max stiffened.

Russell's shadow fell across Max. He looked down at Max seated in the golf cart. "I dropped by Liz's shop. I saw Annie leave in her car and you head this way in that." He jerked his head at the golf cart. "I figured you were coming here. I got a problem with you two."

Max curled his hands into fists. If ever he wished he was standing on his feet, it was now.

Russell talked fast, his voice hard. "Twice now Billy

Cameron's hammered at me because of 'information received.' Billy says he has 'confidential sources.' We all know who's running around the island, poking into people's lives. I'm here to tell you that if you people go around talking about me, you're going to regret it."

"Are you threatening me?" Max met his gaze directly.

Russell's face flushed. "I'm telling you I've had enough. Stop trashing me."

"Not trash. Truth." Max met his gaze without wavering. "Whether you want to admit to it or not. And whether you like it or not, Annie and I will do everything we can to help solve Iris's murder. Somebody told Annie about you and Jocelyn at the sports picnic. Jocelyn wanted to talk to you and you tried to stay away from her. Jocelyn was crying. Today someone else confirmed that. Another classmate overheard you and Jocelyn. Jocelyn told you she wasn't talking to you about the baby."

Russell's face was suddenly unreadable. "There's no proof." His voice was a rasp. "There will never be any proof."

Max fought a wave of anger. "Why don't you tell your side? If you have a side."

"Back off, Max. My life is none of your business." Russell leaned forward. "Things get ugly for people who go looking for trouble."

The moment stretched and held.

Max's muscles tensed. He was ready to launch himself, head down, and butt Russell in the gut when Russell swung away and strode rapidly toward his truck.

The gong sounded mellow. Annie had intended to hurry to her computer, see if Fran had e-mailed a memory for Iris's

spirit poster. Instead, she stopped near the cash desk to look
in amazement at the throng of women in the coffee area.
The gong sounded again. Annie moved down the central
hallway. Dim lighting turned Death on Demand's nooks
into shadowy enclaves. Not good for reading, but soothing
to a harried soul.

At the fringe of the crowd, Annie slipped out of her shoes
to join the other barefooted women. Although she scrambled
to keep up, she felt she did a good job of moving the moon
across the sky. Fifteen minutes passed. Peace touched her
as they concluded with a slight bow, left hand cupped over
right on the lower abdomen.

An aura of contentment permeated the coffee area even
as the tai chi enthusiasts chattered and drank coffee or tea,
each clutching a book purchased before the exercises.

Henny rapped smartly on the coffee bar. "Ladies."
Henny's alert dark eyes gleamed with enthusiasm. "Our
new Mystery Club will meet next Monday evening. We will
discuss"—she held up a hand for silence—"Peter Robin-
son's Inspector Alan Banks series. You'll want to buy the
new book. At a discount, of course. We've ordered them
especially for you and if you'll take your place in line—"

Annie watched in amazement. The dutiful readers—
maybe tai chi was the answer to the world's angst—swarmed
into an orderly queue leading up to the cash desk and a big
stack of beautiful books. Hardcovers. If each customer
bought a hardcover in addition to an earlier purchase, Death
on Demand might set a one-day sales record.

Laurel and Henny swooped to the cash desk. *Ka-ching,
ka-ching.*

When the front door closed behind the last mellow mystery lover, Annie clapped. "You're wonderful. Both of you.

Thank you for keeping the store going. Since Duane is back, I can take over now." Life would almost be whole again. Someday maybe she would sleep through the night and not awaken with a start, remembering the crackle of flames and smell of smoke, fighting away a sweep of terror.

Henny led the way down the central aisle. She radiated eagerness, dark eyes gleaming, narrow intelligent face alight. Laurel high-stepped behind her, silver blond hair swirling, red tai chi uniform perfectly draped on a figure that any chick might envy.

Laurel gave a final kick. "Dearest Annie, Henny and I have wonderful plans."

"Plans?" Annie hoped the word didn't resemble a desperate mouse squeak. "Some special getaway as a reward for all your hard work here?"

Henny patted Annie's shoulder. "We have a mission. We have always loved Death on Demand, but now we know we can make a difference for you."

Annie leaned against the coffee bar. They were wonderful, but they overwhelmed. Death on Demand was her world, hers and Agatha's and Ingrid's. How would Ingrid feel if Henny and Laurel became permanent fixtures?

Laurel beamed. She curved her arms up, pulling down yang. Or was she pushing up yin? "You will be thrilled, dear child."

Henny moved comfortably behind the coffee bar, obviously at home there. She filled three mugs, set them on the counter.

Annie noted the names on the mugs: *Tell You What I'll Do* by Henry Cecil, *Shoot a Sitting Duck* by David Alexander, and *The Takeover* by Richard Wormser. Were they portents of her future?

Henny beamed. "We have a new schedule planned. Subject to your approval, of course. Laurel and I will be in charge every Monday. Ingrid has talked for years about creating reading lists with brief summaries of the books. This will give her time to do the research. Mondays off will afford you and Max long weekends. Mondays will be special." Henny clapped her hands together. "Tai chi every morning, the Mystery Book Club at night."

Laurel beamed. "Isn't it wonderful, dear child? We call ourselves The Tai Chi Mystery Mavens."

Once a week.

Delight made Annie euphoric. Only on Mondays. Of course she was always interested in improving Death on Demand and Laurel and Henny provided a dash of color. Moreover, they were adept at parting customers from their cash. But how glorious that they would invade her domain only on Mondays. "That's great! Oh, how can I thank you?"

"Oh well, if you insist." Eyes gleaming, carrying her steaming mug, Henny headed directly for the collectibles.

Laurel waved her hands like clouds and looked thoughtful. "I've been dreaming of a very special treasure hunt. I don't quite have it worked out, but this would be a good place for the hunt to end."

Henny returned with two books.

Annie left them at the coffee bar, Henny trying to decide between a seventy-dollar good-condition edition of *Fingerprint* by Patricia Wentworth or a forty-two-dollar somewear edition of *A Is for Alibi* by Sue Grafton.

Annie smiled as she slipped behind her computer in the storeroom. How lovely to think about tai chi and mysteries. Those thoughts helped hold at bay the somber moments they'd endured. Tonight she and Max would be safe and comfortable at Emma's. Soon the Franklin house would be ready. Nothing could be wholly right with their world until Iris's killer was found, but she intended to savor this happy moment.

Annie clicked on her messages: forty-three. Sometimes she wished for the good old days of letters or phone calls. Combined, she had never received forty-three letters and phone calls in one day. Annie scrolled, deleting, saving, occasionally responding. She was midway down the list when she stopped, clicked print. Fran's message would help complete the spirit poster for Iris:

Please forgive me for being upset when you came to the shop. If only Iris hadn't come back to the island. She called and wanted to talk about the sports picnic at the pavilion. I've been trying to forget that night for years. I begged Iris to let things be. We can't change what happened and everyone's gone on and made a good life. She wouldn't listen. She asked if I knew who went into the woods with Jocelyn. How would I know? None of us ever talked about the sports awards picnic. If I knew, I wouldn't say because that person might be innocent. Don't you see? No one will ever know what happened.

I'm sorry. I'm upset again. Will everything ever go back to where it was and we were happy?

Annie could see Fran's irregular features with their sur-
prising charm, imagine her impatiently brushing back a
tangle of dark curls. Annie was sorry that Fran was upset.
But Jocelyn and Iris were dead. Annie doubted anything
would ever be quite the same for that tight group of friends
locked together then by a fatal night, pushed apart now by
suspicion and uneasiness and fear.

I didn't see much of Iris in high
school. I was working hard to go to
college, making good grades, saving
money. She never seemed to look ahead so
we didn't spend much time together. She
didn't care about school. Ever since her
mom died, she was sad. I tried to tell
her that lots of people have hard times.
I didn't grow up easy, but I decided I
wasn't going to be like my family. My
mom dumped me on my grandmother. All
she did was complain about how much it
cost to feed me. Iris was lucky. Her
grandmother kept a nice clean house and
she was sweet to everybody. My house
was trashy and my grandmother drank
too much. Iris never got over her mom
dying. Iris kind of drifted around and
she never had much to say. She wasn't
like that when we were little. We were
best friends in third grade. After
school, we'd go to her house and have
tea parties. We pretended we had shops.
I had a jewelry store and I sold gold

rings. I saved the bands from my uncle Joe's cigars and put them on a plate I decorated with foil. Iris found an old stack of *National Geographics* that someone threw out. She cut out pictures and pasted them on art paper. She called them her brochures. She had a travel agency. When she grew up, she wanted to go around the world. She'd be the first person ever from Broward's Rock to go to Zanzibar. She found it on the atlas, saved the *National Geographic* pictures. Zanzibar. She loved the sound. That's how we said good-bye. "I'll see you in Zanzibar."

When she ran away, I always wondered if somehow she'd gone to Zanzibar. Instead, she never made it farther than Savannah. That's how I'll always remember her, smiling and waving, saying, "I'll see you in Zanzibar."

ᴧ∴ *Fifteen* ∾

THE FRONT DOOR to Confidential Commissions was locked, which indicated Barb was out and about. Max used his key and maneuvered the wheelchair inside. He turned on the light and paused to admire the new decor of the anteroom, which was replicated in his office, spare, angular furniture and black-and-white-tiled floor. The new decor reflected the vitality of faraway New York. He'd never regretted his move to Broward's Rock. Where Annie lived would always be home for him, but New York's magic remained a part of him and often beckoned, the rhythm of blaring horns and hurrying crowds, life lived full throttle.

He wheeled to his office, still thinking about Annie and New York and champagne breakfasts. He opened the door and stopped, startled to find the light on. He was sure he'd turned the light off when he left. Barb wasn't here and it was unlikely she'd turned the light on.

He shrugged and wheeled toward his desk. The smell struck him first. He stared at the desktop. There wasn't much blood. Blood must have spewed where death had occurred. The long, thin, headless body of an eastern diamondback rattler lay limp and still atop papers and folders.

Max had a quick memory of Russell Montgomery, red-faced, fists bunched, leaning toward Max. Russell would shoot a rattler with ease, had probably done so fairly often. Diamondbacks were no stranger on the island. As if watching a film, Max pictured Russell moving brush and hearing that distinctive warning. Did he keep a handgun in his truck or a rifle? In any event, how easy for a good marksman to shoot the snake. One less dangerous predator to deal with.

Billy looked at the back door. "Jimmied."

Max was furious. "If anybody knows how to get inside a building, it's Russell Montgomery."

"No proof." Billy glanced up and down the alley. "Whoever brought the rattler would have made sure no one was around."

Max looked, too. The alley was beginning to fill with afternoon shadows. He and Billy were the only people in the service area behind the shops. "Like now." Max turned away. In his office, he stood by the desk as Billy used a gloved hand to lift the carcass from the desk, ease the dead snake into a box.

Billy shrugged. "I don't know what the hell good it will do to keep the snake. I'll tag it for the Tilford case."

Max used damp paper towels to swipe away the traces of blood and body fluids. "We may not be able to tie the snake to Russell, but I'm sure he brought it. Maybe that will turn out to be a big mistake on his part. Sure, we knew he had a hell of a motive, but now we know he's ready to get ugly."

Billy tied twine around the box. "Yeah. There's one interesting thing." Billy's tone was thoughtful. "It could have been uglier. He could have left a live rattler."

As the door closed behind Billy, Max's nose wrinkled as

he smelled the musty scent of rattlesnake. He wheeled to the kitchen area and found Clorox wipes. He returned to his office, wiped papers and folders and scrubbed the desk.

The dead snake was not only a warning, its presence in his office was a contemptuous dismissal of locks.

Max pulled the stacks of folders nearer and saw a note in Barb's flamboyant handwriting:

Here are the dossiers on Jocelyn's classmates. I didn't find much new on anybody. I've highlighted stuff you might want to know. Some heartbreak for Cara Wilkes. I don't think it's relevant to the murder.

Nice thing about an island is that everybody's here unless they're not. I contacted the guests who attended the picnic, excluding Iris's classmates. Seven of the guests knew Iris. Only three noticed her or spoke to her Friday night.

Max was disappointed. He'd hoped others attending the oyster roast might have glimpsed Iris walking into the woods with her killer. He scanned the names. Kim Holland, a bouncy blonde, taught fourth grade and never missed an event at Death on Demand. Ruddy and brusque outdoorswoman Joan Kelly raised Afghan hounds and volunteered at The Haven. Amiable Mike Peterson taught golf at the country club ("Keep your elbow straight . . .").

Kim Holland: I was surprised to see Iris. I intended to say hello but I got to talking with Ted Porter and when I looked around I didn't see her. . . . It was about seven-thirty when I tried to find her. I kept an eye out but I decided she'd left.

Max wrote the time on a legal pad. He felt a flicker of hope. Maybe another guest would pinpoint Iris's presence before or after seven-thirty. That would narrow the period when it would be important to establish the whereabouts of Buck, Fran, Russell, Liz, and Cara.

Joan Kelly: Lived next door to her grandmother. Nice woman. Kept cockers. Iris wasn't up to life. No gumption. Weak stock breeds weaklings. Asked her Friday night if she'd come home to stay. Said she was back for a visit. That was about the time I went back for a second dessert. Real Key lime pie. When did I see her? Ten after seven.

Max scrawled the time in large numerals: 7:10–7:30. Maybe a picture was slowly taking shape. The serving line was still open at half-past seven. Darlene was at her station with a clear view of the entrance to the woods during that twenty-minute period. Darlene would easily recognize Iris and her other classmates. Maybe a net was beginning to close around an elusive, swift-moving, deadly figure.

Mike Peterson: It was nice to see Iris again. She was a sweet girl. I ran into her up near the pavilion. She asked how things were going. I told her everything was great and I was having a swell time getting paid to hang around a golf course. She said she'd been in Savannah the last few years. I asked her to come by our table. I wanted her to meet my wife. She gave me the sweetest smile. She said she would. Maybe I'm spooked by everything that's happened, but I get a funny feeling when I remember her face. As she turned

*away, she looked kind of scared but determined, real
determined. I didn't think anything about it at the time.
Now I have to wonder. . . .*

Max sketched the pavilion and marked the site of the restrooms with *X*s. Iris may have been on her way to a restroom
when she stopped to visit with Mike. Someone could have
followed her from the picnic area with gloves and a length
of cord. Iris's expression of fear and decision convinced
Max he was right. This was the fateful moment. Iris saw the
person she suspected. Mike returned to the picnic tables.
Iris and her classmate spoke. Iris was persuaded her fear
was unfounded.

Max immediately pictured familiar faces. Had Buck
beckoned Iris to enter the woods with the promise of truth
to come? Had Fran offered a solution absolving them all?
Had Russell professed to remember that foggy night and
claimed he could explain Jocelyn's sad death? Had Liz
insisted Iris's memory was faulty? Had Cara recalled Jocelyn's distress and said Jocelyn walked away alone toward
the harbor?

Max turned to the dossiers:

Frances Fay Kinnon Carlisle: Mother Emmalou Estes
Kinnon McElroy, waitress. Father Morgan Kinnon.
Parents divorced when Fran was five. She came to
live with her grandmother Eliza Estes, never knew
her father. Mother visited sporadically. Grandmother
Estes was employed at the telephone company. In
high school, Fran worked at Parotti's, then she was
on the wait staff at Frankie's Supper Club on the
mainland. Fran was class valedictorian. She received

the Campbell scholarship to Clemson. She majored in business, graduated in the top ten percent of her class. She and Buck Carlisle married right out of college. She managed a boutique clothing store while Buck was in law school. Upon his graduation, they returned to the island and Buck joined his father's firm. She opened Yesterday's Treasures. She received a state award for top small business two years ago. Fran and Buck adopted a daughter from China, Terry, who is now five.

Max wondered how Jessica Carlisle, Buck's regal mother, dealt with her daughter-in-law's modest origins. Probably with grim reserve. He doubted Jessica had ever eaten at Parotti's with its down-home atmosphere or Frankie's, which had a shady-lane reputation for backroom gambling and introductions to willing ladies. At least Jessica should be impressed by Fran's academic achievements and acquired social graces. Fran had left her shabby background far behind. Max picked up Buck's folder.

Stanley George (Buck) Carlisle IV: Father Stanley G. Carlisle III, lawyer. Mother Jessica Fairlee, homemaker. One sister, Jodie. Parents are movers and shakers on the island, both financially and socially. Average student in high school. Eagle Scout. Accomplished woodworker. Elected social secretary of his fraternity at Clemson. BA, Clemson; JD, University of South Carolina. Active in student bar association, served as secretary. Married to Fran Kinnon. Returned to the island after graduation from law school and joined his father's firm. Adopted daughter Terry.

Buck was distracted and worried the last time he and Max played golf. Buck didn't relax until his cell rang and Fran assured him she'd taken Terry in to see the pediatrician and her sore throat wasn't strep. Buck had earnestly related that strep was always a danger for Terry.

Max shut the folder. Buck always reflected his thoughts at the moment. He had little natural reserve. He wasn't a man accustomed to dissembling. Max was certain Buck had lied about his last conversation with Jocelyn.

Elizabeth Katherine Ames Montgomery: Father Richard Ames, owned Ames Cleaners. Mother Louise Wylie Ames, worked in the store. Six children. Liz was the oldest. Solid student. Majored in education at the University of South Carolina. Upon graduation married Russell Montgomery. She taught second grade when Russell was stationed at Camp Lejeune. Liz and Russell returned to the island two years ago. No children. Liz is active in the china painting society, sings in a church choir, plays bridge.

Max felt impatient. Liz's bio was accurate as far as it went, but there was nothing to reveal the passions that fuel lives. Henny believed Liz hated Jocelyn and had vandalized Jocelyn's car. Did Liz know Russell had fathered a child that was never born? Did Liz push a hated rival from a pier? Would she kill again to prevent exposure?

He picked up Russell's folder.

Russell Robert Montgomery: Father the late Col. (ret.) Michael "Big Mike" Montgomery. Mother Selma, a homemaker. Vice president of the "B" Club, became president upon the death of Sam Howard. Played football, basketball, soccer. Lettered in all three. 4.0 grade average. Graduated ninth in his class from The Citadel, BS in Engineering. Served five years in the Marine Corps, one tour in Iraq. Married Liz Ames upon college graduation. Returned two years ago to Broward's Rock. Used inheritance from his father to found Montgomery Construction. Active in the Chamber of Commerce. Received an award from a state environmental group for a green house with reduced and recycled water usage and energy conservation through design. Plays golf and tennis. Shoots a Glock 34 in International Defensive Pistol Association competitions.

Max wished he had X-ray vision to check out the contents of the car pocket in Russell's pickup. If Russell's Glock 34 had been recently fired, it would be nice to know. He reached for the phone, let his hand drop. Billy didn't have enough evidence to ask for a search warrant. Moreover, Russell owed nobody an answer about his gun. Not unless a crime was proved. So far as Max knew, it was still lawful to shoot off the head of a rattler.

And Russell could continue to refuse to admit anything about his last talk with Jocelyn despite what Darlene Hopper overheard. That came down to "he said, she said" and who could prove anything?

Max picked up the last folder.

Cara Jane Jackson Wilkes: Father Allen Jackson, salesman killed in a car wreck when she was four. Mother Sydney Thompson Jackson, an actress who worked in

Florida in supper clubs. Cara spent most of her time on the island with her grandmother Belle Thompson. An excellent student. Worked her way through Armstrong State. BBS in Marketing. Joined a greeting card company in Miami. Married Richard Wilkes, sales rep for a mosaic-tile manufacturing company, one daughter Melissa Ann. Melissa diagnosed with leukemia at age sixteen months. Died at age two. Wilkes left a year before Melissa died to take a job in Buenos Aires. Divorce finalized six months after Melissa's death. Cara returned to Broward's Rock two years ago, joined Island Realty.

Max gently closed the folder. He'd always found Cara brittle with a sardonic flippancy. Now he understood. He stacked the folders. He'd take them with him, offer them to Annie. Maybe she would see something he'd missed, some fact that might point the way.

Maybe that would be unnecessary. If all had gone well, Billy would have found Darlene Hopper. Darlene may have seen what Billy needed to know, the identity of the person who walked into the woods with Iris. Armed with knowledge and the power that comes with certainty, Billy might now be talking to one of Iris's classmates.

"A dead rattlesnake?" Annie shuddered.

Max's voice over the phone was calm. "As Billy said, it could have been worse. What if he'd left a live one? Not to worry. I'll e-mail the dossiers to you. See if they suggest anything."

Annie put down the phone. At her computer, she opened the attachment and read quickly. She felt sadness for Cara, but she didn't see that any of the information pointed to a double murderer. She closed down her computer.

As she stepped out of the back room of Death on Demand, she checked out her surroundings, ears tuned for a fateful rattle. She shivered as she pictured a dead rattlesnake draped on Max's desk.

Despite her uneasiness, fueled by Max's call, she felt a sense of accomplishment. She'd handled everyday work and organized the stack of materials ready to use for Iris's poster. Death on Demand was empty except for her and Agatha. Now that Henny and Laurel were gone, the bookstore was, though she was loath to admit it, rather lonely. Of course when Ingrid returned, there would once again be a companionable presence.

A sharp meow pierced the air. Agatha paced toward Annie.

Annie hurried toward the coffee bar. "Although," she said aloud, "I don't need anyone other than you, sweetie."

Agatha bared incisors and loped near Annie's ankle.

The front bell rang.

Annie kept going. Customers could wait. Agatha must be fed. Not, of course, that Annie was intimidated. Certainly not. It was simply that Agatha might succumb to impatience and lacerate the nearest flesh. Which happened to be Annie's ankle. Her speed of hand as she opened a can of salmon soufflé mixed with egg and spooned the soft food into a clean red plastic bowl was on a par with a fast-forward DVD and likely as entertaining had there been a viewer.

Agatha ate and growled, growled and ate.

Footsteps sounded in the central aisle.

Annie risked a quick stroke of silky fur. "See, everything's fine now."

Cara Wilkes stopped by the coffee bar. "If only that was true." There was no trace of sardonic lightness. Her clipped voice held an edge of desperation. "Annie, I need help."

Annie looked into a pale face with set features. "What's wrong?"

Cara jammed a hand through her short haircut. The bracelets on her wrist jangled. "What's right?" Her voice shook. "It's bad enough that Iris is dead. That makes me sick. But I'm terrified by what her murder means." Staring eyes looked haunted. "Iris came back to the island because of Jocelyn's death. There was no reason to kill Iris unless"—a hand clutched at her throat—"somebody pushed Jocelyn off the pier." Tears edged down her thin face. "When I pass the high school, I think about Sam and Jocelyn. When I go up my old street, I think about Iris. I see you and Max and I know you almost died and I'm scared. I didn't think it could get any worse and now it has. Somebody's trying to make it look like I did these things."

Annie felt frozen. Cara was obviously scared. She might have a very good reason to be scared.

Cara pressed close to the coffee bar, her eyes beseeching. "You've been talking to Billy Cameron. Everybody knows that. You know what's going on. What did he say about a gas tin?"

"Billy found an empty gas tin on the deck of the cabin. Someone threw gas everywhere. That's why the fire was so fast." Annie's hands clenched. Whenever she remembered the smoke and flames, horror swept her. She stared at Cara's face, so near her own.

Cara's freckles stood out on her cheeks, dark against the paleness. "It's my gas container. I mow my own yard. Billy found my initials scratched on the bottom. It has my fingerprints on it. Somebody took the tin out of my garage. Annie, I didn't set the cabin on fire." Her voice quivered.

"Your garage is unlocked?" But of course that was what Cara would claim.

"No. I keep it locked. A windowpane was broken out. Someone must have gotten in that way. Billy saw the smashed window, but he looked so grim. What can I do?" She sounded frantic. "I've got to do something to show I had nothing to do with the fire at Nightingale Courts."

Annie wondered if Cara was as distraught as she sounded. "What happened that night in the woods between Buck and Jocelyn?"

Cara took a step back. A tiny muscle flickered in her throat.

"You followed them." That's what Max had learned from Coach Butterworth.

Cara looked stricken.

Annie felt as if she pushed against a closing door. "No one saw Jocelyn after that, did they?"

Cara's face crumpled.

Annie pressed. "You can't keep quiet. Not now. Don't you see? Whatever you know, you have to tell Billy."

"I can't." The words could scarcely be heard. Anguish made her face look old and vulnerable.

Annie's heart ached for her. Even though Cara and Buck's high school romance ended, had Cara been aware of his every move at the sports picnic? Max thought Buck was lying about the night Jocelyn died.

Cara whirled away. The clatter of her steps in the central aisle sounded loud and desperate. She banged through the door and was gone.

* * *

Max held the portable phone and listened to Billy. Max's left foot throbbed. He flexed it. "Ouch."

Billy broke off in midsentence. "You okay?"

"Foot twinge. The nerves instructing me not to move it, stupid. I guess I won't be jogging for a while."

Billy laughed, sounding almost like the easygoing Billy who Max and Annie enjoyed. "Get real. Annie's the jogger."

Max was glad he'd provided a light moment. "Man, are you saying I'm lazy?"

"Oh"—Billy could be tactful—"let's just say you could be the billboard dude for laid-back lifestyle."

"I like that." Max looked at the silver-framed photo of Annie. "Laid-back Lifestyle according to Max Darling: One—Marry the most beautiful girl in the world, Two—Play as hard as you work—"

A subdued snort from Billy suggested he didn't think the equation balanced.

"—and Three—Sea, sand, and sun are better than rum."

"Thought you drank Scotch. Black Label."

It was Max's turn to laugh out loud. "That's called poetic license. What rhymes with Scotch. Botch?"

"Botch." Billy once again sounded dour. "I know all about botch. As in botched. I'm up against it, Max. There are leads all over the place, but not a whisper of evidence. Like that damn snake on your desk. How am I going to trace that? And"—now he was angry—"we can't find Darlene Hopper. I've been to her place, to Parotti's, to her folks' house. She's—"

Call waiting beeped, blipping part of Billy's words. Max glanced at the caller ID. "Hold on, Billy. Hey, it's Darlene calling. Let me put you on the line." Max punched buttons.

"Hello." From the hollow tone, he knew Billy could hear as well.

The voice was low and hurried. "Is this the number for the reward? Ten thousand dollars?"

"Right. The reward will be payable—"

She cut in impatiently. "My name's Darlene Hopper. Write that down. I'm the one who found out what happened. If it weren't for me, nobody would know. If I hadn't been looking at the right time, you'd never know who killed Iris and Jocelyn. I want a promise that they put it in the paper that I'm the one who found out. I don't care about the money. If you pay anybody, you should pay me. But that isn't what matters. I've got some help now, but I'm the main one. We're setting up a trap. We'll get pictures. But none of it would have happened except for me." A pause and a shaky breath. "I wish I had a gun. I wish I could watch Jocelyn's murderer die." The line clicked off.

Billy called out, "Wait."

There was no answer.

"We. Is that what Darlene said?" Annie tried to keep her voice steady.

Max sat in the passenger seat of the Volvo, his face grim. "That's what she said. Darlene and somebody are setting a trap. Only, I don't think so. I think a smooth-tongued devil has convinced Darlene someone else was the killer."

Annie remembered Darlene's tears for Jocelyn. Yes, Darlene called Max about the reward, but money didn't matter to her. She wanted justice. Darlene wanted to be acclaimed as the one who avenged Jocelyn. She hadn't saved Jocelyn that long ago foggy night, but now she could be a heroine and capture Jocelyn's murderer. "Oh, Max." Annie sounded despairing. She drove fast. "Billy's probably already at Darlene's cabin."

"I hope so." He stared at the shadowy road, leaned forward as if to urge the car ahead.

Annie pressed the accelerator. The speedometer nudged seventy, a wild pace for the island. She slowed at each curve in case an unwary bicyclist or jogger might be in her path. "Darlene saw someone she knew go into the woods with Iris." Annie slowed for a doe and two fawns to amble across the blacktop. "Darlene called that person."

Max was angry. "Why didn't she notify Billy?"

"I doubt if Darlene is in the habit of going to the police, talking to them. Maybe her idea was to get some kind of admission and call about the reward." Annie slowed for the crossbar to lift. Once beyond the gate, she took a looping side road to avoid Main Street.

Max shook his head. "Maybe we've got it all wrong. Maybe someone is helping her set a trap."

"Maybe." Annie wished she believed that was possible. "I'm afraid she called the murderer and was told something like, 'I walked into the woods with Iris, but I left her there. I heard a noise on the path and I stepped behind a holly bush. I saw one of our classmates come up to Iris. I went back to the picnic. The next day when I heard about Iris, I knew who killed her. I didn't think anyone would believe me. Now the two of us together can get some proof. Here's what we'll do. I'll call and say we know what happened to Iris and set up a meeting. We'll be safe enough. I'll have my cell and we can call for help if there's trouble.'"

Max looked at her. "And then?"

Annie gripped the wheel tighter. "The murderer can't let Darlene talk. But maybe we'll find Darlene in time. Maybe she called from her cabin and she hasn't left yet." The Volvo jounced down the rutted road, came around a curve to the now familiar dusty clearing and row of weathered cabins.

A police cruiser was parked in front of Darlene's cabin.

Annie parked beside the cruiser. As Annie got out the wheelchair for Max, Billy came around the side of the cabin, moving fast. He gave them a brusque nod.

Max held up a hand and wheeled past Annie. "Better wait a minute." He reached Billy. "Is Darlene here?"

Billy gestured at the cabin. "I went all the way around, pounded on the doors, looked in the windows. The back door was ajar. Since I was acting on a tip and there's a possibility of foul play, I went in. There's no trace of her. She doesn't have a car. There's a bike lock on the back porch but no bike."

Annie's faint hope of finding Darlene faded. If the bike was gone, Darlene wasn't in the cabin. Where was she? Who was with her? Could they find her in time?

Billy strode toward the cruiser, he and Max talking. Annie's thoughts skittered like windblown leaves. Darlene could have called from anywhere . . . lots of people didn't even have old-fashioned phones now . . . if she called on her cell she could have been on her way to meet that faceless figure who slipped through woods unseen, dealing death. . . .

The radio in the cruiser crackled. ". . . no trace yet, Chief. Lou and Hyla are out looking."

Billy was gruff. "Call Bud Heaston, see if he can round up the Scout troop. We may have to ask for help from the sheriff's office. She could be anywhere. Probably she's somewhere on the north end of the island. Nobody involved lives in the gated area."

Annie stood stiff and still. Cara lived in a small frame house two blocks from Main. Buck and Fran's house was on the marsh a half-mile from the harbor. Russell and Liz lived in an antebellum house that overlooked the harbor. Cara was a real estate agent and the offices were on Main. Liz's and Fran's shops were on Main. Buck's family law office was near the harbor park. Russell was working on their house not far from Main. Everyone was close to town and close to the harbor pavilion. If a trap was to be set, what better place than the dim woods where Iris met death?

Annie reached out, gripped Billy's arm. "The woods by the pavilion."

"Hold on, Mavis." Billy turned to Annie, his expression skeptical. "The old murderer-returning-to-the-scene-of-the-crime?" As he spoke, his tone dismissive, his face changed. "By God, maybe you're right." He spoke fast into the mike. "Alert Lou and Hyla. Send them to the harbor pavilion and the site where the body was found. Warn them. Body armor and guns. If they get there in time, there may be an armed and dangerous suspect."

The Volvo raced a scant six feet behind the cruiser. Red lights whirling, siren blasting, the cruiser and Volvo careened around stopped cars, brought traffic to a standstill on Main Street.

Annie's heart thudded. She lacked the cool-headed nerves required for EMTs and police. She grimly kept the pace even though barreling past stopped cars and through intersections made her palms sweat and her stomach knot.

The cruiser slid to a stop in the pavilion parking lot. Billy was out and running, lightly for a big man, toward the entrance to the woods. Annie felt shaky as she slammed her door and hurried around the car to pull out the wheelchair for Max and set it up.

As he swung from the car to the wheelchair, Max banged

a foot and gave a grunt of pain. Even so, he didn't pause, turning the chair toward the woods.

Annie gripped Max's shoulder. "We'd better wait. Lou and Hyla are armed."

Max frowned. "I'll go. You stay here. I set up that damn reward."

Annie tightened her grip. "Whatever happens, that's not why Darlene called." She drew in a breath as Hyla Harrison, eyes wary, thin frame tensed, edged from the woods, pistol in hand. She glanced at them, swiftly scanned the area near the pavilion, then hurried across the uneven ground. "Have you seen anyone? Any cars? Heard anyone?"

Max gestured toward the pavilion. "There aren't any cars in the pavilion lot, only ours and Billy's."

Harrison nodded. "Thanks. I'll swing around on the perimeter, check the other entrance to the woods." When she came even with them, she gestured at the woods. "The area is closed. No admittance until further notice. Crime scene."

Annie tried to call out, demand to know, but she had no breath. Surely Harrison meant the place where Iris died. That was a crime scene.

The officer passed them, then slowed as she neared the end of the pine grove, once again moving with care, as if danger awaited around the end of the grove.

The woods ran east and west. Pines and live oaks with a mingling of magnolias and bayberries spread from the boardwalk by the harbor to the pavilion parking lot and from the picnic area to an apartment house, running perhaps two hundred yards in length and three hundred in width. Friday night they'd found Iris lying not far from the entrance near the boardwalk. Friday night the crime lab had parked near the harbor entrance. This afternoon as the shadows lengthened and the sun slid lower in the west, Billy had disappeared into the woods from the pavilion entrance. There was yet another entrance near the apartment house that intersected the picnic-to-harbor path.

Max shouted after the policewoman. "Where's Billy? What's happening?"

Sgt. Harrison looked back. She hesitated, then jerked her head toward the woods. "He's waiting for the M.E."

∿ *Sixteen* ∿

ANNIE DREW HER sweater close. She felt drained. The caw of seabirds and the slap of water against Fish Haul pier were a mournful accompaniment to the activity near the woods. Just so had they stood on Friday night. Now, as the sun slipped westward, they waited again.

Red lights revolved atop cruisers. The crime van was parked as near the path as possible. Doc Burford's dusty old coupe came around the corner, slewed to a stop by the van.

Max stared at the woods. "You'd think somebody would come out."

Murder can be quick. Gathering evidence takes time. A painstaking examination had begun, drawing in toward the body after a careful survey, looking for any trace of the killer. Once Doc Burford spoke, the body could be photographed and examined.

It was five-thirty when Doc Burford stumped out of the woods, big and burly, his face red with anger. He stopped beside them.

"Darlene Hopper?" Annie waited without hope.

"Darlene Hopper. Age twenty-eight. White, female." He

threw words out like chunks of dirty ice. "Quick. Nasty. Final. Carbon copy. Knocked on the head, stunned, strangled. This time with a strand of wire."

The break room at the police station was spare and simple. John Wayne movie posters decorated one wall. A huge bulletin board held notes, circulars, and alerts. Billy Cameron sat at a long Formica-topped table with three chairs to a side and one at each end. Billy pushed aside a long legal pad and opened the brown paper sack. "Ben makes the best hamburger in the Low Country. Thanks." He unfolded the waxy wrapper. "I sent everybody else home. You two had dinner?"

From another sack, Annie lifted Styrofoam cups filled with Ben Parotti's dark roast Colombian. "We ate at Parotti's." She pulled out a chair and Max took a seat opposite her.

Max flipped off the lid of his cup. "I checked the time. Darlene called me at 3:52 p.m."

Billy spoke with his mouth full. "Lou and Hyla found her dead at 4:26 p.m. Hell of it is, she made only one call on her cell, the call to you. I thought it would be simple. Check out the records, see who she called, break out the handcuffs." Billy sounded discouraged. "It looks like she didn't call anyone. She must have tracked down one of the classmates she saw walk into the woods with Iris. Or she found a phone we don't know about, at the library or in an office."

Max turned his cup, watched a circle of steam. "Have you tracked the pay phone on the boardwalk?"

"No calls to any of the classmates." Billy shrugged. "We don't get an easy lead." His gaze was dark and cold. "I've checked them all out." He glanced at Annie and Max. "I don't discuss live investigations. But," his tone was wry, "sometimes I think out loud." He ate half of his hamburger, ignored them, staring at the opposite wall. "We got a time frame of thirty-four minutes. Buck Carlisle had told the secretary not to disturb him. He decided to take a walk to clear his head. He didn't know what time he went out or when he got back. Buck said he walked out to the pier. He has a French door. Easy out, easy in. Fran Carlisle delivered a gold cherub to St. Mary's. The church secretary wasn't in her office, but the door was unlocked. Fran left the cherub on the counter. Who's to say she didn't park by the south entrance to the woods, meet Darlene there? Ditto Russell Montgomery. Claims he was scouting a new job site a half-mile from the park. Didn't see anybody. Liz Montgomery had closed her shop, claims she was painting a plate in the rear room. Cara Wilkes was on the north end of the island, setting up her sign in front of a new listing. Nobody home. Maybe she did, maybe she didn't. Maybe she had time left over for a detour by the pavilion." Billy took a last bite of hamburger, ate with no apparent pleasure.

Annie turned the cup in a circle. "Cara came to the store. She swears somebody stole the gas tin. She's scared you'll arrest her. I told her the only way for her to be safe was to tell the truth about the night Jocelyn died."

Billy's gaze sharpened. "What did she say?"

"She ran away." Annie took a deep breath. "She's protecting Buck." She paused, added sadly, "Or herself."

Max massaged the back of his neck. "It always seems to come back to Buck. He was late to work this morning. He said he overslept. I'm sure he was lying about that night in the woods with Jocelyn."

Annie remembered fire and smoke. "The murderer was

out late." She turned to Billy. "I'd know if Max left our bed in the middle of the night. What do Buck and Fran say? And Russell and Liz?"

"According to their statements, nobody stirred. As for Cara, there's no one to say." Billy stirred two packets of sugar into coffee pale with half-and-half from the break-room refrigerator. He drank half the cup and looked at Max. "You talked to Buck this morning. You think he lied?"

Max looked somber. "He lied."

Max's folders with the bios were spread across the square teak coffee table. Emma's blue caftan swirled as she came around the sofa with a tray. She placed a glass of sherry in front of Annie, handed Max a Scotch and soda, then settled on the red velvet cushions in her matching teak chair. She sipped a rum and Coke. "Mmm, good stuff. Maybe it's time to take *Marigold's Pleasure* and head south again."

Annie almost blurted out how wonderful it would be if Emma took Laurel and Henny with her as she had on a recent trip. The words trembled on Annie's tongue, then she glanced at Max. It wouldn't do to infer that she always welcomed his mother's absence.

Emma perched half-glasses on her blunt nose and reached for a folder, and the opportunity passed. "First, we have crimes to solve. And I have a book to finish." Emma's stubby hand waved a folder. "Marigold is making progress. It is quite interesting how our cases parallel."

Annie maintained a bright smile. Emma had welcomed them to her home. It was no time to tell their hostess in a strangled voice that Marigold Rembrandt wasn't real and suggest that Emma stop including Marigold in the conversation as if the supercilious redhead, whose adventures had begun so long ago she must be nudging ninety, sat on the sofa between Annie and Max. As for a parallel, how big a surprise was that?

As if sensing Annie's hostility, Emma turned blue eyes on Annie. Her square face was set in determined lines. She spoke with the tiniest hint of an edge. "Marigold excels at picking out the apparently minor fact that matters. Now, we've all read the dossiers which Annie has nicely supplemented with Henny's memories of our suspects as high school seniors. We have a wealth of information. Anyone with true insight should be able to discern the driving compulsion of each person. I will announce a name and in turn, beginning with Annie, each of us will pinpoint the most important fact. This should be done quickly. No ruminating. The mind is always at its best if the immediate thought is revealed. I"—a satisfied smile—"will speak for Marigold." She picked up the first folder, looked at Annie and snapped "Fran."

"Fran's terrified." That was the overriding emotion Annie sensed when Fran came to Nightingale Courts Saturday morning. "I think she's scared for Buck. Why else would she come to tell me Russell and Jocelyn were angry with each other?"

Emma's gaze turned. "Max?"

"Fran commuted on the ferry to a job on the mainland when they were seniors so she didn't spend much time with her school friends. How would Fran have any idea about Iris dealing drugs?" He gingerly shifted a foot. "Why would Fran care if Jocelyn was pregnant?"

Emma pursed her lips. "Marigold notes that Fran quit working on the mainland that spring. Could that be related to the deaths of Sam and Jocelyn? There doesn't seem to be any correlation, but it is an anomaly. Why give up the job that gave her extra money?"

Annie couldn't resist contradicting Marigold. "Where's Marigold's sense of romance? Cara and Buck broke up, Fran quits working on the mainland, and pretty soon Fran has good old Buck in tow. Buck didn't have the quarterback cachet, but Fran could always see past high school. Who was the most eligible bachelor from one of the best families on the island?"

"Possibly." Emma's tone dismissed the suggestion. She slapped the folder on the table, picked up the next. "Buck."

Annie felt sad. "He was a yellow bird. He and Iris. They struggled in school. But"—she struggled to put a nebulous thought into words—"whoever killed Jocelyn and Iris was decisive, quick. Merciless. Could Buck plan that well?"

Max stared into the amber gold liquid in his glass. "Buck's a lawyer. He may be slow, but he's capable of planning. Everybody likes Buck. I do, too. I would have said he was honest, that he could be trusted. Now I'm not sure."

Emma poked her glasses higher on her nose. "Marigold adores big burly guys who are hapless. But nice guys turn rough if they're backed into a corner. Why, in *The Case of the Terrified Tenor* there was an opera star who was an absolute dear, charming as Pavarotti. I hated making him the murderer. Marigold and I tussled over that one. As for Buck, he claims he told Jocelyn that Iris gave the cocaine to Sam. Maybe he was the hidden figure. Maybe he supplied the cocaine to Iris."

Annie tried to picture Buck as a fledgling drug dealer. She shook her head. "Buck seems too transparent for that."

Max shrugged. "It could have been something exciting to do. Until Sam died."

Emma put down Buck's folder, lifted a cream-colored folder. "Liz."

Annie didn't hesitate. "Scary. Fran's scared and Liz is scary. Liz would do anything to protect Russell."

Max shook his head. "Liz strikes me as utterly conventional. Would she marry Russell if she knew about Jocelyn's pregnancy?" He looked from Annie to Emma.

Their answers came together, Annie's decisive, Emma's brusque. "Yes."

He looked puzzled.

Annie reached out, touched his knee. "If a man is your man, you take him on any terms." She glanced at Emma and knew she understood. Beneath Emma's crusty exterior a memory of passion still burned bright. Emma once enjoyed a rollicking adventurous marriage. As a widow, she married a man who betrayed her. That husband fell to his death from *Marigold's Pleasure*. Some still wondered if Ricky's drowning was an accident.

Emma's eyes narrowed. "Marigold strikes to the heart of relationships. If Jocelyn threatened Russell, Liz might have quarreled with her. At the end of the pier." She added Liz's folder to the stack, picked up the next. "Russell."

Annie blurted, "He couldn't go to The Citadel if he had to marry Jocelyn."

Max looked angry. "He followed me to the Franklin house, threatened me. He blames Annie and me for Billy's suspicions. Whatever else Russell's done, I know he shot that snake, put it on my desk."

Emma flicked a bright red nail against the green folder. "Interesting how things turn out for Russell. Jocelyn's pregnant and first thing you know she's dead and cremated. Iris comes back to the island because of Jocelyn's death and now

Iris is dead. Darlene witnessed a quarrel between Russell and Jocelyn. Now Darlene is dead. There's no proof at all against Russell." She slapped down the folder, picked up the last. "Cara."

Annie felt hollow inside. "The gas tin found behind our cabin belonged to her. She insists someone broke into her garage and stole it."

Max nodded. "I think she's telling the truth. Cara's not dumb. Why would she leave the tin? She mows her own yard. She had to realize her fingerprints were on the tin."

Emma was impatient. "Marigold points out a double bluff isn't a bad strategy. Maybe Duane startled her and she tossed the gas tin to be able to move faster. Even more telling"—Emma's gentian blue eyes were cold—"she told Annie she was scared—but she wasn't scared enough to reveal what she knew about the sports picnic. That suggests two possibilities to Marigold. Cara is protecting Buck. Or she's protecting herself. When we consider everyone, Russell appears to have the strongest motive. Jocelyn's death may not be connected to drugs. Jocelyn may have died because she was pregnant."

Annie felt a swell of repugnance. Some fathers did kill women carrying their children. Scott and Laci Peterson were a sad example.

Emma absently turned the ruby ring on her left hand and the stone flashed in the light. "Liz had a powerful motive. However, if Jocelyn died because of drugs, Buck may be hiding information. Here's Marigold's take. Buck is hiding the truth about his talk with Jocelyn. Fran knows more than she's telling or why would she be worried about Buck? Liz is terrified for Russell. We might"—Emma looked like a cat ready to pounce on a mouse—"be able to use her fear to our advantage. Russell's tough and turns ugly when he feels cornered."

Max's face was drawn in the firelight. Annie knew his feet hurt. Pain was worse at night. So were heartbreak and memories of death.

Max's eyes narrowed. "Don't worry. I'm going to watch out for Russell. But we have to remember someone used Iris in dealing drugs. I don't know which one of them is the most likely to have dealt drugs."

Annie felt like a gerbil on a familiar wheel. They needed fresh insight. She looked at Emma. Maybe they needed—difficult as it was to admit—Marigold's counsel. The story unfolding in Emma's head was based on fact, Emma's stealthy entrance to Cabin Six. "What's happening in your book?"

Emma again touched her ruby ring. Annie had often wondered where she had obtained the magnificent ring in its ornate gold setting with a circlet of diamonds. In the light of the fire, it blazed with a glow equal to sunrise on the desert.

"I keep rewriting that scene when Marigold steps into the cabin. I don't have a picture in my mind. I must drop by Nightingale Courts and look into a cabin." Emma looked grim. "I don't remember a thing after I picked up that stack of towels. I'm not sure I really remember that. You told me I'd taken the towels to the cabin. So I suppose I did. Yet, at the hospital something reminded me of the moment before I was hurt. Marigold keeps trying to think what it could be. A sound? A smell? A reflection?" She looked hopefully at Annie.

Annie concentrated. "Your attacker came from behind the door. But the door didn't make a noise." She smiled. "There are no squeaky doors in Duane's world. As for a smell . . ." Annie's sharpest memory was of Clorox, but she'd been cleaning a cabin. The cabins themselves were bright and fresh. Duane and Ingrid disdained deodorizers. "The cabins all smell fresh with a hint of the marsh. As for seeing your attacker, the mirror doesn't face the door." Annie stood up. She pointed at a Navajo rug in front of the fireplace, touched the fringe with the tip of her shoe. "This is the doorsill." She reached forward, grasped an imaginary knob, swung the door open to the right. "When you stepped inside, you were only a few feet from the bed. In a quick glance, that's what you would have seen and perhaps the door to the bathroom. There was scarcely any evidence the cabin was occupied. Iris only had a few things with her and they were in the closet or the dresser."

"I almost remembered." Emma was irritated. "Something in the hospital took me back to the cabin." She lifted a hand, touched the small gauze bandage on her forehead. "Well, it hasn't come. Perhaps it will. In any event, I know what we must do."

Annie looked at her with interest and Max with a touch of amusement. Emma sounded utterly confident. As far as Annie could see, they'd made no progress and were no nearer knowing the identity of their elusive quarry.

Emma's aggressive gaze sharpened. "I propose a gathering of friends. At the pavilion. Tomorrow night. All of them profess distress at the deaths of Jocelyn and Iris. The two of you will invite them. You will confide oh so charmingly that you know everyone wants to learn of the progress being made in the investigation, that startling new developments will be revealed." Now her smile was coldly triumphant. "No one will dare decline even though the night holds terrors for those afraid."

Annie realized Emma was quoting from *The Bishop Wore Scarlet,* admittedly one of her better books. Marigold Rembrandt enjoyed gathering all the suspects for a denouement. So did Nick and Nora.

Annie knew it was a thin hope, but there was a chance they might actually discover something new.

Max looked energized. "They kept things secret for years. Think what a shock it will be when we lay everything out."

Emma nodded as if at a bright pupil. "Exactly. We will have a most instructive evening."

Annie moved restlessly, trying not to waken Max. Everything hinged on tomorrow night. But oh how wonderful it would be if they had some inkling before they all met at the pavilion. Maybe tomorrow she could come up with something concrete. She remembered the expression on Emma's face in the hospital. Emma knew something that mattered. Tomorrow Annie was going to look that hospital room over. Something there . . . Her eyes began to close. She tugged on the cover.

"Ouch." Max jerked up a foot.

She pushed up on an elbow. "I'm sorry. Did I hurt your foot?"

"Not a problem." He murmured drowsily as he turned toward her. "As a matter of fact"—he didn't now sound sleepy—"I know a cure for all hurts, big or little."

Annie turned toward him. Love cured many ills and pushed away dark memories. She came into his arms.

The morning was picture-perfect April, the air soft and fresh and only slightly cool, sweaters sufficing in the shade of Emma's terrace. Sea oats wavered on the dunes. The jade green sea was placid. A gleaming white yacht rode at anchor far out toward the horizon.

Annie wished they could while the day away, walk out onto the sand, plunge into the surf, come up feeling fresh and fine and free. Staying at Emma's was like a holiday in a posh hotel, superb meals arriving on carts and a sense of endless time. They'd already lingered over breakfast for more than an hour.

Max poured coffee into Annie's cup. "Even if Emma's dramatizing herself and creating her own version of a fictional denouement, gathering at the pavilion is a good idea." He filled his own cup. "Once we get the ball rolling, who knows what will happen." He looked concerned. "Are you worried?"

Annie had the starring role. She'd never envisioned herself as lead prosecutor, but it was Annie who had heard Darlene's revelations. "I'll handle it." Perhaps she spoke only a shade too quickly. Could she bring Darlene to life before that reluctant gathering, make them see her sadness and grief and anguish?

∻ *Seventeen* ∾

ANNIE STEPPED INSIDE Yesterday's Treasures.

Fran stood near a counter, one hand on a cobalt blue crystal perfume bottle. A garnet necklace blazed against the creamy beige of her tailored linen dress. Embroidered eyelet on the neckline and hem transformed the dress from ordinary to chic. Fran was the epitome of elegance except for her drawn face and shadowed eyes. She stared at Annie without a word of greeting.

Annie felt a pang of unhappiness. Where was the Fran she knew, laughing and energetic and always busy? Annie didn't know this stone-faced woman with burning eyes.

Annie steeled herself to speak. The sooner she finished, the sooner she could hurry away from the hurt of a friendship that had apparently ended. "Max and I have learned a great deal about the night Jocelyn died."

Fran's eyes never left Annie's face. Her fingers tightened on the sterling silver screw top of the perfume bottle.

Annie spoke into cold silence. "We know everyone who cared for Jocelyn and Iris and everyone who knew

Darlene"—her classmates hadn't been Darlene's friends, Darlene made that clear—"are hoping the truth will be discovered." Annie felt as if she tossed words into a well.

Fran unclasped her grip from the bottle. She spun turquoise-studded silver bracelets in a nervous jangle. Finally, she spoke. "How can anyone ever know the truth? It's nonsense to say someone killed Jocelyn. She either fell or jumped from the pier. She wasn't herself that night. Everyone knows she was upset. As for Iris and Darlene, they could have been involved with sleazy people."

Annie wondered if Fran believed what she was saying or if she was trying desperately to turn the investigation away from those who had good reason to wish Jocelyn dead. If the former, she was due for heartbreak. If the latter, she was motivated by fear either for herself or Buck.

Annie shook her head. "The murders of Iris and Darlene resulted from Jocelyn's death. Tonight we're going to share what we know. Seven o'clock. At the pavilion."

Fran wrapped her arms across her front. Her face was drawn, her eyes empty.

Annie pushed through the door, hurrying into April sunlight and the bustle of Main Street. She carried with her the image of a desolate woman.

Max stopped the golf cart near the French door of Buck Carlisle's office. Max leaned out and knocked on a pane.

Buck looked toward the sound. He stared, then put down a sheaf of papers and pushed back his chair. When he opened the French door, he blocked the way inside. "Sorry, Max. I've got a deadline." Buck looked tired and defensive.

Max nodded. "I won't interrupt. Tonight Annie and I are going to explain everything we've discovered about Jocelyn.

Seven o'clock. The pavilion." Max turned the wheelchair. When he reached the sidewalk, he looked back.

Buck stood like a statue. He wasn't looking at Max. Buck stared across the bay at Fish Haul pier.

Liz Montgomery sacked up a middle-aged tourist's purchase. "I put plenty of bubble wrap in the box. You should be able to check this in your luggage or mail it. Please think about us when you're next on the island."

Annie waited near a rosewood cabinet filled with Dresden figurines.

As the gray-haired shopper bustled past, Liz slowly turned toward Annie. Liz's face was heavy and cold, her blue eyes bleak.

Annie wished they'd called everyone on the telephone. That had been her suggestion, immediately vetoed by Max and Emma. Both hoped for some revealing response to the invitation. Annie knew she was getting a good idea of just how upset everyone was. Was that a plus? She returned Liz's cool gaze with equal frost. "There's going to be a meeting tonight at the pavilion for Jocelyn's friends. Seven o'clock."

She turned to go.

A sharp voice stopped her. "Why should I come?"

Annie swung around. Her answer was rock hard. "Why shouldn't you?"

Max thanked Russell Montgomery's secretary, slipped his cell phone in his pocket. He steered the silent electric golf cart off the main drive. Once again he enjoyed the delights of his new mode of transportation, the dappled shade on the bike paths, the scent of pine, the cheerful chitter of birds and squirrels. The path was circuitous, but it brought him in only a few minutes to Sand Dune Road, home to the island's lumberyard and a half-dozen modest warehouses.

Russell Montgomery stood on the flat roof of a weathered wooden building. He gestured as two workers used brushes to sweep a sticky black mass of coal tar across the roof. The pungent odor of hot tar overrode the smell of pines.

Max stopped the cart far enough from the structure that Russell would be able to see him. "Hey, Russell."

At his shout, Russell slowly turned and looked down. Perhaps the slighter stature of the Latino workmen, though obviously wiry and strong, made Russell appear even larger, more formidable. He stood with his broad shoulders back, his feet planted apart, his blue work shirt rolled to his bulky forearms. After an instant of immobility, he moved swiftly, reached the parapet, swung over the side, and came down the ladder with familiar ease.

When he reached the cart, he stood with his arms folded. His strong face was studiously unrevealing. "You can take occupancy on the Franklin house next Monday. I'll make a final check Friday, but everything looks on track." He spoke with constraint. "There won't be any charge for the repairs."

"Or for the dead snake?"

Not a muscle moved in Russell's face. There might have been a glint of satisfaction in his eyes. "Snake? You've lost me."

"Right. Nobody shot a rattler and threw it on my desk. Maybe we can talk about that tonight." Max's look was level. "I didn't come about the Franklin house."

Russell's hands dropped. "In that event, our discussion is over." He turned away, walked toward his truck.

Max called after him. "You might be interested in coming to the pavilion tonight. Seven o'clock."

Russell kept walking.

"Everyone there will hear about the baby who never got to live."

Russell stopped. His shoulders bowed. His hands clenched into huge fists. He jerked around. "Damn you. Damn you to hell."

The anguished shout hung in Max's mind long after the truck roared to life and jolted down the gravel road to disappear in a cloud of dust.

Cara Wilkes's gamine face twisted in a scowl. "Why don't you leave me alone?" She lifted the hammer and pounded on the top rim of the For Sale sign. Behind her a modest gray bungalow looked comfortable and welcoming in the soft morning sunshine though it had the air of emptiness common to uninhabited structures.

Annie would have liked to wrap her arms around Cara's thin shoulders, offer comfort. "I'm sorry."

Cara lifted the hammer, let it fall to her side. Her lips trembled. "Everything's horrible. Hideous. Hateful. I used to have bad dreams about Jocelyn. You don't think you are going to die when you are eighteen. It was as if all the color bled away, as if the world was strange and everything familiar was off-kilter. The stars at night made me feel as if everything could disappear in an instant. I left the island and it got better and then everything was worse. You don't know"—she looked at Annie with eyes glazed by sorrow—"what I would give if Melissa could have lived to be eighteen or twenty-eight. My baby was two when she died."

Annie did reach out now, touched a rigid arm. "I'm sorry, Cara."

"Sorry's nice." Cara's voice was once again brittle as

Annie had so often heard it, aloof, disengaged, distancing her from pain. "Nice, but it doesn't help. Nothing helps. Except God. I know Melissa's fine now. I'm the one who isn't fine."

Annie moved closer, slipped her arms around Cara's stiff body, held her for an instant, then stepped back.

Cara rubbed her eyes with a thin hand. "No one should have to die young, not Melissa, not Jocelyn, not Iris, not Darlene. I'll come tonight."

Annie stood with her back against the door. It was an ordinary hospital room, at the moment unoccupied. Small. Narrow. A TV mounted on the wall opposite the bed. Open door to the bathroom. One window, a western exposure.

There had been three of them present, Annie, Pamela Potts, and Emma. Annie pictured Emma in the bed, head bandaged, face pale, spiky hair drooping, frowsy in a wrinkled hospital gown, one arm linked to an IV, but her blue eyes were alert and searching. She'd looked at Annie, snapped a crusty complaint. "My head hurts."

Annie had placed the vase with three dozen pink carnations next to the planter with Liz Montgomery's lavender blooms. Pamela had held out both the Homestead Purple and Annie's carnations for Emma to admire. The room had been fragrant with the scent of flowers, including roses from the Altar Guild.

Emma's eyes had fluttered closed, then opened. She spoke a few words, stopped. She'd started to remember what had happened to her and the memory fled.

What in this unadorned room had brought back the circumstances of her injury?

Nowhere in the confines of the room did there appear

to be anything to trigger Emma's memory. Annie looked outside at a majestic magnolia. In the afternoon, the glossy green leaves would shine. This was an old hospital. Had the window been lifted for fresh air? Pamela was a firm believer in fresh air.

Annie nodded. There had been a slight fresh breeze. Perhaps Emma heard the clack of magnolia leaves, a quick snapping sound like a step. Annie walked to the window, lifted the sash, heard the rattle of magnolia leaves and the faint clink of the metal rings on the flagpole.

Billy built a steeple with his fingers. When Max finished speaking, Billy took his time answering. Finally, he shrugged. "I don't think this murderer's going to be rattled by a confrontation, no matter how unpleasant it is. But it can't do any harm for you to talk to them." Billy's smile was dour. "It should be safe enough with the whole group there. Let me know what happens."

Shadows from the pines threw the picnic ground in dark shadow, broken only by occasional lamplights and the gleam from the interior of the open-air pavilion. In the distance, the lights on the boardwalk were in bright contrast to the darkness of the water beyond. The last vestiges of sunset streaked the sky with tendrils of crimson.

Emma led the way, marching up the pavilion steps as if to a throne. Annie wondered if she'd ever achieve the mystery author's compelling presence. The answer was swift. Not in this lifetime or any other.

Balanced on the edge of a foot, Max swung the crutches over the last step into the pavilion. Annie was afraid he was rushing his progress and knew from the tightness of his face and the careful way he placed his feet that walking was hard.

Annie came last. Only a few days before, she'd been eager to greet their guests, a cheerful milling throng. Would she ever come to the harbor pavilion again without a feeling of dread? In the distance, mourning doves gave their soft cry.

Emma appeared affected by the silence of the cavernous pavilion and the stark metal-shaded lights that hung from the ridgepole, affording occasional spots of brightness that emphasized the gloom of the perimeter. She stood with hands on her hips, tonight's fringed caftan a swirl of georgette with alternating blocks of orange and green enlivened by embroidery of bold black dragons.

Emma swung a dismissive hand at the pavilion's picnic tables. "Those aren't suitable. People sitting on either side reminds me of a boardroom." She scanned the area, gave a decisive nod.

Emma pointed at the low brick wall that separated the fireplace from the main expanse of the pavilion. "Excellent. The overhead light shines there. We'll invite everyone to sit on the wall. We'll stand there." She gestured to a spot a few feet away.

Obediently, Annie's gaze followed. Maybe Emma had a talent. Definitely she had a gift for the dramatic. If their guests complied, they would be in harsh relief, their hosts—interrogators?—in shadow.

They walked up the pavilion steps, footsteps echoing. Not one of the five classmates spoke.

Annie knew she would never forget their silence, five faces that struggled to reveal nothing, five classmates forever bound to the pavilion by heartbreak and violence.

Cara came last, walking by herself. She stood a little distance away from the two couples. Emma looked about, as if seeking inspiration. Her gaze stopped at the low wall. She gestured. "Please take a seat on the wall. We'll be brief."

After a disdainful look at the dusty bricks, Liz shrugged and gingerly sat. She folded her arms, her face hostile. Russell sat heavily beside her. He had an old athlete's look of dominance, shoulders bullish, hands planted on his thighs. He looked ready for a fight.

Fran dropped down next to Russell. She pushed back a tangle of dark curls, jingling her silver bracelets. She was pale, though she'd obviously made her usual effort to be stylish. Ebony linen trousers emphasized the Florentine orange of her floral jacquard top. A glum Buck settled beside her. He stared at the floor. Cara was last. She left extra space between her and Buck. To Annie, the space emphasized Cara's awareness of him.

Emma moved nearer the wall. She was impressive, character and determination in her square face, cool intelligence in her gaze. "One of you decided ten years ago that Jocelyn Howard had to die." Her brusque voice was intimidating.

Annie expected denials, recriminations, exclamations of innocence.

The only sound was the cry of the doves.

"From that decision flowed Iris's murder"—Emma's indictment was inexorable—"the attempt to kill Annie and Max, and Darlene's murder. All of you know some part of what happened ten years ago. Tonight the innocent will have an opportunity to speak out and bring an end to a desperate murderer who lashes out at any perceived threat." Emma looked at each of the five in turn. "If you are reluctant to reveal what you know, understand that no one is safe until Jocelyn's killer is found."

Cara shivered. She gave a soft cry of distress. She looked shrunken, as if her black silk jacket was too large.

Buck's turn toward her was immediate. And immediately halted.

Fran's eyes were dark. A muscle flickered in her slender throat.

Buck hunched his shoulders and again stared down at the floor.

Emma was crisp. "Annie will share newly discovered information that tells us a great deal about Jocelyn's last night."

Annie clasped her hands together. She was aware of anger and fear. She felt her own wash of fear. Billy had warned them. *Don't taunt a tiger.* What choice did they have? She took a breath and spoke, trying to keep her voice steady. "Everything goes back to the sports picnic ten years ago. You were close friends." Annie looked at each in turn. "Liz. Russell. Fran. Buck. Cara." She took another breath. "And Sam and Jocelyn. Darlene Hopper was in your class. None of you had anything to do with her. Except Jocelyn. Jocelyn was nice to Darlene. Darlene loved Jocelyn. I talked to Darlene yesterday." Yesterday Darlene had been alive.

Annie looked from face to face, Fran wary, Buck grim, Liz angry, Russell bleak, Cara frightened. To some who listened, the revelations would be shocking. Others knew only too well. Yesterday in the alley, sullen Darlene had shed her toughness, her loneliness. Long-ago passions had awakened. She set out to avenge Jocelyn's death, but she'd run to meet her own. "At the sports picnic, Russell made every effort to avoid Jocelyn. Darlene said Russell looked mean."

Russell's hard face revealed nothing. His steady gaze never wavered.

Liz's eyes glittered with anger. "Russell didn't look mean. He was upset. His best friend was dead."

"Darlene told me." Annie's voice was sad. "Darlene said Jocelyn came up behind Russell, caught his arm. She was crying."

"Of course she was crying." Liz's voice was harsh. "Her brother was dead, you fool."

Annie shut out Liz's voice, but she couldn't escape Russell's anguished eyes. "Darlene followed Jocelyn and Russell when they left the pavilion. They went on the path toward the woods. When they were far enough from the pavilion not to be heard, Jocelyn told Russell she needed help. Russell said he couldn't do anything. She grabbed his arm and said, 'I'm not talking about the baby.'"

Cara's lips parted in an *O* of surprise. Liz's pale face flushed. She sat rigid as stone. Russell folded his arms, appearing massive and immovable. He did not look toward his wife. Buck's eyes widened. Fran watched warily, turning the thin silver bracelets on her wrist.

"Darlene cried out in shock." Annie wondered if they could hear that piteous cry in their hearts. "Jocelyn saw her and screamed at her to go away. Darlene ran. That was the last time Darlene saw Jocelyn."

Annie looked at Russell with grave, questioning eyes.

Russell said nothing. His face was empty, defeated.

Liz turned to him, clutched at his arm. "Tell them what happened."

Russell jerked toward her in surprise.

Liz's voice was sharp. "Tell them, Russell."

Russell tried to speak, stopped. His face crumpled.

Liz struggled to control her breathing. She was dangerously flushed. "I went after Russell when I saw Jocelyn pulling him into the fog. Darlene was ahead of me. I stayed off the path. No one heard me. I heard every word. When Darlene ran away, I came nearer. Jocelyn didn't ask Russell for help for the baby."

Russell turned a tear-streaked face to his wife. "You knew? You've known all these years?"

She took his big hand, held it tight. Her face was open and vulnerable. "I've always known."

His voice was uneven. "You don't despise me?"

"Oh God, honey. You were only a boy. I don't know what you should have done. That night I hated her. I wanted her dead."

The words hung in the silent pavilion.

Emma's blue eyes were cold. "She died."

Liz shuddered. "I didn't kill her. I know Russell didn't. His dad . . . Russell couldn't have gone to The Citadel. It was his dad's dream. Maybe Jocelyn could have had the baby, put it up for adoption. I don't know. All I know is that Russell didn't go into the woods with Jocelyn. Tell them, Russell."

With Liz's hand in his, Russell spoke in short, harsh bursts. "I've gone over that night in my mind. A million times. I let Jocelyn down. I should have stood by her. She and I weren't right for each other. I'd already realized it was Liz I wanted, but I should have stood by Jocelyn. I don't think she wanted to marry me. She had plans, too. I don't know what she would have done, but she didn't come to me because of the baby. She wanted help because of the note. She found a note in Sam's letter jacket. He wore the jacket the night he died. The note was dated Friday. The message was brief: Pick me up at midnight at the foot of the drive. It was signed by Buck. The last Friday Sam wore the jacket was the night he died, a week before the picnic. Jocelyn wanted me to come with her to confront Buck. I told Jocelyn it didn't matter if Buck was with Sam that night. Buck didn't snort cocaine for him. I asked Jocelyn to drop it." He took a deep breath. "She wouldn't agree. I told her I wasn't going to go after Buck. She said she'd go by herself."

Fran came to her feet. "You aren't going to make Buck the fall guy. Buck may have known something about Sam's death, but he wasn't the father of a baby no one wanted." Resentment burned in every word.

Liz was implacable. "Jocelyn left Russell and went to find Buck."

Fran flung out her hands, her bracelets jangling. Her ravaged face twisted in anger. "You and Russell have had plenty of time to invent whatever you please. Ten years of time. The baby would be pretty big by now. Ten years old. But daddy wouldn't be a Citadel man, would he?"

Russell rubbed at reddened eyes. "Shut up, Fran."

"Ten years old . . ." Fran's voice wavered. She began to cry. "Oh God, I'm sorry."

"You think you're sorry." Russell's voice was unsteady. "How do you think I feel? All these years I thought Jocelyn jumped off the pier. But now . . ." He looked toward Buck.

"I didn't hurt Jocelyn." Buck's big open face looked haunted. "She told me she asked Russell for help and he refused. She and I went into the woods, but Jocelyn wasn't scared of me. She was furious. I told her to let it go, that Sam was dead, that nothing would bring him back, to let him rest in peace." Buck's hands opened and closed, opened and closed. "I wish to God I could rest in peace.

I've kept that night when Sam died a secret for ten years. I've always felt sick and ashamed. I'm tired of feeling like a coward. Oh hell, I was a coward. My dad would have kicked me out. I guess I could have gone to jail. I don't know. I would have been in big trouble. I tried to make Jocelyn understand. I couldn't have helped Sam." He came to a full stop, swallowed hard. "But I left him there, dead in the forest preserve."

Max's tone was sharp. "Did Sam pick you up at midnight?"

Buck avoided looking at Max. "I had a midnight curfew. There was an old live oak near my window and I used to climb down and meet Sam at the foot of the drive. My folks went to bed at ten. They never knew. That night was like any other. Sam was in a great mood. When I first started sneaking out, we'd take a couple of six-packs to the forest preserve and drink and think we were studs. Pretty soon Sam started bringing whiskey. He had no trouble getting bourbon at his place. His mom never knew how much she had, she just bought more. Then Sam started snorting cocaine. I never did. He ragged me, told me I was chicken. I told him I liked bourbon better. That Friday night we went to a clearing in the preserve like we always did. We got out of the car. I was pouring some bourbon into a plastic glass. I heard a choking sound and looked up. Sam was shaking and then he fell face forward. I rolled him over." Buck looked sick. "He was dead." He looked up in appeal. "Even if I'd called nine-one-one, it was too late. He was dead. I tried pushing on his chest. Maybe I didn't do it right, but it didn't matter. Nothing helped."

Emma cleared her throat. "What did Jocelyn threaten to do?"

Buck looked hapless. "She was going to tell the police. I don't know what they would have done. My dad would have kicked me out. Conduct unbecoming a gentleman." His tone put the stiff words in quote marks, as if he'd heard them and hated them for many years. "I told Jocelyn it wasn't my fault. Sam got the cocaine from Iris. Jocelyn said it didn't matter how Sam got cocaine, I shouldn't have gone off and left him like a dog that had been hit by a car. Yeah, that's what I did. I was scared. I know that's no excuse. But I couldn't have saved him. He was dead, lying there in the moonlight, his face like marble." He shuddered. "It happened so fast, he was laughing and swaggering like he always did, and then he died."

Emma was blunt. "You were in the woods alone with Jocelyn. You were desperate to keep Jocelyn quiet."

Buck straightened, his broad face earnest. "I didn't hurt Jocelyn. I swear I didn't. When she wouldn't listen, I didn't know what was going to happen. But there was nothing I could do. I left her there in the woods and went back to the picnic. Coach Butterworth asked me what was going on and I told him Jocelyn was upset about Sam. I thought he'd probably go and see and then I'd be done for. Instead he turned and went back to the picnic grounds. I told Jodie I was feeling sick and wasn't going to stay for the awards. She was getting a letter in swimming. She said a friend would bring her home. Mom and Dad were in Atlanta. I went to the parking lot behind the pavilion and got my car and went home. I sat up all night in my room in the dark, looking out the window, waiting for car lights to turn into the drive. I thought the police would come and get me."

Max's face was sad. "Did Iris see you walk into the woods with Jocelyn?"

Buck turned strained eyes to Max. "I don't know. But I never hurt Iris. Or Darlene."

Cara stood and stepped toward them. "Buck is telling the truth." Her voice was steady, weary. She glanced toward Liz. "I guess Liz and I wore our hearts on our sleeves back then. It paid off for Liz." Cara's angular face was passionless, as if she spoke of times so distant they didn't matter. "Liz followed Russell and Jocelyn. I followed Jocelyn and Buck. Buck told you the truth. He ran back toward the picnic grounds."

Annie looked at Cara and felt cold. When Iris came back to the island, Cara visited her at Nightingale Courts. Had Cara been summoned because she was the last person to be with Jocelyn? But how would Iris have known?

Cara ran nervous fingers through her tousled short curls. "I talked to Jocelyn."

Was there a ripple of fear in the pavilion?

Annie looked quickly from face to face. All of them bore signs of strain and despair and regret. Fran's cheekbones jutted. Her eyes locked on Cara's face. Buck's shoulders slumped. His expression was a mixture of misery and shame. Liz clung to Russell's arm, ready to defend him. Russell had an air of exhaustion, a man nearing the end of his endurance.

Cara spoke softly. "I begged Jocelyn not to tell on Buck. I told her how he'd grieved for Sam." Cara looked at Buck. "Buck was sick at heart. But Jocelyn . . ." Cara shivered. "She was angry, white hot with anger, like a fiery sword. I've always thought how sad that she died being angry. Anger sucks out your soul. I was angry when Melissa died, angry at the emptiness of my world, angry for the years she didn't have, angry at her father for running away. I had to root out the anger or it would have killed me. But Jocelyn was set on vengeance. She told me it didn't matter if Buck was sorry. Being sorry wasn't enough. She was going to talk to Iris and then she was going to go to the police."

Cara pulled her sweater closer. "That's the last time I saw her. She left me there and ran back toward the picnic to find Iris. I walked to the boardwalk and went home." In the silence, she said abruptly, "I didn't walk to the pier with Jocelyn and push her in the water. When Iris came back to the island, she called and asked me to come and see her at Nightingale Courts. I went there and we talked. I told her all that I knew. I told her that Buck left Jocelyn alive and I left her alive."

No one moved or spoke. The silence pulsed with anger, hurt, sadness, and despair. Liz's creamy complexion was tinged by gray. Russell slumped like a man who'd run too far and too fast. Fran's cheekbones were hard and sharp, her eyes brilliant. Buck looked diminished. Cara moved uneasily like a horse scenting danger.

Annie felt sickening disappointment. Even if every word they'd heard was true, there was not to be an answer. Iris had admitted that she told Jocelyn the name of the drug supplier. Any of the haunted faces there in the pavilion could have been the shadowy unseen figure who provided cocaine to Iris. Jocelyn may have died because she confronted that hidden dealer of death. But drugs might not be the reason Jocelyn's life ended in cold seawater. She may have died to hide Buck's presence in the forest preserve. She may have died because Russell was determined to escape responsibility for an unwanted baby. She may have died because Liz was possessed by jealousy. She may have died because Cara was determined to protect Buck.

Fran jumped up. "This is intolerable." Her voice was high

and fast. "Buck and I have nothing to do with this. We don't know what happened." She bolted forward.

Buck slowly stood, lifted a hand as if to keep Fran near.

Fran hurried past Emma, then stopped, turned, gestured to Buck. "Let's get out of here." Her bracelets jangled. "We don't have to listen to this." She was perhaps a foot behind Emma.

Emma stood utterly still, as if shocked into immobility, her blue eyes wide, her lips parted. Slowly a hand came up to touch the red scar visible against the purplish bruise on her forehead.

"Emma?" Annie took a step forward. The author wasn't that long from her stay in the hospital. Was she feeling faint?

Emma's caftan swirled as she slowly turned to face Fran. "You."

Fran drew in a sharp breath. Moving fast, Fran hurried to the wall and scooped up her purse. In four quick steps, she stood facing them, her eyes dark and empty.

Emma looked shaken. "I smelled your perfume."

Annie remembered the hospital room and the spicy scent of carnations.

Fran took another step back.

"I heard your bracelets." Emma once again touched her scar.

Through the open window of the hospital, flag rings had clanked against the pole.

Emma pointed at Fran. "You were behind the door in Iris's cabin."

Buck took a step forward. "Fran?" His voice was uncertain.

Russell came to his feet, hands clenched into fists. "Did

you kill Jocelyn? Why? Dear God, why?" His voice was ragged.

Fran's features were rigid. "Iris told Jocelyn she got cocaine from me. Jocelyn was going to go to the police. I got drugs at Frankie's, the club on the mainland where I worked. I dated a guy, a bartender. He sold drugs. He had an MG and cashmere sweaters and a Rolex. I didn't know it would kill anyone. I didn't mean for anyone to be hurt. I never wanted to hurt anyone." There was despair in her voice. "I didn't know Jocelyn was pregnant. We walked through the woods and went out on the pier. I promised I'd never sell drugs again. She wouldn't listen. She was going to tell the police and everything would have been ruined. I begged her not to go to the police. If she did, I would lose everything I'd worked for, going to school, having a decent life. I couldn't help it if Sam died. He didn't have to buy cocaine. If he hadn't bought cocaine from Iris, he'd have gotten it somewhere. But Jocelyn wouldn't listen."

Russell took a step toward her, his face implacable.

Fran yanked open her purse, pulled out a dark blue pistol.

"Fran!" Buck's voice shook. He reached out.

Russell tried to take another step, Liz came to her feet and flung herself toward him, clutched his arm, her face white.

Fran's dark hair stirred as the gentle breeze eddied through the pavilion. Her tone was almost conversational. "Russell, don't make me shoot." She stared mournfully at Buck. "I'm sorry, Buck. I'm sorry for everything, for taking your gun, for . . . everything. I didn't want to hurt anyone." She dropped her purse, held the gun steady with both hands. "I didn't have a choice. I told Iris that Jocelyn jumped, that I'd seen her jump and I'd show Iris what happened if we went to the pier. I'd always been afraid Iris would come home. She was the only one who knew about the drugs. If she told anyone, my life was ruined. If only she'd been willing to stay quiet . . . But she said she had to tell the truth. She had to die. I thought I was safe until I saw the story in the paper." She turned her tortured gaze toward Annie and Max. "I was afraid of what Iris might have told you. I got the gas tin from Cara's garage. But you both escaped. When the police didn't come after me, I began to relax. Until Darlene called. I convinced her that I'd walked into the woods with Iris but we talked and when I left her there I saw Russell going after her but I'd been afraid to tell the police. Darlene hated Russell. I told Darlene I'd call him and set it up for him to meet me in the woods and she could be hidden and hear everything and then we'd have proof for the police." Fran's eyes were weary. "Darlene was always a fool."

Emma once again touched her forehead. "Why did you push me?"

Fran flicked her a dismissive glance. "I had to be sure nothing in Iris's cabin pointed to me. No diary or notes. You came in and almost caught me. I didn't have any choice."

"Nothing ever seems to be your fault." Emma's gaze was cold. "And now?"

Fran's face twisted in despair. "I'm going to Fish Haul pier. That's where it started. Let me end it there. Alone." She lifted the gun, briefly touched her temple, then swung it toward them. "If I hear anyone behind me, I'll shoot." Tears trickled unheeded down her gaunt cheeks.

Buck moved toward her.

She again raised the gun to her temple.

He stopped. "You aren't well. Let me help. Let me take you home."

Her lips trembled. "It's too late. Years too late. Kiss Terry for me. Tell her I love her."

Buck's face folded in misery. Tears welled in his eyes.

Fran took one step back, then another. At the far end of the pavilion, she whirled and ran down the steps to vanish in the darkness.

~: *Eighteen* :~

Annie pushed the small mahogany table a little to the left of the fireplace.

"That's good." Henny stepped forward. She set a black cardboard poster in the center of the table. A white sheet was pasted in the center of the poster. Henny read aloud:

HONORED SPIRIT
Iris Tilford

Iris was slender with soft brown hair and brown eyes. She was kind and gentle. Iris struggled in school and was grouped with the slower students, the yellow birds. One day she astounded everyone when she sang, her voice beautiful and clear, sweet as a canary's song. From then on, she was proud to be a yellow bird. Her dream was to travel someday to the far reaches of the earth. Her spirit reeled when her mother died. Her journey became one of misery and pain and she sought oblivion in alcohol and drugs. She fought through the agony of withdrawal from drugs to sobriety. When she died, she was a proud member of AA and NA. She met death when she tried to make amends for her past. Her life was short but she lived and died with courage.

Henny admired the illustrations. Iris's high school year-book picture was above her name. Decorating the margins were a canary, a bright red biplane pulling a banner with the motto "See You in Zanzibar," an iris in all of its springtime glory, a pale purple sand dollar, sheet music of "Magic," and a brown owl. "Very nice," Henny's voice was warm.

"I think Iris would be pleased." Annie arranged books in a semicircle face up: *Witness to the Truth* by Edith Hamilton, *Mother Angelica's Little Book of Life Lessons and Everyday Spirituality* edited by Raymond Arroyo, and *Seeking Enlightenment Hat by Hat* by Nevada Barr.

Henny straightened a printed stack of the Twelve Steps.

Laurel came out of the storeroom with a crystal vase holding a single fresh iris and set it on one side of the table.

Annie walked to the coffee bar, picked up Agatha, and buried her face in sweet-smelling fur. So much had happened in such a short amount of time. It was already the last day in April. There had been the funerals for Iris and Darlene, and, finally, for Fran, whose body was found in the water two days after she fled into darkness to jump from Fish Haul pier and drown. Though they'd called 911 and Billy was there in only minutes, Fran was gone.

Annie touched Iris's poster. So much heartbreak for so many. Buck and Terry had moved to Charleston. Annie had heard he planned to open a woodworking shop. Would Cara someday, not too soon, not too late, move to Charleston and offer friendship to a damaged family? Cara understood loss and pain and melancholy memories.

Henny came around the table, gave Annie's shoulders a squeeze. "We'd better check the coffee bar. It will soon be time for tai chi." She chattered brightly all the way down the central aisle.

Annie was grateful for her kindness. Every happy day that passed helped push away dark memories. At the coffee bar, Annie slid onto a seat. Laurel sat beside her.

Henny expertly brewed cappuccino, topped three cups with whipping cream and maraschino cherries.

Annie glanced up at the paintings over the mantel. No winner as yet. "I believe I'll carry the contest over into May." She shot a quick glance at Henny.

Henny grinned, a devil-may-care, saucy grin. "I have generously refrained from announcing the winners because I understand there is a wish for others to prevail. However, I think our customers would be distressed if new paintings weren't hung for May."

"Hear, hear," Laurel chirruped, lifting her mug in affirmation.

Henny pointed at each watercolor in turn and announced the titles in a clarion tone. "*Thistle and Twigg* by Mary Saums, *Death of a Musketeer* by Sarah D'Almeida, *Bring Your Own Poison* by Jimmie Ruth Evans, *My Heart May Be Broken, but My Hair Still Looks Great* by Dixie Cash, and *Handbags and Homicide* by Dorothy Howell."

Annie laughed aloud. "Henny, I love you." She looked at Laurel. "And you." Swept by happiness, Annie lifted her mug. "To Henny and Laurel and Death on Demand."

*Turn the page for a sneak peek at the next
Death on Demand mystery,*

LAUGHED 'TIL HE DIED

Available in hardcover from William Morrow

HUBERT SILVESTER, BETTER known as Click, patted his pocket as he climbed the tall tower toward the platform. Two hundred bucks. That was more money than he'd ever had at one time. The minute the deal was made, he'd priced a used Ninja 49cc Super Bike for a hundred and fifty dollars. A bright silver one. He'd have almost fifty bucks left over for gas. When he had the scooter, he'd have everything he'd ever wanted. Life had been great ever since Ms. Hughes helped him land the part-time job at José's Computer Repair. He had a computer he'd put together himself with old parts. José had given him a used laptop for a Christmas bonus. Pretty soon the silver scooter would be his. He'd give his bike to his little brother.

The job itself couldn't have been easier. At first, he'd been a little worried. Still, once he had the handwritten note in his hand that explained who hired him and why, he'd agreed to give it a shot. He wished he could go along in the morning and watch, but he'd find out everything at the program tomorrow night. What was really neat, he was going to be announced as the brains of the outfit. That would be cool.

He figured Mr. Wagner couldn't fuss too much. He played more jokes than anybody.

His face furrowed in thought as he climbed the steep steps to the platform 28 feet above the lake. He's have to come up with a story about the scooter for Uncle Arlen. He'd tell him he was using money he picked up from computer repair jobs to rent the scooter from another guy at the Haven. Uncle Arlen settled into a beer-sodden stupor after dinner every night anyway. He never paid much attention to his dead sister's sons. He gave them a place to sleep and food to eat and was glad they spent their free time at the Haven.

Click swatted at a dragonfly. Sweat beaded his face. He'd never been to the nature preserve before. He'd lived on the island all his life and he took egrets and herons and alligators and dank still waters for granted. He spent most of his time inside, either working at José's Computer Repairs or using the Wi-Fi at the Haven for his laptop.

He climbed, panting a little. So he carried a little extra weight. The jocks made fun of him, but he sneered at the jocks. Why run when you could walk or stand if you could sit? Most of them weren't good enough to play in college, but, if everything went well, he'd have a scholarship to the technical college. Mr. Darling had promised to write him a good rec. Someday he'd have his own repair store and show those stupid jocks.

On the platform, he looked out at the lake, shimmering in the heat. Three alligators sunned on the far bank. There was nobody else around on a muggy July afternoon. People had better sense. They were inside where it was cool or on the beach where the breeze dropped the temperature about ten degrees. Although he understood the plan to keep everything secret until the last minute, he wished they could have met somewhere cooler.

He pulled at his sweat-dampened Braves T-shirt. The weather would be hot tomorrow night at the program, but the sun would be going down and shadows everywhere. The program was going to be lots of fun. Everybody would have a big laugh. He'd bet Mr. Wagner laughed loudest of all.

Scuffing sounds signaled someone climbing the ladder.

Click turned, exited and eager. His eyes widened when the climber reached the platform. Click wondered if he'd have a costume for the program, too.

"Agatha, you really shouldn't." Annie Darling moved toward the coffee bar.

The plump black cat lifted a paw to swipe at her elegant face.

"If the health department finds you on top of the coffee bar, I'll get a citation."

Agatha's ears folded back.

Annie realized her somewhat chiding tone was not being well received.

Annie approached cautiously, a veteran of many losing skirmishes with her gorgeous, but iron-willed cat. The choice of Agatha to honor Agatha Christie had perhaps been a mistake since the celebrated Queen of Crime had been known as a kindly person. Maybe she should have named Agatha, gender aside, for Mickey Spillane.

"I know." Annie softened her tone, added a coo of adulation. "I let you sleep on the coffee bar in the winter and you don't see why summer makes any difference. It's the people." Not that her beloved mystery bookstore was currently teeming with readers, much less buyers. This summer's slow traffic reflected the tourist downturn since the financial bust.

Agatha flattened like a snake. A guttural growl rumbled in her throat.

Annie swerved away from the coffee bar. Her mama hadn't raised no fool, as they liked to say in west Texas where Annie grew up. Living on a South Carolina sea island with alligators and snakes had reinforced her cautious nature. It wouldn't do any harm to let Agatha remain on the countertop as long as they were alone in the store.

Annie paused in front of the fireplace and looked up. If she had been a ballerina, she would have danced to a memory of Strauss's lovely "You and You."

She hummed the melody and waltzed across the floor of the coffee bar and back. Sometimes, when she was happy she had to dance. She was happy today, happy to be in her wonderful bookstore, happy to adore her demanding cat, happy that she and Max had planned a very special evening tonight, and happy with the watercolors hanging above the fireplace mantel.

Every month a local artist provided Death on Demand with five watercolors depicting memorable scenes from wonderful mysteries. This month's paintings represented the first books in series that Annie considered among the best in the mystery world. The first customer to correctly identify author and title received a free book (noncollectible) and free coffee for a month. Annie refused to add up how many months of free coffee had been enjoyed by Henny Brawley, the store's best customer and Annie's good friend. Maybe this month would be different . . .

In the first painting, a tall, slim young woman with striking reddish-blond hair stared in horror at the overflowing bathtub. She clutched a maid's cap in one hand and wore a black maid's uniform. A fully clothed man, even to a black overcoat, lay submerged in the water, staring upward with dead glassy eyes. His dead face was unprepossessing.

In the second painting, a petite young woman with reddish-gold hair leaned against the side of a lakefront cottage, looking up at the porch and two burly men, one with blond hair held by a bandana do-rag, the other with a massive wiry brown beard. In the yard, a dozen motorcycles were bunched. Their riders looked big, rough, and dangerous.

In the third painting, a small African woman, her back twisted, one leg shorter than the other, struggled to mount the steps of a wooden scaffold where a noose hung waiting. A crowd of thousands, black faces and white, watched in frozen silence. Not far from the wooden structure stood a young white woman, her face strained but determined.

In the fourth painting, a young woman with short dark hair, dressed all in black from her polo sweater to her black leggings, crouched behind the balustrade of the minstrel gallery to peer down into a candle-lit village hall at seven figures in black hooded cloaks drinking beer. A black cloth covered a table near the back wall.

In the fifth painting, protective face visor lifted, a woman stared in horror at putrefying human remains scattered on the ground. She was a startling figure in the desert moonlight, her head bristling with electronic wires and probes, her body encased in a lightweight metal contraption of arm and leg braces, a web vest fastening her to a computerized spine.

Each book was utterly original. Annie loved recommending these authors and she was thankful for mysteries, old and new, that made her bookstore a magnet for mystery lovers. Annie was convinced her customers also came for the ambiance, a molting raven perched above the children's section near a photograph of Edgar Allen Poe's tomb, comfortably

cushioned wicker chairs and potted ferns a la the days of
Mary Roberts Rinehart, and posters from famous mystery
movies, including *The Cat and the Canary*, *Charlie Chan
Carries on*, *The Thin Man*, *Ellery Queen and the Murder
Ring*, and *Murder by Death*. Pride of place went to the vin-
tage poster for *The Maltese Falcon*, worth a cool $3,500.
Humphrey Bogart was the quintessential Sam Spade, wary,
suspicious, battered but never broken.

As she made another graceful swoop, the storeroom door
banged open.

"Some people get to dance." Max Darling stood in the
doorway holding a sturdy cardboard box.

As always, Annie's heart danced, too. Was there a man
anywhere as handsome, sexy, and fun as her tall, blond
husband?

At the moment, he was trying hard not to smile, attempt-
ing, in fact, to appear apprehensive. "Other people steal
sand from the beach. I wonder if I broke any laws. At least
I didn't take a sand dollar."

"Max, you're here!" Her exclamation indicated sheer
delight. "Bring the sand up to the front. I've got the books
ready."

Annie walked swiftly down the central corridor, her flats
slapping on the heart pine floor. She hurried to the front
window, humming *Summertime*. Quickly she removed the
books that had celebrated the Fourth: *Roanoke* by Margaret
Lawrence, *Blood and Thunder* by Max Allan Collins, *The
Red, White, and Blue Murders* by Jeanne M. Dams, *Murder
on Lenox Hill* by Victoria Thompson, and *The Drop Edge
of Yonder* by Donis Casey. No books were more American
than they.

Annie never tired of showcasing mysteries sure to please.

Well, they might not please everyone, but they pleased Annie.

A thud sounded behind her. "Damn." Max's exclamation was anguished. Perhaps a trifle too anguished?

She turned. "Are you all right?"

Her husband bent to massage a sandaled foot. "Dropped on my big toe." He gave the sand-filled box a kick, grimaced again. "I may never walk again." He reached out to drape himself against her. "I need solace. Lots of solace."

Mmm. Trust Max.

But she smiled. It never mattered when she saw him, movie-star handsome in a tux, sleepy eyed with bristly cheeks in a tee and boxers, muscular and tanned in swim trunks, sweaty in a polo and shorts on a tennis court, every glimpse evoked the same swift, passionate delight. Her husband, her wonderful husband.

His blue eyes gleamed, and his arm slid more firmly around her shoulders.

She wriggled free. "Your toe will be fine. Get some ice from the coffee bar. I need to arrange the sand." She spread a drop cloth and troweled beach sand from the box.

Agatha suddenly appeared and with an effortless leap landed in the display. One swift paw whipped out to bat at the trickle of sand.

"Uh-oh." Annie put down the trowel and reached for the cat, who eluded her grasp. "Agatha, don't even think about it."

Behind her, Max laughed.

It took some effort and a tempting dish of cat salmon to entice Agatha out of the window and down the aisle to the kitchen area. Annie returned, somewhat breathless. "In a little while, maybe you could put up a lattice so she can't jump into the window."

"A lattice, the woman says. Presto." He snapped his fingers. "One lattice coming up. Where's the lattice store?"

"Try the lumberyard." There was a plea in her voice. "Maybe you could go get it while I arrange the sand."

He leaned against the wall. "I buy lattices and you arrange sand. You can't say we aren't original." His tone was musing. "Now, what would anybody say if they heard you announce that you were arranging sand? Doesn't that have a Laurelesque quality?"

Annie laughed. "I'm not in Laurel's league." Was that ever true. Max's mother, a gorgeous blonde who enchanted men from eight to eighty, was, to put it kindly, a free spirit who was ever and always unpredictable.

"Even Laurel never asked me to carry sand. Do you have any idea how heavy that box was? Why not just put up a beach chair? People who read books can imagine anything. Show them a beach chair and a stack of books and they'll make the connection: Beach Books! That would only take a few minutes and then we could go home and make some beach music of our own. As for a lattice, that comes later."

This time his hand started at the back of her neck and began slipping . . .

Annie ducked away. "Look how much I've taken out. Now you can pick up the box and pour."

He moved with alacrity. "Then we can go home?" His dark blue eyes told her that she was desirable, that they could be home in their splendidly restored antebellum house in a matter of minutes, that the sun would spill into the master bedroom . . .

She should finish setting up the new display. There were orders to fill and e-mails to answer. But Max was so near and she ached to tangle her fingers in his thick blond hair and lift her lips—

The front bell jangled as the door opened.

"Max." Jean Hughes's strident voice broke a golden spell. She burst into the central corridor, attractive yet with a frowsy look, a bit too much makeup, clothes a little too tight.

Jean rushed toward Max without a glance or murmur to Annie.

Annie folded her arms, determinedly maintaining a pleasant expression.

Max took a deep breath, then managed a quick wry grin and a promissory glance before he turned.

Before he could speak, Jean blurted, "I saw you through the window. I'd been to your office. I don't want to bother you, but please, can I talk to you?"

Annie considered clearing her throat since she was apparently invisible to Jean.

Jean reached out and gripped Max's arm, tugging him toward the door. "Please. Oh, please. I need help. You're a nice man. Everyone says so. Please help me."

Annie's resentment was abruptly swept away. The quaver in Jean's voice was real, and the desperate appeal in her eyes revealed a depth of misery.

Jean held out a trembling hand. "I've seen your ad in the paper. Confidential Commissions. Problems solved in a heartbeat."

That was a new ad in which Max took great pride. He did not hold himself out to be a private detective nor was he offering legal counsel. He was a member of the New York bar, but had never taken the South Carolina bar. Max was firm in insisting that no special qualification was needed to provide advice to those in travail.

"I've got an awful problem." There was nothing artful in Jean's language, but her stricken face told a tale of despair. "Please help me. I don't know what to do."

Max recognized heartbreak. His resistant look faded. He nodded toward the door. "Sure. Let's go over to my office. Maybe it will help to talk."

The door closed behind them.

Annie watched until they were out of sight. What had reduced the woman to such a pathetic state? Although Annie was well aware that their South Carolina sea island of Broward's Rock wasn't a paradise, even if it often seemed so, the island certainly wasn't the proper background for an Ibsen drama. Still, she didn't like the possessive way Jean had clung to Max's arm as they walked on the boardwalk.

Annie shrugged. She'd know soon enough. She worked briskly on the new display, artfully placing the titles faceup on the sand. The books, all superb mysteries, had the added cachet of offering stories set in South Carolina: *Mercy Oak* by Kathryn R. Wall, *Hush My Mouth* by Cathy Pickens, *Mama Pursues Murderous Shadows* by Nora DeLoach, *Too Late for Angels* by Mignon Ballard, *Monet Talks* by Tamar Myers, and *Murder in the Charleston Manner* by Patricia Houck Sprinkle.

Of course, Jean had been a disaster from the first. Hiring her to be the new director at the Haven had been on a par with choosing a chorus girl to head up a nunnery. Max wasn't on the board at the Haven, though he'd been invited. As a volunteer, he wanted to avoid any conflict of interest, but he'd regretted that decision when Jean Hughes was appointed.

What were the board members thinking?

Annie didn't need to be a mystery expert to know the

answer. Not for the first time in human annals, when money sizzled, good sense fizzled.

Max still volunteered, teaching sailing and tennis, and coaching basketball, but he avoided gatherings attended by board members. That wasn't accurate. When possible, he avoided one particular board member: Booth Wagner. Island bigwigs, including the mayor and heads of charities, had been ecstatic when Wagner had retired to the island and turned his considerable energies to island affairs, his energies and his apparently limitless wallet.

Jean as Haven director was a fait accompli when Max came home to tell Annie that the board, responding to Wagner's offer to fund a new gym, selected her on his recommendation. Max had been wry. "She's about as qualified to run anything as a panda."

Annie brushed sand from her fingers. Maybe Max would finish soon and they would close up their respective shops and go home for more fun than even the best mystery provided. After all, Jean Hughes wasn't their problem.